ENEMY LINES I
REBEL DREAM

Books by Aaron Allston

Star Wars: X-Wing Series
WRAITH SQUADRON
IRON FIST
SOLO COMMAND
STARFIGHTERS OF ADUMAR

Star Wars: The New Jedi Order: Enemy Lines
BOOK I: REBEL DREAM
BOOK II: REBEL STAND

Doc Sidhe Series
DOC SIDHE
SIDHE-DEVIL

Star Wars: Legacy of the Force
BETRAYAL
EXILE

ENEMY LINES I
REBEL DREAM

AARON ALLSTON

BALLANTINE BOOKS • NEW YORK

A Del Rey® Book
Published by The Random House Publishing Group

Published in the United States by Del Rey Books, an imprint of The Random House Publishing Group, a division of Random House, Inc., New York, and simultaneously in Canada by Random House of Canada Limited, Toronto.

Del Rey is a registered trademark and the Del Rey colophon is a trademark of Random House, Inc.

www.starwars.com
www.starwarskids.com
www.delreybooks.com

ISBN 0-345-42866-8

Manufactured in the United States of America

First Edition: April 2002

OPM 9 8

ACKNOWLEDGMENTS

Thanks go to:

My personal Inner Circle, Dan Hamman, Nancy Deet, Debby Dragoo, Sean Fallesen, Kelly Frieders, Helen Keier, Lucien Lockhart, and Kris Shindler;

My Eagle-Eyes, Bob Quinlan, Luray Richmond, and Sean Summers;

Caitlin Marlow, for offering inspiration;

The authors of New Jedi Order novels past and future;

My agent, Russ Galen; and

Shelly Shapiro and Kathleen O. David of Del Rey, and Sue Rostoni of Lucas Licensing.

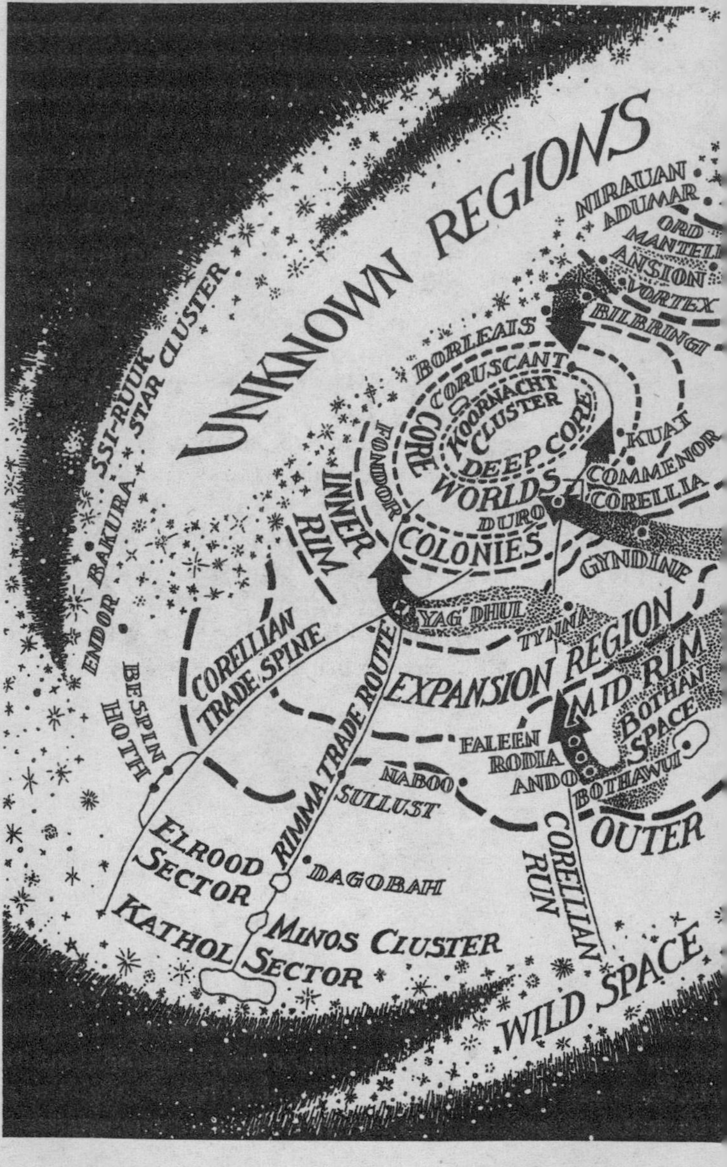

UNKNOWN REGIONS
SSI-RUUK STAR CLUSTER
BAKURA
ENDOR
BESPIN
HOTH
NIRAUAN
ADUMAR
ORD MANTELL
ANSION
VORTEX
BILBRINGI
BORLEAIS
CORUSCANT
KOORNACHT CLUSTER
DEEP CORE
CORE WORLDS
FONDOR
INNER RIM
COLONIES
DURO
KUAT
COMMENOR
CORELLIA
GYNDINE
YAG'DHUL
TYNNA
EXPANSION REGION
MID RIM
BOTHAN SPACE
BOTHAWUI
FALEEN
RODIA
ANDO
NABOO
SULLUST
CORELLIAN TRADE SPINE
RIMMA TRADE ROUTE
ELROOD SECTOR
DAGOBAH
MINOS CLUSTER
KATHOL SECTOR
OUTER
CORELLIAN RUN
WILD SPACE

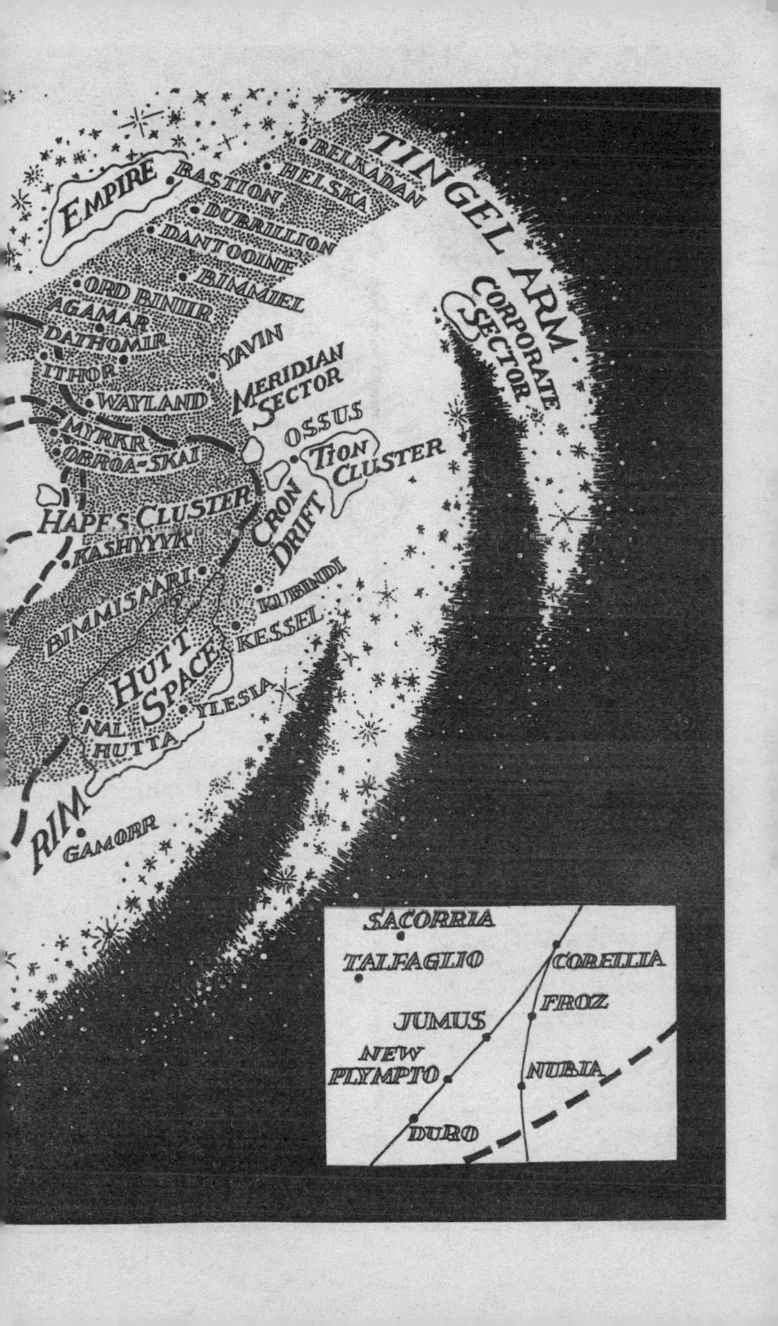

EMPIRE
BASTION
BELKADAN
HELSKA
TINGEL ARM
DUBRILLION
DANTOOINE
BIMMIEL
ORD BINIIR
AGAMAR
DATHOMIR
YAVIN
ITHOR
MERIDIAN SECTOR
WAYLAND
CORPORATE SECTOR
MYRKR
OSSUS
OBROA-SKAI
TION CLUSTER
CRON DRIFT
HAPES CLUSTER
KASHYYYK
BIMMISAARI
KUBINDI
KESSEL
HUTT SPACE
YLESIA
NAL HUTTA
RIM
GAMORR
SACORRIA
TALFAGLIO
CORELLIA
FROZ
JUMUS
NEW PLYMPTO
NUBIA
DURO

THE STAR WARS NOVELS TIMELINE

1020 YEARS BEFORE *STAR WARS: A New Hope*

Darth Bane: Path of Destruction

33 YEARS BEFORE *STAR WARS: A New Hope*

Darth Maul: Saboteur*

32.5 *YEARS BEFORE STAR WARS: A New Hope*

Cloak of Deception
Darth Maul: Shadow Hunter

32 *YEARS BEFORE STAR WARS: A New Hope*

STAR WARS: EPISODE I
THE PHANTOM MENACE

29 *YEARS BEFORE STAR WARS: A New Hope*

Rogue Planet

27 *YEARS BEFORE STAR WARS: A New Hope*

Outbound Flight

22.5 *YEARS BEFORE STAR WARS: A New Hope*

The Approaching Storm

22 *YEARS BEFORE STAR WARS: A New Hope*

STAR WARS: EPISODE II
ATTACK OF THE CLONES

Republic Commando: Hard Contact

21.5 *YEARS BEFORE STAR WARS: A New Hope*

Shatterpoint

21 *YEARS BEFORE STAR WARS: A New Hope*

The Cestus Deception
The Hive*

Republic Commando: Triple Zero

20 *YEARS BEFORE STAR WARS: A New Hope*

MedStar I: Battle Surgeons
MedStar II: Jedi Healer

19.5 *YEARS BEFORE STAR WARS: A New Hope*

Jedi Trial
Yoda: Dark Rendezvous

19 *YEARS BEFORE STAR WARS: A New Hope*

Labyrinth of Evil

STAR WARS: EPISODE III
REVENGE OF THE SITH

Dark Lord: The Rise of Darth Vader

10-0 *YEARS BEFORE STAR WARS: A New Hope*

The Han Solo Trilogy:
The Paradise Snare
The Hutt Gambit
Rebel Dawn

5-2 *YEARS BEFORE STAR WARS: A New Hope*

The Adventures of Lando Calrissian

The Han Solo Adventures

STAR WARS: A New Hope YEAR 0

STAR WARS: EPISODE IV
A NEW HOPE

0-3 *YEARS AFTER STAR WARS: A New Hope*

Tales from the Mos Eisley Cantina
Galaxies: The Ruins of Dantooine
Splinter of the Mind's Eye

3 *YEARS AFTER STAR WARS: A New Hope*

STAR WARS: EPISODE V
THE EMPIRE STRIKES BACK

Tales of the Bounty Hunters

3.5 *YEARS AFTER STAR WARS: A New Hope*

Shadows of the Empire

4 *YEARS AFTER STAR WARS: A New Hope*

STAR WARS: EPISODE VI
RETURN OF THE JEDI

Tales from Jabba's Palace
Tales from the Empire
Tales from the New Republic

The Bounty Hunter Wars:
The Mandalorian Armor
Slave Ship
Hard Merchandise

The Truce at Bakura

6.5-7.5 YEARS AFTER *STAR WARS: A New Hope*

X-Wing:
- Rogue Squadron
- Wedge's Gamble
- The Krytos Trap

The Bacta War
Wraith Squadron
Iron Fist
Solo Command

8 *YEARS AFTER STAR WARS: A New Hope*

- The Courtship of Princess Leia
- A Forest Apart*
- Tatooine Ghost

9 *YEARS AFTER STAR WARS: A New Hope*

The Thrawn Trilogy:
- Heir to the Empire
- Dark Force Rising
- The Last Command

X-Wing: Isard's Revenge

11 *YEARS AFTER STAR WARS: A New Hope*

The Jedi Academy Trilogy:
- Jedi Search
- Dark Apprentice
- Champions of the Force

I, Jedi

12-13 *YEARS AFTER STAR WARS: A New Hope*

Children of the Jedi
Darksaber
Planet of Twilight
X-Wing: Starfighters of Adumar

14 *YEARS AFTER STAR WARS: A New Hope*

The Crystal Star

16-17 *YEARS AFTER STAR WARS: A New Hope*

The Black Fleet Crisis Trilogy:
- Before the Storm
- Shield of Lies
- Tyrant's Test

17 *YEARS AFTER STAR WARS: A New Hope*

The New Rebellion

18 *YEARS AFTER STAR WARS: A New Hope*

The Corellian Trilogy:
- Ambush at Corellia
- Assault at Selonia
- Showdown at Centerpoint

19 *YEARS AFTER STAR WARS: A New Hope*

The Hand of Thrawn Duology:
- Specter of the Past
- Vision of the Future

22 *YEARS AFTER STAR WARS: A New Hope*

25 YEARS AFTER *STAR WARS: A New Hope*

Boba Fett: A Practical Man*

The New Jedi Order:
- Vector Prime
- Dark Tide I: Onslaught
- Dark Tide II: Ruin
- Agents of Chaos I: Hero's Trial
- Agents of Chaos II: Jedi Eclipse
- Balance Point
- Recovery*
- Edge of Victory I: Conquest
- Edge of Victory II: Rebirth
- Star by Star
- Dark Journey
- Enemy Lines I: Rebel Dream
- Enemy Lines II: Rebel Stand
- Traitor
- Destiny's Way
- Ylesia*
- Force Heretic I: Remnant
- Force Heretic II: Refugee
- Force Heretic III: Reunion
- The Final Prophecy
- The Unifying Force

35 *YEARS AFTER STAR WARS: A New Hope*

The Dark Nest Trilogy:
- The Joiner King
- The Unseen Queen
- The Swarm War

40 YEARS AFTER *STAR WARS: A New Hope*

Legacy of the Force:
- Betrayal
- Bloodlines
- Tempest
- Exile
- Sacrifice
- Inferno

*An ebook novella

DRAMATIS PERSONAE

The Jedi

Luke Skywalker; Jedi Master (male human)
Mara Jade Skywalker; Jedi Master (female human)
Jaina Solo; Jedi Knight (female human)
Kyp Durron; Jedi Master (male human)
Corran Horn; Jedi Knight (male human)
Tahiri Veila; Jedi student (female human)
Alema Rar; Jedi Knight (female Twi'lek)

With the New Republic Military

General Wedge Antilles (male human)
Lando Calrissian; merchant (male human)
Colonel Tycho Celchu (male human)
Commander Eldo Davip; captain, *Lusankya* (male human)
Colonel Gavin Darklighter; Rogue Squadron leader (male human)
Captain Kral Nevil; Rogue Squadron pilot (male Quarren)
Captain Garik "the Face" Loran; Wraith Squadron leader (male human)
Captain Yakown Reth; Blackmoon Squadron leader (male human)
Iella Wessiri Antilles; Intelligence director (female human)

Jagged Fel; Twin Suns Squadron pilot (male human)
Voort "Piggy" saBinring; Twin Suns Squadron pilot (male Gammorean)
YVH 1-1A (masculine droid)

Civilians

Danni Quee; scientist (female human)
Wolam Tser; holodocumentarian (male human)
Tam Elgrin; holocam operator (male human)

With the Yuuzhan Vong

Tsavong Lah; warmaster (male Yuuzhan Vong)
Czulkang Lah; commander (male Yuuzhan Vong)
Viqi Shesh; former Senator (female human)
Maal Lah; commander (male Yuuzhan Vong)
Denua Ku; warrior (male Yuuzhan Vong)
Wyrpuuk Cha; commander (male Yuuzhan Vong)
Kadlah Cha; warrior (male Yuuzhan Vong)
Takhaff Uul; priest (male Yuuzhan Vong)
Ghithra Dal; shaper (male Yuuzhan Vong)

ONE

One Month Ago, Pyria System: Borleias Occupation, Day 1

"A god cannot die," Charat Kraal said. "Therefore it can have no fear of death. So who is braver, a god or a mortal?"

Charat Kraal was a pilot of the Yuuzhan Vong—humanoid, a little over two meters in height. His skin, where it was not covered by geometric tattoos, was pale, marked everywhere by the white, slightly reflective lines of old scars. Some years-ago mishap had eaten away the center of his face, eliminating even the diminutive nose common to the Yuuzhan Vong, leaving behind brown-crusted cartilage and horizontal holes into his sinus passages. His forehead angled back less dramatically than many of the Yuuzhan Vong and looked a trifle more like the forehead of a human, for which two warriors had taunted him, for which he had killed them. He disguised the trait as much as he could by yanking out the last of the hair on his head and adding skulltop tattoos that drew the eye up and back, away from the offending forehead. One day he would earn an implant that would further mask his deformity and end his problem.

He wore an ooglith cloaker, the transparent environment suit of Yuuzhan Vong pilots, over a simple warrior's loincloth. Both garments were living creatures, engineered and bred to perform only the tasks demanded of them, to aid the Yuuzhan Vong in their pursuit of glory.

He sat in the cockpit of his coralskipper, the irregular rocklike space fighter of his kind, but he did not wear his cognition hood at the moment; the masklike creature that kept him in mental contact with his craft, that allowed him to sense with its senses and pilot it with the agility of thought rather than muscle and reaction, was set to the side while his coralskipper cruised on routine patrol.

He and his mission partner, Penzak Kraal, were in distant orbit above the world Borleias. The planet had been recently seized from the infidels native to this galaxy so that it could be used as a staging area for the Yuuzhan Vong assault on the galactic throneworld of Coruscant. Borleias was an agreeably green world, not overgrown with the dead, crusty dwellings of the infidels, not strewn with their unnatural implements of technology; only a military base, now smashed, had affronted the Yuuzhan Vong with evidence of infidel occupation.

The voice of Penzak Kraal emerged from the small, head-shaped villip mounted on the cockpit wall just beneath the canopy. Though most coralskippers were not equipped with villips, relying instead on the telepathic signals of yammosk war coordinators for all their communications, long-distance patrol craft did call for a means for direct communications. "Don't be an idiot. If a god is the god of bravery, then by definition he must be braver than any Yuuzhan Vong, than anything living."

"I wonder. Let us say then that you could become immortal as the gods, and never die, but remain one of the Yuuzhan Vong. You would never face death. Could you then be as brave as the Yuuzhan Vong? You could kill forever but never truly risk death, defy death, choose your time and place of death. Which is better, to be brave for a lifetime or to kill forever?"

"Who cares? The choice is not ours. But if I were to choose, I think I would choose immortality. Live long enough, and you might learn how to be brave as a Yuuzhan Vong again. Kill long enough, and you could perhaps learn to kill a star."

Charat Kraal sobered. "I have heard . . ."

"What?"

"That the infidels did that. Learned to kill a star."

He heard Penzak Kraal hiss in irritation; in the villip he saw his partner's lopsided features go even more off center as his mouth pulled down in an expression of contempt. "So what if they did? They killed it the wrong way, with their wrong minds and their wrong devices. And, like idiots, they must have lost the secret. Or they'd be destroying the worldships one by one."

"I have also heard . . ." Charat Kraal lowered his voice, a foolish instinct, since no one but Penzak Kraal could be listening to him. "That gods may smile upon them, too. On the infidels."

"Ridiculous."

"Can you know the minds of the gods?"

"I can no more know the minds of the gods than summon one of the enemy battleships to destroy for my personal glory."

In the distance, away from Borleias, many kilometers from them, an enemy battleship winked into existence, its bow pointed toward them. The ship was already up to speed; it grew rapidly as it neared them, as it approached Borleias.

"Penzak, you *fool.*"

"My words did not summon it, you idiot." The villip's face blurred and adjusted, reflecting a change to Penzak's features; Penzak had pulled on his cognition hood.

Charat did likewise. His surroundings, the cockpit interior, seemed to become transparent, giving him a view in all directions through the senses of the coralskipper, showing him in breathtaking detail the onrushing enemy ship.

No, now it was *ships*. More and more of the loathsome things of metal were dropping out of hyperspace, all aimed at Borleias. At Charat and Penzak.

A moment later, Charat could feel a buzz through the cognition hood, a telltale sign that Penzak was sending a warning to the Domain Kraal commander on Borleias.

The foremost New Republic ship, a sharply angled triangle in white, passed over the two coralskippers, blotting out the sun, casting them into shadow. Nowhere near so large as a Yuuzhan Vong worldship, it was still of impressive size, and so near that Charat felt he could reach out and drag his finger along its hull as it passed.

Penzak Kraal sent his coralskipper into a dive and turned to match the larger craft's course. Charat paced him. Above, he saw thruster gouts from the ship's belly herald the launching of the hated infidel starfighers.

"How do we hurt them worst?" Charat asked.

"Follow me in," Penzak said. "While they're launching. Don't engage the fighters; bait them so they follow us. The ship won't fire on us with the fighters in close proximity. We'll enter their launching bays and destroy the facilities there, then gut the ship from within." He looped around, rising and angling in toward the ship's belly. Charat followed.

Mon Mothma, one of the newest cruisers in the New Republic's fleet, a Star Destroyer refitted with gravity-well generators capable of interfering with the short jumps made by Yuuzhan Vong craft, cruised straight toward Borleias from the point where it had dropped out of hyperspace. This hadn't been a timed drop—they'd plotted a course straight for the planet Borleias, and the planet's gravity well had dragged them into realspace when they'd come close enough. And now before them was the blue-green world they had come to recapure.

"No sign of a Yuuzhan Vong worldship in orbit," reported the sensor officer, a Mon Calamari male with deep blue skin. "The two coralskippers are turning to engage."

General Wedge Antilles, a lean man with a careworn face and military posture, commander of the fleet group for which *Mon Mothma* was the flagship, nodded. "Gunnery, stay on them, vape them if they come against us. Fighter control, continue launching starfighter squadrons."

"Yes, sir."

"Yes, sir."

Data screens lit up with colored blips as New Republic starfighters—X-wings, A-9s, B-wings, E-wings, and more—streamed out of the docking bays and turned toward the planet. Wedge, standing at the captain's station toward the rear of the spacious bridge, ignored the screens. He concentrated instead on the live view of Borleias, which filled the main viewport at the bow end of the bridge.

I hope the Vong here have come to love this world, he told himself. *Because I'm going to take it from them. They're going to learn what it is to lose the things they love.*

Luke Skywalker hit his thrusters. His X-wing roared out of the main docking bay, losing altitude relative to the *Mon Mothma*. Behind him, eleven pilots of Twin Suns Squadron, the temporary X-wing squad that was his command, formed up on him. "Twin Suns away," he said.

"Twin Suns, copy." That would be the controller on *Mon Mothma*'s bridge. "Be advised, two coralskippers are maneuvering into your flight path."

Luke glanced at his sensor board. Two red blips were indeed turning from below to head toward them. "Squadron, follow me out, let's give these two the gauntlet treatment."

He heard a chorus of acknowledgments. There was tension in some of the voices, but not alarm. All his pilots were veterans, survivors of the Sabers, the Shocks, and other squadrons that had been reduced to shield trios, wing pairs, and solo pilots during the Yuuzhan Vong attack on Coruscant mere days earlier. Two of them, forming with him a shield trio, were his wife, Mara Jade Skywalker, and the Corellian-Security-officer-turned-pilot-turned-Jedi named Corran Horn. All his pilots were disciplined and competent. Many wanted revenge.

Luke understood how they felt. The Vong, aided by their human agent Viqi Shesh, had almost managed to kidnap his and Mara's infant son, Ben, just days ago. They had killed his nephew Anakin, and his nephew Jacen was missing. The losses, especially that of his apprentice Anakin, created an ache within him that he could not soothe.

In his youth, Luke would have been anxious for payback, but today he set that portion of himself aside. That was dark side thinking, immature thinking. It had been a long time since he had been a smooth-faced innocent; the scars of combat and lines of age had accumulated on his face, matching the weight of experience and calm that had accumulated on his spirit.

He extended his perceptions and sought Mara with them. He found her and almost flinched away from the contact; she was now an icy presence, concentrated totally on their mission.

He shrugged. Iciness was better than one alternative. Mara, despite her cool and controlled manner, was as anguished as he by the near loss of Ben and the loss of their nephews, and it would be no surprise to find her lit like a lightsaber with a desire for revenge. The fact that she wasn't meant that she was in control.

"S-foils to attack position," Luke said, and suited action to words by flipping the switch that split the X-wings' flight surfaces into their familiar X-shaped attack profile. "First and third trios, take the leader, the rest on the wingmate. Fire at will." He linked his lasers to quad fire, so that all four would fire with a single press of the trigger, and opened up on the lead coralskipper. Four red streams of destructive laser energy lanced out against the coralskipper—

No, it was *eight* streams. Luke's burst, aimed at the starboard side of the skip, never reached its target; a blackness appeared before it, distorting space around it like a gigantic magnifying lens, drawing the laserfire into it. Those four red lances of energy simply bent and disappeared. But Mara's burst, aimed at the port side, hit the coralskipper an instant after Luke's vanished. He grinned; she must have been using her own Force abilities to monitor him, as well. She couldn't have timed it so expertly otherwise. Her lasers raked across the enemy starfighter's hull until the distortion flicked over to interpose itself, then Luke fired again, chipping away at the coralskipper's stern. His blasts were joined by Corran's. The coral-like material of the skip's hull superheated and the lasers tore red-hot gouges along the surface.

Luke sent his X-wing into evasive maneuvers, moving back and forth, up and down with the randomness of a flying insect. He saw his target's counterattack, a glowing missile from the coralskipper's plasma cannon, flash by to port, far enough away to be no danger to himself, Mara, or Corran. In fact, there were no cries of alarm from his squadmates, no sudden and tragic disappearances of New Republic blips from his sensors.

"They're not engaging." That was Twin Suns Eleven, a Commenorian woman named Tilath Keer. "Turning to pursue." Luke saw the blips of Twin Suns Four through Six and Ten through Twelve turning back, following the coralskippers straight in toward *Mon Mothma*.

Luke felt a little tingle, but whether a warning from the Force or from his own years of combat experience he could not tell. "Negative, break off," he said. "Do not engage. Twin Suns, turn to original course and form up on *Record Time*. *Mon Mothma,* these skips are yours."

"Copy, Twins One."

Luke turned back toward Borleias, saw his pilots breaking off from pursuit of the coralskippers and maneuvering to form up with the squadron. The moment his fighters were clear of the coralskippers, *Mon Mothma*'s laser cannons opened up. One of the coralskippers was destroyed instantly, its dovin basal unable to absorb all the incoming damage with its void; the craft was reduced in a flash to glowing, molten particles no larger than a fingernail. The other, apparently more skillful at soaking up damage with its void, still sustained a grazing impact and spun away from *Mon Mothma*, out of control, no danger to the Star Destroyer.

Luke shook his head at the Yuuzhan Vong's pointless sacrifice, at the sad waste of life, and formed his fighters up in an assault wedge in front of *Record Time*.

Record Time was an armed troop transport. At nearly 170 meters, with two bulbous main portions—the larger stern housed the bridge and personnel bays, the smaller stern the engines—connected by a narrow access tube, the vessel looked impossibly vulnerable, impossibly fragile. But its captain-owner, a private trader—a smuggler, Luke believed—had volunteered its use to General Antilles during the fall of Coruscant, claiming it was the fastest, toughest vessel of its type. Now its bay was clear of trade goods and was filled with soldiers instead.

Luke's comm unit hissed with a moment of static, then a woman's voice: "*Record Time* to Twin Suns Leader, all set."

"Twin Suns to *Record Time*, you set the pace. We won't have any trouble staying where we need to be."

The transport surged forward, not fast by starfighter standards, but quickly enough for a freighter. Luke calculated its rate of acceleration and brought his X-wing up in front of the freighter's bridge. Mara and Corran settled in with him. Another shield trio dropped back to the port side of *Record Time*, a third to the starboard side, and the last astern of the transport.

All around Twin Suns Squadron, starfighter squadrons, frigates, destroyers, transports, and shuttles began accelerating to battle speed.

Luke heard Colonel Gavin Darklighter's voice over the operation channel: "Rogue Squadron to Borleias. We're back. We kicked your butt twenty years ago. Now we're here to do it again."

Luke grinned.

Squadrons of coralskippers were already climbing to their altitude by the time Twin Suns Squadron began its descent into atmosphere. Slightly longer than X-wings and comparable spacecraft, the coralskippers were far more massive. They were dense constructions of yorik coral, tapering toward the bow, broadening and deepening toward the stern, with rough exteriors reflecting their organic origins.

They could be quite beautiful, Luke had decided. The

ones rising against them and the two they'd seen after leaving the *Mon Mothma* shared a color scheme, a pastel red and a pearlescent silver swirled together in a mottled pattern. At the bow, tucked into a sort of niche grown into the coral surface, was the round reddish shape of the dovin basal, the creature whose gravitic powers dragged the coralskipper from point to point in space and also brought up defensive voids that drank in damage like a Tatooine bantha drank water. On the top surface, just ahead of the point where the ship's body swelled to its greatest width, was the canopy over the cockpit; this one was tinted blue.

Their beauty was irrelevant. As soon as they came within range, they opened up with their plasma cannons, life-forms that spewed superheated materials that could eat through a starfighter's hull. "Break and engage, cover the transport," Luke commanded, and suited action to words; he spun out in a rapid descent relative to the planet below and opened fire, trusting his wingmates to stay with him, to fire out of phase with him and at different portions of his target to overload and baffle the dovin basal. This time the creature defending his target skip intercepted Mara's shot, fired from slightly below the skip's centerline, but couldn't whip the void around fast enough to counter Luke's and Corran's shots, which scoured the yorik coral all around the pilot's canopy.

Superheated blobs from his target's wingmate flashed toward Luke's X-wing. Luke heard a squeal of alarm from R2-D2, who was tucked into the astromech bay behind his canopy, but ignored it as an irrelevant detail. He continued his rolling descent, varying the speed of his roll and distance covered each half a standard second, and saw the plasma flash between his snubfighter and Mara's.

Then the three of them were well below their targets

and rising again behind the coralskippers' sterns. The skips' voids swung around, hovering at the sterns, ready to soak up infinite amounts of weapon energy.

The first engagements between coralskippers and New Republic starfighters had been terrible for the New Republic. Even seasoned pilots had been thrown off balance by the skips' incredible durability, by the failure of proton torpedoes and laser blasts sucked into the voids to do any harm to the vehicles, by the tenacity of the damage done by plasma cannons, which kept on eating away at vehicle surfaces well after they'd hit.

Now things were different. The surviving pilots had adjusted their tactics and passed their information along to their fellows. The rules of the game were to overload the dovin basals, striking them from several directions at once to ensure that some damage got through to hit the coralskippers' surfaces. Starfighter pilots had to avoid taking any hits at all from skip weaponry; any hit could eat through shields and prove fatal.

And there were new tactics all the time, in every battle. Mara surged ahead of Luke and Corran, flying in a pattern that was oddly predictable, and drew fire from both coralskippers. She became suddenly erratic in her flight, as random as only Force skills could make a pilot, and flashed ahead until she was just behind the skips. She sideslipped to port, and as both streams of plasma cannon fire followed her, the fire from the starboard skip crossed the body of the port-side skip; two balls of fire thudded into the skip's belly before the starboard pilot compensated.

The port skip's void whipped around to shield the skip's belly. In that instant, Mara drop-fired a quad-linked burst of laserfire.

The skip detonated, hiding Mara's X-wing from sight for a moment, and Luke fired a laser stutter-burst at the starboard skip's underside. He hoped that the pilot's confusion at having hurt his own wingmate, along with the dovin basal's effort to shield this skip from the damage from Mara's attack, would leave it momentarily vulnerable.

He was right. His lasers hit the skip's underside and chewed through. That skip vectored away, trailing fluids that instantly froze at this near-vacuum altitude.

He checked his sensors. Two skips down. Mara was coming around to rejoin him and Corran. Diagnostics said his X-wing was undamaged.

Farther out, two of his Twin Suns snubfighters were gone. The pilot of one of them was extravehicular; Luke hoped that the flight suit would keep the pilot alive until a rescue shuttle could arrive. "Good tactics, Mara," he said.

"You always know the sweet thing to say."

Luke grinned and came around toward a new set of opponents.

Starfighter squadrons held the Yuuzhan Vong response to three points of conflict in orbit. The Twin Suns group took advantage of the opportunity and roared down through the atmosphere in an undefended zone, then banked toward the coralskippers' launch point, which had been detected on gravitic sensors. It was, not coincidentally, the same map coordinate as Borleias's New Republic military base. Luke didn't relish seeing what had become of the base during the Yuuzhan Vong occupation.

As they dropped low over the jungle canopy, Luke could make out the target zone ahead. It didn't have the same profile as the holocube he'd studied. The main building seemed to be lower, broader.

Small chips of yorik coral were rising above it, angling

toward them. His sensors said there were six of them.

"Twin Suns, up front," Luke said. "Engage all those skips. *Record Time,* it's your call whether you want to hang back with us or move on to the target without us."

"Twin Suns One, this is *Record Time*. We're here to fight. We'll see you at the landing zone."

"Copy."

Lando Calrissian, in *Record Time*'s troop bay, stood next to the ramp access and tried not to look concerned.

He was sweating. He didn't like sweating. It suggested hard work, something he wasn't fond of, and just didn't give the impression of someone who was infinitely cool, infinitely in control.

He looked over the units of men and women in the bay. Most were seated in rows of high-backed troop couches, strapped in against the turbulence that was likely to come. Their commanders walked up and down those rows, issuing last-minute instructions, advice, encouragements, jokes, insults.

He looked over his own troops. They stood in a circle, each with a hand on the metal post at the circle's center, and stared at him. They were impassive, fearless.

"Ready?" he asked.

In unison, they answered, "Ready, sir!"

He knew that once they left the bay he'd never see some of them again. Unlike the other commanders present, he was content with that knowledge. His troops would serve their purpose.

The bay shuddered as enemy fire finally began to strike *Record Time*. Lando saw fear, even nausea, on the faces of some of the other troops.

Not his. They continued to stare at him, waiting.

* * *

Luke, with Mara and Corran tucked in beside him, roared along in *Record Time*'s wake. He grimaced. He had lost his top starboard laser cannon and engine to plasma fire. His power, maneuverability, and fighting strength were reduced.

Ahead, *Record Time* was settling down into the jungle canopy, or perhaps into the open field just before the base; from here, it looked the same. Little flashes of light were pouring up from the ground and hammering into the transport's hull, blackening it. Though he was situated directly astern of the transport, Luke thought he could see the edges of *Record Time*'s bow distorting as combat damage ate away at it. Then the transport turned to port and Luke saw that he was right; the bow had sustained terrific damage from plasma cannons. He'd be astonished if the transport was spaceworthy now.

After the last lurch and vibration, Lando knew the transport was down. He could barely hear over the systems alarms. He took a last deep breath and nodded at his troops, then slapped the button on the hull panel beside him.

The top portion of the entry slid instantly up out of sight. The bottom portion lowered, becoming a ramp. Warm, humid air flooded into the troop bay. Beyond the entryway was field, its stringy grasses calf-high, and beyond that was some sort of reddish Yuuzhan Vong construction, a large cylindrical building with arms radiating outward at regular intervals.

"Go, go, go!" Lando shouted, and his troops released the bar they'd been holding. Shouting an inarticulate battle cry, they surged for the ramp, readying blaster rifles.

As they reached the top of the ramp, incoming fire began to rain in. Lando heard the rear wall of the bay ring as ammunition pocked it. No, it wasn't ammunition, he reminded himself, but creatures hurled by the Yuuzhan Vong—thud bugs, the hard-hitting insect projectiles, and razor bugs, which sliced whatever they hit and came around again to attack whatever they missed.

One of his troops took a concentration of thud bugs, several of them hitting the man in the throat. The force of the impacts was enough to shear through. That soldier's body collapsed and his head clanked to the bay floor, rolling unerringly toward Lando.

Lando stopped it with his foot like a player trapping a ball and looked dispassionately at it. His first casualty of the day. The combat droid's features stared up at him with no more expression than they'd shown a moment ago. The damage didn't look too bad, he decided. This one would be easily repaired.

The unhurt nineteen droid troops charged down the ramp and into the field, turning to head toward the right flank of the big red building. Their war cry changed from a simple roar to words that Lando didn't understand.

But he knew what they meant. He'd arranged for the war cry to be installed in his droid troops. It was in the language of the Yuuzhan Vong, and it meant, "We are machines! We are greater than the Yuuzhan Vong!"

On the bridge of the *Record Time*, the communications officer, a Rodian, his green scaly hide immaculately clean and the mouth at the tip of his pointed chin puckering, said, "Captain, it's working. They're breaking cover, showing themselves."

The captain, a tall human woman with copper-colored hair tucked up under an officer's cap, extracted herself from her chair and stood. This put her head squarely in the smoke accumulating against the bridge's ceiling. She coughed, ducked, and moved to stand over the Rodian's shoulder.

On the screen was a panoramic view collated from the holocams situated on the transport's hull. It showed the ground all around the *Record Time*, jungle to port and open field to starboard.

Lando Calrissian's droid troops were off the ramp and charging across the field, firing in a defensive screen all around them. And Yuuzhan Vong warriors were popping up all over the field, emerging from the jungle at a dead run, heading toward them, ignoring the transport—lunging like maddened animals toward the droids that insulted them by words and mere presence.

"Transmit this visual to all vehicles and vessels in our engagement zone," the captain said. "Transmit to *Mon Mothma* that the tactic does work. Then tell—oh, blast."

On the screen, something huge was approaching from the far side of the building with the radiating arms, moving around it. This was a living creature, vaguely reptilian, itself the size of a large building. Its skin was a blue-green, but patches of red and silver yorik coral grew over its head and along its spine. From the spine grew huge sail-like plates, and plasma cannons protruded by the dozens from the yorik coral.

The captain's voice rose into a commander's bellow. "Get the troops off this ship *now*. Nonessential personnel, follow the troops off. All weapons come to bear on that target. Fire at will. And vent the smoke here. We've got to breathe to fight."

This had to be one of those creatures that had fought in the Dantooine engagement. The captain had an ugly presentiment that *Record Time* would not survive to lift off again.

TWO

Borleias Occupation, Day 1

The living troops poured out of *Record Time*'s bays, their war cry an inarticulate roar. Lando steered his bodyguard, another of his droid troopers, in the wake of his main body of troops while the others surged toward the main building, spread out to set up a perimeter, or stopped to set up equipment.

Ahead, his droids were experiencing heavy incoming fire; their laminanium armor was pocked with small impact craters from thud bugs, stained with the juices of razor bugs that had smashed harmlessly into them. Lando watched as a warrior of the Yuuzhan Vong hurtled between two of them, his vonduun crab armor dark but gleaming, and whipped his amphistaff back and to the right as he passed. The staff, rigid, swept toward the droid's midsection, but the droid caught it with a free hand, its own motion a blur. The droid aimed its heavy blaster and fired, a burst of energy tearing through the Vong warrior. The warrior jerked backward, convulsed by the outpouring of blaster damage, and hit the ground steaming.

A blow to Lando's back not hard enough to be a thud bug hurled him onto the grass, and he dimly heard his bodyguard say, "Down, sir." Then the droid was firing.

Lando half-rose and saw a Yuuzhan Vong warrior approaching at a dead run, zigzagging to avoid the droid's blasterfire.

From his knees, Lando aimed to the right of the onrushing enemy and fired, spraying laser energy up and down into open space, then traversed left. His shots flanked the droid's, and the Yuuzhan Vong warrior, now five steps away, dodged into them, taking a blast in the knee. He fell forward and skidded toward Lando and the droid, his amphistaff whipping around, pliant.

Lando stood. He and the droid backed away at divergent angles and continued to pour fire into the fallen warrior. The warrior rose, his armor blackened in several places, and drew back his hand to throw something, but a blast—Lando wasn't sure whether it was his or the droid's—caught it in the throat. It toppled backward.

Lando nodded at the droid. "I'm a businessman," he said.

"Yes, sir."

"You know what that means."

"You hate being here, sir."

"You've got that right." The two of them circled around the smoking body, continuing toward Lando's force.

Now the armor-plated beast was visible around the building's edge. The muscles beneath and surrounding its armor plates rippled and the plasma cannons all over its back tilted, taking aim—directly toward Lando, it seemed to him.

He dropped to the ground and began firing.

Luke, Mara, and Corran took a high-speed run over the base area, giving them a split-second view of the Yuuzhan Vong building, of the *Record Time*, of the tremendous beast hurling plasma into the transport's side.

Luke sighed. The last time he'd faced one of these creatures, which Jaina Solo had nicknamed "ranges," and later was known by its Yuuzhan Vong name, a *rakamat,* and saw the tactic he'd used to destroy it had knocked him out for hours. He couldn't afford to do that now. "Let's do what we can to distract the thing from the ground troops," he said. "Two Flight, Three Flight, Four Flight, whenever you get through playing with those skips back there, we can put you to work up here where the fight is."

He led Mara and Corran in a tight loop back toward the engagement zone. All three X-wings began juking just before they cleared the jungle canopy, and plasma danced up through the air all around them. He fired linked lasers at the enormous beast and saw his blast and those of his flightmates swallowed by the creature's void defenses. Then they were over jungle again.

Lando elbow-crawled forward, chanting, "I'm too old for this, I'm a businessman, I'm too old for this, I want a drink." The rhythm of his own words kept him from being fully aware of the sweat dripping from him, of the fear radiating from him as plasma fire flashed by mere meters over his head and into the side of the *Record Time*. Return fire crossed from the other direction, heavy laser cannon blasts that would evaporate him if they grazed him. His droid kept pace, walking slowly so as not to leave Lando behind.

He'd crawled into a circle of troops before he knew it—six of them, five humans and a Twi'lek, only three of them with shoulder arms. "Where are your blasters?" he asked.

The Twi'lek, a red-skinned female, huddled against the mound of her pack. "We're engineers."

One of the others, a long-faced male with a blaster

rifle, said, "*They're* engineers." He fired at the legs of the giant creature lumbering in their direction.

"Engineers?" Lando asked. "With explosives?"

The woman nodded.

"*You're hiding behind your explosives?*"

She nodded again, her dismayed expression suggesting that she understood the insanity of it.

"Dig," Lando said. "A shallow hole. Large enough to put all those explosives in."

"No," said the trooper with the blaster. "We'll just leave them behind and get clear of them."

"No, we're digging." Lando glanced at the Twi'lek woman, who was frozen, her hand halfway to her field shovel, looking between him and the trooper.

The trooper gave Lando an ingratiating smile. "I'm only a noncommissioned officer, but that beats a civilian on the battlefield. We leave."

Lando grabbed him by the collar of his tunic and dragged him close. The trooper had to be younger than twenty, despite his apparent poise. "Listen to me, bantha fodder," Lando said. "I blew up a Death Star before you were born. In twenty seconds I can conclude a conversation with General Antilles, who blew up that Death Star with me, and I'll be General Calrissian again, and and you'll spend the rest of your military career cleaning refreshers on Kessel. Or you can dig. Which is it?"

The trooper looked at him for one long moment, during which streaks of plasma began to look like solid lines in the air above them. "I guess we dig, sir."

"Right." Lando released him. He looked at the Twi'lek engineer and gestured at the trooper. "Give him your shovel."

"Yes, sir."

Lando stretched out, took up his blaster rifle, and took the trooper's place at the perimeter. He fired a few times at distant Yuuzhan Vong warriors and once at the creature. Then he turned to his bodyguard and smiled. "You know, that's the kind of worker negotiations I really love."

The droid nodded. "Yes, sir."

The latest flyby of Luke and his wingmates, during which some of their shots were again absorbed by the *rakamat's* voids and others hit the side of the Yuuzhan Vong building, showed one party of soldiers in a circle directly ahead of the oncoming *rakamat*. The soldiers seemed to be digging a hole. "What do you think?" he heard Mara ask. "Idiots?"

"Picnickers," Luke offered.

"There's a thought."

Luke led Mara and Corran back toward the Yuuzhan Vong base. A moment later, three more Twin Suns settled into formation with them.

"Good to see you," Luke said. "Split off and approach the base from the far side so that you reach the edge of the canopy half a second after we do. They're only expecting three of us. Ready, break."

The ground here was soft; they had the hole dug and three engineers' worth of explosives loaded into it in less than a standard minute. The eight of them crawled away from the hole and toward the *Record Time*.

The Twi'lek woman wasn't crawling. She was flat on her back toward the rear of the column, fiddling with a remote detonator, while Lando's droid dragged her by the feet. The droid kept up sustained fire aimed behind them, toward the *rakamat* and the main engagement area of the infantry fight.

Lando, elbow-crawling at the head of the column, heard the roar of the returning X-wings. He knew their attacks on the beast were futile, but was grateful for their strafing runs, which had kept him and this unit from falling under constant fire.

Three X-wings flashed by from the right, unloading laserfire on the beast's left side. The voids flicked around into the path of the attacks, and Lando thought he saw the snubfighters' red laser beams actually bend as they entered the voids.

Then three X-wings flashed by from the left, pouring laserfire into the beast's right side. The six snubfighters crossed like a demonstration of trick flying and disappeared beyond the jungle canopy.

Lando saw yorik coral superheat and explode, propelled out as the flesh beneath the coral was instantly transformed into steam.

Blackish blood poured down the beast's right flank. The creature roared, a noise like the offspring of a groundquake and distant thunder, and poured plasma fire after the six snubfighters. But still it came on, toward them, toward the *Record Time*.

"Got it," the Twi'lek engineer said.

"Get ready," Lando said. "We'll try to time it to the X-wings' next pass if they're back in time."

The woman began elbow-crawling, freeing Lando's droid.

Lando suddenly found two stumps in the way before him. He looked up. They weren't stumps. They were the legs of a Yuuzhan Vong warrior, encased in vonduun crab armor. The warrior's amphistaff was straight as a spear, its tapered tail pointed right at Lando's back; the warrior held it up, ready to plunge.

The point came down and a dark shape shielded Lando from it, from the dazzling display of plasma and laser energy overhead. Lando heard a human scream, and abruptly the Yuuzhan Vong warrior was flat on the grass, his feet kicking centimeters from Lando's nose. One of the soldiers was atop him, but was already going limp, the amphistaff driven clear through his back.

From his position, Lando had a view under the skirt plates of the Yuuzhan Vong warrior's armor. As the warrior tossed aside the soldier's body, Lando angled his blaster rifle in and fired, hitting the warrior where neither leg armor nor skirt armor protected. This time it was the Yuuzhan Vong who cried out in pain. The warrior jerked and writhed, agony twisting his body apparently beyond the level that even a Yuuzhan Vong could endure.

Lando's bodyguard droid landed between Lando and the warrior. It kicked out against the amphistaff. Its blow hurled the weapon away, though the amphistaff, pliant again, bit the droid; the attack, faster than Lando's eye could follow, did not penetrate the droid's armor and would not have damaged the droid if it had. The amphistaff flew meters away.

The droid stood over the warrior, aimed carefully, and began firing.

Lando twisted around. The giant creature behind them, still pouring blood, had picked up speed. Knowing it was injured, perhaps dying, it was charging the *Record Time*.

The Twi'lek engineer had the detonator in her hand, her thumb over the button.

"Wait," Lando said.

She turned an anguished expression toward him, but didn't argue.

The roar of the returning X-wings began to rattle everyone and everything in the field. Lando watched the skies with a small part of his attention and kept the rest on the oncoming creature. Its front feet were over, then past the buried cache of explosives, and its main body was moving into place above the disturbed ground that marked its location.

Lando swallowed. If he was successful, the beast would die. Innocent, and Lando found it painful to watch it lumber toward him, toward its death.

He put the blame on the Yuuzhan Vong. It was better than accepting every bit of responsibility for killing a tremendous creature that, but for its controllers, might never have endangered him.

The X-wing roar rose in volume, and the plasma cannons on the beast diverted their streams of fire from the *Record Time* into the air. Lando saw the vehicles flash in from two sides, north and south this time instead of east and west. He saw red lasers flash down into the blackness of the beast's voids, saw return plasma fire clip an X-wing's underside and begin burrowing in.

Then the snubfighters were gone, the plasma cannons sending fiery destruction after them. "Now!" Lando shouted.

He didn't even see the woman press the button; he was aware only of the fire, reddish yellow and as evil looking as anything produced by the Yuuzhan Vong, roiling out from under the beast. It engulfed the creature and slammed Lando with heat and noise; he buried his face in the grass to escape it.

A moment later, he could look again. The creature was down on its side, its belly ripped and blackened by the force of the explosion. Blood streamed from it, but amazingly, it still lived, at least for the moment, its sides heaving with the effort to breathe.

It was not firing on X-wings or the troop transport now. Lando could hear and see the transport's lasers picking up again, not concentrating their fire on the creature, now picking off individual Yuuzhan Vong warriors within sight.

Lando's droid was firing, too. Lando looked over to see the droid placing shot after shot into the body of the Yuuzhan Vong warrior who'd come so close to killing him. The warrior was dead, the neck and top torso portions of his armor burned away by repeated blasts.

"One-One-A, you can stop now," Lando said. "What's wrong? Is your threat-recognition software on the blink?"

The droid looked at him. "Yes, sir. I suspect so, sir. I still register this one as a threat."

"Override control twenty-seven aye aye six, flag this target as no threat."

"Understood, sir." The droid stopped firing.

"We'll get you in for repairs," Lando said. "But don't feel bad. You did well."

"Yes, sir."

The situation was largely under control by the time Wedge descended to the planet's surface in his shuttle. He made a pass over the site of the Borleias New Republic base.

Once upon a time, it had been an Imperial base, housing TIE fighters and stormtroopers, charged with the duty of defending a nearby biological research facility managed by the Imperial general Evir Derricote. Then Rogue Squadron, at the time commanded by Wedge himself, had come as the spearhead of a mission that had wrested control of the world from Derricote. The Imperial base had become a Rebel Alliance base, and then, once the Rebels had taken Coruscant and become the legitimate government in this part of the galaxy, a New Republic base.

Now it was rubble. Wedge doubted that any part of the original base was more than two meters in size.

Where the main facilities buildings had once been now

rested another sort of building, pastel red and pearl, several stories in height, a circular core from which eight more or less evenly spaced extensions radiated, like arms on a sea creature. Wedge didn't have to ask to know that the building was something organic, a living creature bred by the Yuuzhan Vong to serve as a dwelling. Had it been dropped on the former base like a bomb, crushing it flat, or had it grown out of the middle? Wedge didn't know.

Lying beside it was a gargantuan creature, another of the Yuuzhan Vong's fighting resources, the reptile the *Record Time* had reported. It lay on its side in an immense pool of black blood. Wedge's troops reported that it was dead and awarded the kill to Lando Calrissian and the group of engineers.

The main building was surrounded by numerous smaller buildings, these shaped like the curved shells found on the backs of oceangoing arthropods and some land-based snails. Each was the size of a small house, aesthetically pleasing in muted color and curving design—so long as one didn't remember that they housed beings who killed other sapient beings without mercy and injured themselves for pleasure.

The rest of the old base was in ruins, docking bays and outbuildings turned into blackened, crumbling shells. It looked to Wedge as though they'd been used for target practice by the coralskippers' plasma cannons.

The area was swarming with New Republic troops. Dead men and women in New Republic uniforms lay at various points on the ground; there were many dead Yuuzhan Vong among them. Wedge saw his troops leading prisoners into open patches of ground surrounded by other troops. Many of the prisoners were human, their foreheads, even at this distance, clearly bearing the coral-like twin horn growths that signaled they were slaves of the Yuuzhan Vong. Other prisoners were Yuuzhan Vong, but their skins were smooth, unadorned by the extensive tattooing or scarring he'd seen on Vong pilots; Wedge assumed that they were members of the Shamed Ones, the pariah caste of Yuuzhan Vong society, whose bodies rejected modifications and who could thus never climb the ranks of the Yuuzhan Vong social hierarchy.

The base was a loss, and, even though it was captured, the new Yuuzhan Vong base on top of it was not the sort of place Wedge wanted to use as a ground-based operations center. It might contain numberless traps and dangers for New Republic occupants, and it certainly wouldn't reassure the New Republic refugees he expected to begin streaming in from Coruscant.

He keyed his comlink. "Rogue One, this is Antilles. Give me an escort. We're going to visit the biotics facility."

"Will do." A few moments later, two X-wings, one belonging to Gavin Darklighter and the other to his wingmate Kral Nevil, maneuvered to flank him. Wedge heeled about toward the biotics facility and hit his thrusters. Not long after, he hovered over the site of that base.

General Derricote's biotics facility was a long single building, several stories tall, its eastern facing a sheer drop, its western facing graduated downward in an aesthetically pleasing slope; the top story was a narrow strip, wide enough for a corridor along one set of rooms, the next story down wider, the next story down wider still, so that the whole thing seemed to be a gigantic wedge whose sharp edge pointed at the sky. Officially, it had been a site where Derricote preserved and studied samples of rare plant species from the world of Alderaan. Secretly, it had been used to engineer a deadly disease, the Krytos virus, which afflicted and killed members of nonhuman species. It was spread by the Imperial forces when the Alliance captured Coruscant.

From this height, Wedge could see that the building was still intact. The jungle had grown right up to it, trees surrounding it, vines draping over the turquoise-colored banks of viewports. But those viewports were unbroken; it didn't surprise Wedge that Derricote had used transparisteel instead of some lesser material.

Wedge transmitted a holocam view of the site, adding coordinates to the data stream accompanying the transmission. "*Mon Mothma,* this will be our ground facility. I want an occupation force and engineers here from our battle reserves as soon as possible. I want the jungle burned away for a kilometer around on the north, east, and south faces, two kilometers to the west—with escaped Yuuzhan Vong in the jungle, I want a substantial kill zone. Once that's done, have the ground forces enter and clear it of Yuuzhan Vong and other predators, then bring in personnel to clean it up, get its generators working, and so on. The field immediately west will be our landing zone.

"Issue the order that all the Yuuzhan Vong dead are to be stripped of gear for study, but their bodies are to be left where they fell." This was not an act of insult on Wedge's part. The Yuuzhan Vong had several times in the past demonstrated a need to retrieve the bodies of their dead. By leaving the bodies, Wedge hoped to reduce the number of assaults that his troops would suffer, since there would be no assaults while attempting to retrieve bodies.

"Keep a detachment on duty to contain the Yuuzhan Vong base while another detachment, plus Danni Quee's people and Lando's droids, searches it for prisoners and hiding Vong. When they're done evacuating the site, have the engineers blow it up."

He sighed to himself. After a brief respite from it, he

was back to niggling administrative details. He'd rather be retired or fighting again.

Borleias Occupation, Day 2

A day later, the biotics building was secure and operational.

The occupation forces hadn't found any Yuuzhan Vong hiding within the structure, but it was obvious the enemy had been here on a few occasions, breaking up machinery, smashing furniture—warrior-vandals. The bad news was that the building's generator had been smashed. Currently a small freighter was situated next to the building, heavy cables running from its engine compartment into the building's basement and to field shield units set up to protect the complex.

The building was now surrounded by six square kilometers of destroyed jungle growth. His forces had used fire, lasers, defoliants, whatever they could get their hands on. The biotics facility, a secret home of ugliness, was surrounded by obvious ugliness. To step out of the building was to step into a hot, humid environment that stank of burned vegetation and offered no view but char, ships that had landed for repairs, and distant jungle.

Luke, returning from a perimeter sweep around the Yuuzhan Vong settlement—a sweep in which they'd encountered no Yuuzhan Vong, but suspected, from the behavior of Borleias's animal life, that Vong were out there—learned that Wedge had requested his presence at a general meeting of his senior officers and personal allies. He joined the crowd in the biotics building's ground-floor mess hall. Mara was already there, baby Ben in her arms; at her feet was a baby carrier she'd jury-rigged from a backpack. On one ankle was a cast, immobilizing it against the bone break she'd sustained when she crash-landed during Coruscant's fall.

Luke headed for a seat beside her, but Wedge waved him up to the head of the table, to the other seat beside him. Luke gave Mara a smile of apology and moved to sit by Wedge.

"Our stay here is going to be short," Wedge said to the entire assembly. "But it's going to be longer than we'd like. There's going to be more fighting. I'd like to have some tricks up our sleeves to offer the Yuuzhan Vong when they come, so I want you to be thinking about it. Transmit your ideas to your commanding officers. The commanding officers will transmit them to me—and I don't want there to be too much editing of them. Now's not the time to think conservatively."

A naval officer Luke did not know, a woman in a lieutenant's uniform, spoke up. "General, if I can ask—"

"Go ahead," Wedge said.

"Why do we want to stay here at all? The garrison has to have alerted their commanders that they were being overrun. The Yuuzhan Vong will be coming."

Wedge nodded. "Well, there are several reasons. The first is this: because Borleias—rather, the Pyria solar system—is an important hyperspace crossroads, the convenient intersection of a lot of routes, it's on a lot of people's nav computers. It's inevitable that many refugees fleeing Coruscant—or arriving there and suddenly discovering that the Yuuzhan Vong have taken it—will be coming here as the first stage of their escapes. Someone needs to help them. A lot of them may be in damaged craft. We can't have them clogging up our repair facilities in space, not when they're needed to repair combat craft, so they'll have to put down on the planet's surface.

"Second, we need to catch our collective breaths. We left Coruscant with just the ships on our backs. We need to take stock, take inventory . . . and calculate the enormity of the disaster that we've just experienced." Wedge's face, for a moment, expressed a pang of pain, and Luke felt it, too. Wedge hadn't been able to get in touch with his wife, Iella, or daughters, Syal and Myri, before duty had forced him to leave Coruscant. Not knowing what had happened to them, the shame of not being able to carry out both his duties to the New Republic and his duties to his family, had to be eating at him. Wedge swallowed hard, then his features were schooled once again into impassivity, and he continued.

"Third, yes, the Yuuzhan Vong will be coming here. They can't permit an enemy garrison so close to the planet they've just taken. And if we can hold their attention for a while, that's even more time for others fleeing Coruscant to get away, and for our other fleet groups, the ones bel Iblis and Kre'fey command, to gather themselves, too.

"Fourth, and last, it's a morale issue. Our people have just taken a tremendous kick in the teeth—the loss of Coruscant. We're going to kick in return. If you run from neks, or Vong, they won't respect you. They'll chase you, drag you down, and kill you. Only if you stand your ground do you have a chance of survival. If we dig in our heels here and slap the Yuuzhan Vong across the face, it may do some harm to their morale. It may do some good for ours. Luke, I'd appreciate it if your Jedi could be not just as active as possible, but also out there for everyone to see—a constant reminder to our forces of the strength and versatility they represent."

"And of one of our most important roles," Luke said. "Protectors of the people. Consider it done, General." Luke left unstated the fact that a higher profile for the Jedi could mean more lost to the Peace Brigade, fewer able to reach the escape routes Han and Leia were establishing. This was a necessary risk.

"Thanks." Wedge turned his attention away from Luke and to the gathering before him. "Colonel Darklighter, I want to keep Rogue Squadron on high guard in Borleias orbit for the time being."

"Yes, sir."

"Captain Deevis, I want at least two ships with good sensor systems on-station in the Coruscant-Borleias approach corridor, one just on this side of the point Borleias's gravity well would cause incoming ships to come out of hyperspace, one at a distance, our best-guess projection based on previous tactics as to where a Yuuzhan Vong sortie might drop out of hyperspace." He began looking among the assembled officers and civilians, not waiting for confirmations of his orders. "Captain Birt, while *Record Time* is being repaired, you're in charge of the injured. Find a portion of this facility you can set up for triage, surgery, and wards. Coordinate with *Haven Jace*, our medical frigate. Lando, the rest of the facilities are yours to apportion, and you'll act as quartermaster. Booster, you're in charge of communications. Make sure we make the best use of whatever equipment we have on hand, and coordinate it through the *Errant Venture*. Danni—is Danni Quee here?"

"I'm here." Luke saw a hand waving from the back.

"You're in charge of just about everything Vong. You'll get the prisoners, the gear, and vehicles we've captured from the Yuuzhan Vong garrison. First priority, in my opinion, would be freeing the prisoners from the blasted coral things. Corran Horn?"

"Here." Another hand waved from the back of the crowd. Horn was no taller than Luke and wasn't always easy to spot in a large group of people.

"Corran, Gavin did receive your request to rejoin

Rogue Squadron, and he and I both welcome it, but I've got another assignment for you for the moment. We know there are Yuuzhan Vong out in the jungle. I want you to help set up security for this facility. Your combination of Jedi, Corellian Security, and Starfighter Command experience is just what we need. In the meantime you can continue flying with the Twin Suns until you transfer back to the Rogues."

"Understood."

"Tycho, you're in charge of starfighter forces. I remain in direct command of space navy forces. I want preliminary status reports downloaded to my datapad in half an hour and a meeting of officers and divisional heads in the conference room in two hours. Lando will let you know where the conference room is." Wedge clapped his hands together sharply. "Let's move, people."

The crowd dispersed with military rapidity, leaving behind only Wedge, Tycho, Luke, and Mara. Mara joined the other three at the table.

Luke made his voice mild. "You didn't ask anything of me. Well, you asked me to do what I was going to do anyway. You didn't have a specific task or duty for me."

Wedge gave him a puzzled look. "Luke, you're more or less the guiding light of this whole operation. I don't mean just my fleet group. All three groups are looking to you for advice. I can't make demands of you, or of the Jedi."

"You can make demands of friends."

Wedge blinked, then offered up a slight smile. "True. And I'd be happy to do that." He offered an apologetic shrug. "As drained as we are of resources, I want the *Errant Venture* to stay here. I've already asked Booster. But that means that if the Jedi trainees stay aboard her—"

"It's no longer a safe haven for them, I know. I'll be

dealing with that. I have some ideas on where we can put the students."

The Maw, he thought, with the Jedi haven under construction there, with its surrounding screen of black holes and mad gravitic interactions, would be best for now.

"Then I want you in charge of special forces, special operations. Mara, I know this is a lot to ask of a woman with a small baby—"

Mara straightened, holding Ben to her. "Trust me, my capacity for mayhem is undiminished."

Wedge's smile broadened. "I didn't spot any ranking Intelligence officers in that crowd. I'd appreciate it if you could act as our Intelligence head for the time being. When we get in an officer from Intelligence, you can move over to Luke's department of special forces and mayhem."

Luke hesitated before speaking again. "Wedge, has there been any word about Iella or the kids?"

Wedge shook his head. "None. But if there's anyone in the New Republic who could smuggle herself and two children offworld—"

"It's Iella, I know. They'll be fine, Wedge."

"Are you—" Wedge's voice was suddenly hoarse. "Does that mean you've seen something? With your Jedi perceptions?"

Luke shook his head. "I'm sorry, no."

"Oh." Wedge schooled his features back into impassivity, but to Luke, he looked as though another hope had suddenly died within him. Luke felt a crushing shame at having given him a false hope, however inadvertently.

Wedge rose. "Yes. I'm certain they'll be fine." He left the chamber, Tycho with him.

"He's hard to read," Mara said. "How is he?"

Luke shrugged. "Holding on. Relying on all that military discipline. But not knowing about his family is chewing away at his guts. "C'mon, let's find out what sort of resources special operations and Intelligence can put together. And we need to find someone who can baby-sit while we're off doing our duties."

Mara shook her head. "I'm not going to accept any duties that take me away from Ben. Not anymore. Flying yesterday, that was the last time. I couldn't stand it again."

"Mara—"

"No, listen to me, farmboy. There's no one, other than you and Karrde, that I'd trust more than Leia. But she couldn't protect Ben. Viqi Shesh took him back on Coruscant, and we had to rely far too much on luck to get him back. I'm not going to let him out of my sight. Period. Anyone who comes after him, I kill personally."

Luke looked at her, taking in her calm demeanor and the wild eruption of emotions it hid, emotions he could feel through his Force-bond to her, and knew he wouldn't win this argument today. As if on cue, Ben woke and erupted into wails of distress. "We'll talk about this later," Luke said.

Mara gave him a frosty little smile. "Sure, if you like reexperiencing the same conversation and the same results."

THREE

Yuuzhan Vong Worldship, Coruscant Orbit

They were two Yuuzhan Vong guards assigned to march her to her last interview. Assigned to conduct her to the meeting where she would be condemned to death.

She was afraid of them, for either could kill her on a whim, and neither had the slightest regard for her life.

She knew contempt for them, for they were ugly, anonymous creatures, drones whose names would never be known. Somewhere, and perhaps very soon, they would die in battle and be forgotten.

She envied them. The remainders of their lives, however short, would probably be longer than hers.

She was Viqi Shesh. Once the Senator representing Kuat before the New Republic, she had for a long time also been a spy for the Yuuzhan Vong, funneling them crucial information about the planet Coruscant and the workings of the New Republic's government. Long and faithfully had she served her new masters.

But long and faithful service hadn't meant much to them. As the Yuuzhan Vong invasion of Coruscant had begun, she had attempted to carry out her latest assignment—the kidnapping of Ben, the infant son of Luke and Mara Jade Skywalker—and had failed. Her enemies had been a step ahead of her and had swept the brat off to safety. She had pursued and had been within meters of retrieving the baby, but a counterattack by Lando Calrissian and his combat droids had left her disgraced and friendless, in the grip of the Yuuzhan Vong she had failed.

Until that moment, she'd confidently anticipated receiving great rewards from the Yuuzhan Vong for her service and effort. Instead, her reward had been to be arrested and hustled up to Domain Dal, the worldship that served Tsavong Lah, Warmaster of the Yuuzhan Vong, as his flagship.

She was in pain. Neathlats, a sort of living bandage, clung to her right forearm, where Princess Leia's Noghri bodyguard had bitten her to the bone, and to her back, where Leia's lightsaber had slashed and burned her. Neathlats promoted healing but did not diminish pain. That was not the Yuuzhan Vong way. Instead, they irritated nerve endings, causing the pain of injuries to be sharper.

She was without allies. No one would speak for her. She had failed to produce Ben Skywalker for the Yuuzhan Vong, and her betrayal of the New Republic was by now certainly common knowledge among the refugees from Coruscant.

But she was not weaponless. Not while she had her intelligence, her political experience. She still had a weapon she could aim at Tsavong Lah.

The guards led her along a lengthy corridor. Its lines were not truly straight, its corners not quite right angles. Its surfaces were a mottled red reminiscent of muscle tissue. It smelled like raw meat, and Viqi forced herself to keep an expression of disgust from her face.

It was deep within the Yuuzhan Vong worldship. It had to be well away from the ship's centers of command, for there was no other traffic along it. Viqi was pleased that she could still think analytically.

They reached a large chamber, its walls identical to those of the corridor, with an ivory-colored set of double doors opposite, a matched pair of Praetorite Vong guards standing before them. The guards drew the doors open to let them pass.

Beyond was a large oval chamber in the same mottled red. Its floor sloped downward in a gentle curve, its lowest point being a circular opening some three meters across. The opening surrounded blackness; Viqi found she could not focus on the darkness. It seemed fuzzy somehow, rising above the level of the floor a quarter meter or more.

Beside the pit stood Tsavong Lah, the great planner and guiding light of the Yuuzhan Vong invasion of this galaxy. A heavily scarred and tattooed example of high-ranking Yuuzhan Vong, his lips had been slit into tatters that stirred whenever he exhaled heavily, and his body was marked everywhere with bloodred scales, implants that spoke of his importance. His left arm had been replaced at the elbow by a radank claw, all reddish scales and spines, with fingers that were segmented and articulated in a manner not natural for Yuuzhan Vong or human; spines and scales were emerging from the flesh above his elbow as well, and small black dots, carrion-eaters, swarmed around them. She repressed a shudder. Despite all of Tsavong Lah's mutilations and decorations, she had found him somewhat attractive—power and ambition in males being a lure for her, a secret weakness—but the rot that afflicted him, which threatened both to rob him of both his radank claw and his power, disgusted her.

The guards and Viqi came to a halt before Tsavong Lah. He turned to fix his stare on her. "You may feel honored," the warmaster said. "It is not customary for one of my position to witness the disposal of waste."

She looked at him, and then again at the pit overfull of darkness. In the blur of that darkness, at its edges, she saw motion that seemed suddenly familiar. It was identical to that of the little black dots, the carrion-eaters, that infested Tsavong Lah's arm.

She concealed a sensation of revulsion. "This is the fate you've chosen for me?"

"Yes." The warmaster gestured at one of her guards. "Denua Ku will kill you. If you are polite in these last few moments of life, I will let you choose the means of your death. He could break your neck, stab you with his amphistaff, have the staff bite you. Then your body will be tossed into the pit. The creatures there will ignore it for a time, until it begins emitting the odors of decomposition, and then they will fall on it, slowly eating it away to nothingness. You will disappear into darkness, Viqi Shesh, and cease to be, as though you never were."

Viqi's stomach knotted, but she kept her expression calm, emotionless. "Why don't I just jump in? I can drown as your little bugs fill my lungs. That way, these two nameless nothings beside me don't get to participate."

She could sense anger in the increasing stiffness of her guards' postures, but Tsavong Lah merely widened his eyes and looked a bit surprised. "You are anxious to provide compensation for your failure?"

"Of course. I will do it this way if it is what you require; it is my obligation to serve. But I'm more anxious for you to stop lying to me. To end that particular torture, I'll jump in right now."

"Lying. An interesting accusation. A deliberate offense." Tsavong Lah smiled again. "One you can offer because you think nothing worse than death could await you. If that is your belief, you are wrong."

"I say you are lying for this reason: you are not disposing of me because I failed you. Others have failed you and been permitted to live . . . because they were still loyal resources you could rely on. You're having me put to death because you think I'm no longer valuable to you. No longer a resource."

To the extent that they could, Tsavong Lah's features became thoughtful. "I am impressed. You make your point. I am killing you because you *are* no longer a resource, Viqi."

"But I am. My most powerful weapon is still with me, Warmaster—my brain. While I sat in my cell, I used it, and I uncovered a threat to your control of the Yuuzhan Vong, to your plans for this galaxy, to everything you consider a goal. You are in danger you don't even know about. Only I have uncovered the secret."

"Name it, then."

"No." She looked at her guards. "Not while these unworthy ones can hear my words. Not while *anyone* other than you can hear them."

Tsavong Lah gestured. Viqi's guards took her by her arms and, seemingly without effort, lifted her. They held her over the pit. Black dots leapt up from it, settling on her feet and lower legs. Some leapt off again.

"Anything you have to tell me, they can hear," Tsavong Lah said, "in the final moments of your life."

Viqi returned her gaze to his. She was able to keep the fear she felt out of her voice. "You and I are the only ones in this chamber I *know* are not your enemies. I will not speak what I know before strangers, because it might spell your doom. If I die now, with my secret unspoken, you might figure it out yourself, and survive anyway. *I will not betray you.* So drop me." She made her expression fierce, and the ferocity was not just a show—the fear she felt was real, and fueled very real anger.

Tsavong Lah considered her for a long moment, then made a shooing gesture to his guards. They withdrew a step, bringing Viqi back over solid flooring, and released her. She fell awkwardly, almost collapsing when she landed; a stumble and she might have pitched forward into the pit anyway. Then they turned and left the chamber.

Viqi felt the first, faint stirrings of hope. She was in charge of this situation, for the moment at least. If she could hold on to her tenuous advantage, she might live.

Tsavong Lah regarded her steadily. "Well?"

"Your body rejects its latest modification," she said, her words coming out in a rush. "I know what you're thinking. You believe it's your gods talking to you, telling you to figure out the correct path to their approval. But that's not what's happening.

"You're being betrayed, Warmaster. By the shapers. They've put a faulty limb on you. It threatens to turn you into a Shamed One. Soon, they'll start recommending courses of action to you—military action, political action. When you start doing what they say, the problems with your limb will diminish. But anytime you fail to do as the shapers demand, new problems will begin. You're going to be their slave, Warmaster."

Tsavong Lah fell silent. His eyes were unreadable.

You contemptible, predictable fool, I have you. Viqi clamped down on the rush of elation she felt—she could not afford for it to be reflected in her expression.

In her cell, she had used her skills of fabricating and anticipating treachery—not to figure out the source of the problems afflicting Tsavong Lah, but to concoct an accusation that explained all of them, a story that would take time and effort to disprove. She would use that time to find some way to escape the Yuuzhan Vong.

"An interesting notion," the warmaster said. "What if you are wrong?"

"I am *not* wrong." Viqi gave him her most unconcerned expression. "I just ask for the opportunity to see my theory proven right. Kill me *then* if you choose. At least I'll die victorious."

Tsavong Lah regarded her for long moments. Then he nodded to himself. "We will see. I will give you duties to perform until proof is in my hands . . . or my patience ends." He called out a few words in his language, and the guards returned to flank Viqi. At the warmaster's gesture, the guards took Viqi by the shoulders, spun her around, and led her back out the door.

Every step was more distance between her and the pit. Every step was a loosening in the tight grip that fear had on her heart. Every step was a drumbeat accompanying the words that pulsed through her mind: *I live. I live. I still live.*

Borleias Occupation, Day 3

Wedge's comlink beeped, awakening him. His booted feet slid off the desk before him and hit the floor with a too-loud clatter. He sat up, wondering for a moment where he was and what he was doing there.

His office was dark. He'd fallen asleep before making it back to his temporary quarters. He grabbed his comlink and held it up before him. "Go." He rubbed sleep from his eyes and wondered how many minutes of rest he'd had.

"General, this is *Mon Mothma*. One of our wing-pair patrols reports a transport with fighter escort arriving insystem."

"Yuuzhan Vong or refugee?"

"Neither, sir. Its communications officer says it's the

official transport of the New Republic Advisory Council. Their authentication code checks out."

Wedge frowned at the comlink. It was inconceivable that the Advisory Council was still functioning in any capacity. Until the fall of Coruscant, they'd been Chief of State Borsk Fey'lya's handpicked advisers, a lubricating layer between him and the grinding machinery of government. But with Fey'lya's death during Coruscant's fall and the collapse and flight of the New Republic Senate, Wedge had guessed that the Advisory Council would have been scattered to the space routes, each member racing home to prepare for Yuuzhan Vong pursuit. "Have they done anything other than request clearance to land?"

"Yes, sir. They've, um, requested a meeting with you and your general staff, as soon as possible. They say they've brought your orders."

Wedge made a face. As if he needed interference from a now-irrelevant group of politicians. "All right. Set up two starfighter squadrons in a circle illuminating a landing field well away from the facility. Tell the Advisory Council that it's a military honor display. If they ask why they've never heard of such a thing, tell them it's a Rogue Squadron tradition. The starfighters are authorized to attack without further confirmation if this turns out to be some sort of Vong trick. If it's not, conduct the Advisory Council here, to the conference room, as fast as possible. Begin reprovisioning and repair of their transport immediately—and put some technicians aboard to sweep the ship and make sure it doesn't have any surprises for us. Got that?"

"Got it, sir."

"Out." Wedge rose with the uneasy feeling—one that had come to him every time politicians had a surprise for him, one that had almost never been proven false.

* * *

When Luke and Mara reached the conference room—he with a cup of steaming chocolate in one hand and a cup of caf for Mara in the other, as her arms were occupied holding Ben—it was already half full of Wedge's officers and advisers. They occupied seats around two-thirds of the main table and chairs behind; several seats at the table, those nearest the main doors, were being kept conspicuously empty. Wedge sat at the head of the table, facing the door, Tycho beside him; they were huddled in conference, though Wedge spotted Luke as he entered and waved the Jedi Master up to the head of the table again.

The expressions of most people in the room suggested they'd only recently been roused from sleep. Luke knew how they felt.

Mara dropped into the seat closest to the chair reserved for Luke, next to Lando. Lando looked pained, his brow creased in a frown, his eyes bloodshot.

"Hangover?" Luke asked.

Lando winced. "Stop shouting."

"I could whistle you up some caf."

"If you were to whistle, my head would explode and there would be brains everywhere."

Mara shook her head, deadpan. "No brains. Just skull fragments."

Lando shot her a betrayed look. Luke grinned, waited until Mara had settled Ben in her lap, and handed her the caf. Then he joined Wedge and Tycho.

There was noise from the hall, a clattering of boots, and a group of ten or twelve people turned into the conference room.

Luke knew several of them by sight.

Pwoe, first of the council to enter, was a Quarren. Quarren, roughly humanoid in shape, sometimes tended to unnerve humans and near-humans because of their looks; they were an aquatic species with squidlike heads from which trailed four tentacles where a human's lower facial features would be. The Quarren as a culture did not deserve this reaction, but, in Luke's estimation, Councilor Pwoe did; Luke knew him to be a grasping, politically carnivorous being who was no friend of the Jedi. It would not have surprised Luke to find out that Pwoe had something to do, either directly or indirectly, with the formation of the Peace Brigade, the collaborationist forces who kidnapped Jedi and handed them over to the Yuuzhan Vong. Today, Pwoe wore a full-length green robe that contrasted nicely with his leathery orange skin. As he entered the room, his turquoise eyes scanned the chamber, found Luke, fixed on him for a moment, and then moved on. Pwoe sat in the chair directly opposite Wedge.

Chelch Dravvad of Corellia sat to Pwoe's right, and Fyor Rodan of Commenor sat beside him. The two human males, both of middle age and with the confident, artificial aura of politicians on display wrapped tightly around them, tended to keep their attention on Pwoe, rather than making eye contact around the room.

Niuk Niuv, the fourth councilor to enter the room, was a Sullustan. If some long-ago biological engineers had created a race to resemble a child's stuffed toy, they could not have done much better than the Sullustans, who had round heads, large round ears, wobbly jowls, and charming nonhuman features; only Ewoks were more likely to produce squeals of glee in a child seeing them for the first time. But, like Ewoks, Sullustans could be dangerous foes, and Niuk Niuv was dangerous even for a Sullustan. He'd been an opponent of the Jedi ever since joining the Advisory Council. He sat to Pwoe's left.

Niuv was the last council member to enter. The remaining members of the council's company appeared to be aides, datapads in their hands and worried expressions on their faces, and guards, faces impassive, blaster rifles held at the ready position.

Luke rose as the others did, a customary show of respect for Senators and members of the Advisory Council, but he felt a wave of irritation or offense roll off the people already present in the room. So many council guards present suggested that the council didn't trust Wedge's security arrangements. It was an insult; Luke simply didn't know whether it was accidental or deliberate.

Wedge said, "Councilors, welcome to Borl—"

Pwoe held up a hand. "General Antilles, you address not only the Advisory Council but the Chief of State."

Wedge blinked, then his gaze moved to the clasp being used to hold Pwoe's robes together. Made of gold, it was the New Republic symbol surrounded by stars. Borsk Fey'lya had occasionally worn it. Luke saw Wedge struggle with his response—Pwoe's rise to the position of Chief of State was not by any stretch of the imagination a legal one, but in these unsettled circumstances, it might just be a practical reality.

"Congratulations on your promotion," Wedge said. He gestured for the others to sit, and did so himself. "If I may ask, where are Councilors Cal Omas and Triebakk?"

Pwoe spread his hands, a gesture of ignorance. "Alas, we do not know. We suspect that they perished during the assault on Coruscant."

"Two more tragedies to add to the list."

"Indeed."

That, potentially, was bad news. Omas, a Senator representing the relocated people of Alderaan, and Triebakk, a Wookiee from Kashyyyk, were sensible beings who did not have an irrational dislike of the Jedi. They had been a moderating influence on the Advisory Council. Now, if they were indeed lost, all the members left to the council were largely opponents of the Jedi, advisers who had often argued in favor of finding a way to accommodate the Yuuzhan Vong—to settle the war with negotiation.

Luke felt a surge of suspicion. Had the two missing councilors perished on Coruscant? Or could they have been left behind deliberately by these deal-making bureaucrats—or even been pushed out of an air lock on the trip here? He shook his head, willing those thoughts away.

Mara leaned over, nearly touching foreheads with him. "I felt that," she whispered. "That was my thought, too."

Lando leaned into the huddle. "You don't need the Force for that," he whispered. "I could read it in Luke's expression."

"Shh," Luke whispered. "Or I'll make a loud noise."

Lando leaned away again, his motion hurried.

Pwoe continued to stare at Wedge, impatience evident in his body language. "We should begin."

"We'll start in a minute," Wedge said. "Members of my general staff are still in transit." His face was fixed in a slight smile. Luke could tell that it was nothing but veneer, a mask covering agitation, irritability.

Pwoe fixed him with an admonishing look. "I understood that you'd be ready for us. Time is pressing."

There were footsteps in the hall. Booster Terrik, glowering, entered and moved to sit near the table, close to Tycho. There were more footsteps, running footsteps, and Danni Quee skidded through the doors, juggling datapads and portable screens; her hair was an unruly blond mess tied in an off-center ponytail. She slid into a seat near the door, directly behind Corran Horn, and looked at Wedge. "Sorry," she said.

"Nothing to be sorry for," Wedge said, and looked up at one of the council's guards. "Doors."

The guard looked at Pwoe, received his nod, and closed the doors.

"Now we can start," Wedge said.

Pwoe nodded. "Yes, of course. First, I want to reassure you all that the government of the New Republic is in fine working order. Drawing on the emergency authority that has fallen to us with Borsk Fey'lya's death, and with the temporary disarray the Senate finds itself in, the Advisory Council has assumed the reins of power. We are now formulating plans to reorganize our armed forces and retake Coruscant. We are in communication with planetary governments from all over the New Republic, which are acknowledging our leadership and awaiting orders."

Luke and Mara exchanged glances. She took a sip of her caf and then winced, as if the bitterness of the drink were the reason.

Wedge responded to Pwoe's statement with only a nod.

Pwoe waited, as if expecting more, and then, after an uncomfortable silence, continued, "We wish to congratulate you on your success here at Borleias, General."

"Thank you . . . but we haven't had any success yet. We seized this facility through use of overwhelming force, which says nothing about either side in the conflict."

"Yes, of course. Still, I need to hear details of what you have accomplished here."

With little evident emotion and no extraneous words, Wedge briefed the Advisory Council members on the situation on Borleias. Luke saw the councilors nodding and whispering to one another as he spoke.

When Wedge was through, Pwoe said, "You've done

very well in seizing the initiative, in anticipating the needs of the New Republic and acting on them. Not that I wouldn't expect that of you. But now we need to bring your operation back into the New Republic command structure so that it can be coordinated with the rest of our response to this disaster. Sien Sovv remains Supreme Commander of our armed forces, and you'll continue taking orders from him. Here is the first set."

Niuk Niuv sent a data card skidding across the tabletop. Wedge caught it, then slotted it into his datapad.

"Since these are your own trusted advisers, I will share your orders with them," Pwoe said.

Wedge looked at him. His face was impassive, but the look was still a warning, a rebuke. To announce a leader's orders in this manner to his subordinate officers was to question that leader's competence, to deny that leader the right to limit the information reaching those subordinates.

Pwoe ignored the look and continued. "What we need from you, General Antilles, is for Borleias to stand as a fortress against the Yuuzhan Vong, even beyond the point that the stream of refugees from Coruscant ends. The Yuuzhan Vong won't be able to tolerate the thought of a New Republic–controlled military base so close to Coruscant, on such a prominent hyperspace crossroads, and so they'll come against you here. This will give us crucial time to regroup and then to come and relieve you. Once we've done so, we can use Borleias to stage the recapture of Coruscant. You must hold here at all costs. Can we count on you?"

Instead of answering, Wedge asked, "What forces and matériel will I have for this assignment?"

Pwoe blinked. "Most of Fleet Group Three is currently away from here, is that correct?"

"Yes. At deep-space rendezvous, on operations, coordinating with the other fleet groups, and so forth. I'll have to bring portions of them back here for the sort of operation you describe."

"Not at all. You underestimate yourself, General. We'll leave you with a large proportion of the matériel you currently have in the Pyria system. That should suffice until you're relieved. Of course, you can commandeer additional forces arriving from Coruscant, and any volunteer units that choose to join you."

Wedge nodded. "Councilor Pwoe, I'm afraid I have to turn down your assignment."

All whispered conversation stopped in the conference room. Luke felt a slight sense of unreality. Through the years, he'd seen Wedge reinterpret orders and bend them in his efforts to do what was best for the Alliance and New Republic, but never *refuse* orders.

Pwoe straightened, becoming taller and somehow seeming to swell in his chair. His voice became deeper, projecting better to those in the far corners of the chamber. "Perhaps I made a mistake in couching what I was saying in the form of a request, General Antilles. You must understand, that actually constituted an order."

Wedge nodded. "Nevertheless, I'm refusing it."

"As an officer of the New Republic, you cannot do that."

"I'll resign my commission."

"In this period of crisis, that could be construed as an act of treason," Pwoe said. Luke could actually feel outrage pouring from the Quarren, but it didn't feel quite right—Pwoe was outraged because he was being refused, not because he actually believed his charge of treason.

For the first time since the meeting began, Wedge smiled; it looked to Luke as though he were clamping down on a laugh. But the smile wasn't a cheerful one.

Luke imagined, with a flash of insight from the Force, Wedge drawing his blaster, a fast, smooth move, and shooting Pwoe right in the face. Luke twitched, his hand automatically seeking his lightsaber hilt, before he realized that this vision was not what Wedge intended to do—just what he *wanted* to do. Luke found himself startled by the violence Wedge was obviously keeping under restraint.

But Wedge merely said, "Treason. Now *there's* a curious charge in this circumstance. But we don't need to get into that. Or into the legitimacy of your claim to be the Chief of State. Instead, I'll make you a deal, Councilor Pwoe. I'm going to mention a set of military forces and privileges. Give them to me for this assignment, and I'll accept command. Otherwise, I'll transmit you my resignation of commission before you can walk a hundred paces."

Outrage crept into Pwoe's voice. "You can't dictate terms to your superiors."

"Actually, given these circumstances, I can."

Pwoe turned to Tycho, who sat beside Wedge. "Colonel Celchu. I'm promoting you to the rank of general. Your assignment will be the one I just described to this traitor . . ." His voice trailed off as Tycho shook his head.

Pwoe took a deep, long breath. His eyes flicked back and forth as he evaluated other officers in the chamber. He relaxed, settling against the back of his chair. "All right, then, in the spirit of cooperation, I'm prepared to hear what it is you want to ask for."

Wedge began counting off on his fingers. "First, all matériel currently in Pyria system, including extraneous forces we picked up in our retreat from Coruscant, and any currently in transit here remain under my command for this operation."

Luke could see, though the councilors could not, Wedge

give Tycho a light kick under the table. Tycho opened his datapad and began typing, glancing at Wedge occasionally as though transcribing the general's words, but Luke was certain that Tycho was performing a very different task.

"Second, I want the *Lusankya.*"

Pwoe almost rose out of his chair. "The most powerful ship remaining in our navy? I don't think so."

"I *do* think so. And since, once the Yuuzhan Vong decide to besiege the Pyria system, getting supplies will be somewhat problematic, I need a three-month supply of food, medical gear, fuel, and ordnance for the entire force. I'll give you three days from the time you depart this system for that to arrive. If it doesn't, we leave. And one other thing."

Pwoe's voice turned frosty. "There's always one other thing."

"I want the right to communicate directly with any officer in the armed forces, to invite him or her to join us here, and the right to accept his or her transfer—without having to go through the commanding officer."

"Antilles, you are obviously deranged. You should have been put out to pasture years ago."

"I was, Pwoe. I should have been *left* there. And if the Advisory Council had conducted its part of the war with the Yuuzhan Vong in any competent fashion, I *could* have been left there." Wedge held his hands out, palms up, a gesture saying, *There we are.* "Well?"

"Refused, of course."

"As you wish. When this meeting is done, I'll order the forces here to abandon Borleias. By the time you can get another occupation force here, the Yuuzhan Vong will hold this world. And, no, I'm not bluffing."

Pwoe locked stares with Wedge, and whispers began

again in the conference chamber. Finally Pwoe said, "A moment."

"Take two."

Pwoe turned to huddle with the other Advisory Council members. Wedge turned to Tycho. The murmurs rose in volume.

Luke leaned back toward Mara and Lando. "Sometimes," Luke said, "I wish I had my sister's political insight, or yours. What's Wedge doing?"

"Pwoe is lying," Mara said. "He wants Wedge to shore up Borleias so that the Yuuzhan Vong will come here to crush it. But he won't be sending forces to reinforce Borleias. No one will. It will fall, and everyone here will die."

Luke frowned. "Then what's the point to holding it?"

"It gives the Advisory Council members time to go home and make preparations there. Preparations for war, or preparations so they can make the best deal possible with the Yuuzhan Vong. It gives the surviving members of the Senate the same time. And if they did their job right and convinced Wedge to fight ferociously, the Yuuzhan Vong might even be impressed with this little battle, might offer better terms in their negotiations."

Luke gave Wedge a look. "So all he just negotiated for was enough military strength to let us hold out longer."

"That's right."

"But everyone who stays here is still dead. Pointlessly dead. Just dead a little later."

"That's right."

"I'm sorry I asked."

Mara managed a slight smile. "If he's negotiating, he has a skifter up his sleeve. You know that."

The huddled members of the Advisory Council leaned away from one another and Pwoe turned again toward Wedge. Conversation in the chamber immediately died down. "General, I deplore your methods and your arrogance. I don't imagine you can expect much in the way of a military career once this assignment is done."

Wedge nodded. His expression was kind, solicitous—or nearly so. Luke suspected it was actually mockery of those emotions. "But you accept."

"Yes. We accept. It is my pleasure to relieve you of command of Fleet Group Three, even if I must leave you your current rank and command of this garrison."

"Once your orders confirming the terms I specified have been broadcast over the HoloNet to our armed forces, you can consider me to have accepted, too." Wedge glanced at Tycho's datapad. "But I recommend that it be soon. Rogue Squadron has reported sighting what may be a Yuuzhan Vong scout ship. This planet will be a war zone very soon." He straightened and looked around. "This meeting is over. In five minutes we'll have a quick operational planning meeting." He gestured at Luke, Mara, Lando, Booster, and others, indicating that they were expected at that meeting.

The members of the Advisory Council, suddenly kicked free of the activities at hand, rose, looking a little uncertainly at Wedge, who paid them no further attention. The guard Wedge had called upon earlier opened the door again and Pwoe led them through. Luke could feel both irritation and smugness from the Quarren.

Luke shook his head. Smugness. Pwoe was smug because he knew Wedge would soon be dead. Luke felt anger rise within him. He shook his head and dispelled the anger—not forcing it from him, simply releasing it, feeling it dissipate.

Mara smiled. "I felt that."

"It's hard to be the serene Jedi Master all the time."

"I don't want you to be serene *all* the time, farmboy."

* * *

Gavin Darklighter moved up toward Wedge. He heard the general whispering to Tycho, "What results?"

Tycho whispered back, "All Fleet Group Three ships within four hours' travel of Borleias are now in hyperspace on their way here."

"Good work."

Gavin leaned over his commander and lowered his own voice. "General, none of the Rogues on patrol reported anything to *me* about sighting a Yuuzhan Vong scout."

"Of course they did. Five or six hours ago. In orbit around Borleias."

Gavin frowned, remembering. "Wait a minute. That was just the burned-out hulk of a coralskipper. One that we vaped when we arrived."

"Correct. And a coralskipper can be used as a scout ship."

"Sure."

"And Rogue Squadron *did* report sighting it."

"Sure." Gavin felt his confused expression give way to a rueful smile. He looked across the room, where the last members of the Advisory Council were leaving, haste and nervousness evident in their body language. "Sir, how you can be so deceptive without actually lying is beyond me."

Minutes after the Advisory Council's shuttle left orbit, Wedge had the conference doors locked and guards posted outside. He looked across the faces of those he'd asked to remain behind—Tycho, Luke, Mara, Lando, Booster, Danni, Gavin, Corran. "Is anyone not clear on what just happened?" he asked.

Luke spoke up. "Are we sure, are we *absolutely* sure, that we've just been thrown to the neks?"

"Think of it this way," Wedge said. "Pwoe just handed

me the navy's biggest surviving warship and enough matériel to noticeably diminish the New Republic's ability to defend itself from the Yuuzhan Vong. From a coldly analytical political perspective, do the Coruscant refugees' lives or Borleias's military importance warrant that sacrifice?"

Luke shook his head. "No."

"Then the only thing we can conclude from this is that the so-called Advisory Council has given up on the New Republic. That band of connivers has already concluded that we're going to lose, that the Yuuzhan Vong are going to become the dominant force in this galaxy. *They've given up.* And considering how much political power they hold, their giving up could well doom the New Republic."

"I suppose so."

"Now, back to the subject of Borleias. We're worse off than we thought we were," Wedge continued. "Before, we thought we'd be able to blast off this rock, rejoin bel Iblis and Kre'fey, and lay in plans to help the New Republic rebound. Now, we can't. I would very much like to hear any ideas about what we can do to counteract the damage the Advisory Council seems very prepared to do to our chances for survival—both here on Borleias and in the galaxy as a whole."

"Before we do that . . ." Luke frowned at his old friend. "Wedge, if there's no good to come out of it, why did you accept this assignment?"

"Well, because in a sense, the council is right. Pyria does have to be held. The Yuuzhan Vong have to be slowed. And if you'll permit me a little ego here, I don't think they'd appoint someone as skilled as I am to replace me here. It would be some commander who followed their orders with blind loyalty and nothing but the death of this garrison at the hands of the Yuuzhan

Vong." Wedge shrugged. "I don't plan to die here, Luke. And while I don't think I can hold Borleias, I might be able to make it a name that causes little Vong children to whimper." He returned his attention to the room in general. "So, back to my original question."

No one spoke at first. Then Luke cleared his throat. "There are two basic styles of fighting, hard and soft. Back in the Rebel Alliance days, we fought soft. The New Republic fought hard. You're expected to stay here and fight hard. But, ultimately, hard obviously isn't going to work.

"I think that the model extends into our politics, too. If we continue to devote ourselves to the hard style, we're going to doom ourselves."

Wedge nodded.

Lando said, "So what you're saying—what *are* you saying?"

Mara said, "What we're saying is that you should stop attacking the Yuuzhan Vong with the New Republic. Attack them with the Rebel Alliance instead. Both here and in the wider theater of war."

"But the Rebel Alliance is gone," Danni said. "It *became* the New Republic."

Luke nodded. "Correct. What I'm proposing . . ." He took a deep breath. "I'm proposing that it's time for a new Rebel Alliance. Something that's unbounded by the traditions and the shortsighted thinking of the current government of the New Republic. Something different."

"That's treason," Booster said. "I like it."

"A resistance force," Wedge said. He gave Luke a sharp look. "But it would have to be a secret resistance. We can't just declare independence from the New Republic and march off to fight the Yuuzhan Vong. Secret units in hidden locations. Operations not discussed with the New Republic High Command."

"That's right," Mara said. "Which, if we decide to do this, makes you the weak link, Wedge."

Tycho frowned at her. "Perhaps you'd better explain that comment."

"Because in the legal sense, it *is* treason, Tycho. Wedge has already demonstrated that he's willing to bend the rules—misappropriating a sizable fraction of the New Republic's armed forces and using them in a manner inconsistent with his orders. This goes well beyond that. He'd be misappropriating munitions and matériel and giving them, not loaning them, to a private force. Even if we win, he could end up with the stamp of traitor in all the historical records. So could you. Can you do that, Wedge?"

Wedge looked troubled and did not respond at once. The others kept silent.

Finally, Wedge met her gaze, then looked at the others. "I think that we're right at the edge of annihilation. Not just the government. Our entire culture, our history. If the Yuuzhan Vong win, they won't necessarily wipe us out . . . but they'll ingest us. Digest us. We'll *become* the Yuuzhan Vong, and everything we stood for, everything we aspired to, will vanish. It would be as if we were a hologram and the power was suddenly cut off. Gone without a trace." His voice hoarsened. "I'm not going to let that happen to my daughters, or to your children. So here's what I propose."

He drew his blaster and shoved it, spinning, to the center of the conference table. "Anyone need a blaster? That's mine. I'm willing to put it out there because there's no one in this room I'd hesitate to give it to, or to put my life in the hands of. And that's how I propose we build this Resistance. For the time being, don't bring in anyone you wouldn't trust your life to, or your children's lives. We'll set up contacts, bases, and cells the old Rebel Alliance way. While the New Republic hits the enemy where they're strong, we'll figure out how to hit them where they're weak. And if—or when—the New Republic finally falls, we'll be here to hit the Yuuzhan Vong both ways, mixing hard and soft styles.

"Are we in agreement?" He caught the eye of each of the others in turn.

Each person nodded or raised a hand, all but Booster, who drawled, "I *suppose* so." The others laughed.

"All right." Wedge leaned back. "From now on, we're the Inner Circle. Things said here don't go outside. People outside will think it's my own group of advisers, rather than the start of a resistance movement. If there's someone you think can hear the treason we're plotting, tell the rest of us . . . and we'll vote to bring him or her into the Inner Circle, or not. Others we know we trust and need, like the Solos, will join us when and if they arrive.

"Now, let's think about soft-style fighting. The Yuuzhan Vong are going to hit us here at Borleias. We need to draw them in, give them some success they don't deserve, so they'll grow to depend on and anticipate tactics that we can abandon when we need to. I need a me and I need a them." He turned to Tycho.

Tycho took a long breath. "Well, I can be them probably as well as I can be you. And, of course, you can be you better than I can be you. But if you're them and I'm you, everyone is thinking outside the box."

Wedge nodded. "Good point."

Lando said, "I'm really lost."

Wedge grinned. "A game of tactics, Lando. When they decide to send a serious military commander against us—whether it's right away or after a few engagements—that commander is going to be analyzing our tactics so he can implement the best strategy possible against them. In other words, to have an idea of what he's going to be doing, we have to figure out how much of our thinking and tactics he predicts. So if we can give him exactly what he expects from us, reinforce his prejudices about our strategic skills—"

"You can abandon them later and give him a surprise," Lando said.

"Right. So in our planning sessions, Tycho is going to be General Antilles, and I'm going to be whoever the Yuuzhan Vong commander is, and we'll see just how far astray we can lead him."

"I get it," Lando said. "In fact, I get it better than you realize. You're playing sabacc."

Wedge considered that statement, his expression thoughtful. "I suppose so. And for bigger stakes than I've ever seen before."

FOUR

Borleias Occupation, Days 4–5

For the first time in years, Luke found himself facing an opponent whose very nature made him waver in courage and resolve: bureaucracy.

Meetings were among the most ferocious weapons of his opponent. He would spend one hour, two, three discussing anti–Yuuzhan Vong starfighter tactics with Colonel Celchu and a board of military advisers, then rush to a similarly lengthy, tedious, and tiring gathering with scientists pondering yet again the reason the Yuuzhan Vong and their creatures were invisible to the Force. Luke learned to alleviate his frustration by taking charge of the meetings and conducting them along with other activities—exercise, inventories of supplies, training sessions for the Jedi students aboard *Errant Venture*.

And yet plans progressed as the Inner Circle formulated the structure of a Resistance that could settle deep into hiding as the Yuuzhan Vong came and could then spring up to gut the invaders when the time arrived.

Similar in structure to the Jedi underground that Leia and Han had been organizing, the Resistance would be broader in nature and greater in numbers. The Inner Circle would land one or more trusted members on every world it could. Those members would set up Resistance cells of personnel. Each cell would set up more cells. No member of a cell would know the identities of more than two Resistance members outside his or her own cell, the better to contain damage if a cell were to be compromised. Each cell would try to establish a base that the Yuuzhan Vong could not find, a place to store vehicles, weapons, tools, droids, anything that the Resistance would need when the time came to return the fight to the Yuuzhan Vong.

The existence of the Inner Circle was known throughout Wedge's fleet group and nicknamed the Insiders, but it was commonly believed that it was a board of military advisers. Its true purpose remained a secret.

Luke offered what knowledge and tactics he could, and it turned out to be more than he'd expected.

In the years since he'd become a Jedi Master—and for years he'd been the *only* Jedi Master known to the galaxy—he'd searched tirelessly for knowledge about the Jedi as they had been before the rise of Emperor Palpatine to power. Palpatine and his right-hand servant, Darth Vader, Luke's own father, had systematically destroyed the Jedi and tried to eradicate all knowledge of their existence. Luke had sought to recover that knowledge. He'd searched out the remaining traces of the Jedi, finding scraps here and rumors there, and had learned to run those trails to ground. Most had led nowhere—as the Jedi he'd sought had either successfully vanished or had disappeared temporarily, only to be found, at last, by Palpatine's minions and expunged.

In learning how Jedi who had survived the initial sweeps of the Emperor's Purges had done so—how they'd gone to ground, erased their official identities, concealed their Force powers, smuggled their lightsabers, and eluded their hunters—Luke had, without knowing it, accumulated a tremendous, if only theoretical, knowledge of those techniques. Now, in meetings and recording sessions, that information poured from him and was added to the Intelligence training of Mara and others, becoming part of the handbook of establishing Resistance cells, as it had when he and his allies had begun setting up the Jedi underground across the galaxy.

Eventually, realizing what good they might do for the Resistance's cause, Luke became resigned to, even comfortable with, the meetings. And they kept his mind away from the worry and ache he could feel growing within him.

More than twenty-five years ago, when Luke's Uncle Owen and Aunt Beru had died on faraway, insignificant Tatooine, Luke had found himself alone—surrounded by new friends, but possessing no family. Then, over time, he'd gathered a family about him. His father had not been among those gathered; Anakin Skywalker had died months after the revelation of his true identity. But in Leia, Luke had found his true sister; then his friend Han Solo had become his brother-in-law. Their children, Jacen, Jaina, and Anakin Solo, had followed. Then Luke's relationship with Mara, which had evolved from a murderous hatred on her part to love on both their parts—love, and a bond, expressed through the Force, that blurred the edges between them, between their thoughts and hopes—had culminated in their marriage. Finally there had been Ben, born mere months ago, and Luke's family numbered eight, all calling Coruscant home.

Now "home" was a conquered battlefield. His family, gathered after so much sacrifice and effort over so many years, was scattered. Young Anakin Solo was dead, and all the hopes Luke had invested in him were gone. Jacen was missing; most were convinced he was dead as well. Jaina had not come to Borleias; she was off on a personal quest of vengeance, and such quests often led to ruin, the dark side of the Force, or death . . . or all three. Han now recuperated from an injury at a secret Jedi base, and Leia waited with him. The only ones Luke could hold to him each day were Mara and Ben, and the three of them lived surrounded by enemies.

Each time this realization hit Luke, he gently moved it away from his conscious thoughts and meditated, focusing himself on his purpose, his tasks, those he loved. But these Jedi techniques merely put off his worries for a while longer. The worries endured, waiting patiently to claim his attention and erode his confidence. They were the Yuuzhan Vong of his own mind.

Luke found himself surrounded by foliage and thought for an instant that he was on foot patrol in Borleias's jungles. But he realized within an instant that the air here was even danker than was customary on Borleias, and the precise nature of the plants and trees around him was wrong for that world. Here, the trees were darker, larger, their limbs drooping, while opaque pools of groundwater concealed furtive movements of their occupants.

Dagobah. It was the world where he had trained with Yoda, a lifetime ago.

So this was a dream. He shook his head. No, in dreams he was not usually so lucid. It was a vision, then, a vision through the Force.

He turned and faced the opening into the cave. It was there that he had confronted a vision of Darth Vader—of himself in Vader's distinctive dress. Now, there was no Yoda to warn him against taking weapons into this place of evil and confrontation, and Luke felt sad that this vision would not give him even the momentary pleasure of seeing his old Master again in the one context where his presence was appropriate.

Luke found he was dressed in black. His lightsaber hung at his waist. He removed it, depositing it in the crook of a tree branch, and entered the cave.

Within, he found only darkness and silence. But he knew something was there, a few steps from him, a deeper darkness. He could neither see nor hear it, but could feel it within the Force. He stepped toward it and felt it move to the side, circling him.

Then it brushed past him, a contact that sickened him, reawakened in him every great hatred of his life—for Darth Vader, for the Emperor, for himself when he had stumbled too far down the path of the dark side—and left the cave. Luke followed.

He emerged into brighter light than he'd seen outside a moment ago, and now he was surrounded by soaring buildings, construction so high that the sky was visible only as a faint sliver of light. All around him, duracrete surfaces, crashed landspeeders, and giant blocks of unrecognizable debris were coated with green algae and waving grasses in a more pallid green hue. At his feet, a human body was covered with the same stuff.

The darkness he'd pursued was ahead of him, farther down the narrow aperture between skyscrapers, still invisible to the naked eye, still nauseatingly tangible within the Force.

It roiled and spun like a tornado. It increased in size until it brushed against the buildings to either side. The algae and grasses there changed when it touched them, suddenly bearing large, malformed fruits as black and slick as old oil. Then every surface in sight was covered with the fruits, and as he watched they began to drop from their stems. They struck the ground and then struggled to newly developed feet, walking in every direction with the awkwardness of babies.

And each of them was filled with misery and dark side longing for ruin.

One opened its mouth and let out a piercing wail. Then another did, and a third. Suddenly the air was full of their cries.

A hand gripped Luke's shoulder. He opened his eyes. Mara was shaking him; her face was pale. The air was still filled with cries, but they were Ben's, and Mara held the baby away, as if to protect him from Luke. "What is it?" she asked.

"A vision." Luke brought his breathing under control and found that one part of his vision still lingered; dark side energy and malice still surrounded him. Ben, as sensitive to the Force as only the child of two eminent Jedi could be, wailed in protest. "There's evil on Coruscant. Tremendous dark side evil."

Borleias Occupation, Day 5

The hologram showed a familiar sight: the daytime skyline of some portion of Coruscant. The enormous, soaring buildings and the mottled orange clouds in the sky were distinctive to that world, though there were so countless many different planetary vistas like this that no one present could precisely identify the portion of Coruscant being displayed.

Things were different, though. The more distant skyscrapers seemed to be a uniform shade of green, and the reason why was evident on the nearer buildings: they were coated in a material that looked like algae. From the algae protruded things that looked like grasses, tree branches, umbrella-topped fungi. Up close, their colors were different; only in the distance did they blur together into a single hue.

Luke found the hologram unsettling. The algae and grasses were identical to those of his vision.

In the darkened conference chamber, a man stepped up next to the holoprojection. In the light cast by the projection of Coruscant, his face was luminous, the green from the algae lending color to his pale skin, white hair, mustache, and beard, giving him a nonhuman aspect. He was lean with age, though not to the point of emaciation. His garments were black, covering all but his head and hands, leaving viewers with the impression that those body parts were floating free in the chamber.

But this wasn't an eerie image. Many of those present had known his face for years. Wolam Tser was a political historian whose holodocumentaries had cataloged every stage of the New Republic's development from when it was nothing but a poorly funded, chaotically disorganized Rebel Alliance.

"I've stopped the image here for a moment," Wolam said, his rolling voice and upper-class accent instantly familiar to those in the chamber, "so you can see what is happening on Coruscant's surface. Some sort of planet shaping has begun. Those growths cover much of the planet's surface. They spread incredibly swiftly; everything you see in this image was bare duracrete the day before this was recorded. The darkest green material, some sort of pastelike scum, secretes acids that break down the chemical composition of duracrete. The fungi, I suspect, are related to the exploding fungi of Yavin Four; when struck, they detonate. The hardier-looking growths send deep taproots into the surfaces beneath them. In short, they are rapidly destroying the construction on Coruscant's surface—and, of course, construction covers almost every square centimeter of the planet's surface. The air, though this image doesn't suggest it, is increasingly noxious, and the remaining population is staying in ever-lower city levels, huddling near air scrubbers that provide them with adequate atmosphere."

Luke asked, "What about Yuuzhan Vong intrusions?"

Wolam peered in his direction, squinting in a futile effort to see deeper into the shadows. "That is the distinctive voice of Master Skywalker, isn't it?"

"It is."

"The Yuuzhan Vong are indeed performing raids into the lower levels. Some seem to have objectives, such as the destruction of air scrubbers, while others seem to be nothing but hunting expeditions. But the most fearsome of their assaults are not raids; they occur when the Yuuzhan Vong remove themselves from an area. They evacuate to a distance of many kilometers. And then this happens." Wolam brought up a small handheld device and depressed one of its buttons.

The frozen image suddenly flickered back into life, though nothing changed other than the motion of nearby planet-shaping growths in the wind and a brief flash of lightning in one of the clouds.

Then something did change. A patch of that cloud became brighter. Something erupted from it, a small flaming dot with a trail, descending at an angle toward the planet's surface.

The dot disappeared behind the buildings in the distance. There was a moment in which nothing occurred other than the dissipation of the dot's smoke trail high in the atmosphere.

A flash of light from that point in the distance briefly overloaded the holocam's ability to record; the image burned away to brightness. Then it returned.

The buildings still stood in the foreground and the distance, but now there was something behind them: a tall column of smoke spreading out toward the top into a shape reminiscent of many forms of fungus.

And something was racing toward the holocam, a shock wave. Nearest the smoke column, the buildings blurred and vanished. The wave of destruction, a distinct semicircle, flashed across the intervening kilometers faster than a starfighter could fly, eradicating every structure in its way. As the leading edge came close to the holocam's viewpoint, Luke could hear members of the audience drawing breath and leaning back as though to put more distance between them and the wave.

The vision of Coruscant shook and faded to blackness.

Someone brought up the lights in the chamber, and once again it was a cozy meeting room rather than a vision of doom.

Wolam stood near the head of the table, to Wedge's left; he was the only one standing. "That event nearly cost the life of my holocam operator, Tam." He gestured to a man at the rear of the chamber; the fellow, young and bulky enough to look awkward in a normal-sized chair, gave him an indifferent wave. "Tam lay unconscious for two days before finding his way back to me, and was sick for days after because he'd breathed in so much of the toxic atmosphere. He's still feeling the effects."

Wedge asked, "What sort of weapon did they use to achieve that result?"

Wolam gave him a thin smile. "Our own. That was a Golan Defense Platform. A few days ago, it defended Coruscant against the Yuuzhan Vong. Then, after it was destroyed, it was nudged from orbit to come down upon the planet's surface. I can't estimate . . ." He stopped, and there was no indication on his face of what had caused him to hesitate, but Luke felt a sudden flash of pain from the man. "I can't estimate how many died when it hit. Millions, tens of millions, hundreds of millions. That impact zone was a couple hundred kilometers southwest of the Imperial Palace. They're pushing more satellites and skyhooks down, one after another. And since only a few million of Coruscant's citizens have found passage offworld, the vast majority are in mortal peril—in the short term, from the falling satellites, and in the long term from the planet shaping."

"We appreciate the information you've brought us," Wedge said, "and the samples you've given us have been forwarded to our team of scientists specializing in Yuuzhan Vong techniques." He consulted the datapad before him. "Your shuttle's damage—that was sustained during your departure from Coruscant?"

Wolam nodded. "One reason it took me a few days to depart was that several of us clubbed together to make a mass departure. The idea was that, since their starfighter analogs would inevitably come after us, some of us might survive where one ship wouldn't." He looked apologetic. "Mine was one of the few that made it out."

"Your damage is being repaired. Your shuttle should be ready in a day or two. We can send you out with the next batch of refugee departures; you'll have starfighter cover for your trip."

Wolam glanced around. Luke saw his attention freeze, for the barest of moments, on several of the faces present at the meeting, including Luke's own. Then Wolam returned his attention to Wedge. "If I may, I'd like to stay instead. I'm a historian. Here is where history is being made. We won't be much of a draw on your resources. We have quarters aboard my shuttle."

"Very well." Wedge stood. "Now, it's back to work. I'm sorry it's all bad news today, but we need to be kept updated."

On his way out the door, Tam accepted congratulations from many of those who'd been present—congratulations on bringing valuable information, congratulations on surviving. He nodded and gulped, uncomfortable at being among so many people—at being among so many *famous* people—and moved as quickly as he could. His size, for he was tall enough to brush his hair against the top of the doorjamb and bulky enough to bring a smile to the face of a smashball team owner, acted against him, as it usually did; he managed to catch chair legs with his feet and inadvertently brushed some smaller people out of the way as he staggered for the door. Then he was out in the hall, where at least the traffic was moving in the direction he wanted to go, and a few moments later was outside, gratefully gulping in Borleias's moist, warm air.

"Not much for crowds, are you?" The speaker—female, young—had moved up beside him as he'd recovered.

He took a look at her and his stomach lurched again. She was right. Crowds were bad. But attractive females didn't help either. They, too, made words stick in his throat and made his heart hammer. This one was slender, her hair a cascade of blond curls now tied back in a tail. Her eyes were a lively blue, her features the sort that brightened any chamber they entered.

Tam took a moment to remember what it was she'd said. He managed a smile that, he hoped, suggested he was at ease. "That's right. I'm a *field* holocam operator, not a city boy. How I ever let Wolam persuade me to come back to Coruscant with him really baffles me."

"I suspect that he's pretty persuasive."

"He is." Tam thought furiously, trying to remember what normal people did in these situations, then extended his hand. "Tam Elgrin."

She shook it. "Danni Quee."

"Say, I know your name. You're almost famous." Then he winced. "That came out wrong."

Her smile said that she was amused rather than offended. "Listen, Tam, I have a question for you. Do you have any recordings that Wolam Tser didn't show us back there? Any recordings of the Yuuzhan Vong?"

"I—" He felt the onset of a headache but ignored it. He hadn't been told that he couldn't share his recordings. Wolam Tser might fret about it, but then again, in these times of war, when it was vital to share information with appropriate parties, he probably wouldn't. "I do. I have some recordings of a Yuuzhan Vong hunting pack. In the midlevels of Coruscant. I was with some people. After I stopped recording and really started running, I got toward the front of the pack and the Yuuzhan Vong fell on those in the rear." He shrugged. "So I got away." He pulled up the bag he always carried with him, the one that held his holocam, his miniature backup holocam, his recordings, his recording blanks. He found the recording he was looking for and pressed the data card into her hand. "That's the one. I'd like it back."

"I'll copy it and get it back to you soon. Today, even."

"Thanks."

"Nice meeting you." She flashed him a smile and headed back into the building.

"Likewise." Finally able to get his heart rate under control, Tam headed away from the building, out into the kill zone.

Within the half kilometer nearest the front of the building, the burned-out area that had once been jungle was heavily occupied by vehicles and vessels; two large docking bays were under construction, duracrete being poured, prefabricated metal walls being raised. All around them were shuttles and starfighters, speeders and hovercrafts, transports and one large freighter with extensive damage to its bow.

Tam brought out his holocam and took a few moments to record the scene. Someday, if the New Republic survived, people would want to know how these events played out.

The headache grew in strength so suddenly that it felt as though he'd been stabbed. He cried out, clutched his head, and struggled to keep from falling.

He knew why the headache was back. It was because he wasn't obeying. His instructions were clear. He dropped the holocam back into his bag.

Tam weaved his way between the ships in the kill zone to reach his—well, really, Wolam's—shuttle.

Of course, it was a shuttle in function, not a shuttle in design. It had begun its career as a Sienar-built Skipray blastboat, an Imperial four-person gunship. An ungainly-looking thing, it had a bow that looked like an eccentric cam gear, the narrowest portion pointed forward and broadened by a pair of fixed wings angled downward at a sharp angle. The bow was attached to a stern that was little more than a huge axle. Mounted on the axle were the stabilizer fins, forward-sweeping wings that could rotate to be horizontal for landing or vertical for stabilization in atmospheric flight.

When it had been a machine of war, it had been heavily armed. But years ago, after Wolam Tser had stolen it when escaping with recordings of Imperial base-building activities that the Empire didn't want him to retain, he'd begun modifying the boat. The proton torpedo and concussion missile tubes had been removed to give the boat more cargo and cabin room. The laser cannon turret on top had been replaced with a transparisteel dome, opening up more cabin room and offering those beneath it another view of the stars. The controls had been simplified, making the optimum crew size two instead of four.

Behind the command cabin, room that had been

needed for missile racks was now converted into two smallish cabins, one for Wolam and one for his holocam operator.

Tam offered a false smile and a wave to the mechanics now welding metal plates over the holes in the wings, repairing damage sustained when one of the boat's companion vehicles had exploded under coralskipper fire. He climbed up the port-side bow wing to the main hatch and entered, his movements hurried. Only if he hurried would the headache be kept at bay.

He didn't pause as he entered the command cabin but headed into the aft passageway. In two paces he was at the door to his cramped cabin. He entered in a rush—*Hurry, hurry*—and sealed the door behind him.

He lifted the mattress of his bunk to reveal the storage compartment beneath. In it was a large, roughly spherical piece of rock—"A souvenir of Corellia," he'd explained to Wolam.

Of course, he'd lied. He'd had to.

He set the stone, which was lighter than it should be, atop his bunk and rapped three times on its surface. A moment later, he rapped again, twice.

The stone split along an invisible center seam. It opened like an ocean bivalve, but instead of revealing two linings of flesh and perhaps a pearl, it showed only an amorphous blobby mass of material in the bottom.

His stomach lurching at the thought of touching it again, Tam reached out and found the slight protrusion at the top of the blob. He stroked it, feeling the living thing react to his touch. He snatched back his hand and wiped it on his pants, though there was no residue on his fingers from the smooth thing.

Moments later, the blobby material stretched up and assumed the approximate shape of a human head. Tam didn't think it was a Yuuzhan Vong female's head; the forehead was too pronounced, the features not made irregular by mutilation.

The villip looked at him with the face of his controller. "Report," it said, its speech unaccented.

Tam felt his headache fade to almost nothingness, but the turmoil in his stomach, the turmoil in his emotions kept this from being the relief it otherwise would have been. "We are on Borleias," he began.

Borleias Occupation, Day 6, Predawn

There was a rap at the door. Wedge jolted upright, his eyes opening, his mind momentarily cloudy about where he was, what he should be doing.

He was still in his office, in his chair, but he'd fallen asleep. He couldn't let himself do that. Every moment he didn't push himself, more people might die.

He rubbed sleep from his eyes and turned to the door. "Come."

The door slid over and out of sight, but there was no one in the corridor beyond. Then his visitor showed himself, peeking in from around the doorjamb.

The man was of average height and bald—shaven bald, Wedge knew, rather than prematurely bald. His mustache and goatee were close-cropped and black, giving him a sinister appearance, but his smile, all cheer flavored with wicked humor, dispelled any sense of dread. He was handsome in a way that only celebrities and a few extraordinarily successful businessmen and criminals could be.

Wedge rose. "Face! I was afraid you were lost back on Coruscant. Come in."

Garik "Face" Loran, leader of the covert Intelligence team known as the Wraiths, shook his head. "Later. For now, I'm just here to drop off a package."

"What package—"

She moved around Face, entering the office at just short of a dead run. She was tall, Wedge's average stature making them the same height, and slender, with dark blond hair now frosted attractively with gray. In her youth she'd been an extraordinary beauty; now, to Wedge's perception, lines of laughter and worry accentuated that beauty rather than detracted from it.

Suddenly he was on the other side of the desk—by running or vaulting, he could not recall—and enfolding her in his arms. "Iella . . ."

There was more noise than two voices could account for, cries of "Daddy!" Wedge released his wife, crouched, and grabbed up his dark blond, blue-eyed daughters, who had magically appeared on either side of Iella; he stood with one in either arm, Syal in the left and Myri in the right.

A few days before, when he'd picked them both up in their quarters on Coruscant, he'd complained that they were getting big, too heavy for him to lift. Now, their arms around his neck, he could barely detect their weight.

A moment ago he'd had nothing but a mission. Now he had a future again, a future he could hold to himself, a future he could squeeze and hear and smell. Wedge glanced over at Face, but the Wraith leader had, appropriately, vanished while attention was elsewhere, and the door was sliding closed where he'd been.

They lay in the darkness of Wedge's quarters. Moonlight spilled in through the turquoise transparisteel, casting everything in shades of blue, bed and walls and skin.

"It's not the same as watching your home dying," Iella said. Her voice was thoughtful. She stared at the bluetinged ceiling as if staring far beyond it, staring all the way back to Coruscant. "Not the same as if they'd descended on Corellia. But seeing orbital platforms drop onto the city, knowing that millions were dying with every impact, knowing that the few who were streaming into space in private vessels and leaving their homes behind were the *lucky* ones . . . Coruscant is dying. Wedge, I don't know if I can describe the misery of it."

"You don't have to," he said. "I know what it was like to leave you behind. To have to tell myself, 'I *can't* find them, I *can't* help them, I *can* keep people alive up here.' "

She turned a smile on him. "Didn't you trust me to get us out alive?"

"Yes. But trust doesn't keep worry from eating you up from inside."

She kissed him, rested her head on his shoulder. "What do we do now?"

"Well, you were just promoted to head of Intelligence for my operation here, which frees up Mara to make the Vong suffer in her own inimitable way. I'm going to need you to spread information among our people and see if the Yuuzhan Vong act on any of it—if we have any traitors among us, I want to find out who they are as fast as possible, to use them for our own purposes or eliminate them as a threat."

"Is that going to be here or at some other station?"

"Here." And he told her of the meeting with the Advisory Council.

She was silent for a long time as she thought about what he'd said. "Wedge, you're doing what you never like to do. Fighting a two-front war. The Yuuzhan Vong on one side and the Advisory Council on the other."

Wedge smiled. "The Advisory Council doesn't know we're at war with them."

"They know they're at war with us; they just don't

know *we* know it. But they may figure it out more quickly than you imagine. Even without Borsk to lead them, they have a lot of political smarts. Which means that Yuuzhan Vong spies aren't the only spies you have to worry about. One of my jobs is going to be leaking information and seeing how our supposed *allies* respond to it . . . so we can use them for our own purposes or eliminate them as a threat."

"I knew I was keeping you around for a reason."

"At least two reasons."

"Don't tickle."

FIVE

Yuuzhan Vong Worldship, Coruscant Orbit

The villip stared at Viqi Shesh with the face of a human man, large-boned, the angle of his head suggesting fear and pain. "I'm not in a position to learn any secrets," the villip protested. "I just follow Wolam Tser around, recording his observations and interviews."

Viqi made her voice a purr. She hoped its tones and nuances would carry across the villip. This voice excited men, made them long for her, and the notion that desire for her would torment this man amused her. "You met Danni Quee. Become her friend. Her lover, if you're capable of it. Convince her to confide in you. Volunteer for additional duties when Tser isn't making use of you. You can do simple electronics repairs, can't you?"

Tam's voice sounded pained. "Yes."

"Get a job doing that. Put recorders or transmitters in devices that will go in critical places. Iella Wessiri is good enough to find anything *you* might plant, so don't try to harvest the information those devices might bring you; instead, leave counterpart objects where blame will fall on people within their command structure, people Antilles and Skywalker don't quite trust yet. Cause paranoia. Do you understand?"

"I understand."

"Prove it, simpleton." Viqi stroked the villip and it contracted, cutting off the communication.

She sighed and stretched. The skin of her back, still healing, protested, but she did not let that minor pain show on her face. Then she turned, the bloblike material that served her as a chair accommodating itself to her motion, and faced her own controller.

He was dressed in the loincloth of a warrior, amphistaff in hand. His nose had been smashed flat, an oddly symmetrical mutilation for a Yuuzhan Vong, and part of his right upper lip was gone, revealing teeth beneath. His skin was decorated extensively with tattoos.

But his most extensive mutilation was a single puckered scar. In most places it was an angry red, sometimes graduating to a scabrous brown, everywhere standing out starkly against his skin. It started out at the top of his bald head, wound down his right cheek to his chin and up the other side, then turned downward again just short of his left eye. It continued down his neck and wound back and forth across his chest before disappearing beneath his harness. It reemerged on his right thigh, ending in a circle around his knee. It must have been among his earliest decorations, for his tattoos paralleled it, never running across it.

His name was Denua Ku, and Viqi knew from the few words she had exchanged with him that he had no grasp of Intelligence operations. He was here to guard her, not to help her with her assignment. She gave him a smile that was all contempt and mockery. "All done," she said.

"Then you will return to your quarters." His voice suggested mutual contempt, even through the tizowyrm, an organic translator of the Yuuzhan Vong, implanted in her ear.

"I'm sick of my quarters. I do half an hour's worth of work a day managing this idiot of an operative and spend the rest of my time in chambers that smell like half-cooked bantha tripe. I want something to *do*."

Denua Ku said nothing. Viqi took that as a good sign. If he'd been under strict orders to keep her in her quarters, he would have immediately demanded that they go there. But he wasn't going to suggest any sort of recreation to her; she'd have to find her own diversion.

She knew they'd never agree to a diversion that would get her near spacecraft or pilot training, so she'd have to find some other way to get her into other parts of the worldship, places where she could meet other Yuuzhan Vong—or even some of their prisoners.

"I want to learn how coralskippers and buildings and armor are grown. How everything is grown. I suppose I'll need a skill for when the Yuuzhan Vong have subjugated everything and don't need an Intelligence division anymore." Denua Ku didn't answer, so she added, "Take my request to the warmaster. I suspect he'll agree to it."

It was the carrion-eaters' hour, or so Tsavong Lah thought of it, the hour in which he permitted visitors to come before him on miscellaneous errands, the hour in which he cleaned away his visitors' petty difficulties so they didn't accumulate like carrion. He steered his attention away from that customary thought, as it came too close to his problem with his new arm.

The warrior Denua Ku came before him with Viqi Shesh's request. Tsavong Lah authorized it. The human woman would never abandon her manipulative ways to learn a productive trade.

Next into the small reception chamber was Maal Lah, his kinsman and one of his best military advisers. Maal Lah's features were surprisingly regular, his jawline unbroken, but his face was meticulously decorated with red and blue swirls.

"Yes, my servant?" the warmaster asked.

"I have learned a curious thing," Maal Lah said. "The infidel fleet that took Borleias has not yet begun its withdrawal. And the surviving warriors of Domain Kraal report that the tool-users are digging in as if against a siege."

"That makes little sense from a military viewpoint," the warmaster said. "They cannot hope to hold it. They cannot hope for relief." He considered the matter. "Send Wyrpuuk Cha's fleet to crush them. Domain Kraal despises Domain Cha; having to admit a debt to Cha will be additional punishment for not holding Borleias as they should."

"Yes, Warmaster."

"Was there anything else?"

"No, Warmaster." Maal Lah withdrew.

Next to receive an audience was Takhaff Uul, a priest. Highly placed within the order of Yun-Yuuzhan, the great god of the Yuuzhan Vong, Takhaff Uul was young for his duties; others of his age in the same sect were low-ranking priests, servants and aides to senior priests, while he was already a well-respected interpreter of the god's will. His tattoos were not geometric designs or exaggerations of deformities; his designs were of eyeballs, small clawed hands, tentacles, all rendered in realistic detail as if to suggest he had had dozens of transplants in his short life. He bowed low before the warmaster.

"Speak," Tsavong Lah said.

Takhaff Uul straightened. "I speak out of place," he said, "bypassing the high priest to bring words directly to your ears, so I have come prepared to die if my words displease you."

"You should always come prepared to die," Tsavong Lah said. "You should not try to predict when your words will displease me."

"Yes, Warmaster."

"Speak your mind."

"I speak not my mind, but the will of the Creator, Yun-Yuuzhan. My visions of him in last night's dreams led me to thoughts of you and your . . . affliction."

Tsavong Lah lifted the hand of his radank claw and studied its grasping digits. With this limb, he could rend the throat of a Yuuzhan Vong warrior . . . assuming the limb did not tear free of him with such an exertion. "What did he say of me?"

"Only that your pursuit of this war brings much pleasure to the heart of the slayer Yun-Yammka."

"I do not see how this relates to my arm."

"It was what he did *not* say, Warmaster. I felt—and this was only a priest's intuition—that the Creator believed himself to be separate from the glory you are achieving. That he is not receiving his due share. That he is displeased."

"And what did you feel would correct this measure?"

"A dedication, Warmaster. A gift. Something offered to Yun-Yuuzhan alone. An entire world devoted to the Creator and his priests and concerns."

"But the priests of Yun-Yuuzhan have haven everywhere, among all domains and colonies."

"Yes, Warmaster. I know you are correct. But who can know the mind of a god? I can only interpret the dreams I have, and hope that I am correct."

"I will consider this." With his radank claw, Tsavong Lah made a shooing gesture, and the young priest withdrew.

As soon as the priest's back was turned, Tsavong Lah nodded to one of his trusted guards and made a gesture that only the warmaster and his personal guards understood. That guard followed Takhaff Uul to the chamber portal; when the priest was well down the corridor, the guard spoke quietly to another guard, then returned to stand behind Tsavong Lah's seat.

The warmaster dealt with another pair of administrative matters. Then the guard who had followed Takhaff Uul returned and presented himself before the warmaster.

"Well?"

"He went to the chambers of Ghithra Dal, the shaper," the guard said.

Tsavong Lah sat in contemplation for long moments. Ghithra Dal was the shaper who had attached his radank claw.

Viqi Shesh might have been correct.

He would have to find out.

Borleias Occupation, Day 9

The fleet of Wyrpuuk Cha slowed as it entered the outer limits of the Pyria system. The system's distant sun was visible through the amber-colored shell that served the bridge as a viewport, but Wyrpuuk Cha paid it no attention, concentrating instead on the cloud of blaze bugs that hovered in the black hemispherical depression at the rear of the chamber.

The insects, capable of hovering in flight and glowing or growing dark at the mental command of the fleet's yammosk, formed glowing patterns and shapes within that depression. A spherical cluster of them represented the system's sun. Others formed smaller balls representing the planets of the system. Numberless glowing mites of a related species, too small to see but for their bluish glow, arrayed themselves to represent the crisscrosses of ionic trails that decorated the solar system, indicating where the hated metal ships of the enemy had recently made runs.

Other blaze bugs hovered singly or formed into small, irregular patches. These, Wyrpuuk Cha knew, constituted groups of enemy ships. Knowledge of their whereabouts came from villip transmissions from the Yuuzhan Vong refugees on Borleias and from the gravitic senses of the yammosk, but the information was incomplete; fleet elements too near gravity wells would not be detectable, nor would ships situated at distant points in or just beyond the solar system. The enemy could have hundreds of ships located here; it would take time and sacrifice to root them out and destroy them.

Time he had, and warriors in great number willing to make that sacrifice. Depending on the enemy forces and commanders, it might prove a struggle, but Wyrpuuk Cha would be able to take this system.

The question was whether he'd be able to take it swiftly enough, efficiently enough to please Warmaster Tsavong Lah. He could not afford to spend too much time or expend too many resources. He needed, strategically speaking, to bare his belly, invite his enemy's attack, and gut his opponent while that opponent was outstretched, out of balance, out of position. He could afford one feint, maybe two.

"They have not reestablished shield platforms in orbit around the planet." That was a female voice. It belonged to Kadlah Cha, a military analyst belonging to his own domain.

He spared her a look. Her facial tattooing was startling even by Yuuzhan Vong standards, darkness around her eyes and below her lower lip suggesting, at first glance, that those features were grossly oversized. Her decorations were a mirror image of, and copied from, his own, though his were accentuated by scarring from warfare and a slit at the center of his upper lip, rising nearly to his nose, that acted as an artificial harelip and perpetually bared his upper teeth. "So they will have situated a minefield around Borleias, and simulated a shield with their metal ships."

"No, Commander." She moved to the blaze bug depression and extended her hands into it, waving many of the images aside, waving the spherical cluster representing Borleias toward her. The dismissed insects swarmed toward the sphere, expanding it, adding details representing vessels in orbit around the planet. "See? They have capital vessels in what looks like geosynchronous orbit above one point on the planet, not far from the Domain Kraal touchdown point, and other vessels in more typical orbits. Nothing else. And the Kraals report no buildup of ground-based shield generators except at this site."

"A hardpoint defense of one location." Wyrpuuk Cha considered that, reevaluating the situation. He reached into the depression and gestured to return the image to its previous magnification. "And see here. Recent, repeated travel to this orbit above the sixth planet, an orbit corresponding to one of its moons. Yet no indication of ships here now. A hidden base of some sort? They're not protecting the primary world from intrusions that could drop planetshaping materials, so they don't care about the world itself . . . just what is to be found at that one site. We must find out what they protect there and on that moon."

The alarm jolted Wedge and Iella out of their sleep. It was a shrill, keening thing, not the sort of alarm installed in a military installation; it had to be some sort of biological hazard alert that was part of this station's original equipment. Wedge groped on the table beside his bed for his comlink and found it was already beeping for him, the sound drowned out by the alarm. "Antilles here."

"We have a major Yuuzhan Vong intrusion." The comm officer's voice was a disinterested drawl in distinct contrast with the importance of his message. "Dozens of capital ships entering the system at its outer fringes from Coruscant's bearing. No sign yet of coralskipper launch."

"Issue a systemwide alert condition. I'll be there immediately." Wedge rose, mind already clear and focused on his task, and began to dress.

He saw that Iella was already one jumpsuit ahead of him. She sealed her suit's main seam and asked, "What's the plan for today?"

"Bad tactics. We're leaving a gap in our coverage of the sensor station on the fourth moon of Pyria Six. We'll beat back whatever comes at Borleias but let them chase us off that moon. I'll be coordinating from the ground so they can *detect* that I'm coordinating from the ground. Reinforces the impression that there's something important down here, too."

She helped him seal his suit and gave him a quick kiss. "I hate it that you're going to lose, even on purpose."

"Why?"

"Because you're such a bad loser."

He gave her a grin. "Ultimately, I intend to be a very, *very* bad loser."

SIX

Borleias Occupation, Day 9

Saba Sebatyne, a Jedi Knight of the Barabel people, tapped her way through the power-up checklist of the Wild Knights' lead blastboat. Her fingers moved deftly and surely for such a large and bulky creature; Barabels were reptilian, covered in scales, with large eyes protected by heavy, protruding brow ridges, but otherwise somewhat inexpressive faces.

Danni Quee covertly watched Saba. Danni's position on the ship, sensor operator and sometimes ship's weapons, didn't call for as much preparation as Saba's. Saba's efficiency and speed with her task were undiminished, but Danni knew she had been through much pain recently—the loss of her Jedi Master, Eelysa, to a Yuuzhan Vong–bred monster called a voxyn on Corellia, and then the loss of two of her kin, hatchmates to her own son, during Anakin Solo's successful but costly mission to destroy the queen—the source of the voxyn. But Barabels were very different from humans in their expressions of pain and grief, inviting no sympathy, so Danni could offer her no condolences.

Saba came to the end of her checklist. "Pilot station ready," she said.

"Sensor station ready," Danni responded automatically, and the other Wild Knights aboard called out their readiness. Danni was not technically a Wild Knight, nor technically a Jedi Knight like the others, but she had flown with them on many occasions now and found that her duty station, when she wasn't occupied with critical scientific projects, was aboard the Wild Knights' blastboat.

Saba called in the squadron's state of readiness and immediately received the unit's orders. With a hiss, she turned her attention away from the screen before her as if rejecting its presence.

"What is it?" Danni asked. "If you can tell us, I mean."

"We are to defend, and lose, and quit the field," Saba said. "To act as a shield. Conservative tacticz. This one is a hunter. This one does not know how to defend or flee."

"*This* one is a scientist," Danni said. "This one didn't used to know how to kill."

Saba regarded Danni levelly, then returned her attention to the screen. "Danni can return to using human grammar now," she said.

Twin Suns Squadron, Rogue Squadron, and the Wild Knights blasted off from Borleias's surface. The fuel it took to reach orbit, though not a substantial portion of the starfighters' capacity, could well be missed in the later stages of today's battle, but Luke agreed with Wedge that allowing the Yuuzhan Vong to detect the launch of three preeminent New Republic squadrons from the planet's surface would reinforce the enemy's impression that this was a significant site.

As they reached high orbit, their astromechs and onboard computers received detailed orders. Luke reviewed them and nodded. Twin Suns was to stay in geosynchronous orbit above the biotics facility and vape anything that came at it. Rogue Squadron would set up above Borleias's moon and make a speed run against any promising target of opportunity. The Wild Knights would move to reinforce the lunar station at Pyria VI. "Twin Suns on station," he announced. "Rogues, Knights, good hunting."

"Good hunting." That was Saba Sebatyne's voice, made even raspier by the limitations of the comlink. Her starfighters and blastboats peeled off for their run to Pyria VI. Gavin Darklighter responded with a mere click of his own comlink before Rogue Squadron looped away for the short run to Borleias's moon.

Luke glanced behind him, to port and starboard. To port, Corran Horn waited with a calm he had never enjoyed as an X-wing pilot, a calm he had attained only after becoming a Jedi Knight. But to starboard, where Mara should have been, was Zindra Daine. She was a Corellian pilot, green as grass, barely out of her teens, not a Jedi. Luke winced at the thought of himself and Corran having to cover for a novice. Mara's absence would be keenly felt today and in subsequent engagements. Though he sympathized with her desire to stay with Ben, to protect him against all possible dangers, he hoped Mara would realize that her desire was irrational, her goal an impossible one—and that her absence from the battlefield might just result in the loss of good people.

Wedge stood before the hologram at the center of the command room. This was an unlovely lozenge-shaped chamber with a curved ceiling two dozen meters below the biotics building. It had once been intended as a blast shelter, but now it was crammed with mobile consoles and their operators.

The chamber's duracrete walls, not well designed for acoustics, rang with noise, the voices of military officers doing their duties, the beeps and chirps of computers demanding their operators' attention, live sound feeds from unit leaders up there in the battle zone. Wedge ignored them and concentrated on the continuously updated tactical holo.

It showed Pyria at one edge, Borleias a little out from it, Pyria VI farther out, and the fringes of the solar system at the far edge. Red blips representing the Yuuzhan Vong invasion force clustered at that edge and streamed toward the other sites.

"The Rogues are on-station," Tycho said. As chronically unable as Wedge was to run his operations from a seated position, he stood before the console devoted to starfighter coordination. "The starfighters on the target moon are standing by. Vong intrusion there anticipated in two minutes."

"Have those fighters launch," Wedge said. "Make it erratic. They can form up in time, but they should look as though they were caught off guard."

"Done." Tycho turned back to his screen.

Wedge's attention flicked across the hologram. Some ships lay dormant, well away from the action, monitoring the situation with their sensors, ready to step in should reinforcements be needed. Frigates, cruisers, and other capital ships were situated above Borleias. Starfighter units maneuvered to head off the Yuuzhan Vong approach.

The main Yuuzhan Vong force stayed coherent, a reserve fleet situated not far from where it had entered Pyrian space. The units moving against the New Republic forces were, Wedge knew, mere probes, sent out to test the strength of the defensive forces. This battle wasn't about winning or losing; it was about gathering information on enemy capabilities.

"Pyria Six reports contact," Tycho said.

* * *

Captain Yakown Reth was not a happy man.

It wasn't enough that, of all the up-and-coming officers in Wedge Antilles's command, he'd been assigned the unpromising duty of guarding a shuttle load of scientists, engineers, and construction specialists building a subsurface habitat on an airless moon. Yes, he'd been assigned two full squadrons of starfighters to defend the base. But his E-wings were not equipped with proton torpedoes—the brass said that these weapons were in short supply—and Reth wasn't even authorized to know what the scientific personnel were up to.

And now, as Yuuzhan Vong coralskippers hurtled toward him, came to wipe out this idiotic little facility, Colonel Celchu was micromanaging him, dictating that wing pairs launch only as they came ready after going through a second checklist. His forces were straggling into space like an undisciplined mob. If General Antilles was monitoring the action here, he'd assume that Reth was an idiot.

Finally, as the incoming blips on the sensor screens reached the outer limits of his starfighters' range of fire, the last two E-wings of Green Squadron struggled into formation and announced their readiness.

"Remember, no individual heroics," Reth said. "We have to overwhelm their defenses and overlap our own. Break by wing quads on my command, three, two, one . . . now." He suited action to words and spun down a few hundred meters toward the jagged and unappealing surface of the moon he was protecting. Green Two through Green Four followed him, in loose, imprecise formation. This was not surprising for a group that had been cobbled together from units shattered back at Coruscant. But it was aggravating. It made him look sloppy.

Coralskippers too distant to see opened fire; trails of

glowing redness lanced out toward Green Squadron. Reth nudged closer to Green Two, his wingmate, and saw Green Three and Four crowding in, allowing their shields to overlap. Reth grimaced. Working with unfamiliar pilots in such proximity was as distasteful to him as the thought of trading unwashed clothing with them.

"Accelerate to full," he said. "We'll punch through and come back. Set lasers to stutterfire. I'll designate a target and we'll all hit it. Ready . . . mark." He put his targeting reticle on an incoming coralskipper, not the first in the line coming toward him but the third, and fired a burst.

Red laser beams erupted from his E-wing's nose and wingtips, an irregular drizzle rather than a hard-hitting burst of concentrated energy. Bursts from his wingmates followed his in, drenching his target. Reth hated the new stutterfire configuration. He knew that it did damage around the coralskippers' blasted void defenses, but it prevented the lasers from hitting with any sort of satisfying power.

An incoming stream of lava balls angled across his formation. Three or four hit the overlapping shields of the E-wings, and the audible sensor interpreters of his vehicle noted the impacts with sharp bangs. His diagnostics didn't light up, and his sensors showed his target followed by a cometlike tail consisting of bits of yorik coral chewed away by their laserfire.

Though that coralskipper was still sound, Reth switched targets, pouring his damage and that of his wingmates on another skip. This coralskipper, angling straight into the path of his lasers, was distantly visible, and Reth saw his unit's lasers chewing at it, at its edges, across its canopy; though its void flashed in front of much of the laserfire, swallowing it, enough curved around the singularity's edges and penetrated the skip's surface. That skip suddenly became as luminous as the distant Pyrian sun and then was gone.

Reth managed a tight smile. So far, so good.

"Sensors show a formation looping around the moon toward us." The voice, quiet and controlled, was Corran's, and it came across Luke's private comlink, not the one built into his X-wing. Corran's X-wing was several hundred kilometers behind the Twin Suns Squadron's formation in lunar orbit, trailing it and acting as rear guard.

Luke nodded. The main sensor relay from the ground stations showed a column of coralskippers and frigate analogs on a straight approach toward Borleias, but the Yuuzhan Vong had obviously detected Twin Suns and sent a detachment around the moon to trap them between two forces. "Get back up here," he told Corran. "Prepare a shadow bomb to drop." The other pilots of Twin Suns weren't Jedi and so weren't capable of utilizing the shadow bomb weapons—proton torpedoes with their propulsion units removed, shoved across space merely by the powers of the Jedi mind—so he didn't have to transmit these orders to them. He activated his snubfighter's comlink on squadron frequency. "Prepare to follow me in." He switched back to the scrambled frequency he shared with Corran and Zindra. "Thirty seconds before our pursuit gets into firing range, we accelerate straight toward the enemy column . . . but Corran and I leave the shadow bombs behind."

Corran and Zindra responded with comlink clicks.

Sensors showed Yuuzhan Vong vessels far ahead, crossing the plane of lunar orbit on their approach toward Borleias. Luke could distantly see the running lights, or whatever the organic equivalents were, on the Yuuzhan Vong frigate analogs. Corran was much closer, approaching fast from the rear, and now Luke could detect the first blips indicating the detachment coming up behind Corran. "Drop shadow bombs," he said, and kicked his accelerator into life as he dropped his own shadow bomb.

Twin Suns Squadron roared out from lunar orbit on a straight approach toward the main Yuuzhan Vong column. Their course had to be absolutely straight if the trick was to work.

His Force perceptions irrelevant, Luke kept his eye on the sensors. They showed the distant blip of Yuuzhan Vong pursuers growing less distant; they showed the tiny, coded comlink transmission from the shadow bombs left behind; they showed the alien column ahead, also getting closer and closer.

"They're firing," Zindra said, the high-pitched excitement of a novice in her voice, and Luke saw flashes of distant lava cannon misses in his peripheral vision.

Luke began juking and jinking, his attention divided between controlling his X-wing and and the shadow bomb he had launched.

The trailing force of coralskippers numbered about thirty; at this range, it was hard to get exact numbers. They were approaching the point where the Jedi had dropped the shadow bombs and were in a narrow approach formation, a speed formation. Luke nudged the shadow bombs into a line, each a few kilometers from the next, and watched their blips separate and line up in anticipation of the approaching skips.

He didn't feel the coralskippers pass the rearmost shadow bomb; his Force perceptions couldn't detect them. But the sensors showed the line of skips reach and begin to superimpose itself on the line of shadow bombs. He waited until the foremost skip reached the leading bomb, then reached out and squeezed with a small measure of his Force powers.

On the sensors, the clean line of coralskippers behind became a fuzzy mass, then began to fade. Where perhaps thirty skips had been in pursuit, half that number now looped away from the detonation point, in search of whatever mystery ship must have attacked them.

Luke snapped back to the here and now. Zindra's X-wing was directly above him, its mass blocking his direct view of the fight, but he could tell that they were in the midst of the main coralskipper column, had maneuvered into the midst of the enemy while most of his attention was locked up with the shadow bombs. Corran was still tucked in to port, his shields overlapping Luke's and providing additional support, patiently waiting for Luke to snap back to full attention so they could deal with the enemies ahead.

Zindra's voice crackled over the comlink: "Great shooting! Um, are we going to do anything about that frigate ahead?"

Luke suppressed the urge to grind his teeth. "Yes, we are. I'll take lead." He goosed his thrusters; he and Corran maneuvered ahead of Zindra. "Follow me in."

Luke peeled off on a strafing run against the frigate analog. Corran and Zindra followed.

Saba fired and a pulse from the Wild Knights' ion cannons washed across a tight formation of coralskippers, causing them to spin out of control; the skips veered out of the main engagement area above the moon of Pyria VI.

The blastboat shuddered. Saba checked her diagnostics screen, saw nothing, and glanced at Danni, who was on the main sensors.

Danni shook her head. "No damage. But . . . well . . . it's a good excuse."

Saba hissed in vexation, but said, "Do it."

Danni activated a control on her console board. Saba, unhappy, added a little wobble to the blastboat's motion as it looped around toward another patch of coralskippers.

"Wild Knights One, this is Green Leader. You're venting atmosphere, repeat, venting atmosphere. Can you hear me? Over."

Saba stared unhappily at her controls. Of course they were venting atmosphere. They'd rigged the rear of the blastboat with a couple of new valves to do just that—to eject a compressed oxygen and nitrogen mix to suggest they'd been hulled.

Danni activated her comlink. "Green Leader, this is *Wild One*. We've taken major grutchin hits. Venting . . . they're chewing through toward the engines . . ." Her voice sounded pained, and she added a racking cough to her performance. "Smoke in the cabin . . ."

"*Wild One*, get out of here. Get to ground, now. We'll hold here."

"Thanks, Green Leader. Wild Knights are—" Danni clicked the comlink off and then added, unnecessarily, "away." She looked up at Saba, guilt in her expression.

Saba hissed again and banked around back toward Borleias.

Behind them, over the next few minutes, the other members of the Wild Knights would follow suit. As each took a minor bit of damage, he or she'd behave as though the craft had sustained a major hit and turn toward home. Eventually the other units defending the moon over Pyria VI would find their situation untenable and have to abandon their post.

That was the plan. But it felt like losing. It felt like abandoning comrades to the enemy.

And that was something Saba Sebatyne did not do. Had she been a human, the pressure she exerted on the controls would have turned her knuckles white.

* * *

Captain Reth grinned after the departing Wild Knights leader. Certainly, the blastboat's departure weakened their position. But the almighty Jedi leader of that famous squadron was fleeing the battle zone, her tail between her legs, and he, commander of the lowly cobbled-together Green Squadron, was still in the fight.

He returned his attention to the enemy before him. It wouldn't do to receive his medals posthumously.

"Analysis," Wyrpuuk Cha said.

Kadlah Cha joined him again. "We have caught their outpost off guard," she said, and gestured at the engagement zone most distant from Borleias. "They supported it with insufficient numbers. No matter what they choose to throw at us, we can bring units to it faster and in better condition from the reserve fleet."

"Good. Go on."

She gestured at the main battle zone, above Borleias. "Here, matters are not so promising. Their defense of the hardpoint site on the ground is ferocious, and we are losing forces, coralskippers especially, at a far greater rate than they are losing analogous forces."

"Have they demonstrated any new tactics, new weapons?"

She shook her head.

"Good. They're fighting with spirit, but don't seem to have any surprises for us. We can break their spirit." He considered. "We'll continue until this outpost has fallen to us, and break off the assault on Borleias for now. We'll use the outpost as a staging area. Break any prisoners found at the outpost, and arrange for all information, all memory, found there to be sent to the warmaster."

"It shall be done."

* * *

"Arrival in three . . . two . . . one . . . mark."

Right on the navigator's spoken cue, the swirl of lines in *Lusankya*'s forward viewport straightened out and contracted into stationary stars, one of them barely near enough to be recognized as a sphere instead of a mere pinpoint of light.

Commander Eldo Davip, nearly two meters of space navy gristle packed into a bulging officer's uniform, shook his head, not satisfied with the results. His bridge crew, most of its members new to *Lusankya*, had not so far demonstrated reliable competence, and now they'd managed to drop his new command into the Pyria star system much farther from the planet Borleias than he had indicated.

Then he frowned. Ahead, some stars were disappearing, others reappearing, as objects moved into and out of the way. Did the Pyria system have an asteroid belt? He turned to his navigator to ask that question, but suddenly the bridge was filled with alarm bells and the startled exclamations of officers.

"It's a trap!" That was the sensor operator, a male from Coruscant, his excitement not quite concealing the clipped, upper-class pronunciation that betrayed his origin. "We're surrounded by Vong vessels!"

Davip whirled to face the sensor screen set up near his commander's post at the rear of the bridge's second-level walkway. It showed *Lusankya*'s position with the blip representing *Millennium Falcon* neatly tucked in beneath, but the two spacecraft were surrounded by the blips of dozens of vehicles, mostly capital ships, all either enemy red or winking from unknown yellow to red.

The horror of the situation swelled in Davip's throat, choking him for a brief moment. Then the commands he needed to utter, *had* to utter, forced their way past the obstruction. "All shields up! All batteries fire at will! Fire as you bear! Launch all squadrons!"

As soon as the drop out of hyperspace was complete, Han Solo frowned at his instruments. "We dropped a couple of seconds early," he said.

Leia, looking absurdly tiny in the *Millennium Falcon*'s oversized copilot's seat, pointed up through the cockpit viewport. The underside of *Lusankya* hung there like an irregular ceiling. "It wasn't a mistake. Their nav computers must have sent us faulty data."

"No, I'm showing heavy gravitic abnormalities here. We were pulled out of hyperspace by the presence of—" Han's eyes snapped wide open and he yanked at the *Falcon*'s controls, sending the onetime freighter into a rolling dive its original manufacturers had never intended it to experience. Shouts of surprise—and a couple of thrill-rider glee—erupted from the passenger compartment.

A glowing trail of fire, ejecta from a Yuuzhan Vong plasma cannon, ripped through space where the *Falcon* had just been. Han pitched his voice to be heard throughout the ship: "Take the guns! We're in the middle of a Vong fleet!"

Wyrpuuk Cha nodded, satisfied with the results he was seeing.

The blaze bugs flurried, rapidly changing position in the portion of the depression representing the reserve fleet. Wyrpuuk Cha frowned as he took in the changes. Something triangular, in the same approximate shape as one of the enemy's hated Imperial Star Destroyers but much larger, was now situated in the midst of his fleet. Wyrpuuk Cha wondered if the blaze bugs' representation was actually to scale.

He glanced out the viewport of his bridge. There, to

port, seemingly close enough to touch, hung a vast expanse of darkness decorated by running lights in deep blue, a vastly oversized Star Destroyer.

Jolted by sudden panic, Wyrpuuk Cha opened his mouth to issue commands.

The Super Star Destroyer erupted as if channeling an internal explosion through innumerable tiny ports on its hull.

Wyrpuuk Cha didn't know the numbers, didn't know how many hundreds of laser batteries the vessel carried, had no idea how many hundreds of ion cannons. All he knew was that as his voice had to rise to be heard above the shrieks of the alarms emanating from the bridge's walls as their inarticulate cries indicated where and how badly his matalok, a rough analog of the toolmakers' hated Mon Calimari cruisers, was sustaining damage; that the bridge floor was shuddering under his feet; that nothing could be seen outside the port-side viewports because of the intensity of incoming fire from the enemy monstrosity; that there was no way, short of a personal blessing from the gods, that the voids projected by his ship's dovin basals could protect his matalok from the incalculable damage being directed against it.

He turned to shout a command to his chief pilot, an order to turn directly away from the enemy vessel and present all voids to the rear. Before he could speak, there was a bright flash of light in his peripheral vision and all noise ceased. Wyrpuuk Cha turned toward the bow again.

There was nothing there, only stars and flashes of fire from the ships of his fleet. The seats where his yammosk interpreter and villip officer had been were gone, as were the floor, walls, and ceiling of the bridge, all missing from a point a mere pace in front of Wyrpuuk Cha's feet.

And it wasn't true that all noise was gone. There was a

roaring in his ears, a pain—just none of the sounds of battle that had filled them mere moments ago.

He was cold, suddenly so cold that he involuntarily curled into a ball, and abruptly he found himself floating forward, past the last few handspans of bridge, out into starry emptiness.

"Wild Knights are out of the engagement zone," Tycho said. He reached into the hologram representing the battle zones of Pyrian space and gestured at one bright cluster of colorful, swirling blips. "The Yuuzhan Vong are concentrating their effort on Pyria Six's moon. They're cautious, not trying anything particularly bold, just a standard attritional assault."

"Very well," Wedge said. He stood beside his chair, knowing that his voice was carrying very little expression, that his features must look blank at the moment—that was the way it always was when he was calculating things on a strategic scale. Focusing like this seemed to make him distant, inhuman.

But he couldn't focus. Something was wrong, some noise out of place, and Wedge turned from Tycho to pinpoint the incongruity.

There it was, one of the communications officers. During the last minute, her voice had risen, taken on a tone not of alarm but of confusion, as she'd dealt with the faraway unit leader who was her assignment. But now Iella stood leaning over her shoulder while the comm officer waited. Both women wore perplexed expressions. Wedge didn't like things that could perplex Iella.

Iella looked up and caught his eye. She raised her voice to be heard over the chamber's clamor. "Super Star Destroyer *Lusankya* reports that she's insystem with the *Millennium Falcon*. They're in the middle of the reserve Yuuzhan Vong forces. *Lusankya* has inflicted heavy damage on the enemy and is taking damage. She needs an escort to get through the enemy."

The volume of voices in the chamber dropped by a measurable proportion. Wedge heard Tycho's shout of "*What?*"

Then Wedge got his own voice under control. "Confirm ship identification," he managed, and moved to stand by Tycho. "Bring up that portion of the battle zone."

Tycho manipulated controls on his console and the area of space it displayed contracted and panned to one side. The effect was that of one portion of the battle zone suddenly swelling to dominate the hologram. Wedge could see that the tight formation of the enemy reserve fleet had blurred, diffused, and that in the midst of all the red blips were one large green and one small green marker.

"Identities confirmed," Iella called. "*Millennium Falcon*, Han Solo swearing up a storm. *Lusankya*, Commander Davip commanding."

"*Commander* Davip?" Wedge shook his head and bit back on his next question: Why was Davip, a ship captain whose career had long been characterized by strong-willed indecisiveness, a commander instead of a galley cook now? And why wasn't a ship of *Lusankya*'s military importance under the command of a full admiral? "Who's closest to this engagement? Never mind that. Who's unengaged and far enough out from the sun to make a microjump into that engagement zone?"

"*Mon Mothma,*" Tycho said, not bothering to refer to the hologram or his console. "*Rebel Dream.* In one to two minutes, we can have another six ships ready to jump."

"Danni Quee reports detection of two yammosk kills," Iella said. "One minute apart. The Yuuzhan Vong are not battle-coordinated now."

"Very well." Wedge lowered his voice. "Of course,

they don't need to be coordinated to destroy *Lusankya* and the *Falcon.*"

Tycho nodded.

The tactic he needed clicked into Wedge's mind. In the span of a second, he evaluated it, tested it for major weaknesses, dismissed the weaknesses as irrelevant because of the Yuuzhan Vong's current state of confusion, and decided that he could probably use the tactic again—once—at a later time.

He reached into the hologram and indicated an area of space next to the Yuuzhan Vong reserve fleet, just on the far side of that engagement zone from the direction of Borleias. "Have *Mon Mothma* make a microjump to appear here. When she arrives, she's to broadcast a homing beacon on open fleet group frequencies and defend herself. One minute after she arrives, she's to activate her gravity-well generators and keep them up for one minute. Issue that to *Mon Mothma* directly."

Tycho turned to his console.

Wedge turned to the room. "Attention," he said, and the clamor dropped a couple of notches. "All ships and hyperdrive-equipped starfighters that can get clear of enemies within the next two minutes are to do so. Inform Rogue Squadron and Twin Suns Squadron that they're to abandon their current action and get clear. They'll jump in the direction of a homing beacon they're about to detect. Gravity-well generators will pull them out of hyperspace in the *Falcon*'s and *Lusankya*'s engagement zone. Their orders are to form up on *Lusankya* and escort her to Borleias. Let's do it, people."

Tycho straightened from his console. "*Mon Mothma* has jumped."

"Good." Wedge sighed and lowered his voice. "Tycho, we're about to achieve a tremendous victory we don't want."

Tycho gave him a thin smile. "We'll put that in your biography. General Antilles was so good he couldn't fail when he tried to."

"Thanks."

SEVEN

Borleias Occupation, Day 9

Han put the *Falcon* into a dive toward *Lusankya*. It was like diving into an erupting volcano; *Lusankya*'s hull was incandescent with firing ion cannons and laser batteries, making nearspace around her a blinding kill zone.

But her kill zone was safety compared to what was on the *Falcon*'s tail: half a dozen coralskippers, their pilots determined and vengeful. Plasma cannon ejecta flashed by the *Falcon*'s viewports and hammered into her stern shields.

The *Millennium Falcon*'s own guns fired, sending their damage aft against the coralskipper pursuit. From the shouts bouncing forward from the gunport accesses, it sounded as though Ganner and Alema Rar were in control of the guns. He thought the other Jedi in the passenger area, all survivors of Anakin's raid on the Yuuzhan Vong worldship above Myrkr, were cheering them on.

As the *Falcon* dipped in closer to *Lusankya*, Han could no longer hear the cheering—laser blasts and explosions flashed by close enough to rock her, to batter her shields. Somewhere astern, machinery came free of its housing and smashed to the *Falcon*'s deck, and as Han continued to roll, juke, and dive, he could hear the distinctive sound of shrapnel impacts as components of the machinery began slamming into bulkheads.

"Sounds expensive," Leia said.

Han shot her a betrayed look. Then they were clear of the kill zone, astern of *Lusankya*, where the Super Star Destroyer's lasers no longer crisscrossed over their heads.

The sensors showed no skips on the *Falcon*'s tail, though more were incoming, several seconds from being close enough to fire. Han breathed out a sigh of relief. "If we pick up more pursuit, I'm going back through," he said. "Those guys are good."

Leia frowned. "Who?"

"The gunners on *Lusankya*. They picked off our pursuit and didn't put a scratch on us."

"Han, they were trying to kill us, too. I saw those batteries traversing to follow us. We're nothing more than another blur to them. You just outflew them. The skips didn't."

"Oh." Han looped around to port, away from the incoming coralskippers; he circled *Lusankya* at an almost safe distance and watched the Star Destroyer's cloud of starfighters engaging the Yuuzhan Vong. "Then I'm *not* going back."

"Right."

"Do you have an exit vector for us?"

She consulted the sensor board again. "We're almost smack in the middle of their fleet. The thinnest screen between us and clear space is back that way—" She gestured out along the course by which they'd arrived insystem. Then she peered more closely at her screen. "I have friendly signals there. One Star Destroyer and more ships arriving."

Han snapped the *Falcon* around toward that course so sharply that he and Leia, and presumably all those aboard, were mashed into their acceleration couches. Belatedly, he shouted over his shoulder, "Hang on!"

Luke led Twin Suns Squadron away from Borleias high orbit at top speed and felt his smile withering away. A moment ago, he'd been as close to happy as one can be when caught in the middle of a firefight. The enemy had suddenly become uncoordinated, sure sign that their yammosk had died and that they'd have to quit the battlefield, and Luke hadn't lost a pilot in the engagement. He'd hoped their job was almost done. But the unusual nature of his new orders suggested it was barely started.

A beep from R2-D2 alerted him that *Mon Mothma* was broadcasting her beacon. Luke looped around to be oriented straight toward that broadcast location while his astromech plotted that direction as a hyperspace jump course. He clicked his comlink over to squadron frequency. "Announce readiness," he said, and added, "Leader ready."

"Two." Corran tucked his X-wing in to Luke's port.

"Three." Zindra moved up to Luke's starboard.

"Six."

"Four."

When all other eleven pilots had acknowledged, Luke set a five-second timer and broadcast it to coordinate it with his other pilots. "Clench 'em if you've got 'em," he said.

The counter dropped to zero. The Twin Suns jumped into hyperspace and then dropped almost immediately back into realspace, a jump duration of far less than two seconds.

Ahead, Luke saw *Mon Mothma*, her pointed bow aimed back in his direction, Borleias's direction. Little gouts of red from the Star Destroyer's vicinity suggested that she was being harassed by coralskippers, but before Luke could direct his squadron against them, R2-D2 beeped to indicate incoming orders.

Luke glanced at the text scrawl and led his squadron in a tight loop around toward the Yuuzhan Vong fleet behind them. "All right, people. We're to get to *Lusankya* and punch a hole for her. Anyone gets in the way, discourage him."

Rogue Squadron dropped out of its microjump close to *Mon Mothma*. The Star Destroyer's complement of starfighters already had space secure around her; some of them were accelerating into the engagement zone toward *Lusankya*.

Gavin led the Rogues in a tight loop in the same direction.

His comlink crackled. "Aww, Twin Suns is there ahead of us." That was Volu Nyth, a human woman from Kuat, a new Rogue.

Gavin put some snap into his voice. "No unneccessary chatter!" Then he lowered his tone. "Besides, we had to travel farther to get here."

Han bit back a curse as he sent the *Falcon* through a bewildering series of side-to-side and up-and-down maneuvers, designed to throw off the aim of his pursuers. All eight of them.

It wasn't just the danger to his ship, his wife, his passengers that made him unhappy.

He was getting tired.

Twenty years ago, a fight like this would have just loosened him up and made him ornery. Now sweat was pouring from him and he could feel fatigue in his arms.

"Friendlies ahead," Leia said. She had to shout to be heard over the continuous firing of the *Falcon*'s guns.

Han glanced at his sensors and made a minor adjustment to their course—minor, but so abruptly executed that it slammed Leia rightward. If not for the copilot's harness, she would have been hurled from her seat. He grimaced. He still needed to get that seat replaced with something made to human scale. "Sorry," he said.

The friendly signal ahead broke into four smaller signals, each of them made up of three blips—shield trios, meaning it was probably an X-wing unit. As the *Falcon* neared them, they spread out in attack formation, but not very far apart, and then opened fire.

Their lasers flashed close enough to the *Falcon*, Han thought, to peel paint from her hull. Then the X-wings were gone, and so were four of the pursuing coralskipper signals.

Five. The *Falcon*'s upper gun turret scored a kill, and suddenly pursuit was down to three coralskippers. "Who was that?" Han shouted.

"Me!" The voice was female. So it was Alema in the top turret, Ganner in the bottom.

"Three we can handle," Han said. This time he remembered to shout, "Hold on!" Then he set the freighter into a painfully tight loop upward. He was pushed hard back into his pilot's couch as the acceleration compensator failed to keep up with the maneuver.

In the midst of the maneuver, when the acceleration forces were at their height, he glanced at his wife, expecting her to be crushed motionless against the back of her chair, but she was actually sitting forward against the tremendous acceleration. She gave him an amused, even superior, look.

A Jedi technique, it had to be, something on the order of levitating rocks. He tried to keep jealousy from his expression, and called over his shoulder, "Alema, wait for the booms before firing, one-two-three."

"Understood!"

As the three remaining coralskippers came back into view, Han saw that they were only just beginning to rise in pursuit of the *Falcon*—his maneuver, executed so soon after the Rogues had cut their numbers in half, had confused and delayed the Yuuzhan Vong for a fatal moment.

Han armed the *Falcon*'s concussion missile launcher and fired at the foremost coralskipper. At this distance, he could fire again at the second and once more at the rearmost before the first missile hit.

Then it did, an explosion that should have shattered the skip into flinders of yorik coral but was instead sucked into the void projected by the vehicle's dovin basal.

But Alema Rar's shot with the turret laser flashed past the void and sheared through the skip's coral armor. The coralskipper exploded as its internal mechanisms were superheated, their fluids converted instantly to steam and gas.

The second missile detonated, with the same result, and Alema's second shot punched through the amber-colored canopy. The canopy blew out as though the pilot were about to eject, but Han knew the skips didn't have ejection seats. There was no pilot left behind, just a blackened crater where his body and seat had been.

The third skip pilot, fast on the reflexes, turned and dived away from the *Falcon*, presenting a narrower profile to aim at, maneuvering to be below the top turret's angle of fire. The concussion missile's explosion flooded into the void at the skip's rear . . . and then Ganner's laser shot penetrated the skip's lower hull, shearing through the vehicle, emerging through the top hull amidships. Amazingly still flyable, the skip accelerated away, trailing cloudy debris that had to be body fluids flash-frozen by exposure to vacuum.

"The Rogues?" Han asked. He felt out of breath.

"Reaching *Lusankya*," Leia said. "We have a friendly ahead." Indeed, there was another Imperial Star Destroyer in their path, an older model than *Mon Mothma*; it was maneuvering around from an outbound course to turn toward *Lusankya*.

"What say we tuck into her launching bay and rest for a minute?"

She smiled. "You're the captain."

"I notice you never say that to me when you disagree with something I've said."

As they neared the Star Destroyer, Leia let out a little noise of surprise. "Han, she's the *Rebel Dream*."

Han looked, startled, at the ship before them. *Rebel Dream* had once been Leia's flagship—not her command, since naval officers always captained her, but a vessel at her beck and call, chosen to lend credence to her importance as she conducted negotiations between the New Republic and unaligned planetary systems. The *Millennium Falcon* had rested for some months in one of *Rebel Dream*'s cargo holds while Han had led a military campaign against a rogue warlord.

Leia's expression was open, thoughtful, and years seemed to drop away from her as she revisited those long-ago times. "What do you think, Han? She looks like she's in wonderful condition."

"Yes, she does."

Leia glanced over and realized that her husband wasn't looking at the ship. She flushed but looked amused. "Han. Get your mind back on work."

"Sorry. Getting old. Easily distracted." Han kept his exultation, his victory from his face. For one moment, he'd distracted Leia from the ache that had consumed her since Anakin and Jacen were lost. Maybe if he could do it again from time to time, the poison of that ache would not claim Leia, would not take her from him too.

"Sure. Old. Of course."

"*Lusankya* has her escort," Tycho said. "And with them keeping the Yuuzhan Vong fighters and frigate analogs at bay, she's ripping a seam right through their fleet."

Wedge nodded. The hologram bore out Tycho's statement.

No new friendlies had appeared in *Mon Mothma*'s vicinity for a couple of minutes; she'd finished with her interdiction field generators. "Order *Mon Mothma* to bring up the rear of our force there, and tell her to tuck in close. The Vong will fall on any stragglers; they don't need a yammosk to tell them to do that."

The hologram showed the Yuuzhan Vong fleet, which had grown large and diffuse, gradually contracting as it moved against the group centered on *Lusankya*. But without yammosk coordination, the Yuuzhan Vong were unable to mount any sophisticated tactics or manage any real concentration of fire on the New Republic's capital ships. As Wedge watched, the Yuuzhan Vong numbers began to thin. Wedge felt a professional impatience with the enemy commander, or whoever had taken charge of their fleet after their designated commander had died; if he didn't acknowledge defeat and order a retreat, he stood a good chance of losing his fleet.

Then it came. First a *matalok*-class cruiser analog peeled away from the engagement, then a frigate analog and two or three coralskipper squadrons, and suddenly the battle was essentially done, all the Yuuzhan Vong capital ships outward bound, only a few coralskipper-on-starfighter duels continuing as some Yuuzhan Vong pilots chose a futile but honorable death over retreat.

"Issue the order," Wedge said. "Set up for the fleet's return." He offered Tycho a bitter little smile. "We also need to celebrate our victory."

Tycho looked at him, expressionless. "I'm giddy already," he said.

Han Solo marched down the *Falcon*'s ramp, one arm around Leia's waist and the other raised in a wave as he acknowledged the cheers of pilots and crew in Borleias's main docking bay. "Why are they so happy? I mean, I'm happy, but they're acting like I won this one single-handed."

Leia gave him a little smile, the best she'd been able to manage since—Han turned his thoughts away from the memory. She said, "You dropped into the middle of a Yuuzhan Vong fleet and came out without a scratch. The famous Han Solo. You've just reminded them that they can win."

"Ah."

"Besides, you win every one of your fights single-handed. Just ask your admirers. I'll find you a historian who knows how to appreciate a bribe, and tomorrow you'll be the man who told *Lusankya* to drop out of hyperspace where she did, the man who blew up the enemy flagship with his blaster pistol."

"Don't you dare."

Ahead of them, the *Falcon*'s passengers moved through the crowd, led by one of Wedge Antilles's officers. Many of them were Jedi, but not all of them had ever been the object of a rambunctious crowd's attention before.

Ganner, the dark-haired and all-too-handsome Jedi Knight, was first of them. He waved at the crowd with all of Han's poise but none of Han's self-aware irony, and the smile he turned on some of the ladies in the crowd was nothing if not brilliant. Beside him was Alema Rar, the blue-skinned Twi'lek Jedi; a proficient organizer of rebellion and espionage, she had spent long periods disguised as a dancer, and she demonstrated a dancer's ease and poise now as she smiled at the crowd. Next were Zekk, the former street urchin who had trained as a Dark Jedi before joining Luke's academy on Yavin 4, and Tesar Sebatyne, male Barabel offspring of Saba.

Last but for Han and Leia were Tahiri Veila and Tarc, two worries for the Solos. Han shook his head. No, they weren't worries; they were genuine heartaches.

Tahiri, a slender blond Jedi student, had been one of Anakin Solo's closest friends. In recent months and weeks, they'd been closer than friends, had been on the verge of becoming something more. It had been Anakin who had rescued her from Yuuzhan Vong captivity; Anakin who had helped her overcome the brainwashing that nearly convinced her that she herself was one of the Yuuzhan Vong.

And then Anakin had died. Han could no longer maneuver his thoughts away from the memory. He felt something grip his heart and squeeze; the pain almost caused him to stumble. He spared a glance for Leia; she was looking at Tahiri, too, and the bleakness Han felt was reflected in her eyes.

Though dressed in Jedi robes, Tahiri was characteristically barefoot. There was little strength or pride in her posture now; Anakin's death had hit her hard, possibly as hard as it had hit his parents. She was silent; once upon a time, there would have been no way, short of an order from Luke Skywalker, to shut her up.

Tahiri had one arm around Tarc, guiding him, lending him reassurance. Tarc was twelve, a boy of Coruscant chosen as part of Viqi Shesh's kidnapping plot against Ben Skywalker. Viqi had chosen him as a distraction because of his extraordinary resemblance to the Anakin of a few years before, a resemblance so distressingly close that Han felt his stomach lurch each time he saw the boy's perpetually mussed brown hair, icy blue eyes, and open expression.

It hurt merely to see the boy, but it would be cruel and wrong to abandon him, to reject him. It was a problem Han couldn't solve with a blaster or fancy flying.

Han glimpsed a head of blond hair bobbing up and down as its owner pushed through the crowd. "Incoming flier," he said.

And then Luke Skywalker was on them, embracing both Han and Leia, his grin youthful and infectious. "You picked a good time to visit," Luke said.

"Your sister's fault," Han said. "We broadcast on the HoloNet to find out if you were still on Borleias. We got both confirmation and an invitation to accompany *Lusankya*. 'Let's go with *Lusankya*,' she said. 'More safety for our passengers.' "

Leia gave him a cool look. "You really need to enjoy these rare occasions when you're right." Then she caught sight of something and her expression brightened again. "Mara!" She pulled free to embrace her late-arriving sister-in-law.

"Listen," Luke said. "Wedge is getting quarters set up for you. You have time to clean up a little. But we all need to talk to you."

Han gave him a curious look. "Who's 'we all'?"

"The Insiders."

In as few words as they could afford, Han and Leia told the story of their time in the Hapes Cluster after the departure of Luke and Mara—of Jaina's terrifying drift toward the dark side of the Force and Kyp Durron's unexpected help on her behalf, of the skirmish that had left Han with a skull fracture from which he had barely recovered, of Ta'a Chume's attempts to displace daughter-in-law Teneniel

Djo and persuade Jaina Solo to wed Teneniel's husband, Isolder. "The situation there isn't resolved," Leia said. "But Han and I couldn't make it any better. We have to trust Jaina to make the right choices."

They were in the biotics building's mess hall rather than the Insiders' usual conference room. With Han and Leia were Wedge, Iella, Luke, Mara, and Lando, a comfortable group of intimates. They seemed pleased to see Han and Leia, but otherwise somewhat tense and distracted.

"You're not acting like someone who's won a substantial military victory, Wedge," Leia said.

Wedge made a glum face. "It's the sort of victory that can cost us the war. We were hoping to get a Yuuzhan Vong commander of average skills, with an average fleet, and I suspect that we did. We were going to string him along for as much time as we could, but circumstances today dictated that we wipe him out right away. The next one they send is going to be much tougher, and that's going to make things more difficult for all of us. But you two have come at a good time. We need your skills."

"Leia's skills, you mean," Han said. "Without her, I don't think there's any way the New Republic can hold together."

"Both your skills," Wedge said. "Because the New Republic is dead. An oversized hulk with a decentralized nervous system; the extremities don't realize that the heart isn't beating anymore."

Leia and Han exchanged a glance. "Let's hear it," Leia said.

EIGHT

Yuuzhan Vong Worldship, Coruscant Orbit

Maal Lah paused outside the barrier leading into the tracer spineray chamber. He glanced at the guard who had conducted him here as though to ask, *Are you certain he is here?* But the guard avoided eye contact, whether because he dared not look into the eyes of a superior or because he knew what fate waited beyond the barrier, Maal Lah could not say.

As Maal Lah advanced, the barrier retracted, a fishlike mouth that parted before him, and he stepped into the chamber.

It was a place of knowledge and of training. The tracer spineray was close kin to the provoker spineray that was capable of tracing neural pathways as its subjects thought about certain topics . . . and then directing pain into those pathways to prevent the subject from reexamining those thoughts. The tracer, too, traced neural paths, but had only related functions: to determine how efficiently signals were transmitted along those pathways, and to issue pain to receptors with micromillimeter precision, allowing the subject to gauge the degree to which tissues remained injured or imbalanced once healing seemed complete.

The chamber was poorly lit, bioluminescent glows reflecting from red and black coral walls suggesting thick deposits of half-dried blood. It featured one central table with a gray oval top, the carefully engineered terminus of the tracer spineray, tilted so that one end nearly touched the floor. A male of the shaper caste stood beside the table; Tsavong Lah lay atop it, his feet toward the ground. He was fully clothed, but his left arm lay bare against the leatherlike surface of the table, and Maal Lah knew that the warmaster's visit was purely medical; the tracer spineray had to be evaluating the condition of the radank claw grafted onto his arm. It looked no worse than the last time Maal Lah had seen it, but no better. Perhaps the warmaster wished him to see that it had not deteriorated, so that he might inform others, head off speculation about Tsavong Lah's possible rejection of the graft.

Tsavong Lah glanced at him without moving his head and beckoned. The shaper moved to the side so that they might speak privately, but Maal Lah could feel that one's eyes on him.

"I require your insight, my servant," Tsavong Lah said. "An interpretation of events."

Maal Lah nodded, not speaking. He preferred not to speak much before his warmaster. Those who did inevitably said too much and earned Tsavong Lah's ire; Nom Anor was constantly on the receiving end of that displeasure.

"I dispatched Wyrpuuk Cha's fleet to Borleias to retrieve it from the infidels. We had assumed that the garrison there was simply intent on dying well.

"It was, however, a trap. The infidels demonstrated unusual precision, daring, and savagery in a brilliantly conceived and executed plan. They dropped their largest spacecraft, one that we did not know was part of the fleet there, into the heart of Wyrpuuk Cha's formation and used it to destroy both yammosks. That spacecraft became a lure for our fleet's other ships, which descended upon it, allowing enemy reinforcing vessels to arrive almost unnoticed and fall upon them from all sides." The warmaster was silent for a long moment. "That fleet is all but destroyed. The designated successor to Wyrpuuk Cha's command leads many of the survivors back to us now. A pilot of Domain Kraal has commandeered some of the survivors to bolster his efforts to harass the infidels. Of course, those survivors disobeyed a direct order from the designated successor when they chose to remain with him.

"I have settled on a plan of action," the warmaster concluded. "But I welcome your thoughts."

Maal Lah remained silent for long moments. It would not do to offer half-considered ideas, and Tsavong Lah neither disparaged nor was made uncomfortable by long silences.

Finally he said, "If the ambush was as precisely conducted as you describe, it was unquestionably the work of their greatest tactician, Garm bel Iblis."

"No. Bel Iblis appears to be in command of an entire fleet group, elsewhere. The vessels in Pyria system seem to belong to the command of Wedge Antilles."

Maal Lah fell silent again as he recalculated. "I will need to evaluate the reports of the survivors. But it seems inevitable that bel Iblis planned that ambush. Meaning that he is working very closely with Antilles. Meaning that there is great importance to that site. Before we destroy it, we must learn what that importance is. And then we must destroy it so savagely that every infidel who once smiled at the success of that ambush will flinch in dread."

"Yes."

"Which means, in turn, that you must personally lead the conquest of Borleias."

Tsavong Lah shook his head. "I cannot. It will be too great a demand on attentions needed elsewhere. But you are correct. It does need a warmaster's touch."

Maal Lah frowned, not understanding, then he straightened as the significance of Tsavong Lah's words hit him. "He will not do it."

"He will."

"I think he is the finest possible choice. If he can be persuaded to go."

Tsavong Lah nodded. "Prepare a ship to take me to Domain Lah."

"It shall be done." Maal Lah took the warmaster's tone as a dismissal and turned away.

Old scars on his back began to itch, scars dealt by the one whose services Tsavong Lah was about to employ.

When Maal Lah was gone, the warmaster gestured for the shaper to resume his duties, and said, "What do you conclude?"

Master Shaper Ghithra Dal took a moment to compose his answer before offering it. "There is no sign of change. The tissue where the radank claw joins your original flesh continues to decay, continues to heal."

"There is no sign of rejection with my other implants?"

"None."

"What does that mean to you?"

"I do not know."

"Where your shaper's knowledge fails you, you still have instincts, opinions. I want them. Do not fear my anger on this point. I can distinguish between fact and opinion."

"Were I to offer an opinion, Warmaster, it would be that the true cause of this malady does not lie with the shapers' science . . . but with the will of the gods."

Tsavong Lah felt a little thrill as another piece of

reality clicked into place in the pattern Viqi Shesh had suggested. "Which gods?" he asked.

Ghithra Dal cocked his head, his gesture suggesting that he was not sure. "Any god could manifest anger this way. But in my experience the one most likely to do so is Yun-Yuuzhan. Still, if I might dare to suggest a course of inquiry for you to take . . ."

"Show me no fear, Ghithra Dal, and make your suggestion."

"I would recommend that you speak to the priests of all the myriad gods and ask them which among the great beings might be angry with you. It is a question for priests, not shapers."

Except, Tsavong Lah thought, *when the priests are in collusion with the shapers. What will your reward be? A generous portion of land on the world the Yun-Yuuzhan priests receive? A continent, perhaps?*

"I will consider this," the warmaster said. He rose and allowed Ghithra Dal to bring him his garments. *And I will seek a second opinion. I will find someone who can speak as a shaper . . . but does not owe any loyalty to the main orders of shapers.*

I will bring Nen Yim to me.

Borleias Occupation, Day 11

Luke Skywalker sat cross-legged on the floor of the *Millennium Falcon*'s forward cargo hold, which was empty of cargo. It was one place, in this overcrowded military base, where he could be alone, one place where what he was doing was less likely to distress his son.

He opened himself to the Force and floated within it. He did not think of the question he hoped he would answer—thought was counterproductive to intuition.

But this time, the currents of the Force took him where he wanted to go.

He could feel an enduring manifestation of the dark side. It was not waiting for him, not beckoning to him; it had an agenda that had nothing to do with Luke Skywalker. And in the brief moment before he lost his awareness of it, he knew that it still roamed the broken pathways of Coruscant.

Han Solo watched his wife come slowly back to life.

Not long before, the loss of Anakin and Jacen had shattered her, convinced her that all her works and efforts were meaningless. Once she had realized, at an intellectual level at least, that this was not so, their daughter Jaina's troubles in the Hapes system had reminded Leia that she had duties, obligations. She began to carry them out in her customarily brisk and efficient manner, but without the spark of enthusiasm or the wicked humor that were so much a part of the Leia he loved.

At any time of day or night, her thoughts might return to Anakin, the way he had suffered and died on his mission to the Yuuzhan Vong worldship above Myrkr. Her breath and color would leave her and she would have to lean into Han's arms or curl into a ball wherever she was sitting until the pain eased. Han, too, felt the stab of Anakin's loss, but held himself upright, trying not to show it—he was determined to be there for Leia, to never again let her down the way he had after Chewie's death.

But now, as Leia spent her time with her datapad linked to various ships' libraries and her personal archives aboard *Millennium Falcon* and *Rebel Dream*—cataloging politicians who owed her favors, reconstructing the measures she and the other founders of the Rebel Alliance had taken when laying the groundwork of their movement more than two decades before—a semblance of enthusiasm was returning to her. The pain from Anakin's loss and uncertainty from Jacen's disappearance were still there, undiminished . . . but when they did not completely occupy her, she seemed more vital, more alive. More herself.

Han welcomed the change without entirely understanding its cause; as far as he could tell, she was merely doing the sort of political work she'd been doing for decades.

Leia's exclamation startled him out of his studies: "What happened here?"

He turned and grinned up at her, at the blank expression she directed toward the open space where Chewbacca's seat had been. "I'm having something Leia-sized put in today." The grin was half genuine amusement at her surprise, half mask to hide his own lingering feelings of dismay; replacing Chewie's chair, one of the last tangible mementos of the Wookiee's life, had been among the hardest things Han had ever done. "Are you through reorganizing the galaxy for now?"

She shook her head, finally turning her attention to her husband. She moved up beside him. "I still have some solar systems to move, and I'll be laundering the Hapes Cluster—"

"It could use it." Han dragged her over and onto his lap. "We can start with Isolder, the walking headache—"

But Leia's attention was focused elsewhere, on the planetary data now displayed on the *Falcon*'s computer screens. "Han, what's this?"

"Coruscant."

"I *know* it's Coruscant. I mean, what are you doing studying it?"

He shrugged as though he didn't know the answer, a delaying tactic as he tried to sort among any number of lies he could tell. None of them seemed likely to fool her.

Finally he said, "It's the twins thing, Leia. Twins are sacred to them. They think Jacen and Jaina have meaning to their gods, and that means if you're right that Jacen is still alive, then he's going to be in the hands of their most important people. Their command worldship is at Coruscant. You don't have to be a genius to figure out that Coruscant, either on the planet or in that worldship, is the most likely place for Jacen to be."

She looked him in the eye, all levity gone from her expression. "You're not going to go in there after him."

"I might," he said. *I am,* he told himself.

"Han, no. Listen to me." This was not Leia's voice of command; it was a plea. "You can't help him. If you go, I'll lose you, too."

"I'm as hard to lose as a bad reputation."

Leia didn't bite, didn't respond with any of a dozen glibly appropriate responses, one more sign of her seriousness. "You have to understand. I can't see the Yuuzhan Vong in the Force, I can't see Jacen in the Force . . . but I'm not cut *off* from the Force. It still shows me things, offers me visions, from time to time. When I see either of us going back to Coruscant while it's in Vong hands, I see us failing there. Dying there."

Chilled by the tone in Leia's voice, Han shook his head. "Someone has to go."

"Luke. Luke has to go. He has a chance. We don't." Leia seemed to deflate, as if the admission that she could offer no help, no comfort to her missing son had reduced her in volume. But she straightened again in a moment. "You can't help Jacen, but you can help me."

"How?"

"With politics."

"You know how I feel about politics. You know how good I am at it."

Her smile returned. "The Resistance means it's time

for new politics. The kind where, if the fellow smiling at you is planning to put a vibroblade in your back, instead of smiling in return, you shoot him."

"Really?" He thought about it. "Shoot him just once, or as often as I want?"

"As long as your blaster's batteries hold out."

"Sounds wonderful. What's the catch?"

"I've accepted the assignment Wedge talked about the other night. Pending you signing on, that is. Once we've got a plan worked up, we'll be traveling from system to system setting up Resistance cells. Calling in favors. An extension of the Jedi Underground. Probably blundering into Yuuzhan Vong forces and Peace Brigade units."

"And shooting them."

"Yes."

He opened his mouth to ask if this is what she really wanted to be doing while one of their surviving children was missing and the other was in unknown circumstances on an almost hostile world, but then he caught the look in her eye, the gleam that had often graced Rebel Alliance leader Leia Organa's expression in the darkest days of the first war with the Empire.

The darkest days brought out the best in some people . . . people like Leia Organa Solo. Now the days were dark again. Now, in spite of the pain and uncertainty she struggled through, Leia was at her best again.

She was back.

"I'm signing on, lady."

"Good. We need a scoundrel like you."

"I don't have to be a nice man anymore?"

She shook her head and leaned in for a kiss.

From behind them, the singsong voice of C-3PO blared, "Master Solo! The mechanic with your new copilot's chair is here."

Han and Leia both jolted, then Leia dissolved into silent laughter.

Han glared at her. "As a reactivated scoundrel, I get to shoot Goldenrod, too, don't I?"

She shook her head.

"So *that's* the catch."

"That's the catch."

Danni Quee jumped and straightened in her seat, and in the brief moment after she awoke, she couldn't remember what had awakened her. But then it came again, a knock at the door. "Come in," she said automatically, and brushed hair back from her face.

The door slid open and Tam Elgrin stood there, hands held before him as though he wasn't sure quite what to do with them. He put them on his hips, thought the better of it, crossed them before him, and leaned on the doorjamb. The door hissed partway closed, recognized him as an obstruction, and hissed open again.

"Tam. Hello. I didn't think you could be on this corridor."

He offered her an uncertain smile and gestured at the identichip adhering to the front of his shirt. "I'm, uh, doing repairs with the civilian repair group. So I can be here."

"Ah."

"Do you have anything you need repaired?"

The door tried to close again. Tam ignored it.

Danni shook her head. "Not really. I've been doing most of my own maintenance."

"Oh. Right. Well, if you ever get shorthanded, be sure to, you know, contact me."

"I'll do that."

Tam waited there, through one more cycle of the door

attempting to close, before appearing to realize that the conversation had probably run its course. "Um, can I get you something? To eat or drink?"

"No, that's all right. Thank you anyway."

"Well, then. I'll be going."

"Good-bye."

"Good-bye." Tam's expression graduated to perplexed, then pained. He stood back from the door and reached up to rub one of his temples. "There's that headache ag—"

The door slid shut, cutting off his last word.

Danni slumped. This was the third time in three days that Tam had gone out of his way to talk to her, in his inimitably clumsy fashion. Obviously, he'd developed an interest in her, and that was the last thing she needed.

Oh, it wasn't that she disliked him. But her duties, analysis of Yuuzhan Vong technology, came first. Then there was her as-time-allowed training in the use of the Force, her occasional missions with the Wild Knights. She had meetings with the Insiders and lengthy consultations with others who were knowledgeable in Yuuzhan Vong technology, individuals such as Cilghal, the Jedi healer from Mon Calamari. She had sleep, now her favorite hobby, appreciated because of its scarcity. She just didn't have time for the legions of male pilots, officers, technicians, and civilians who thought that she surely must be interested in spending some time with them.

It was even worse with Tam, who stared at her with big, needy eyes filled with an emotion she couldn't quite interpret. It wasn't love, or affection, or admiration. It was something like longing, only worse.

If she didn't know better, she'd have said it was desperation.

She rubbed her eyes in the vain hope that it would allow them to focus, then turned her attention back to her instruments.

* * *

Preparing for bed, Iella asked, "Wedge, do you have any reason to distrust Luke and Mara? Or does Tycho?"

Wedge lay back on the bed and winced in anticipation of the day's accumulation of aches and pains assaulting him. "Of course not. Why?"

"A couple of days ago, I found a listening device planted in the Skywalker quarters. It was an amateur job, attached with a little patch of duracrete to a water pipe in their refresher. So it would only pick up conversations taking place in that one-person refresher, and only when water wasn't flowing through the pipe."

He gave her a curious look. "Sounds like we're being spied on by someone who hasn't seen enough holodramas."

She slid into place beside him. "Today I found the corresponding listening device. In Tycho's quarters."

Wedge chuckled. "So you suspect Tycho of wanting to listen to fourteen hours a day of crying baby?"

"Certainly not. But I'm taking it seriously because I don't know what it represents. I know what to do when I find signs that a competent agent is working against us. This, this is just confusing."

"Maybe our enemy has two listening devices. One to listen to and one to plant to throw blame on Tycho."

"That's a good guess."

"So what did you do about it?"

"I left the listening device, and told Luke and Mara not to talk in the refresher, and why. I'll script up some false leads for them to say within its range and see what comes of it."

"Problem solved." Wedge reached over to switch off the bedside light.

Borleias Occupation, Day 15

It had been nearly a week since *Lusankya*'s arrival had smashed the Yuuzhan Vong fleet. Since then, squadrons and even smaller units of coralskippers, now based out of the captured lunar station above Pyria VI, had harassed the New Republic ships in orbit and made some daring runs against the biotics station on the ground, but these attacks seemed little more than probes testing for weaknesses.

Luke Skywalker and a man named Kell Tainer worked on Luke's X-wing, patching up the damage done during the last attack. The damage was mostly minor, hull scoring and components shaken loose, but if allowed to accumulate it would gradually render the snubfighter useless.

Tainer was tall and in shape, the leanness of his muscles suggesting that they were for use rather than for show. His brown hair was receding from his forehead but long in back and braided. He wore a droopy mustache and a close-trimmed beard. He looked like nothing so much as an asteroid miner or backworld mechanic, but Luke knew better.

"I thought you were Intelligence," Luke said. A needle-thin stream of lubricant sprayed from the engine he was working on, the one at lower starboard, and left a zigzag red-black mark on his cheek and forehead. He tightened the clamp over the perforated hose and mopped ruefully at the fluid on his face. "A Wraith, right?"

"You're not supposed to know that." Kell's voice was muffled. His upper body was wedged into the snubfighter's tiny cargo compartment; he dangled from the waist down out of the access hatch at the underside of the X-wing's bow. It looked as though the X-wing had decided to begin a career as a carnivorous beast and Kell had been its first, unresisting prey. "Now I have to kill you."

Luke grinned. "What are you doing working with the mechanics?"

"Used to be a mechanic. Worked for a while in a Sluis Van refitting shop that Admiral Thrawn's forces eventually blew up, in fact. But I could ask you the same thing. Thought you were a Jedi Master. What are you doing working with the mechanics?"

"Same answer, more or less. I had to maintain all my machinery on Tatooine when I was a kid and many times since. And this is *my* X-wing."

"Get in there, you little—all right. Your ejector mechanism should be working again. Let me get this panel dogged down so your feet don't drop into the cargo compartment."

"I'd appreciate that. Not that my feet always reach the floor anyway." Luke finished sealing off the second of two valves. He removed the damaged tubing in between and began attaching its replacement.

Kell slid out from the compartment as though the carnivorous X-wing had decided he just wasn't worth swallowing. He landed on his feet, nimble for such a big man. "Want to test it?"

"No, thanks."

"Go ahead, hop in and fire it off. That's the only way to be sure it works."

Luke glanced up at the drooping metal docking bay ceiling five meters above their heads. "No, thanks."

"Spoilsport." Kell grabbed the lip of the hull beside the cockpit—the canopy was raised, allowing him the grip—and heaved himself up, leaning over into cockpit, his upper half disappearing from view again.

"You're Tyria Sarkin's husband, aren't you?"

"Aha, that's how you knew I was a Wraith. Yes, I am."

"How is she doing?"

Kell was silent for long moments. Luke heard the ratcheting sound of the man's hydrospanner. "She's doing well," Kell said. "Mostly she travels with our boy, Doran. Teaching him the ways of the Jedi. She travels so far afield . . . she probably doesn't even know how bad the Yuuzhan Vong invasion has gotten. We have pretty much a long-distance marriage. Months of separation alternating with extravagant welcome-home celebrations. Back when you confirmed her in her rank as a Jedi Knight, that thrilled her for months. Years."

"She earned it." Luke finished fitting the second tube end and reopened the valves. The tube stiffened a little as lubricant coursed through it, but it held.

Tyria Sarkin walked a strange and solitary path for a Jedi, Luke knew, but it was a path he was familiar with; it had been his own. He'd tested her about twenty years ago, when he'd first heard of her, a New Republic pilot candidate with Force abilities, but discovered that her powers were weak, her self-discipline inadequate to the task of shaping her into a Jedi. He'd let her down easy and suggested that she concentrate on her piloting skills. But sometime in the next few years she'd found the discipline she'd needed and resigned from the military to learn the ways of the Jedi. She'd learned mostly on her own, traveling and exploring, experimenting and investigating, reading communiqués and advice Luke had sent her but spending no time at Luke's Jedi academy on Yavin 4. The fortunate thing, Luke reflected, was that she had never rejected Luke's guidance and authority the way disaffected Jedi like Kyp Durron had; she had simply progressed in her own way, at her own rate.

Kell dropped to the ferrocrete floor again. "All done."

"Here, too, just about." Then Luke felt a new presence and glanced over at the docking bay entrance.

Iella Wessiri stood there. "Thirty standard minutes," she said. "Insiders meeting."

"The bantha crows at dawn," Kell said.

Iella blinked at him. "What?"

"You know. 'The bantha crows at dawn.' What's the countersign?" Kell aimed his hydrospanner at her as though it were a blaster. "Or perhaps you're not Section Head Iella Wessiri at all? Pull that ooglith masquer off, or I open fire."

She gave him a thin smile. "My husband never really told me how annoying you were." She turned to Luke. "Thirty minutes. There's news." She turned and left.

Kell adopted an expression of disdain. "No countersign, indeed. What sort of holodrama is this, anyway?"

"You're going to do what?" Mara asked. Her voice had not risen to carry through the doors and into the conference room, but it had become sharper. It was loud enough to startle Ben, but the baby merely looked up from her arms, gurgled, looked at Luke, and reached out for his father. Luke gave him the pinkie of his natural hand to grasp.

Luke steeled himself. "I'm going to Coruscant."

"Your visions?"

"They're getting worse and more frequent. Whatever is happening there, it's building. Getting stronger. Or *going* to build, *going* to get stronger—I don't know if I'm seeing the present or the future."

"Or the past. You could be seeing something about Palpatine's rise to power."

He shook his head. "There wouldn't be a sense of urgency to the visions."

"Well, send someone else. This is an Intelligence-style mission. Sneaking around in the dark. Not exactly suited to a fighter pilot with a glowing sword."

"Maybe you're right. Maybe I should invite some Intelligence types along. But since it's a matter of the Force, there has to be a Jedi there." He gave her a reassuring grin. "Everything's better with a Jedi around."

"Where did you learn that smile? Have you been practicing in front of a holo of Han Solo? Listen, I'm not objecting to a Jedi going on this mission. But it can't be *you*. You can't go."

"Why not?"

"Because *I* can't go. I have to stay with Ben."

"It has to be me, Mara. With the galaxy falling apart and the Jedi needing leadership, and with so many of them looking at anyone *but* me because they believe I'm some sort of passive, prematurely ancient wise man on a mountaintop, I think it would be a good thing for them to hear that I've led a mission into Coruscant. They'll have to rethink my outlook and my opinions." It occurred to Luke that Leia would probably be pleased with the political slant of his reasoning . . . and then he realized that he was once again playing in Leia's battlefield, the universe of politics, where she was a master and he was usually a floundering novice.

"Don't do this, Skywalker."

"I have to. Come *with* me."

"I'm needed here."

"That's what your feelings are telling you. What does the Force tell you?"

Her eyes flashed. "It doesn't tell me anything."

"Then you're not open to it. You're afraid of where it will lead you. You're afraid it will tell you that you need to step away from Ben, however temporarily."

Mara's face closed down, allowing no emotion to escape beyond the event horizon of her features. "I'll tell you what I'm afraid of. I'm afraid that my husband is becoming some sort of dried-up desert mystic, cut off from human emotions."

Luke sighed and abandoned the argument. "The offer's open until I leave." He cocked his head toward the conference room door. "We need to join the rest."

Luke took his customary chair beside Wedge at the head of the table. Mara, still stony-faced, sat beside Han and Leia.

No one was talking; instead, everyone watched Iella Wessiri as she moved the length of one wall, slowly and rhythmically waving an electronic device beside it. The lights on the device blinked a steady pattern in white.

Wedge waited until Iella finished. She nodded at him to indicate that the chamber was free of listening devices.

"Two hours ago," Wedge began, "a refugee ship arrived from the direction of the Hapes Cluster. It had been part of a fleet heading toward Hapes. The fleet had been assembled in considerable secrecy, but the Yuuzhan Vong intercepted it, and this ship was the only one to escape. This coincides with word we've received from Talon Karrde today that the Vong are becoming much more adept at tracking refugee traffic.

"I suspect that the New Republic fleet groups, under direct control of the Advisory Council, are going to be unable to devote their resources to this problem. So I'm going to devote some of ours. I'm looking for ideas."

"The first step," Luke said, "has to be to figure out what the Yuuzhan Vong are doing. How they're getting their accurate information about refugee ship movements. It could be that they've infiltrated one of the Yuuzhan Vong into the refugee ship network . . . in which case you'll want a Jedi to travel on some of those voyages to try to find a crew member who can't be detected in the Force."

"Good point," Wedge said. "Anyone else?"

Danni Quee waved from the back of the room. "They could be using some sort of tracking creature."

"Also a good point," Wedge acknowledged. "What do we do about that?"

Danni considered. "Tracking creatures will probably be using gravitic fluctuations to signal their presence. I can build a detection device similar to what I'm using to track yammosk activities. If we mount it on a refugee vessel, it can record gravitic flux and determine whether a creature like that is aboard. But if the vessel doesn't survive the trip and we can't retrieve the recording, that does us no good."

Corran Horn spoke up. "So we make sure that the vessel survives. We put together a surprise for the Vong and then run the vessel on missions until they decide to take it. This has an additional benefit; the Yuuzhan Vong are preying pretty much at will on refugee ships. If Yuuzhan Vong vessels assigned to this duty start disappearing, they may have to rethink their operations."

"Good," Wedge said.

Corran continued, "But if the Yuuzhan Vong *aren't* using gravitic tracker creatures, we still have to figure out where the holes are in the security of the refugee network. We'll have to root out the problem the old-fashioned way."

"Well, it looks like we have some tactics to employ," Wedge said. "I think we'll need a volunteer to coordinate this effort, and that volunteer can work with me and Tycho to assemble a mission. Anyone?"

Lando's hand was, to the surprise of the others, first in the air. "I think it's about time I made a lot of Vong look bad," he said. "In my own inimitable way, of course."

"Of course." Wedge grinned at him.

"I'll need communications access to Talon Karrde, Danni's device, a starfighter squadron, maybe a Jedi or two, and a lot of brandy. I can't stress the brandy part enough."

Wedge gave him a dubious look. "I think we've accomplished what we needed to here. Does anyone have anything else?"

"I do." Luke gave Mara an apologetic look. "I'm going to Coruscant. Something's happening there, something outside the activities of the Yuuzhan Vong, and I have to look into it. I suspect that once I'm there, I can find a way to get offworld, but what I don't know is how I'd get to the planet's surface."

"Intelligence can get you there," Iella said. "We've been thinking about putting a team on the ground there—we need to set up Resistance cells on Coruscant. We can combine the two missions." She gave him a wicked smile. "I'll give you that extremely annoying mechanic."

"Thank you so much," Luke said, deadpan.

Domain Lah Worldship, Myrkr Orbit

He was a warrior of the Yuuzhan Vong, his face so thoroughly scarred and tattooed that the decorations all but hid his wrinkles of age, his augmented vonduun crab armor concealing the leanness of active venerability. In his hands, coiled like a long rope, was an amphistaff of unusual type—far longer, much more slender than the standard Yuuzhan Vong weapon.

One did not often see a Yuuzhan Vong warrior this old. Most had gone to a noble death long before achieving this age.

He walked behind the black coral benches of his teaching chamber, behind the rows of his students, warrior-officers clad only in loincloths. At the head of the chamber, blaze bugs took on the form of a planet, of its defensive platforms and screens, of attacking Yuuzhan Vong forces.

"See there," he said. "The upper right quadrant of the world Coruscant. The stream of ships against the visible screen, how it flares into incandescence and disappears. These ships held our enemies' refugees, and they disappeared because we ordered them into a region of space protected by the enemy's passive defenses. When they could no longer bear the notion that their innocent relatives were being consumed by their own defenses, they lowered those defenses, and we entered their world-sanctuary." The blaze bugs altered their configuration so that the stream of ships passed through the shield, now accompanied by colors suggesting Yuuzhan Vong attack craft. "Now, what was the most important piece of information we needed to implement this plan?"

For a moment there was silence. Then a young warrior, his body scarcely graced by scars or tattoos, stood. He remained rigid, his back to the elderly instructor. "We needed to know where their passive defenses were."

The elderly Yuuzhan Vong drew back his coil of amphistaff and then snapped it forward. The pointed tail cracked out and stabbed into that warrior's back, punching a hole into the flesh over his shoulder blade. As the elderly one yanked his living whip back, the hole bled.

"Sit," said the old one. "What you have just received is a Czulkang Lah pit. Everyone who studies with me receives several. They become badges of honor, a sign that you have survived instruction with Czulkang Lah. But the more hopeless among you receive many pits, countless pits, and rather than it being a badge of honor, such scars tell other officers that you were an idiot. I recommend you not gather unto yourself too many. Now, who will answer the question I asked?"

No one stood or spoke.

The old warrior sighed. "All stand, all but the one who had the courage to venture an answer."

All the students, except the one still bleeding, rose. Czulkang Lah lashed out at them, methodically and rhythmically cutting two pits in each back. The warriors he struck did not cry out; none offered any sound more dismayed than a grunt. But they would remember this day and how their fear of offering a wrong answer had earned them their teacher's ire.

When he was halfway through the group of thirty students, one who had not yet been struck spoke up, saying, "We had to know that the enemy would sacrifice all to save a few. We had to know how they thought."

"You, sit." Czulkang Lah continued his whip cracking, sparing the one who had last spoken. When all but that one had bloody backs, he said, "All sit.

"Now, all *think*. Tudrath Dyn is correct. We had to understand their weaknesses . . . and their strengths. Their ability to train great warriors despite their daintiness concerning death and pain. Their hateful love of machinery . . . and their correct evaluation of that machinery's effectiveness. We had to *know*. Else we would not have beaten them on Coruscant. Else we would not beat them elsewhere."

A warrior with a bloody back stood. "May I ask a question, Warmaster?"

"I am not Warmaster," Czulkang Lah said. "Not for a lifetime. Yes, you may ask. I punish wrong conclusions . . . not curiosity."

The warrior asked, "How can one understand the ways of the enemy without learning to think like the enemy? And if one learns to think like the enemy, is that one not infected with his thoughts, and a danger to the Yuuzhan Vong?"

"A good question. Sit." Czulkang Lah walked around

to stand before his students. "The answer is as you suspect. For our theoretical tactician to think like the enemy is to be infected with his wrongness. If the infection is not too great, the tactician can cure himself by reimmersion in our ways. If the infection is too great, he can find a way to die honorably, knowing that his sacrifice has enriched us. So his infection is not a problem unless he passes it on to others. Remember—and this is the lesson that the enemy on Coruscant did not understand—individual survival is not important. As soon as you dispassionately place yourselves among those whom you are willing to send to certain death, you take another step toward strategic wisdom." He glanced past the ranks of his students at the figure, a distant silhouette, who had just entered the coral-lined chamber. "We are finished for now. Go."

They rose and marched, nearly silent on bare feet, from the chamber, glancing but not staring at the visitor, who remained at the rear, in the shadows, wrapped in a voluminous cloak.

When they were gone, Czulkang Lah moved forward. "Is it you?"

Tsavong Lah unwrapped himself from his cloak. "Father."

Czulkang Lah offered a nod of acknowledgment. "Son. Or is your visit as warmaster?"

Tsavong Lah moved to stand beside his father. "As warmaster *and* son. As son I ask, how do you fare?"

Czulkang Lah bared his teeth; their irregular and broken lines had been glimpsed through his slitted lips previously, but were now clearly revealed. "How do you think? I am old. But for my augmented armor, I could barely move. Aches befall me that have nothing to do with the marks I have put on myself over the years. And I am little but an honored prisoner here, unable to lead, and begged by my son not to die."

"This has changed."

"You no longer wish me to teach?"

"I wish you to lead."

Czulkang Lah did not bother to conceal his surprise. He leaned away from his son as if the few centimeters of additional distance would give him a better view. "Tell me."

"We have been somewhat embarrassed by a garrison defending a world at a hyperspace crossroads. Borleias, I am sure you know her."

"Pyria system. Staging point for the assault on Coruscant."

"Correct. The garrison defends the world with savagery and tactical brilliance. We are not sure why. Examination of one of their technical facilities in the system we captured indicates that they are developing something there, some new weapon to use against us, but unfortunately their scientists were able to destroy most of the evidence before they fled. The resources they bring to bear, tactics I cannot explain, all suggest that something is afoot there. I need someone to go there, root out the mystery, and *then* destroy the garrison . . . and to do so in such a way that our embarrassment is forgotten and theirs is legendary."

"No. Find someone else."

"Why?"

"When I succeed, it will have been just a bittersweet taste of what I once knew. I will not do this unless, once all is done, I retain a command, return to what I know best."

Tsavong Lah hesitated, and Czulkang Lah continued. "You fear that I will bind the loyalties of officers, of whole domains, to me, and take from you the rank you once took from me. But I will not. I opposed you years ago because I opposed coming to this galaxy, attacking these infidels. *But we are here now.* I have no reason to oppose you, plot against you. All I demand is that you give me a reason to continue living."

His son hesitated a moment longer, then nodded. "When Borleias has fallen, you will retain command, and the stories of new exploits will be added to your legend, as they should be. For now, I wish you to take Domain Hul and all her resources to the Pyria system and do what I have described."

"It will be done." After a moment, Czulkang Lah added, "I am pleased that you came in person to ask."

"No matter what our disagreements, you remain a hero to the Yuuzhan Vong, and to your son. I owe you no less."

NINE

Deep-Space Rendezvous Point

The Gallofree personnel transport *Jeolocas* dropped out of hyperspace exactly where she was supposed to, so far from any star system and from any widely known hyperspace route that the only thing her occupants should have seen was the surrounding expanse of stars and nebulae in all their color and purity.

Instead, as the whirling lines of hyperspace travel straightened and then foreshortened and *Jeolocas* dropped into realspace, clearly visible from the bridge was a Yuuzhan Vong frigate analog, an oblong mass of glistening red-and-black yorik coral, less than twenty kilometers away, easy firing distance.

Jeolocas's captain, a young man from Corellia who had grown up on the exploits of famed Corellian pilots like Han Solo and Wedge Antilles, suddenly felt the kinship he'd always known with those heroes fade away to a cold recognition of his own mortality. For the first time in his life, he felt no ambition to see an enemy spacecraft in his targeting reticle, to dogfight with enemy pilots in the thick of battle. In fact, the merchant corps he served suddenly seemed more dangerous than he could endure. "We're dead," he said, his voice a croak.

The officer next to him, a Twi'lek female with pale blue skin, merely smiled. "Not unless you want to be."

"What?" He stared at her, looking for any sign that she was distressed, confused, surprised in the least. He saw none. He didn't know her well—hadn't known her prior to a day ago, when she'd been assigned to this mission on the direct recommendation of the Talon Karrde organization—and now he understood that everything he *had* known about her, her name, her service record, all had to be a lie. He looked around the interior of the command pod and realized that she'd sent the other five ship's officers off on various duties just prior to arrival, leaving the two of them alone here. "You knew they'd be here."

"That's right."

"You're Peace Brigade, you sold us out—"

"It doesn't matter who I am. It only matters that you do as you're told."

He drew his service blaster. He'd practiced his draw for years until it was as smooth as shimmersilk and faster than the eye could follow. He'd practiced it until Han Solo himself, had he ever met the man, would have been impressed with his speed and deadliness.

As he brought the weapon up, he felt a sharp pain in his wrist.

He looked down. His hand was empty, bent back at a bad angle. His blaster was in the Twi'lek woman's hand and tucked barrel-first under his chin. She looked slightly more serious now, as if deciding whether to forgive him for the minor transgression of trying to kill her. The pain from his wrist jolted up to his elbow, then made more leisurely progress up to his shoulder while he stared, uncomprehending. He cradled his injured hand.

"Do you want to live?" the woman asked.

He nodded.

She smiled again. She reached up with her free hand and took the captain's cap from him, settling it down on her own head. "Then go hide. Don't come out until I call for you."

He turned and marched, his legs stiff, from the bridge. From the corner of his eye, he could see, through the viewport, the Yuuzhan Vong frigate launching a shuttle of some sort.

Suddenly, the thought of being less dashing than Han Solo didn't bother him as much as it used to. He could happily be less dashing than Han Solo for the rest of his life . . . so long as the rest of his life was measured in years rather than minutes.

The air lock opened and the armored warrior led his unit of Yuuzhan Vong into the hateful metal corridors of the transport.

Waiting for him was a single ship's officer, a female of a species he had seen before, a species whose name he could not recall; her skin was a pleasing blue two shades lighter than the bags under his eyes, and her hairless head separated in back into two fleshy tails. She wore a blue uniform jumpsuit and cap, both decorated in gold trim. A blaster pistol lay at her feet.

"I am Bastori Rak," he said. "Who is captain here?"

"I am." The female offered him a respectful nod but did not meet his eyes. Nor did she exhibit fear.

Bastori Rak hesitated for a moment. His usual tactic during such boardings was to instill pain and fear into the ship's officers to eliminate any possibility of defiance, but no defiance was being offered. It was obvious that the female already knew she was a subject of the Yuuzhan Vong. He briefly considered striking her anyway, but decided to test the extent of her willing obedience instead.

He drove the pointed end of his amphistaff into the blaster pistol's grip, shearing through it and into the deck plating beyond, then shook the blaster's remains free from his weapon. "What is your destination, and what do you carry?" he asked.

"We are bound for the Hapes Cluster with a cargo made up mostly of refugees," she said. "We carry seven crew, three hundred twenty-six refugees—three hundred forty if you count the ones who are in hidden compartments—as well as food, personal effects, trade items, and Jedi training materials. Shall I give you the codes to our computer security now?"

"Yes, and then you will follow—*Jeedai* training materials?"

"Yes."

"What sort of materials?"

"I'm not sure. I saw only the contents of one barrel. They include holos of training regimens, holos of Jedi history and philosophy, infectious agents that transform normal beings into Jedi, a lot of lightsabers from their new manufacturing plant, that sort of thing."

For a moment, Bastori Rak could only gape at her. Visions of his future passed briefly before his eyes. A find of this significance would result in his advancement, in his name accumulating long-deserved fame. Finally, he managed, "Are there *Jeedai* here?"

The woman considered. "I don't think so. Though if there are, I expect they'll be back with the training materials, destroying them."

"Take us there at once."

She shrugged and turned down the long corridor leading into the transport's depths.

Two levels down, in one of the forward holds, Bastori Rak and his warriors looked with distaste at the tall stacks of nearly identical cargo containers, obviously the result of mechanical manufacture, as the female led them between aisles of the things. "There," she said, and pointed.

Set out in an open area between two stacks were barrel-shaped metal containers, a bit over a meter tall and nearly a meter wide at their thickest point, arrayed in four rows of four. Each was labeled JEDI ACADEMY PROPERTY. DANGER. DO NOT OPEN.

Bastori Rak felt light-headed. "Can we move them without harm?"

"I don't think so," the woman said. She held her hand up, palm toward the ceiling, a gesture that suggested she was begging for something. "Here, let me show you."

Bastori Rak looked at her. She now met his eyes, her expression one of mocking humor.

In his peripheral vision, Bastori Rak saw something silver moving from above. It smacked down into the woman's palm.

The hilt of a lightsaber.

She said, "Embrace the pain, scarhead," and ignited the weapon; a bright silver blade of energy shimmered into existence.

The weapon's distinctive *snap-hiss* noise jolted Bastori Rak into action. He swung up his amphistaff in a blocking motion.

Her strike, a lateral slice, danced around his parry. It sliced the miniature villip from his shoulder and seared into his neck between the vonduun crab armor on his torso and his helmet. He felt blinding pain, pain too great for him to accept or ignore, and the amphistaff flew from his nerveless fingers as he collapsed.

But he was not dead, and could still see. He saw his second-in-command strike at the woman, saw her graceful parry, heard her laugh. He saw the tops of the *Jeedai* barrels bulge as their contents stood up within them and smashed through the thin metal sheets sealing them.

Their contents were droids, war droids, weapons at the ready. Their blasters opened up, chewing through his warriors.

There was blinding whiteness to his vision now. He struggled to stay focused but could not. He died watching his warriors jittering in the concentrated fire coming from the hated war droids.

Colonel Gavin Darklighter, sitting in darkness relieved only by the glows from his instruments, hit his comlink. "That's the signal," he said. "Launch."

The darkness above his head parted as his X-wing's camouflage—a cargo container bolted to the transport's top hull, immediately before the command pod—parted and folded down to either side. All around, the other eleven snubfighters of Rogue Squadron were also being released, also hitting thrusters as they hurtled toward the Yuuzhan Vong frigate.

The Yuuzhan Vong were quick on the uptake—Gavin could allow them that. Almost as soon as Rogue Squadron cleared the transport, the frigate's plasma cannons were opening up, directing streams of superheated material at his X-wings. "S-foils to attack position," he said, "and fire at will."

The wings of the twelve snubfighters opened into their characteristic X shape. Before Gavin's were even locked into place, Nevil and two other Rogues had fired proton torpedoes.

Gavin and the rest waited for a handful of seconds, slewing their snubfighters around in an effort to keep the plasma cannon trails off them, then opened up with their lasers. Twelve sets of quad-linked lasers flashed, sending their destructive energy across twenty klicks of space in an instant, bypassing the proton torpedoes, hurtling against the frigate—

Hurtling into the voids projected before the frigate. The vessel's dovin basals, responding to the threat of the first attacks to arrive, created their gravitic singularities in front of the laser attacks and swallowed the majority of their energy.

They were still swallowing, in fact, when the late-arriving proton torpedoes flashed between them and struck the frigate's hull. They detonated, one, two, three brilliant explosions, and as the last of them began to fade Gavin could see the mighty frigate cracked in two, each half spitting forth flaming debris. The plasma cannons no longer aimed their energies at Rogue Squadron; two of them still fired, sending burning blobs randomly into space.

"Confirmed kill," Gavin said, "no friendly losses. Do you read, Gambler?"

Lando Calrissian's smooth tones were preserved across the comlink. "We read, Rogue Leader. Likewise, no friendly casualties here. A beautiful execution all around."

"We'll see you back at base, then. Rogue Leader out." Gavin led the Rogues in an easy loop around until they were oriented toward Borleias. A few moments later, his squadron made the jump into hyperspace.

Lando looked over the battlefield that had been a cargo hold. Twenty Yuuzhan Vong warriors lay dead, some of them no longer recognizable as bipedal humanoids, all over the deck plating. Lando's fifteen war droids and Alema Rar, the Twi'lek Jedi, moved among them, dispatching wriggling amphistaffs and the occasional thud bug and razor bug set free by the blaster damage that had killed their owners. Alema whistled to herself as she worked.

Lando consulted his datapad. He sent a signal to query a device elsewhere in the vessel. "Not good. Danni's device isn't indicating any weird gravitic fluctuations. Meaning that there probably isn't a tracking creature on this vessel."

Alema nodded and switched her lightsaber off. "Refugees have to be turning one another in. I'm not sure for what. Violence threatened against their loved ones, maybe. Maybe some sort of bribe." She shrugged. "We'll figure out what they're doing."

Lando turned his attention to his droid aide. "One-One-A, let's get this cleaned up. Get rid of the biological remains only, don't worry about the blaster scorches. Load representative weapons and gear into a barrel and seal it tight, then load it onto the shuttle."

One-One-A saluted. "Acknowledged."

"Would you like to celebrate?" That was Alema. She wore a curious smile, artificially demure.

Lando turned back to her. "What did you have in mind?"

She just continued smiling.

"Oh." He gave her his best smile in return, modulated his voice to its smoothest register. "I find myself flattered. But I am a married man."

She cocked her head as though the answer were incomplete.

"So I have to decline," he concluded.

She shrugged as though it were of no concern. "I'll prep the shuttle, then."

When she was gone, Lando turned back to 1-1A. "Remind me again of the rewards of being virtuous?"

"I have never reminded you of this before."

"That was a rhetorical question."

"Nor have I ever told you of such rewards prior to not reminding you."

"It was still rhetorical. I really need to give you an upgraded conversation module if you're going to be talking all the time."

In the distance, they heard Alema calling, "Captain, captain, wherever you are! You can come out now!"

Borleias Occupation, Day 30

Han came awake with Leia shaking him. Their chamber was dark, and he could feel that only a few hours had passed since they'd gone to sleep. Grogginess lay over him like a second blanket. It occurred to him that perhaps Borleias had never become a true colony world because everyone who lived there was continually sleep-deprived. "What, what?"

"The control center just reached me on the comlink," Leia said. There was a breathless excitement to her voice, a happiness Han hadn't heard in a long time. "Jaina's in-system and headed this way. Get—"

Han was suddenly on his feet, the grogginess evaporated like a snubfighter shield hit by a laser cannon. He lurched toward the footlocker that held his clothes.

"—dressed."

Luke watched them spiral down from the sky, a battered-looking X-wing and a disk-shaped Hapan freighter, landing in the same portion of the field that had briefly served the Advisory Council's vehicles.

Jaina Solo—heir to some measure of her father Han's lankiness, with features as deceptively delicate as her mother's, her brown hair clinging to her scalp after hours in a helmet—descended the freighter's boarding ramp and was immediately enfolded in the embrace of her parents. Behind her was Lowbacca, nose lifted as if trying to scent friends among the crowd; he offered a rumbling Wookiee growl of welcome as Tahiri, Zekk, and other academy friends bolted from the fringe of onlookers to embrace him.

Kyp Durron descended from the X-wing cockpit. Slender and dark-haired, with sharp features that seemed sculpted to convey anger and discontent but currently were calm, he was, for once, not dressed in stylish civilian clothes, but instead wore an anonymous pilot's jumpsuit.

Luke moved up to join Kyp. Mara didn't keep pace with him; Luke knew she was waiting for an opening to talk to Jaina. Luke gave the problematic Jedi a nod he hoped looked friendly. "Kyp."

"Master Skywalker." Oddly, there was neither irony nor anger in Kyp's voice.

"You seem tired."

"No, I don't," Kyp said. "Just different."

They brought out a dark-hours meal for the latecomers and heard their story—a free-form recounting, to be sure, made somewhat random by the way Jaina, Kyp, and Lowbacca tended to interrupt one another with corrections and elaborations—of the days the three had spent on Hapes after the departure of Han and Leia. Wedge, acting more or less as master of ceremonies for the meal, brought in one more participant; Luke was startled to see Jag Fel enter the chamber.

Fel was a tall, wiry young man with close-cropped black hair, a scar running from his right eyebrow upward and then being echoed in a white lock of hair. He was Wedge's nephew and, not surprisingly, a brilliant pilot, having inherited reflexes from both the Antilles and Fel families and having been raised among the militaristic, blue-skinned Chiss, among whom his parents had chosen to live. Fel's black uniform harked back to those of old-time Imperial TIE fighter pilots, but was cut along different lines, with red piping along tunic and pants. Luke had been aware that Jag had been on Hapes with Jaina, but thought he'd departed from there for distant regions of space.

Han tried to find seats near Jaina, but, curiously, Leia chose places far enough away to give her a little distance, a little perspective on their daughter.

"So the Yuuzhan Vong are clustering around Hapes, but Tenel Ka is in charge there as Queen Mother," Luke summarized. "Some good, some bad. Even with her fleets so badly reduced and her danger so close, Hapes could be a strong ally for us. We'll need to offer her whatever support we can manage to keep the Vong from making any further inroads there."

Kyp made a sour face. "I don't think Hapes can ever be sorted out." Then he looked thoughtful and added, "On the other hand, I'm the last one who ought to be offering that kind of opinion."

"We're lucky things turned out as well as they did there," Luke said. "Ta'a Chume could still be in charge, could still be making things harder for all of us." He turned to Jaina. "Seriously, you understand that I wasn't questioning your decision. I wasn't hinting that you should throw yourself on the thermal detonator that a marriage to Isolder would represent."

Jaina offered him an unperturbed smile. "I know what you meant, Uncle Luke. I made the right choice."

Han leaned rightward so he could whisper to Leia. "She's changed. Just in the days since we left Hapes."

Leia nodded, imperceptible to all but him. "She's settled something in her mind. I think she's come through one of the conflicts that was eating at her." She sagged just a little. "But whatever she settled, it wasn't about me. She didn't quite relax when I was holding her out there."

"She'll find the right course through what she's dealing with. Give her time."

Wedge, focused on Jaina, asked, "So, what are your plans now? You're still on Rogue Squadron's reserve roster, but your situation is unique, so I'm not going to call you up for duty if you and Luke feel you'll be more useful elsewhere. I can put you in touch with one of the fleet groups if that's what you want . . . but we could really use your piloting skills on Borleias."

Jaina looked around. Han saw her gaze click to a stop, ever so briefly, on him, Leia, and, curiously, Kyp and Jag. "I'd like to stay," she said. "But I want to do something. I want to form a new starfighter squadron, if I can put together enough pilots and matériel, and practice some tactics involving the Force. Force-based coordination."

Luke's eyebrows rose. "Sort of like what Joruus C'baoth did for Thrawn."

Jaina shrugged. "I'm not talking about ancient history, I'm talking about now." She glanced around at the winces and dark looks she received from everyone present who was over the age of thirty. She offered up a calm smile. "No, I didn't mean it that way. I meant, I'm not talking about something on the scale that C'baoth used. Just within a fighter squadron. The Yuuzhan Vong think that I'm associated somehow with Yun-Harla, their goddess of trickery. I'd like to play on that . . . and this means coming up with methods of trickery. Or what seems like trickery to them. That means the Force to me. The Force, and maybe the best advice from the best pilots, like Uncle Luke and General Antilles."

Wedge considered. "I've heard a little about this Trickster goddess thing. I think it has real potential for psychological warfare. So I'm inclined to move on this idea. But, Jaina, if we're going to have the Yuuzhan Vong believe you're tied to this Yun-Harla, we're going to have to treat you like a goddess."

Jaina turned her smile on him. "That sounds terrible."

"I'm not joking. I suspect it means special treatment to the point of isolation. You'd have to be seen getting benefits and considerations that you haven't earned, which will cause bad feelings among pilots who have earned them. You'd only be able to talk freely with people who were in on the secret, and only in areas that Intelligence has certified are free of listeners. It's going to distance you from people."

"That won't be a problem."

Luke leaned forward. "I also think this is something that ought to be done. Anything new we can do to keep the Yuuzhan Vong off balance is worth exploring. And since I have another mission priority now, why don't I just hand command of Twin Suns Squadron over to her? With your approval, Wedge."

Jaina's head turned as though it had been snapped around by a Wookiee wrestler. "You mean that?"

"I do. And I don't think the symbolism will be lost on the Yuuzhan Vong. Luke Skywalker gives up his personal squadron—"

"A squadron with the word *twin* in the name," Jag said, his tone low.

"Good point," Luke said. "It was actually named in memory of Tatooine, but they don't know that."

Wedge nodded. "Jaina could use some command experience, and I know something she doesn't—which is that Corran Horn has rejoined Rogue Squadron. Meaning that we'd have two starfighter squadrons with Jedi in them. That might allow us some even more extravagant experiments in tactics."

"I brought in a fighter squadron from Hapes," Jag said. "But the notion of learning tactics involving Force coordination—and playing with the minds of our enemies—is an intriguing one. I think I'd like to join your Twin Suns Squadron."

"I would, too." That was Kyp Durron. Han saw a momentary flash of surprise in Luke's eyes.

Wedge didn't bother to conceal his own surprise. "You're both sure? About taking orders from a squadron leader with a lot less command experience than you have?"

"Yes," Jag said. "I know how to take orders as well as give them. And my second-in-command, Shawnkyr Nuruodo, is certainly qualified to lead the squadron I brought."

Kyp nodded. "I suspect I'd benefit from analyzing and advising for a while instead of leading. If I start to chafe, I can always transfer out."

Han felt Leia's breath on his ear, heard her whisper, "It looks like Jaina's not the only one who went through changes."

"Obviously a fake Kyp," he whispered back. "You distract him. I'll shoot him under the table."

Wedge turned a smile, tinged just slightly with amused malice, on Jaina. "There you go. An instant squadron for you to reconfigure as the honor guard of the manifestation of a Yuuzhan Vong goddess. This means that the very first thing you get is bureaucratic personnel matters to deal with. I'll see if I can round up an Ewok pilot candidate to throw your way just to make things more difficult. You'll be my age in no time."

Yuuzhan Vong Worldship, Coruscant Orbit

Nen Yim stood over the warmaster as he lay on the table. She was uneasy, for her life hung in the balance, and everything, including the simple fact that she stood while Tsavong Lah lay before her, was wrong.

She was a woman of the Yuuzhan Vong. A member of the shaper caste, she wore the living headdress of the shapers, and among her living decorations and mutilations was her right hand, not the one she was born with. It was an eight-fingered shaper's hand, each of the digits acting as a tool useful to her profession. Her teacher, Mezhan Kwaad, had been a heretic, disobedient to the rulers of the Yuuzhan Vong, contemptuous of the gods, but Nen Yim had learned many secrets of the shapers' craft. She was soon called by Supreme Overlord Shimrra himself, as his personal shaper, who had temporarily re leased her to the warlord.

Under a curved lens—a living creature that adjusted its shape and therefore magnification at its operator's touch—was Tsavong Lah's left arm. Nen Yim carefully studied it, noting the appearance of the flesh at the join of Yuuzhan Vong arm and radank claw, observing the behavior of the carrion-eaters upon it. They were huge in this view, the size of a thumbnail, possessed of spiky hairs, sharp angular legs, and pincers adept at digging through flesh.

"Well?" the warmaster said.

Nen Yim considered her reply, but she had little to lose by presenting him with the naked truth, so her delay was not long. "There is little I can tell you after one brief examination. But I can give you these facts.

"First, what is happening here is not like any implant rejection I have ever seen."

"Why?"

"These creatures are bred to consume dead flesh. They are useful for cleansing wounds. They are attacking the necrotic flesh of your join. But there should be little or no necrotic flesh there, because both your natural arm and the radank claw are regenerating. In a normal rejection, such as we see with the Shamed Ones, one part or the other begins to fail to regenerate, and carrion-eaters spread through that portion of the unfortunate's body until the connection between original flesh and new flesh is gone."

The warmaster did not interrupt, so Nen Yim felt safe in continuing. "Second, because your Yuuzhan Vong flesh is regenerating at a slower rate than the radank flesh, and because only your Yuuzhan Vong flesh is becoming necrotic at the join, the effect is that the radank claw is increasing in size, occupying a greater portion of your arm as your original flesh diminishes."

"I can see that."

"But it is unnatural. It is especially unnatural because, third, the radank claw, as it grows, appears to be developing characteristics of a radank as it would appear farther up the leg, as if someone were slowly re-creating the entire creature through the absorption of your body. It is an odd pathology."

"If it were deliberate on the part of a shaper, why would it be done this way?"

Nen Yim lifted the optical device away from Tsavong Lah and positioned it over a surface littered with tissue samples she had taken from him. "If I were to guess, I would say that the presence of the carrion-eaters is required to convince casual onlookers and those who are not expert in shaper techniques that rejection is imminent; this requires the sacrifice of flesh to the parasites. But your arm is essentially sound, meaning that if the process can be stopped, it will be as functional as if it were transplanted without difficulty."

"In other words, it promises rejection without harming me extensively."

"That's correct, Warmaster."

"Could you do this? Could you cause an implant to act this way?"

"I believe so. I've never turned my mind to such a task . . . but out of different techniques, techniques designed to accomplish other ends, I believe I could find a way to do this."

"What would you have to do to your victim?" Tsavong Lah sat up, wrapping his cloak about himself, and once again towered over the lowly shaper.

"I would have to engineer the attachment point of the implant to react to certain substances. Then, after the implant was successfully attached, I would have to maintain a supply of those substances into the join."

Tsavong Lah shook his head. "There is no way I could be fed such poisons. The measures I take to keep my food pure are too extreme."

"Does he touch you?" The words left her before she could contain them, before she could remind herself that one at her lowly level did not put a direct question to the warmaster without first performing a complex series of ritual statements. She swallowed against sudden fear, but persisted. "I apologize for my lack of manners. But it occurs to me that if I were to examine such an injury routinely, I could introduce these substances through direct handling. Or perhaps through use of specialized creatures resembling the carrion-eaters, bred to carry these substances and die rather than consume dead flesh."

The warmaster ignored her breach of protocol. "He does touch my flesh and that of the implant in his examinations. Can you counteract his efforts?"

"I do not know. I do not even know for certain that these are the actions of a shaper. This *could* be the signs of a god's displeasure." Nen Yim sensed the warmaster's impatience with her answer, and pressed on. "But assuming that this is the work of a shaper, I would first need to examine your arm immediately after the shaper's next visit, so that I might detect any new substances or parasites that he might have introduced."

"It will be done as you say." Tsavong Lah gestured for her to take up the voluminous cloak she had hidden her features within when being brought to this chamber. "You will be taken to quarters. Assemble a list of what you will need. If anyone asks why you are here, tell them that you will be preparing my infidel servant, Viqi Shesh, for certain experiments." As if divining Nen Yim's thoughts, the warmaster added, "No, you will not be experimenting with her. But this deception should placate the curious."

"As you wish it, Warmaster." She bowed and retrieved her cloak.

Borleias Occupation, Day 37

"What am I supposed to be seeing?" Iella asked. She was in Danni's office, and a little annoyed because Danni was taking up time she needed for Intelligence matters.

Danni tapped a key on Iella's datapad. The image began again—a view of Yuuzhan Vong warriors in a dimly lit corridor. They charged toward whoever was carrying the holocam, their war cries terrifying, their movements just slightly alien. "This is Tam Elgrin's recording. He was with a group of people in a Coruscant building when a Yuuzhan Vong patrol saw and pursued them. He was at the rear of his group when he recorded this. Then he switched off the holocam so he could concentrate on running, and he got away. Most of the other people didn't."

"So?"

"There's something wrong with the recording, and with Tam himself. Tam behaves kind of oddly, more than is normal for someone who is just socially maladjusted, I think, so I've been trying to figure him out. I've played this recording over and over again, first looking for little bits of information about Yuuzhan Vong hunting tactics, then about Tam . . . and I finally realized that this feeling of wrongness I had didn't have anything to do with the Yuuzhan Vong."

"You've lost me."

"I kind of went behind your back and asked the Wraiths to look into it for me. To do analysis on the recording in their spare time."

"They have spare time? I don't remember issuing them any spare time. So what did they find out?"

"There are nine sets of footsteps echoing in that hallway. You can count eight Yuuzhan Vong visible in the recording, so the other one has to be Tam."

"Eight Yuuzhan Vong and *one* human." Iella looked at the recording again. It played on continuous loop. "Meaning that Tam wasn't with a group."

"Right."

"Why would he lie?" The answer was in place before Iella finished the question. "Because if he admitted he was alone, he'd have to have a really good explanation of how he got away from those warriors."

"Right again."

"Meaning he *didn't* get away."

Danni shrugged. "That's my guess. But I'm not in Intelligence."

"You want to transfer?"

Danni smiled. "I don't think they'd let me."

Iella extracted the data card from her datapad. "Mind if I take this?"

"Go ahead. I've copied the recording. Multiply."

"That's good work, Danni." Iella rose and moved to the door. "You let me know if you ever want to get into the Intelligence analysis business."

"Twin Suns Leader ready," Jaina said. "Four lit and in the green." The vibration from her X-wing's engines, the whine of engines from all over the special operations docking bay, cut into her, a familiar and welcome sensation.

"Twins Two, ready." That was Kyp. "Going to shield me a goddess."

"Twins Three, ready." That was Jag, and, as Jaina predicted, he omitted any quip or irrelevant remark.

"*Record Time,* ready to lift."

Moments later, they lifted off, two X-wings and Jag's clawcraft comprising a shield trio, with the *Record Time,* the troop transport damaged during the taking of Borleias and subsequently patched back together, lumbering after them. They moved easily out of the docking bay and lifted toward the starry sky, just starting to blur with dawn, above them.

Jaina spared a look out the starboard side of her canopy at Jag's clawcraft. This variant form of TIE starfighter had the basic cockpit sphere and twin ion engine pods of classic TIE fighters and interceptors, but from the point the engines met the cockpit emerged four forward-sweeping, talon-shaped solar array wings. Jaina didn't know whether to be pleased or irritated at the artistic incongruity of that style of vehicle being included in her mostly X-wing squadron, and tried to think as a Yuuzhan Vong goddess would.

After a few minutes, long after they'd cleared Borleias's atmosphere and were headed to a patch of Pyrian space well away from any naval activities, she keyed her comlink. "Kyp, remind me to issue an order that all starfighters in this squadron are to be individually decorated by their pilots. No uniformity. Their astromechs, too."

"Will do, Goddess."

Jag said, "Coming up on practice zone in ten, nine, eight . . ."

Moments later the starfighters slowed to a stop, relative to distant Borleias, and hung drifting in space as *Record Time* caught up to them.

Jaina asked, "How are you going to decorate your fighter, Jag?"

"Black ball," he answered immediately. "The claws the color of silver metal, with bloodred splashes on them. As though the whole thing were some sort of claw weapon. The metal, of course, is to annoy the Vong; otherwise I might use a more naturalistic claw color."

"You came up with that just in the time since I decided everyone should decorate their starfighter?"

"No. I decided on this design days ago, when I calculated that you'd be issuing that directive."

Days ago? Jaina felt a flash of surprise and irritation. How dare he attempt to predict her this way?

How dare he do it successfully?

But she tamped down on the feeling. Jedi Knights needed to be serene. Squadron leaders shouldn't let their pilots get to them. She needed not to be caught off guard, even when caught off guard. She just smiled. "Well, it's a good design. I approve."

"Thank you." There was the slightest touch of mockery to his reply, and Jaina felt her mood sour slightly. It wasn't true, as some of the New Republic pilots thought, that Jag Fel always acted as though he were superior. What was true was that he always seemed to see through deceptions, always seemed to know the truth behind what was being said to him. No one liked to have their falsehoods ignored, their images pierced.

On the other hand, this meant Jag would have a harder time behaving as though he were serving a goddess made flesh. Jaina smiled to herself. She'd be able to find some way to make him uncomfortable, to penetrate his unflappable manner.

"*Record Time* coming on-station." The announcement blaring through her comlink jolted Jaina out of her reverie.

"Deploy targets," Jaina said. "All right, Kyp, let's show Jag how Force-users do it."

From one of *Record Time*'s bays streamed a series of cargo containers. They were the most-damaged of the containers that had been used to bring garrison supplies into the Pyria system, too badly crushed or corroded to stand up to further use. Now each had two red target zones painted on each long side; sensors were attached to the targets. They tumbled through space at *Record Time*'s arrival velocity.

Jaina led her flight in a loop that would bring them up at a ninety-degree course to the containers' path.

"I'm open, Goddess."

Jaina suppressed a grimace. She should have known that Kyp would be ready for the Force link they were trying. She should have felt it.

But she had been keeping herself a little closed off. It was better that way. She didn't want to be so closely tied to Kyp that he would feel it through the Force, be tortured by it, when and if she followed her brothers into death.

When, not if.

So, though she let him help her back from the dark side path she had recently followed, though she even acknowledged him as a second Jedi Master—though no one would ever replace Mara as her true Master—it was best to keep him at a certain distance.

But she couldn't do so all the time, so, feeling a touch of unease, she extended her Force perceptions toward Kyp, found him, merged with him in a sense.

It was neither as close nor as effective a bond as the one between Luke and Mara. But then, she didn't want it to be. That sort of closeness led to no good.

She frowned at that thought, wondering where it had come from, wondering if Kyp had picked it up. But there had been no flicker of emotion from him. Doubtless he hadn't. "All right, Jag. Kyp and I are going to pick and hit a target. The sensors will tell us how close together our strikes are, how well we're coordinating through the Force. For fun, I want you to see how long it takes you to punch a hole in the target directly between our two strikes."

"Consider it done."

They angled in toward one target, Jaina and Kyp moving together with a precision possible only through the Force. Jag stayed with them, tucked between and slightly behind them, his maneuvers as fast and precise as it was possible for them to be without Force coordination.

Jaina picked her target—a container both tumbling and spinning on its long axis, two containers starboard of the one they were heading toward—and fired. Her quad-linked lasers and Kyp's burned off at what looked like exactly the same instant, hitting the red target zones of the container simultaneously, reducing the container's two ends to molten slag. A fraction of a second later, Jag's blast hit the center of the spinning mess, cleaving it in two.

"Not bad." Jaina consulted her comm board. "Four one-hundredths of a second between our shots, Kyp; yours hit second. We need to get those numbers down.

Jag, you were twenty-six one-hundredths of a second behind Kyp. Pretty good, considering you didn't know which container was going to be our target."

"Actually, I did. I knew it wasn't going to be the one our course was aimed at. Given a fifty-fifty directional choice, you go starboard more than half the time. I figured you wouldn't choose the first target of opportunity in that direction, so I centered on the second. Of course, if I'd been wrong, it would have taken me a much bigger fraction of a second to hit the target you'd chosen."

Jaina heaved a sigh. Jag was determined to annoy her with his efforts to predict her. But she schooled her emotions once more into something like serenity and merely clicked her comlink in acknowledgment. "Let's go around again," she said.

The second run was much like the first. Jaina's and Kyp's shots remained separated by a few hundredths of a second. Jag's follow-up shot was, if anything, faster than it had been on the first target.

"You guessed I'd go left of our course, one target out," Jaina said.

"Yes."

"Let's do it again."

As Luke finished packing his bag for the day's activities, Mara entered their quarters. Ben was awake in her arms, grasping at her hair, pulling it into his mouth, but all of Mara's attention was on Luke. "I'm going to Coruscant with you."

That stopped Luke cold. "What changed your mind?"

"Time. Time to calm down, time to figure things out. Understanding that there's nobody more suited than you are to stopping the enemy that menaces Ben, and there's nobody better than *me* at watching your back." She shrugged, then looked down into the face of their son.

"Ultimately, it was figuring out that if I wait until Ben's enemies are right in front of me before I kill them, I've already failed him."

Mara's expression was so melancholy that Luke felt his throat constrict. "Listen, I'm about to go out into the jungle with Tahiri to plant a few gravitic sensors. Care to come along?"

Mara nodded. "Do you think Leia would baby-sit for us?"

"I suspect she'd be very happy to."

Luke, Mara, and Tahiri moved through the jungle a few hundred meters from the start of the kill zone. They'd entered the jungle, had gone through a series of steps to shake off any likely Yuuzhan Vong observers, and now reached the first of their target zones.

Luke set down his backpack. From within it he drew a short-hafted heavy hammer. "Behold," he told Tahiri, "the favorite weapon of Jedi before the invention of the lightsaber."

She frowned at him, green eyes confused beneath her bangs. "You're kidding."

"Of course I'm kidding. C'mon. The Jedi sledgehammer?" Grinning, he turned to his wife. "Mara?"

From her own backpack she drew a stake, two-thirds of a meter long, made of metal, very broad at the top. She obligingly set it point-first into the ground. "Go ahead. I've always thought that menial labor involving hitting heavy metal things with other heavy metal things was man's work."

With quick, hard blows, Luke pounded the thing until its head was flush with the ground. Then he spread dirt and leaves over it.

"And that's going to transmit gravitic fluctuations?" Tahiri sounded dubious.

"Uh-huh." Luke replaced the hammer in his backpack, then picked the backpack up. It weighed less, several kilograms less, than it had when he set it down. He pretended not to notice, or to recognize that the ground beneath the pack was stirred up, when it had been smooth when he'd set the pack down. "Ready?"

"Ready," Tahiri announced. Mara just nodded.

As they moved from the site, Luke whispered, "Well?"

"I think we were being watched," Tahiri whispered back. "I mean, it felt right. From the Yuuzhan Vong perspective. But I'm not sure."

"I'm sure," Luke said. "Couldn't you feel the insect life go quiet just east, ahead of us?"

"I . . ." Tahiri looked embarrassed. "I could have been able to if I'd thought about it. But I didn't."

"Don't feel bad. You were thinking Vong—"

"*Yuuzhan* Vong."

"—Yuuzhan Vong instead of Jedi. I suspect it's not easy to think both ways at once. Is it?"

Tahiri shook her head. "They're ahead of us, then. That won't be the same group that was watching us, I expect. That group hasn't had time to get into position ahead of us."

"Good work," Mara said. "When do we expect it?"

"They'll wait until we can't hear what the first group is doing back at the site we just left," Tahiri said. "But they'll be impatient. It'll be pretty soon after that. Such as . . . now." Tahiri thumbed her lightsaber on; its *snap-hiss* heralded the lengthening of its glowing blade just in time for that blade to intercept a thud bug. The thud bug flared into incandescence and disappeared with a crackling sound.

Luke brought his lightsaber up but turned away from

Tahiri. He saw, out of the corner of his eye, Mara doing the same, turning the other way. The three of them stood back to back as the Yuuzhan Vong warriors came spilling out of the jungle.

There were five of them, and the first, coming in at Luke, was moving too fast, committed to the charge, depending on the first thud bug to distract the Jedi. Luke spun his lightsaber to intercept his cracking amphistaff, then rolled over backward, propelling the Yuuzhan Vong warrior past him in an uncontrolled tumble. *Yours,* he thought.

Barely looking, Mara brought her own lightsaber blade around, plunging it into the hurtling warrior's face as he tumbled past.

The next one in came at Tahiri, amphistaff rigid in a two-handed grip. She parried his first strike, his second, and kicked him in the knee, but the impact of her bare foot on his vonduun crab armor slowed him not at all.

Two, timing it as a single attack, leapt out from a screen of dangling fronds at Mara. She reversed her lightsaber so that the butt of the hilt was next to her thumb, the blade oriented down, and directed it back and forth against their low amphistaff attacks, using the lightsaber as a defensive umbrella. As one went high to bring his weapon up and over her defense, she kicked out, a beauty of a full-extension kick that caught him under the jaw and tumbled him backward into the fronds.

The last one came in at Luke. He was slower, more patient than his comrades. Luke struck, a feint, then began a reverse strike as he saw his opponent raise the amphistaff to parry . . . then something about the warrior's pose and motion set off an alarm in Luke's mind. Luke dropped to one knee and the poison spat by his foe's amphistaff went harmlessly over his head.

It wasn't entirely harmless. Luke saw it arc toward

Tahiri's side. She withdrew a step, drawing her enemy forward, and the poison splattered against that warrior's mask, dribbling through the eyehole. The warrior gurgled, clamping down on a shout of pain or dread.

Luke rose to a crouching position and then continued the motion, leaping up and over his opponent, inverting as he went, swinging his lightsaber with blurring speed at his foe's head. His enemy caught the blow on his amphistaff and was shoving the staff's pointed tail at Luke even as the Jedi Master landed. Luke caught the thrust on his lightsaber blade, deflected it mere centimeters, and kept the energy blade scraping up the amphistaff's length. His opponent jumped away before the lightsaber could sever his fingers.

Tahiri's enemy was down now, poison flowing from one eye socket and smoke rising from the other, and she moved into position just in time to intercept Mara's second foe as he returned from the verge of fronds. Caught off guard by her flurry of attacks, the Yuuzhan Vong warrior allowed himself to be forced into retreat; both of them disappeared into the fronds.

Luke's foe flicked the serpent head of his amphistaff forward. Luke sidestepped and the poisoned thing snapped to full extension a hairsbreadth from his side. Then Mara's hand closed around it, over the head, and yanked. Luke's foe stumbled forward, off balance for one deadly moment, and Luke swung his lightsaber into the vulnerable gap beneath the warrior's helmet. Flesh boiled and severed. The warrior fell.

Luke spun. Mara was flinging the captured amphistaff into the face of her foe; the warrior contemptuously brushed it aside and raised his weapon.

Luke flung his own lightsaber spinning toward the warrior, then added a deft touch with the Force to make its flight eccentric, unpredictable. The warrior batted it aside as well, but the distraction was too long; Mara drove in with her lightsaber, punching through the warrior's right arm socket, shearing his arm completely off. As he fell, she followed through with a thrust to the face.

Luke beckoned and his lightsaber, depowered, flew back into his hand. He snapped it on again. "Tahiri?"

"Here." She emerged from the screen of fronds, unhurt. "Look what mine was carrying." In her hand was a metal stake.

Luke frowned. "Is that the one we just planted?"

"No, a different one."

Mara smiled. "Success."

"Let's go," Luke said. "Before any more decide to visit."

They headed on to their next planting spot. There, they'd hammer another stake in—a stake that did contain sensor equipment, but which was designed to be found and removed by the Yuuzhan Vong.

For the real sensors were in Luke's bag. Each was a little droid, the size of the ubiquitous little utility droids found all over capital ships. These contained the same gravitic sensors as the spikes, but also burrowing motivators that allowed them to exit the slit at the bottom of Luke's backpack and dig their way into soft soil. The Yuuzhan Vong might see every spike planted, might remove every one . . . but odds were good they wouldn't detect a single burrowing droid.

Luke had fought against many sneaky people, but was usually happy to have sneaky people on his side.

As they executed kills on target after target, Jaina became more proficient at choosing targets Jag couldn't anticipate; the time between Kyp's shot and Jag's grew until it averaged nearly half a standard second. Jaina felt she'd achieved a slight measure of victory. At least Jag couldn't remain confident in his ability to anticipate her thinking. But the gap between Jaina's firing time and Kyp's remained about the same.

"I have an idea on that," Jag said. "About your Force coordination."

Jaina almost laughed. "Jag, you don't know anything about the Force. You're as Force-blind as your uncle."

"Yes, and my uncle would figure this out, too. I'm looking at your Force link as though it were some sort of neural interface between you and Kyp. Assuming it allows speed-of-light communication of impulses, we have your impulse to fire essentially triggering both your firing reflex and Kyp's. Correct?"

"Maybe."

"So perhaps the difference in your times is roughly the difference in your physical reaction times. You're years younger than Kyp. Perhaps you should either hesitate—for as short a time as you can manage—once you've made the decision to fire, or you should let Kyp choose the targets and follow *his* lead."

Jaina looked over her shoulder, through the canopy, to where Jag's clawcraft floated beside and behind hers, and gave Jag a dubious look. "All right, sure. Let's give it a try."

On their next run, the difference between Jaina's and Kyp's shots was one one-hundredth of a second, still in Jaina's favor.

Kyp whistled. "Good thinking, Fel. Let's do this a few more times . . ." His voice trailed off.

Jaina felt it, too. She stared off into space, in the direction of the star Pyria.

"What is it?" Jag said.

"Something . . ." Jaina switched her comlink to fleet frequency and brought up her navigation program. She oriented her X-wing toward the source of her disquiet to give her a close reading on the course toward that distant point. "Twin Suns Leader to Control."

"Control here." It was a man's voice, decorated with a disinterested drawl.

"Do you have anything going on in the spinward side of the system, say on an approximate course toward Arkania?"

There was a delay of a few seconds. "Negative on that."

"Something's up . . . my flight is going to head that way. Keep your ears open for us." She switched back to her squadron frequency. "Come on, mortals."

"As you wish, Goddess."

Jag responded with a comlink click.

TEN

Borleias Occupation, Day 37

Jaina and her pilots flashed across Pyrian space as fast as their thrusters would take them; they angled in close to the star Pyria, picked up a little gravitational momentum from that close passage, and flung themselves toward the source of disturbance Jaina and Kyp could both sense. That disturbance didn't abate. If anything, it grew more clear, more strong.

Within minutes, Iella Wessiri took over the comlink at Control. "What have you got?"

"Not sure. Just a sensation in the Force."

"It can't be Yuuzhan Vong, then."

Jag said, "It can be Vong-related."

"True."

Jaina said, "Can you direct your sensors along our course to see what's out there ahead of us?"

"Negative on that. There's a little matter of a sun between us and your course. However, we're maneuvering *Rebel Dream* into position to track you and anticipate your course. She should be coming on-station in—she's on-station now." Iella grew silent for a moment. "*Rebel Dream* reports one large signal, multiple smaller signals incoming. Gravitic anomalies suggest it's Yuuzhan Vong.

General Antilles requests that you take a look, but be careful."

"We're on it." General Antilles *requests.* Jaina shook her head. Wedge had been right. All this goddess deception was going to take some getting used to.

Soon enough, the distant anomalies showed up as blips on her sensors, and then she began to pick them up on her visual sensors.

Nearest was a Yuuzhan Vong frigate analog with a screen of coralskipper escorts. Behind it, some distance away, surrounded by a screen of Yuuzhan Vong capital ships . . .

Jaina keyed her comlink. "Control, it's a worldship, a big one even by Vong standards." She felt her mouth go dry. This wasn't the worldship that was in orbit around Myrkr, the worldship where Anakin and Jacen had died, but just seeing another of the vast living craft so soon made her feel sick.

"Understood, Twin Suns Leader. Suggest you return."

"Negative." Jaina made a slight course correction to put her flight on an intercept course with the oncoming frigate. "We need to see why they're starting out with such a small probe."

Jag's voice came over the squadron frequency. "That small probe includes a frigate. It's big enough to cause us some trouble."

"Yes, but that's where I'm feeling the disturbance in the Force." The disturbance, she decided, didn't have the feral hunger that was characteristic of a voxyn. No, it felt like pain.

Then they could see the frigate and its escort. Three coralskippers, a quarter of the screen, peeled off from the formation to head their way.

"Three?" Kyp sounded insulted. "They expect three coralskippers to be enough for us?"

"No." That was Jag. "They're just supposed to slow us down. We can either ignore them and take some plasma cannon fire up the exhaust ports, or deal with them and let the frigate past."

"We deal with them," Jaina said. "Then catch up."

The coralskippers came on, firing.

"Let's play with the new tactics." Jaina extended her Force perceptions, found Kyp's waiting for her like an outstretched hand. The three of them settled into their earlier formation, the two X-wings ahead, the clawcraft behind and between. Almost as one, they twisted, rolled, and sideslipped, always eluding the oncoming plasma cannon fire, the oncoming grutchins.

Jaina chose their target, the coralskipper at starboard rear. Kyp chose the moment to fire. The skip's dovin basal created its void directly before Jaina's shot, but Kyp's smashed into the coralskipper's bow, annihilating the dovin basal. Then Jag's lasers stitched their way along from the bow to the cockpit canopy, punching burning holes all the way. That coralskipper continued on a dead ballistic course as the others flashed past the Twin Suns pilots and looped around for another attack.

Jaina looked at her sensor board, at Jag's attack delay. "Three-quarters of a second! Jag, you guessed wrong."

"Rather, I've taught you to be a little more unpredictable."

She managed an amused smile. Trust Jag's personal shields to deflect her criticism. "Let's do it again. Maybe with fifty-fifty odds, Jag can guess right this time."

The Yuuzhan Vong frigate's course took it close to the star Pyria, the reverse of Jaina's outbound course, as it headed toward Borleias. Once Jaina, Kyp, and Jag finished with the three skips sent to delay them, they blasted along in the frigate's wake, catching up rapidly.

The frigate cleared the star's orbit and began a straight-line approach to Borleias. Jaina's sensor board showed *Rebel Dream* vectoring in on an intercept course; comm transmissions indicated that starfighter squadrons were launching both from planetside and from *Lusankya.* There was no way the frigate would get close enough to Borleias to do any harm.

"Frigate's slowing," Kyp reported. "Vectoring. It's changing course. It knows it's a futile attempt."

"Wait, wait," Jag said. "Put your visuals on its underbelly."

Jaina did, and saw a long slit appearing in the frigate's underside hull. It was a moist-looking opening, as unlovely as a Hutt's mouth that had been pressed shut and was slowly beginning to gape.

As she watched, the gap began issuing shapes, tiny irregular things that spilled forth, streaming along the frigate's original course.

Jaina grimaced. The shapes were wiggling. More organic weapons. Probably worldshapers of some sort, if they were being released at this distance toward Borleias in general instead of at a military target in specific.

Then she realized that the disturbance she'd felt in the Force was traveling with those shapes. She felt her stomach sink. She put more power into acceleration, roaring toward the cloud of wiggling shapes, ignoring the frigate and coralskipper escort as they vectored away.

In moments, she could see what the Yuuzhan Vong had discharged.

People. Mostly humans, the occasional Sullustan or Rodian or Devaronian. They were male and female, of all ages, naked—

No, not quite naked. As she got closer, Jaina could see the transparent covering on their bodies, a transparent sac inflated over their heads. They were wearing some variation of the ooglith cloaker, the Yuuzhan Vong environment suit; doubtless it would give them a few more minutes of life as they soared through space. They might freeze to death, they might run out of air, they might reach Borleias's atmosphere and burn up in reentry. But they were all minutes from death, a score of them or more.

A Sullustan female saw Jaina's X-wing approaching. The Sullustan twisted her head around and looked at Jaina, her eyes wide with fear, her expression imploring. Jaina could only stare back, helpless.

She became aware that Jag was talking.

". . . ejected hostages. They appear to be in some sort of ooglith cloaker suits. They're on ballistic approach toward Borleias. I don't think the planet's microgravity is perceptibly accelerating them yet. I can't estimate the survival time their suits give them. I read twenty-two, repeat two-two of them. Standing by."

The words, so calm, so clinical, snapped Jaina out of her reverie. She looked after the departing coralskippers and frigate.

"Don't do it." That was Kyp's voice, and she felt it through the Force as much as she heard it over the comlink. "They're trying to dictate your responses."

"Serenity," she whispered. She felt as though if she spoke more loudly, the volume would tear open a hole in her and let out the anger growing within her. "The way of the Jedi is serenity." She reached out through the Force, found the Sullustan female, and tugged at her.

She could detect no change in the Sullustan's velocity. She tugged harder. "Kyp, can you save any of them?"

"Maybe. That's a tremendous amount of kinetic energy to absorb." Kyp's presence in the Force diminished as he turned away from her to the problem at hand. On her sensors, she saw one of the hurtling shapes begin to slow down.

She pulled harder at the Sullustan and was finally certain that the female was slowing. “Jag, you can't do anything here. Get back to Borleias, escort some shuttles up—”

“I've called for shuttles. And I'll let you know when I'm useless. I recommend you follow *my* lead and discontinue trying to slow them to a stop.” Jag's clawcraft darted ahead of the X-wings, maneuvered with delicacy into the cloud of victims, matching and then slightly surpassing their speed.

Then, with skill that was on the wrong side of impossible, Jag rotated his clawcraft and sideslipped it until it was mere meters to the side of a dark-skinned human male. Jag flicked his thrusters and the clawcraft slowed. The clawcraft slammed into the human at somewhere between twenty and thirty kilometers per hour; the man, stunned but not completely incapacitated, flailed around frantically as he was vectored away from Borleias.

The clawcraft rotated; as soon as that victim was clear of any possible ion wash, Jag touched his thrusters again, and maneuvered until he was alongside a second victim. That one, too, he rammed, as delicately as possible, an impact that appeared to hurt the Twi'lek woman's arm, but sent her off at an angle that would not propel her into Borleias's atmosphere.

Jaina's flight was able to vector every one of the twenty-two ejected victims away from entering Borleias's atmosphere. They couldn't save all twenty-two; four died from exposure before the shuttles could reach them, and the remainder were all removed to the biotics facility's medical ward, in varying stages of cold exposure. But none ended up as gruesome meteors flaming into incandescence in the planet's atmosphere.

The flying it took to save the survivors was remarkable enough to draw applause from the ground crews when Jaina's flight and the shuttles landed just after midday, but the pilots waved off the appreciation and did not lose their grim demeanor.

Word came that the Yuuzhan Vong worldship had taken up distant orbit, beyond the orbit of Pyria's farthest planet. It remained on-station there, its capital ships and coralskippers clustered near it.

Through the special ops docking bay's holocam feed, Wedge watched Jaina and her pilots arrive; then he switched off the view. "I was right," he said. His voice was pitched low enough that it would not carry far in the perpetual babble of sound that was the operations center.

"You were right," Tycho said. "The Vong have brought out big guns and someone with a certain amount of personal style to fire them."

"Have the recovered victims, including the ones who didn't make it, and anyone who has been in direct physical contact with them go through decontamination. Have Danni or Cilghal supervise the decontam. I want the surface of Fel's clawcraft to be checked out and similarly decontaminated. They *might* have anticipated Jag's tactics, so they might have booby-trapped all of the victims."

Tycho nodded. "I'm on it."

One more thing." Wedge caught Tycho's eye. "You were listening to Jaina's comm traffic. Her desperation to save those people."

"Yes."

"That's not dark-side behavior, at least as I understand it. I queried Kyp privately, and he's pretty sure that she's bouncing back from her brush with the dark side."

"Meaning," Tycho said, "is she trustworthy? Maybe even enough to be one of the Insiders?"

"Right."

Tycho's face revealed no emotion other than careful consideration of the question. Finally he nodded. "The brain and the gut are in agreement. I think she's worth our trust. She's a Solo."

"I think so, too. She goes on the list."

Yuuzhan Vong Worldship, Pyria Orbit

The Yuuzhan Vong pilot with the absurdly human forehead and its concealing tattoos remained bowed with his arms crossed over his chest in salute until Czulkang Lah gestured for him to straighten. Czulkang Lah said, "Your name?"

"Charat Kraal."

"And you are a pilot of Domain Kraal and its colony on this system's most habitable world?"

"I am, Warmaster."

"Do not call me warmaster. My son is warmaster. And answer this: Why have you seized elements of Wyrpuuk Cha's fleet, suborning those elements to mutiny against his designated successor?"

Charat Kraal stared back unblinking. "My goals and his diverged. His goal was to save the remnants of his crippled fleet. Mine was to improve the Yuuzhan Vong situation within this system. I believe that mine had precedence."

"You had best establish that you have done considerable damage to the infidels' warriors and machinery with the resources you commandeered, then."

"I would say that I have done negligible damage to them. My *intent* was to do negligible damage to them."

Czulkang Lah suppressed a smile. Charat Kraal was marching toward his execution with the plain speech and courage appropriate to a Yuuzhan Vong pilot. "Explain."

"Both before and after the arrival of Wyrpuuk Cha's fleet, I used my forces to harass the infidels—not because I imagined I could defeat them with the resources I had, but because this harassment revealed information about them, about their intentions." Charat Kraal gestured toward the pilot who had accompanied him, the blameless pilot who would, if things went badly, conduct word of his death back to the Kraal. That pilot brought him the recording villip, a spongy creature nearly the size of a Yuuzhan Vong torso. "If I may."

Czulkang Lah gave him a curt nod.

Charat Kraal lay the recording villip on the floor of the command chamber and gave it a stroke to awaken it. It flattened into a disk and then began to glow with a harsh yellow light. The light flowed up from it until it illuminated the air above it, then began coalescing into three-dimensional pictures.

Charat Kraal continued stroking and prodding the creature, and the pictures changed above it. First was an image of a grashal habitat, doubtless the primary home of Kraal on Borleias, then images of infidel spacecraft performing planetside attacks, images of nighttime spacecraft launches, images of infidel capital ships in orbit.

Finally the image settled on an aerial view of the infidels' headquarters, a tall curved building with many outlying buildings and a burn zone that, close to the constructions, was thick with spacecraft. "This is their habitat," Charat Kraal said. "Their general and his staff live here. He conducts all operations from here instead of from the comparative strength and safety of one of his triangle ships. Many *Jeedai* live here, and constantly patrol the jungles around the site."

"How many *Jeedai?*"

"Unknown . . . perhaps a dozen. The numbers slowly increase. Two of them are Luke Skywalker and his mate Mara."

"What of Jaina Solo?"

"She is here. I think perhaps there is some change in her stature. Before, Luke Skywalker seemed to be the preeminent *Jeedai.* Now it appears to be her."

"Continue."

"The infidels' interest in this site initially puzzled me, but now I think I understand. When the Kraal first occupied this world, interrogation of prisoners who once defended it revealed that it was a site where secret medical projects were conducted. New life-forms were created. It was, in short, the infidels' equivalent of a shaping facility, and they defend it so fiercely that I suspect they are doing some shaping now."

"Of what?"

"I do not know. It seems to me that whatever they are doing would be safer on one of their triangle ships, so the project obviously must be done here. This suggests that either the equipment they are working with is too delicate to move, or the creature they are designing must be created upon a living world. And since they are masters at creating and operating equipment, the latter possibility seems more likely."

Charat Kraal advanced the images above the villip through several sequences of spacecraft takeoffs, then slowed to show an odd-looking craft leaving the biotics facility. It did not have the smooth lines of most infidel machinery. It looked like a segment of metal pipe, tall as a human and twenty meters long, bent at the middle in a right angle, with another pipe, a meter in diameter and five long, bisecting the angle. A twin-seat cockpit that appeared to have been liberated from a starfighter was attached to the point of the bend, facing away from the smaller pipe, and thruster engines had been mounted on the two larger portions of pipe, oriented in the same direction as the smaller pipe. The pipe ends were capped with a device that looked as though it would iris open.

"There are three of these," Charat Kraal said. "And a fourth with three protrusions that extend at even, identical angles and a fourth protrusion that extends at a right angle from all of them; I have seen it but not been able to record it. My scouts, who eavesdrop on the infidels whenever they can get close enough to do so, call them 'pipefighters' and say they are part of an operation called 'Starlancer.' All three fly very badly. They go up into space and situate themselves at very precise points in relation to one another, far apart from one another, so that the three craft like this are points of a triangle and the fourth craft is at the center of their array. Then they communicate for several minutes. I do not know why."

"Speculate."

Charat Kraal hesitated. "I am only a pilot, not a shaper, and not one of their infidel scientists. But I had one of my advisers, who understands their mathematics better than I, analyze what they are doing. She says that if the center craft's right-angle protrusion is precisely a right angle from the triangle represented by the other three craft's positions, then it traces a course back to the Coruscant system. Perhaps it is a spy device, a communications device, or a weapon aimed at their old capital."

"Interesting." Czulkang Lah evaluated the pilot for a moment.

"Great One, if I may . . . if it is your intent now to order my death for my presumption, I ask that you order me to kill myself, rather than having me executed. That way I will have achieved a great ambition: to serve, even for a moment, Czulkang Lah."

The old Yuuzhan Vong allowed impatience to show in his expression. "Be quiet. Charat Kraal, I am advancing you to the rank of wing commander. Your forces will be replenished to full fighting-wing status. You will perform special missions for me, often in association with the other fighting wings. One of your tasks will be the capture of Jaina Solo; I will issue you other orders, as well. You will report to me. Do you understand?"

"I do, Great One." Charat Kraal's face twitched as he struggled to retain an impassive expression.

"Go."

Borleias Occupation, Day 39

The pilots of Twin Suns Squadron piled out of their X-wings, E-wings, and one clawcraft. They drifted off through the special ops docking bay, toward the main building, joking and recounting, pleased to have gone through a mission with no casualties. They'd escorted the cobbled-together Operation Starlancer pipefighters up into space, had escorted them to their precisely plotted positions while their pilots ran a few tests, and had come home without loss. Coralskippers had maneuvered out to take a look at what they were doing, but had not attacked . . . suggesting that they were studying the activities of the Starlancer ships but were not yet ready to move against them. The betting was that, no matter how slow moving and cautious the new Yuuzhan Vong commander was, he'd take action against the Starlancer ships soon.

Jaina lingered behind in the docking bay, putting some distance between herself and her pilots. *A supposed goddess can't be too chummy with her servants,* she told herself. And a voice from deep in her thoughts, one she listened to when no other Jedi was around to detect it, whispered, *And a doomed woman shouldn't get too close to people who might miss her when she's gone.*

She leaned against her X-wing, ignoring the sounds of the mechanics around her.

There was something within her, an alien thing she couldn't seem to rid herself of. It was a cold hatred of the enemy. Perhaps it had been with her since the start of the Yuuzhan Vong invasion, since the death of Chewbacca and its effects on her father and her family, but she had only truly become aware of it when Anakin died. Then the arrival, two days ago, of the worldship, and the attempted showering of Borleias's atmosphere with innocents, had caused it to swell within her.

Hate wasn't the way. It was wrong for a Jedi. And it was pointless for someone who was not likely to survive long in this war, not with all the enemies she was accumulating; she had better things to spend her time on than hating.

On the other hand, perhaps hate was right for a fighter pilot; it could keep her focused, give her an intensity she needed in combat.

But it was still emotion, still painful. She didn't want it. Didn't need it. She pushed it down, tamping it under the weight of her logic.

As she calmed, as she opened herself again to the Force, she felt a familiar presence, a reassuring one. Well, it was meant to be reassuring; it was projecting an aura of reassurance.

Jaina turned to see Tahiri approaching. She gave Tahiri a smile, but she knew it to be uncertain.

Tahiri had been on the verge of becoming closer to Anakin, might even have become a Solo someday. Now that would never happen, and Jaina sometimes thought Tahiri might just drift away like a planet that had suddenly escaped its sun's gravity. Jaina knew she was supposed to care, but that was just more emotion to pile on top of what she was already trying to rid herself of. One more relationship to maintain when she knew it was better to begin trimming those away.

Tahiri's clothes and the skin of her arms and legs were decorated with patches of green—stains from leaves and grasses, Jaina decided. "You've been on patrol?"

Tahiri nodded. "I spent a couple of hours playing hide and seek with some Yuuzhan Vong warriors out there. I never really caught sight of them. They must have seen me once, since I had to knock a thud bug out of the air. When I got back, I heard that your squadron was coming down. I thought maybe you'd want to talk."

"No, not really."

"Or maybe you'd want to get in some relaxation. A bunch of Rogue Squadron boys have converted a bioreactor tank into a heated tub. They're off on patrol, so it's unguarded—"

Jaina shook her head. "I don't have time. I have a session with an Intelligence group, the Wraiths, coming up. We're discussing psychological warfare and Yun-Harla, the Vong Trickster goddess. And then I have something to do I don't want to."

"What's that?"

"Talk to Kyp Durron. I'm going to hand Twin Suns Squadron over to him."

"You just took command, and already you're giving it up?"

"For a few weeks only, I hope. I'm going to—you know about Uncle Luke's expedition."

"Yes."

"I'm going to invite myself along."

Tahiri was silent for a few moments. Then she said, "Jaina, I don't think that's such a good idea."

"I expect everyone to tell me that. But Dad and Mother think Jacen's . . . " Jaina suddenly lost the breath to speak. Why was it so hard to say the word *alive*? She knew the answer as soon as she asked herself the question; it was because she desperately wanted to believe what Leia believed, and couldn't bring herself to. She couldn't allow herself to hope. She had a Force-bond with her twin, and it had been severed. He was dead, and to dream otherwise was just a way of distracting herself with delusion at a time when distractions could be fatal. She found her breath and continued, "They think Jacen's there. I have to go there . . . to prove that's not where he is."

"Don't do it," Tahiri said. There was quiet urgency to her voice.

"I have to."

"No, you don't. In fact, you stand a greater chance of getting Luke and Mara killed."

"You don't think very much of my skills."

"Yes, I do." Tahiri didn't sound apologetic or contrite. "But if it were just a matter of skills, or power for that matter, you'd be trying to send Kyp Durron, wouldn't you?"

"Kyp would never work. He and Luke have too much disagreement between them—"

"Exactly. Which makes my point. Just skills aren't the only thing you have to look at."

"So what are *you* looking at?"

"Well, there's this whole twins thing. The Yuuzhan Vong want you and Jacen together, and whatever they plan for you can't be good." Tahiri looked away for a moment. "Jaina, all I have to do is to think a certain way and I *become* Yuuzhan Vong, for as long as I can stand to. This thing about twins, it's not a casual interest. It's an obsession. Where twins are, the eyes of the gods look down. Twins distort reality around them. It's a sacred thing."

"So what?"

"So, let's say Jacen *is* alive. I hope he is. Let's say you go with Master Skywalker to Coruscant. You're seen but not captured. The Yuuzhan Vong suddenly know that both the twins are on Coruscant. They'll devote a *lot* more resources to finding Jaina Solo than they would to just finding a party of invaders, even *Jeedai*—Jedi—invaders. Right or wrong?"

"Well . . . right. But they might not recognize me."

"True. So you're going to risk Luke and Mara on a 'might not'?"

Jaina felt a growing sense of desperation. It was like so many of her fights in early Jedi training with her Uncle Luke. She'd press hard, put him on the defensive . . . and then realize the degree to which his superior skill was turning her lunges into awkward, off-balance, losing strategies.

She was losing this argument. Losing to Tahiri, who was both years her junior and all bottled up in pain because she'd lost Anakin.

"Luke and Mara aren't as close to Jacen as I am. I'm his twin." Deep down, she knew that the statement was insupportable, that Luke and Mara had skill, experience, and Force sensitivity enough for this task. But it was the argument she'd chosen, so she stubbornly stuck with it.

"So I'll go instead of you."

"You?"

Tahiri nodded, solemn. "Other than you, who'd be better? I don't know Jacen as well as you do. I can't feel him in the Force as well. But I know him better than any Jedi who wasn't in a Force-bond with him the way we were on that Yuuzhan Vong worldship. And no one, *no one*, knows the Yuuzhan Vong, at least the way they think, better than I do."

Jaina just looked at her, unable to argue that point. "I think . . ." She felt the heat of her argument slip away from her. She dropped almost effortlessly into a reflective state. She was sure Luke would approve of the transition. "I think you'll let your emotions get the better of you."

"I could say the same thing about you. Which brings us back to the point. Does neither of us go, or do I go?"

Jaina sighed, defeated. Oddly, the defeat didn't anger or irritate her. She just felt more tired than before. "You go." She felt Tahiri begin to lean forward for an embrace, but Jaina turned away before that feeling could be translated into action. She didn't want Tahiri to feel closer to her. It would only hurt Tahiri more once she was dead. "Thanks for caring."

"You're welcome . . . but you may not want to thank me after the other thing I have to say."

There was something in Tahiri's voice, some reluctant warning, that caused Jaina to turn back to look at her more closely. Tahiri's expression was an odd mix: concern, apprehension, a reluctance to hurt.

"All right," Jaina said, dubious. "Let's hear it."

"First, believe me, I understand that what I'm saying is none of my business. But I have to say it anyway." Tahiri took a deep breath to compose herself. "I think you should stop avoiding your mother."

"Avoiding her?" Jaina offered Tahiri an incredulous expression. "She's everywhere. I bump into her a dozen times a day."

"You know what I mean. You're not avoiding her as a defender of Borleias. You're avoiding her as your mother."

"That's ridiculous. I haven't started calling her 'Leia' or 'Hey, you,' or 'What's-your-name, Han's wife.' "

"You *have* started calling her 'Mother' instead of 'Mom.' "

"Have I?" Jaina frowned, trying to remember.

Tahiri just stared at her, and Jaina had the uneasy feeling the girl was staring right through the screens of logic she'd erected for herself as though they were the most highly polished transparisteel.

Jaina relented. "Look," she said. "I love my mother. But we don't have, I don't know, the kind of connection most mothers and daughters have. We were apart so often when I was a kid . . . she was trying to hammer the New Republic government into shape, and Jacen, Anakin, and I were on lonely little worlds with Chewbacca, or Winter, or on Yavin Four."

"Did that keep you from having a connection, or did it simply make you mad at her?"

"That's a stupid question."

"If you say so. But you can reach out to her at any time, and, click, you'll be connected again." Tears filled Tahiri's eyes and she turned away. "There's a point where you realize that you've had the last talk you're ever going to have with someone you love. That he's gone. Have you realized that about your mom? Has she realized that about you?"

Jaina's own vision blurred with tears. Her resolve finally gone, she reached out for Tahiri and pulled her close. "It's not that way," she said, the words having a hard time working their way around the sudden knot in her throat. "It isn't."

"If you say so." Tahiri held her in return for several long moments, then pulled away, not meeting Jaina's eyes. "I need to go get cleaned up."

ELEVEN

Borleias Occupation, Day 39

"My name," the man said, "is Sharr Latt. I'm a Wraith."

He was a bit over average height, with hair that was just a few degrees of color away from pure white, worn in a slightly shaggy haircut. His eyes were blue and amused; his features belonged to the sort of comic entertainer who abused his audience and got laughs from it. He wore red pants and vest, a sky-blue long-sleeved shirt and boots; a broad red swath of cloth, more decorative than functional, served him as a belt, and a matching headband circled his brow. His accent belonged to the lower-class humans of Coruscant, and the smile on his face could have been interpreted as insincere or mocking—or both.

Jaina turned to the man's companion. This being was a Gamorrean, one of the thick-bodied, snout-nosed, tusk-mouthed humanoids to be found fighting battles or doing low-complexity jobs all over the galaxy. This Gamorrean wore anonymous brown garments of human styling. "And is this one a Wraith, too?" Jaina asked, joking.

"I am," the Gamorrean answered. Jaina jumped. Many Gamorreans understood Basic, but their vocal cords were not adequate to let them speak it. The

Gamorrean continued, "My name is Voort saBinring. You can call me Piggy."

There was a certain mechanical inflection to Piggy's voice that led Jaina to believe his speech was artificially augmented. That would explain things. To cover for her sudden discomfiture, she shook each of their hands in turn, then asked, "So, what are we doing today?"

Sharr pointed through the blue-tinted window out into the jungle beyond the blackness of the kill zone. "We're going out there. We'll find a pool fed by cool underground springs. We'll bathe one another while Piggy stands guard, and see what develops from there." He shrugged. "Or, we can talk about psychological warfare and how it is applied to the Yuuzhan Vong."

"I'll take the psychological warfare."

He nodded. "That's pretty much what I figured. And since Piggy won't need to guard us, I expect he'll be tutoring you in small-unit starfighter tactics."

She gave Piggy a narrow look. "Did you used to be a starfighter pilot?"

The Gamorrean nodded, causing his jowls and rolls of belly fat to wobble. "I did. I served your father on one campaign."

"I think he told me about you when I was very young. One of those 'you can be whatever you want when you grow up' stories. 'The Gamorrean Who Became a Fighter Pilot.' I thought he'd made it up."

"I have kept a low profile since those days. I have not done much flying."

"That sort of suggests that you might not have much to teach me about small-unit tactics."

The Gamorrean smiled, a broadening and curving of his mouth that revealed more teeth—teeth far cleaner and straighter than most Gamorreans enjoyed, Jaina saw. "I think I will surprise you," Piggy said.

* * *

"Your work in the Hapes Cluster was pretty good," Sharr said. The three of them were now on top of the biotics building. Below them in the near distance were the landing fields; beyond, stretching to the horizon, was jungle. The afternoon sun bore down upon them, but Jaina welcomed the heat after the coldness of space she'd experienced in the morning's mission.

They were in clear sight of any Yuuzhan Vong observers that might be lurking at the jungle's edge, but the Yuuzhan Vong traditionally did not employ snipers.

" 'Pretty good,' " Jaina said. "Meaning you think it could have been better." She lay facedown on a blocky duracrete protrusion, staring off into the ship berthing area of the killing field, and watched the mechanics working on the *Record Time*. The surface she lay upon vibrated; within it was air-circulation machinery.

Sharr, leaning with his back against a smaller protrusion housing pumping equipment, kept his attention on his datapad and nodded absently. A few meters away, Piggy lay sprawled on his back on the roof surface, hands behind his head, eyes closed, enjoying the sunlight. His shirt was off, his belly expansive enough that Jaina suspected she could probably set a landspeeder down on it. She entertained the notion of painting landing stripes on it.

"How?" she persisted.

"Your tricks were good ones," Sharr said, and met her gaze. "But they weren't layered. You'd have one trick, and it would baffle them and kill them, and that would be it. Sometimes two. You need to have trick after trick available, so there's never any end to them; that's what they expect of their Trickster goddess.

"The second problem is that the Yuuzhan Vong could eventually figure out how you performed your tricks.

That bit with the tracers, where each Yuuzhan Vong ship broadcast the distinctive signal of *your* ship, so they'd fire on one another—good thinking. But if you'd had a little charge in each one that would detonate it, leaving behind a scorch pattern like a laser hit—then they'd never have understood how you caused them to fire on one another. And it's incomprehension, never figuring out the trick, that fills them—or us, for that matter—with supernatural dread."

"I like the sound of 'supernatural dread,' " Jaina admitted. It was a pleasing enough thought that she didn't take offense at Sharr's criticism of her efforts.

"We want them to suspect, not that you're somehow associated with Yun-Harla, not that you're a priestess or something, but that you *are* her." Sharr closed his datapad and tucked it into a pocket. "Everything you do should promote that impression, even in extremely minor ways. In fact, you're doing it now."

She gave him a curious look. "How?"

"A goddess does not work. And here you are, lounging around, being lazy in clear view of all the pilots and mechanics in the field below. A goddess does not fear. And here you are, in plain sight of the Yuuzhan Vong, unconcerned. A goddess is superior to mortals. And here you are, resting on a higher level than your two companions. Speaking of companions, goddesses have strange ones. Hence a Gamorrean and some idiot in nauseatingly bright colors." Sharr looked down at his outfit and shuddered.

"I get it," Jaina said. "This is why Piggy is here even though he's not talking about starfighter tactics yet."

"Very good." Sharr nodded. "From now on, you're on stage every minute of every day. We're not going to *say* you're a goddess. We're just going to treat you as though you are one, and you're going to act accordingly."

"Never ask when you can order," Piggy said.

"Never work—except the work Yun-Harla would perform," Sharr said. "Putting together tricks, that is. Don't carry things for yourself. We'll get you a porter if you don't have someone who'll do it for you."

"Don't be subtle in your motions," Piggy said. "Big, generous gestures, as though you were used to conducting an orchestra."

Jaina grimaced. "People are going to hate me. They're going to think I've become horribly stuck up."

"That's right." Sharr gave her another smile, this one more genuine, though still definitely tinged with mockery.

"But in private—"

"In private," Piggy said, "you continue the illusion. Though you can tell anyone you trust absolutely."

"No, she can't," Sharr said.

"Yes, she can."

"I'm the psychological warfare expert here, and I say she can't."

"I'm three times your mass, and can take off your head with a single bite, and I say she can."

"Excuse me?" Jaina let a little shrillness creep into her voice. "In case you haven't noticed, I'm still here."

Piggy opened his eyes to glance at her, then he and Sharr exchanged looks.

"She has us on that one," Sharr said to Jaina.

"She is indeed still here."

"Listen, Great One," Sharr said.

"Don't call me that."

"I need to. We all do. The thing about telling people—inevitably, the Yuuzhan Vong will have spies here. In our camp, in our base. The more people who know that you're not really becoming as arrogant as a Kuati merchant-princess, the more likely it is that those spies will notice. Tell whomever you want—but be aware that every extra person means the chances increase that the truth will spread."

"General Antilles has already broken Twin Suns Squadron out of the normal command structure," Piggy said. "Which makes sense, as a goddess wouldn't have a formal rank within New Republic hierarchy."

"Good point." Sharr pulled out his datapad and keyed in a few words. "That means we can arrange for your pilots to be called by whatever maximum rank they've attained, since it has no bearing on your unit's command structure. Colonel Jagged Fel. Jedi Master Kyp Durron." He frowned. "No, not just Jedi Master. Kyp Durron, the Destroyer of Worlds, is subordinate to Jaina. To the Yuuzhan Vong, that will be significant." Then he returned his attention to Jaina. "What do you think?"

She gave him a smile. She hoped that, to some distant observer watching her through organic optics, it would look as wicked as it felt. "You mentioned a porter. Can I have anyone I want as my manservant?"

Sharr nodded. "That's what it is to be a goddess."

"No," said Jag Fel. He didn't raise his voice or even look at them. He continued ratcheting the hydrospanner on the lower starboard claw of his TIE clawcraft, improving, with millimeter-by-millimeter precision, the alignment of that claw's laser.

All around them, mechanics tinkered with damaged starfighters, pilots lifted off in courier shuttles, messengers flashed by on landspeeders; the cacophony kept their words from carrying very far across the docking bay.

"It's important." Sharr leaned against the claw. At Jag's glare, he straightened away from it. "Don't give us some sort of idiotic excuse that your pride won't take it. Lives may depend on it."

Jaina, a couple of steps back, not deigning to speak directly to a mere mortal, merely smiled. She held up her hand as though to admire her nails; Yuuzhan Vong spies were not likely to see that they were unpainted, cut short, and—she finally noticed—dirty.

"I'm happy to participate in any plan so long as it's the best plan to accomplish its goal," Jag said. He straightened and slapped shut the hatch that had allowed him access to the claw's internal systemry. He ignored Sharr and addressed Jaina directly. "This isn't the best plan. You haven't thought it out."

Jaina gave him a cold stare. "Yes, it is. You just don't want to do it."

"No, I have a better idea."

Sharr snorted. "Better than what an expert on psychological warfare and a Jedi Knight have assembled. Of course."

Jag turned an unfriendly smile on him. "Kyp Durron."

Sharr's expression changed as he considered the suggestion.

Jag continued, "To your presumed Yuuzhan Vong spies and observers, I'm just an unknown quantity—a pilot from a place the Yuuzhan Vong haven't encountered yet. But Jedi Master Kyp Durron, if they see him bowing to her, carrying her baggage, digging dirt from beneath her nails—"

Jaina tried very hard to keep her outrage from being reflected in her expression. She didn't think she succeeded very well.

"—they'll be impressed. Who else would a Jedi Master bow to but a goddess, right? It'll create rumors among *our* people, as well as theirs." Jag turned half away from them and dogged down the panel he'd shut.

More than just finishing his point, Jag had also signaled an end to the discussion. But to turn away and leave with no further discussion would be to lose points.

Jaina waited until she was sure she had her voice under control, had lowered it to something like Leia's political voice, and said, "I'd like you to work up the events of two days ago as a sim. Maybe more of us can learn to save extravehiculars just with vehicle maneuvering."

Jag tucked his hydrospanner into a belt loop, turned toward her, and executed a salute so sharp and meticulous that Jaina could detect no sign of resentment or irritation in it. "It will be done," he said.

She returned the salute, spun on her heel, and headed back to the main building.

Sharr caught up with her. "I've only known him for five minutes and already I hate him," he said.

Jaina made an exasperated face. Despite the irritation she felt, she had to admit—to herself, anyway—that Jag had been right. "Oh, he's not so bad."

Luke's Coruscant expedition came together with startling speed.

Iella offered him the services of the Wraiths, the most experienced Intelligence cell on Borleias. Luke met Face Loran, the unit leader, and already knew Kell Tainer. Face introduced him to the other Wraiths who'd been on Coruscant when it fell.

Elassar Targon was a middle-aged Devaronian with a bounce to his walk that suggested a much younger man. He wore a flamboyant jacket, military in its cut, in reflective black with gold fringe, red piping, and numerous medals hanging from it; the fringe and medals swung as he walked, and he accentuated the effect by often making a circular gesture—"To ward off bad luck," he explained. "It really works. Try it." But Luke noted that the man's shirt, trousers, and knee-high boots were a matte black, and suspected that Elassar could lose or reverse the jacket to become instantly inconspicuous. Inconspicuous, that is, anywhere Devaronians were to be seen.

Baljos Arnjak was a human; he spoke with the clipped, precise accent of a Coruscant native, or one who aspired to Coruscant ancestry. He was tall and lean, with dark hair, mustache and beard that made his pale skin seem absolutely pallid. He was dressed in a multiply stained orange pilot's jumpsuit that suggested he was a mechanic who wore only hand-me-downs, but Face introduced him as the team's biological expert—a man with nearly as much expertise in Yuuzhan Vong technology as Danni Quee.

Piggy saBinring was the Gamorrean pilot assigned to tutor Jaina in battle management. Perhaps the only one of his kind, he had, in childhood, been modified by a biologist working for the Warlord Zsinj. The biologist had altered his brain structure, giving him patience and an extraordinary mathematical acuity, the latter being necessary for him to learn the complex astronautics and astrogation required of starfighter pilots. Sharr Latt was the pale-haired Coruscant native who had been assigned to work with Jaina on her role as avatar of the Trickster goddess; he and Piggy were just back from their first session with her.

Bhindi Drayson was a human female. She spoke in the same deliberate way, and with the same innocuous accent, as the late and former Chief of State Mon Mothma, suggesting a background on Mon Mothma's homeworld of Chandrila. Bhindi was unlovely, as lean and sharp-featured as a naked vibroblade, with dark hair and eyes that contributed to a perception of her as someone brooding and menacing, but Luke felt no aura of menace from her, just a quiet watchfulness.

"Are you any relation to Hiram Drayson?" Luke asked

her. Admiral Hiram Drayson was a former military officer and Intelligence leader, and a friend of Mon Mothma.

"His daughter," she said.

"You have a noble family history."

She gave him a brief smile. "And that's only the parts you've heard about."

"Bhindi is one of our two tactics experts, with Piggy," Face said, "and she's been learning whatever she can about Yuuzhan Vong tactics. Unfortunately, we're going to lose her on Coruscant."

Luke frowned, wondering for a moment if Face was somehow both prescient and extremely inconsiderate, then realized what Face meant. He turned to Bhindi again. "You'll be staying there when we leave?"

She nodded. "I'll be setting up Resistance cells on Coruscant."

Luke suppressed a shudder. Going into Coruscant would be bad enough. The thought of being left behind among enemies so antagonistic and alien, deliberately staying there, was not a pleasant one. Bhindi looked faintly pleased at having discomfited a Jedi Master.

They'd gathered, the Wraiths and Luke, in a chamber deep within the Borleias complex—a chamber that, from its pristine condition, had not, Luke suspected, been found by the Yuuzhan Vong during their brief occupation. How the Wraiths had discovered its existence was not something he knew; all he did know was that it was accessed through a sliding panel in the back of a laboratory. The hidden chamber, too, had been a laboratory; on the shelves on its walls were the left-behind remnants of biomedical gear. Luke saw bacterial culture dishes, injectors, neural monitors . . . at the back of the chamber was a full-sized bacta tank, empty, the transparisteel of its main compartment scuffed and abraded through hard [illegible]e so that many portions of it were almost opaque.

"So," Face said, seating himself on one of the stools at the chamber's main table. "Let's show him what we've got. Kell, you first."

The big man hefted a green cloth bag roughly two meters long. From its open top he pulled an object like a very shallow one-person boat. It was thick, perhaps thirty centimeters in depth for most of its length, thinning to some ten centimeters all along the edge. Its red underside was both gummy and reflective; it took Luke a moment's study to see that a thick layer of transparent red material had been closely fitted over a smooth silvery surface. Its top side was a dull gray, with two shoe-shaped clamps protruding from it.

Kell dropped this apparatus on the table in front of Face. It made a boom as it hit the table; it had to be heavy. Face shot Kell a sardonic look and said, "Thanks."

"Don't mention it." Kell turned his attention to Luke. "This is something we've been working on for some time. We mount them in shells resembling meteorites or debris. Together with the shells, they act as individual atmospheric intrusion pods."

Luke gave them a skeptical look. "Meaning what, exactly?"

"Meaning you ride them from orbit into a planet's atmosphere."

"In what?"

"In the shells I mentioned. Nothing more. The red stuff is an adhesive that affixes to the interior of the shell. The shell doesn't even have to be airtight. One person rides it in a vac suit, his feet gripped here." Kell indicated the clamps. "The underside is an ablative heat shield. Slowly ablative, you understand. Layered between the heat shield and the top are a simple repulsor unit and a power cell. The repulsor keeps it angled correctly toward the planet's surface. You drop into atmosphere at the correct angle and ride it all the way down. The shell burns up from friction with the atmosphere—it's designed to keep the heat from cooking the occupant. The heat wash also conceals your true nature from most sensors—ours and theirs. When the shell gives way, the silvery surface is your secondary heat shield; it's ablative, too, so the visual illusion that you're a burning meteorite continues. In other words, you look and act just like a piece of space debris punching into the atmosphere."

"Until you get near the planet's surface," Face added. "At which time the repulsor puts out its final effort and slows you down so you crash quite slowly into the surface."

"Crash," Luke said.

"Quite slowly."

"And these have been successfully tested."

Face glanced around, looking a bit nervous. "Well, tested, sure. They've been *tested*. Each time they're tested, we assemble what data we can, and the next generation of pods comes back just a bit more intact."

"We're sure they have them right this time," Bhindi said.

Luke looked among them, and it was Bhindi who broke first, losing her worried expression, snickering at Luke's.

"We've made insertions with them," Kell said, relenting. "They're pretty new, but Sharr and I have used them twice, Face and Elassar three times. We've never fried anyone yet."

Luke shook his head. "I have to say, this sounds like the worst idea in a thousand generations of bad ideas."

"You haven't heard all our ideas," Bhindi said.

"Next," Face interrupted, and nodded at Baljos.

The scientist rooted around in a bag of his own. From it he drew something that he threw atop the atmospheric [illegible]rusion unit. It looked like what would result if someone carefully removed all the skin from the head of a Yuuzhan Vong and meticulously reattached it into the shape of a head. It twitched when it hit the pod, then settled into stillness.

"An ooglith masquer," Luke said.

"Right the first time," Baljos said. "I'm the inventor. Well, the developer. I was working from captured ooglith masquers."

"But this one looks like a Yuuzhan Vong face."

Baljos nodded. "Each one is unique. I give them all names. That's Brand. So called because most of the mutilation decorations come from a technique that resembles branding. They hurt like anything to remove . . . but you can wear them for hours or days, unlike holoshrouds, where your batteries give out after a few minutes."

"This, I like," Luke said. "It'll help us move among them without being detected."

"Next," Face said.

Bhindi rooted around in her own pack. From it she extracted a brown object made up of a thick, curved disk at the top, bent down into the approximate shape of a canopy, mounted atop a thick stem that grew thicker at the other end. It was approximately the size of a human head.

Luke gave it a close look. "It's some sort of fungus."

"We'll all be carrying them," she said.

"In case we get hungry?"

"It's not a fungus," Bhindi assured him. "It's a droid."

"You've got to be kidding."

"It looks like a type of fungus found in dank places in Coruscant's undercity," Bhindi said. "We're hoping that the Yuuzhan Vong won't destroy them, precisely because they look like something organic. In fact, their covering *is* organic, a type of mold. Their circuitry is heavily shielded.

They have an epoxy reservoir so they can cling to whatever surface they're on if they get grabbed, and an epoxy solvent so they can detach themselves later. They're mobile and have very advanced sensor arrays and tactical programming."

"Meaning," Elassar said, "that they're going to sneak around, find Yuuzhan Vong installations, try to get inside, and relay information to one another. They'll establish a relay chain up to the surface, and the one on the surface will transmit to surviving comm stations there."

"It's a long shot," Bhindi said, "but any piece of information we get could prove vital at some point. And we have four different shape and coloration schemes on these, including two that look like Yuuzhan Vong worldshaping plants. If the Yuuzhan Vong discover that one is a droid and destroy everything that looks like it, the others could survive undetected."

"Fungus droids. I always thought that Intelligence work was supposed to be, I don't know, sophisticated and charming."

Face snickered. "That's what you told me the first time we met."

Luke frowned. "When did we ever meet before?"

"It was . . ." Face reconsidered. "Oh, that's right. I was in disguise. You wouldn't recognize me now."

"But when was it? Now I'm curious."

"I can't tell you."

"We have a few sets of vonduun crab armor," Bhindi interrupted, "and a few more sets of armor faked up to look like the real thing. If they get close enough to touch it, they'll know the fakes are made of manufactured materials, of course. And we have lots of tizowyrms—their translator worms."

"And we have explosives," Kell said. "Lots and lots of plosives."

"And a Jedi," Piggy said, his voice a mechanical rasp.

"Three Jedi," Luke corrected. "Mara and Tahiri are going with us. All right. Let's figure out exactly how we're going to get into Coruscant orbit, where we want to land, and what our priorities are. If we're crazy enough to do this, we need to be sane enough to do it well."

TWELVE

Borleias Occupation, Day 39

In the hallway of the senior personnel quarters, where most of the Insiders kept their chambers, Jaina was held up by a crowd—Wedge, Iella, their daughters, Luke, Mara, little Ben, the Jedi Kam and Tionne Solusar from the Jedi academy, Han, Leia, and C-3PO. They were crowded into the hall in a mass of good-byes and last-minute instructions.

"I don't want to go." That was Syal, Wedge's older daughter. Her voice was not raised in the high-pitched whine of the wheedler; though she couldn't be older than ten, she was expressing a feeling rather than complaining. She was speaking as befitted a child who'd been trained to think, to express arguments logically, to express emotions clearly.

"I know," Wedge said. He knelt beside both daughters and took them in his arms. "But where you're going, I'll worry less about you and can do my job better."

"We'll take good care of him." That was Kam Solusar, to Mara and Luke. But Mara did not seem to hear; she was totally focused on her infant son, whom she held to her. Mara was whispering to her boy, and though Jaina strained to hear, she could not; Jaina wondered if Mara was perhaps not using words, but communing directly through the Force. Luke held them both, watching his son with a wondering expression.

Mara's own expression contained none of the edginess and dark humor that were the parts of her everyone saw. This was not exactly a softened Mara, but it was a different Mara, one whose angles and thoughts were unfamiliar to Jaina. Jaina wondered what the baby was seeing, whether this view was, like some optical puzzles, something that only made sense or was recognizable when viewed from one specific angle.

For a moment Jaina felt a flash of emotion—her own, rather than Mara's or the baby's, but it was still unfamiliar to her. Envy, she thought, as it faded, but whom was she envying? Mara, or the baby?

"Hey, kid." That was her father, finally noting her presence. "You here to see us off? Or are you running interference?"

"Uh . . . I didn't even know you were going. I'm part of the main task force."

Wedge reluctantly released his daughters and rose. "Jaina, this is the first mission to take the Jedi students, and some of the civilian children, such as mine, to the new safe zone. Han, I've got Nevil and Corran running interference for you."

"Well, blast. Thought I was going to be able to give my daughter some much-needed flying lessons."

Jaina didn't rise to the bait. She just shrugged. "Some other time, maybe."

With extraordinary gentleness and a reluctance she couldn't conceal, Mara handed her son to Luke. She bent to kiss Ben's forehead, then turned away . . . not swiftly enough for Jaina to miss the flash of pain in her features. Then Mara was walking back to her quarters, her stride long and her boot heels clicking in a manner that seemed absolutely normal, as if nothing out of the usual had just occurred.

"Come on, Junior Corellians." Han turned away from the crowd, stooped just a little, and looked back over his shoulder. "Who wants a ride to the *Millennium Falcon*?"

"Me!" That was Myri, closer to Han than her sister. She jumped onto Han's back; he locked his arms under her knees so she could ride piggyback.

Han scowled at C-3PO. "Come on, Goldenrod."

"I am as ready to depart as I was at the beginning of this discussion, four minutes and thirty-eight seconds ago."

"No, you pile of parts, I mean, do what I'm doing." Han flexed, emphasizing his odd posture.

"As you wish, but I fail to see what will be gained . . ." C-3PO bent in an imitation of Han's position, then added "Oh" as Syal, grinning, jumped onto his back.

"That's it," Han said. "Syal, don't be afraid to use the whip, he's willful and skittish."

"Sir, I protest. These are adjectives that cannot properly be used to describe my behavior . . ."

Han set himself into motion, heading down the hallway, but rolled his eyes at Jaina. "I should have known better. She weighs as much as a wampa."

"I do not!" Myri said.

They passed down the corridor, C-3PO and Syal following. Jaina watched them go. So many times she'd ridden her father's back that way. The last time . . . when had it been? Only a few years ago. He'd said she was getting too big, or that his back was getting too old. Probably another Han Solo fib.

The gathering in the hall was breaking up, Leia accompanying Wedge and Iella toward the complex's main hall, saying, "I need to talk about some additional matériel." Luke followed, little Ben in his arms, talking to Kam and Tionne.

And then Jaina was alone. She followed Mara's path to the door of the Skywalker chamber and knocked. At Mara's "come in," she did so.

Mara stood in the center of the main chamber. All the chamber's furniture had been placed against the walls, giving the room a large open area in the middle, doubtless a place for Mara and Luke to exercise or meditate. Perhaps Mara had just started an exercise; she looked a little flushed, her hair slightly disarrayed.

"I guess it's a bad time," Jaina said. She jerked her head back toward the door and the corridor beyond. "I didn't know all that was going on."

"It's all right. They're taking the Jedi academy students to a new hiding place. Somewhere they'll be safe while the *Errant Venture* is on-station here. Ben is going with them, and Wedge's kids, and the boy Tarc." Mara shrugged, and seemed about to add something, but no more words came.

"Are you all right?"

"I feel like I've had the wind knocked out of me. I just can't seem to find my breath."

This sudden candor, the way Mara seemed to be just short of in control, was unnerving. Jaina tried to find some words to help but realized the ridiculousness, the futility of it. She didn't have any experience to compare to it.

Other than losing Anakin and Jacen. It was not the same. On one hand, they were her brothers, not her son; on the other, the loss was permanent. She steered herself away from those thoughts. "You could go with him," she said.

"Don't think I haven't considered it. Don't think I won't be considering it until the moment your parents blast off. Or even after." Mara swallowed hard. "But my work here, and this mission to Coruscant, is more important than my feelings. If I'm not here to do something I'm supposed to do, the Yuuzhan Vong could take another few strides toward victory. Down the line, when it counts, that might be the difference for us. It might be the difference between Ben having a galaxy he can grow up in . . . or not having one. If I just do what I *want* to, and go running after your father, Ben could end up dying. Or becoming a slave of the Yuuzhan Vong. I can't do that."

Mara's eyes were closed now, but she was in control—in control of her physical self, anyway. Nothing could control the anguish she was feeling.

Jaina felt it through the Force, an outpouring of pain that roared out of Mara like water through a shattered dam. It washed across Jaina and she was suddenly lost in it—

years alone the cold of space in her heart the Emperor's hand avenge his death and then Luke what does hate become Ben so small so small was I ever that small will I ever see him again do I deserve to be his mother

It folded Jaina over like a snap-kick to her stomach. She lurched back into the door, but Mara, eyes closed, somewhere deep within herself, didn't seem to hear.

Jaina resisted the urge to go to her mentor, to put her arms around her, to comfort her. The numbers had to catch up with Jaina sooner or later, as they had with her brothers. Mara would be better off not having her emotions divided as finely as they were. By stepping away, allowing Mara to concentrate just on her immediate family, Jaina would be helping her. She backed into the doorway and out into the hall.

The door slid closed in front of her, but the wash of thoughts and emotions from Mara continued. Jaina moved away and began to catch her breath, but Mara's ache still permeated her, mingling with her own ache from the loss of her brothers, and she wished she could keep from ever hurting that way again.

With every step she drew away from Mara's quarters, she felt the pain slip away. At the end of the corridor, where it intersected with the main corridor leading to the administrative sector, she was herself again . . . but with her thoughts and emotions still whirling like clouds of piranha-beetles on Yavin 4.

Her thoughts were still not settled minutes later as she went through her X-wing checklist.

All around her, starfighters and larger spacecraft in the special operations docking bay roared, whined, or rumbled into life, the sounds and vibrations cutting through her despite the insulation provided by X-wing hull and flight suit. Normally she found it comfortably familiar, even soothing, as if everyone affected by the noise and vibration were united by them into a single mind with a single objective, but just now it was distracting, intrusive. She couldn't focus.

The *Millennium Falcon* was in sight off to her port, and she could see her mother and father in its cockpit. Leia caught sight of her look and waved, smiling. Jaina waved back, absently, and forced a smile.

The starfighters of Jaina's own squadron were arrayed around her, with Kyp and Jag situated nearest. She could see Kyp going through his own checklist, gaze flicking back and forth across the controls. Jag was already done with his, leaning back in his pilot's couch, anonymous TIE fighter helmet on, his posture relaxed.

Some of these people loved her. Others at least respected her. They would be hurt when she followed her brothers into death, but she had a handle on that, putting them all increasingly at arm's length so the sting would be less when she was lost to them.

She could help things further along. Kyp had suggested some time ago that she become his apprentice. If she accepted, it would probably sting Mara a bit, but then Mara would be able to withdraw from her life and perhaps wouldn't feel the greater sting when Jaina died. And if she became Kyp's apprentice, she could insist that he maintain the distance suitable to a Master-apprentice relationship and stop expressing his personal interest in her.

That left only Jag. She didn't know what he might have meant to her had things been different. She suspected that pursuing this question was one of the reasons behind his joining her squadron. But he was disciplined enough, too accustomed to loss to be drastically affected if Jaina died. He'd be all right.

She settled back, a trifle calmer. She had a plan for all the people she could currently affect. When the numbers caught up to her, all these people would be able to endure her loss a little better, a little more easily.

Her comlink clicked. It was Kyp, a direct, pilot-to-pilot transmission routed through their respective astromechs. "You all right?" he asked.

"Just using a calming technique."

"I don't think it's working. I can feel you from over here. You're in turmoil."

"No, I'm not. It just seems that way." To cut the conversation short, she clicked over to squadron frequency. "Twin Suns Leader to squadron. I have four engines at full power, ready to scramble."

"Two, four lit and waiting for a target."

"Twin Suns Three, ready."

"Four, starboard upper showing its usual power flux, but ready to dance . . ."

A minute later, the go-code flashed across her board. Twin Suns was first out of the special ops docking bay, its starfighters surrounding one of the kludged, right-angle-shaped craft the defenders of Borleias referred to as pipefighters. They set up on the killing field and waited for the other squadrons to deploy.

Next were the Rogues, reduced in number by the absence of Nevil and Corran, with their pipefighter, and the Wild Knights, guarding theirs. Fourth was Blackmoon Squadron, the renamed E-wing squad that had previously protected Pyria VI's moon, under the command of Captain Yakown Reth; they escorted the triangle-shaped pipefighter that was the centerpiece of the Operation Starlancer experiments. Finally, the *Millennium Falcon*, its two Rogue Squadron escort X-wings, and a larger freighter lumbered out of the docking bay, practically emptying it.

Jaina switched her comlink over to fleet frequency. "This is Twin Suns Leader to Control. Test-fire mission is ready to launch."

"Twin Suns, this is Control. Launch at will. Best of luck."

Jaina led the Twin Suns and their pipefighter up in a gentle ascent through Borleias's atmosphere. No one was entirely sure how much stress the experimental pipefighter could endure. After every test mission, mechanics descended on the cobbled-together vehicles, with their space station angle segments and their old Y-wing cockpit and engine components, and managed to patch them together for yet another launch. No one was yet suggesting that this was a losing battle, but Jaina knew the experimental vehicles were soaking up a lot of repair and maintenance resources. She hoped the project would be successful enough to warrant the effort.

The squadrons reached high planetary orbit and went

their separate ways, each navigating to a different point in the Pyria system—all but the *Falcon* and the vehicles with her, which remained behind in orbit.

Tam Elgrin scrambled into his quarters on the shuttle and fumbled with his concealed villip. Pain made his fingers clumsy; it took several tries for him to get the device open, to stroke the villip surface itself so that it would correctly expand into the shape of his controller.

"Speak," the woman said.

"Jaina Solo has just taken off," Tam said. With every word, his headache eased just a bit. "With her entire squadron. I was able to fling that thing, that bug, at her X-wing as she was flying out of the docking bay. It stuck to the side. As ordered." He was getting very good at following orders. Not long before, he'd walked to the limits of the kill zone permitted to civilians and used his holocam to record the bleakness of that destroyed landscape, waiting there long enough for Yuuzhan Vong warriors at the kill zone's edge to throw a packet to him. It was a jellylike gob of transparent material, wiggling, filled with bugs and worms and things that couldn't escape except when he jammed his fingers into it to pry them free, and subsequent communications over the villip had told him what all the various creatures within it were for.

"Excellent. You're doing very well, Tam."

His controller's words of praise, her encouraging tones, made Tam feel better. He hated himself for it.

"Was there anything else?" his controller asked.

"Nothing," he said. His headache was gone now.

"Contact me when you've had a chance to evaluate the morale of the garrison once Jaina Solo is taken," the woman said. Then the villip inverted.

Tam closed its container. He stood in place, shaking.

He now had an idea of how the leash that had been put on him worked. When he failed to carry out his orders, the pain began. It worsened as his failure continued. When he was able to report success, it diminished. But since his controller couldn't know, until he reported, how successful he was, the only stimulus for the pain could be his own knowledge of failure. Some portion of his brain that lit up when he felt guilt, some hormone discharged into his bloodstream when he was under a specific kind of stress, triggered the headaches.

He had no doubt that the pain, if allowed to grow too great, could kill him. He'd been told so. He'd felt it grow to the point that he believed it signaled an imminent explosion in his head, a fatal aneurysm or other deadly failure within him.

If only he could find some way to think himself around the pain, to feel no guilt or acknowledge no failure, so that the pain never came . . . but even with that thought, throbbing began in his temples and the pain returned.

He slumped, defeated. He wasn't even allowed to think such things.

He was a slave and he would always be a slave.

He left the shuttle, head down, to return to his duties.

Han slouched in his pilot's seat and stared, in unaccustomed contentment, at the stars.

"What are you thinking?" Leia asked from the copilot's seat.

Han glanced at her. She looked far more comfortable in the Leia-sized seat they'd installed for her. At the very least, she wouldn't be slipping back and forth during high-performance maneuvers. "You know me," he said. "I wasn't thinking."

Leia nodded. "I *know* you. What were you thinking?"

"I was thinking about what would happen when we finally got rid of the Vong. I was thinking about taking up the old trade again."

"*Sure* you were."

"In an elder-statesman way, of course. And I was thinking that someone with *your* skills and connections, Leia, could be a tremendous asset to that sort of operation."

She just looked at him for a moment, her expression somewhere between amusement and outrage. "You think *I* should be a smuggler?"

"Sure, why not? You're through with politics, you said so. Maybe you should follow *me* around for a few years. Like I did with you, when you were busy helping rule the galaxy."

"You didn't follow, you visited."

"Well, that's as close to following as I could manage. I'm sure you'd be better at it than I was."

"I may not be a politician anymore, but I'm still, well, honest."

"Mistress Leia, Captain Solo . . ." They were the musical tones of C-3PO.

Han and Leia looked to the back of the cockpit, where the Protocol Droid stood in his usual posture of nervous diffidence. "What is it?" Han asked.

"It's the children, sir. I was wondering what sort of games and entertainments I should find for them. They are, well, bored."

"They can't be bored yet. We've only been here two minutes."

Leia nodded. "It takes Han at least three."

Han shot her a glare. "Break out the hologame board."

"Well, I did, sir, but they appear to think it's somewhat old-fashioned."

"Old-fashioned? That's one of the few systems that was installed *new* in the *Falcon.*" Then Han frowned. It had been new when installed, which was, oh, nearly three decades ago.

Leia smirked at his expression. "See-Threepio, let the younger ones train with lightsabers against the remote. They won't want to, since it's so antiquated, but tell them it's the same one Luke first trained on, and bring up his scores to give them something to compete against. The older ones . . . um, put up some simulations on the quadlasers and let them run through those."

Han nodded. "That's more like it."

"If they don't want to work with equipment that old, tell them it's a history lesson."

"Yes, Mistress Leia." The droid returned the way he'd come.

Han glared at her. "Leia, you're just asking to walk from here."

She just smiled at him.

Twin Suns Squadron came on-station in an empty region of Pyrian space. The twelve members of the squadron broke into four shield trios and moved out from the center of their zone while the pipefighter remained behind, maneuvering itself to be more and more precisely at the exact mathematical point the Operation Starlancer coordinators required of it. They directed their sensors outward to give them earliest possible notification of a Yuuzhan Vong intrusion.

Occasional, low-volume comments crackled up from the comm board, which was set to squadron frequency. At the four stations of the Starlancer mission, nothing was happening—nothing but pipefighters setting up.

"I like your design." That was Kyp, the volume of his voice louder than the settings she'd set up for her comm system. She glanced down and saw that he once again was routing a message through their astromechs for privacy.

Jaina turned to look through her canopy at Kyp's X-wing, which was floating mere meters off to her starboard. He was also looking back at her. "What design?" she asked.

"Your X-wing coloration. I like it for its effectiveness."

"Oh, right." She'd arranged for her X-wing to be painted a glossy white; on each flank was a picture of a running voxyn. The reptilian beasts, designed by the Yuuzhan Vong to detect and slaughter Jedi, had all been killed or doomed by the young Jedi Knights' expedition to the worldship around Myrkyr, and Jaina did not remember them fondly—they had killed too many of her friends and colleagues. But she did like the idea when Sharr had expressed it to her. She liked the mixed signals it sent, appreciated its ambiguity. Did it mean that she identified with a creature created by the Yuuzhan Vong? That though she was a Jedi, she did not fear it and had participated in its destruction? That she admired its ferocity and cunning? Its presence as a symbol on her snubfighter would confuse the Yuuzhan Vong. It was certainly confusing the New Republic fighters and Jedi who did not belong to the Insiders.

Kyp's own X-wing was now individually decorated as well, with a design that had to be as unpleasant to him as the voxyn were to Jaina. On either side of the fuselage was painted a sun in the throes of going supernova, a reminder to the Yuuzhan Vong that it was Kyp Durron who had destroyed whole worlds, years ago, through use of a superweapon called the Sun Crusher. Kyp had been driven by rage during that time, and had not been old enough for maturity to have restrained him. Even today, many people thought he should pay for his crime against those Imperial worlds—pay the ultimate price, sacrificing his life—but Luke Skywalker had disagreed, and Kyp had, in the intervening years, found a sort of uncomfortable and incomplete redemption in his role as a Jedi.

For a moment, Jaina thought about adding, *I like your design, too.* That would confuse Kyp, help keep him at bay. But her resolve softened and she could not bear to inflict that little wound on him. She kept her mouth shut.

"Contact, bearing three-three-seven, incoming." That was Gavin Darklighter's voice at the muted volume of the squadron frequency.

"Wild Knights here. We have incoming targets from Rimward." This was Danni's voice.

A moment later, Captain Reth called in a sensor contact for Blackmoon Squadron.

Jaina's sensor board was still empty of unfriendlies, but three simultaneous approaches against the other units protecting the Starlancer vehicles suggested that she'd have incoming coralskippers soon as well. She switched to squadron frequency. "Keep your eyes open," she said.

"Awww." That was the mechanical voice of Piggy, who was now flying as Twin Suns Five and doing squadron tactics evaluation. "I wanted to sleep a while longer." Then his voice became suddenly alert, as though he realized his jest might not be appreciated. "I mean, to hear is to obey, Great One."

Jaina grinned. If she were leading this unit like a military squadron, she'd snap at him for making irrelevant comments over his comlink, but the Twin Suns pilots were supposed to be looser, more idiosyncratic.

"Starlancer Leader to squadrons, we are ready for test-firing."

Jaina switched back to fleet frequency. "Starlancer Leader, this is Twin Suns Leader. Fire at will."

Several kilometers behind her, the ends of the two larger

pipelike extrusions from the pipefighter flared into incandescence. A bright red bar of light, a meter-thick laser beam, leapt out from each one. Instead of flaring once with a short burst of energy, like a starfighter weapon system, they continued pouring out laser light.

Acknowledgments came in across her comm unit, indications from two other Starlancer triangle-corner vehicles that they, too, had fired. Then there were updates from them: "Estimated two minutes until impact . . . One minute forty-five seconds . . . one minute thirty seconds until impact . . ." All four Starlancer craft were fitted with voice-only holocomm units, allowing them to coordinate at transmission speeds greater than the speed of light, and their respective guardian squadrons were piggybacking their own communications through those holocomms.

Jaina tuned out the updates and concentrated on the fighter-pilot chatter. The Rogues, Wild Knights, and Blackmoons all reported detecting inbound squadrons, but now indicated that the squadrons were not coming in at attack speed. This seemed to be a slower, more deliberate sortie.

"Fifteen seconds until impact . . . Impact. We have positive connection on both leads with Vehicle Two, with Vehicle Three . . . with Vehicle One. All three are positive. Fire central units."

Behind Jaina, the pipefighter fired off its third extrusion, the one that bisected the right angle; it, too, emitted a meter-thick stream of laser light. At the moment it fired, the project controller began transmitting, "Estimated one minute twenty-two seconds until impact . . . one minute fifteen . . ."

"Wild Knights engaged." Danni Quee's voice rose in pitch. "We have two squadrons of coralskippers."

"Same here, two squadrons." The Blackmoon leader,

Captain Reth, was calmer than Danni. "Standard incoming tactics."

"Rogues have two complete squadrons incoming." Then Gavin Darklighter's voice took on a slightly amused tone. "Correction, two incomplete squadrons."

Jaina frowned at her sensor board. Why weren't the Yuuzhan Vong attacking her position? It didn't make sense for them to attack three of four Starlancer positions. They should be attacking only one, to acquire a Starlancer pipefighter, or all four.

Then she saw it, a blip at the extreme range of her sensors. "Incoming enemies," she said, "from this position. Twin Suns shield trios, form up on me."

Han and Leia listened to the comm traffic from the Starlancer positions—when it wasn't drowned out by the shrieks of amusement from the more distant portions of the *Falcon*, where novice Jedi practiced deflecting remote blasts, shooting down computer-generated targets with computer-generated laser blasts, and ran amok. Han and Leia could also hear C-3PO's ineffective protests. "That should be enough distraction out there," Leia said.

"I think so, too." Han keyed his comlink. "Kam, Tionne, get them settled in and strapped down. We're jumping out of here in one minute." A moment later, he could hear the deeper tones of Kam Solusar addressing the boisterous passengers.

"Can I sit up here?"

Han and Leia turned to see Tarc standing at the opening into the cockpit. The boy looked uncertain, unhappy.

Leia said, "You don't want to sit back there with the others? We won't have much time to talk to you, honey."

Tarc shook his head. "They're better at everything than I am. Even Syal and Myri."

Leia exchanged a look with Han. Han cleared his

throat. "Sure, kid, strap into the seat behind mine. And cinch everything down tight."

The two coralskipper squadrons came laser-straight toward the Twin Suns pilots. As Twin Suns broke again into four shield trios, the coralskippers broke into four units of six, one each to a shield trio.

"Standard procedures," Jaina said, and angled toward one of the six coralskippers heading her way. She reached out for Kyp within the Force, found him and grabbed him as easily as catching a comrade's hand, then waited for him to select a target.

He did. They fired together, Jag firing an almost undetectable fraction of a second later. Kyp's lasers found the target coralskipper's void; Jaina's blasted through the bow, Jag's through the pilot canopy. Then they hurtled past, the remaining five coralskippers turning in pursuit.

As she banked around for another pass, Jaina spared a glance for her sensor board. It showed all the coralskippers still engaged with the starfighters; the six skips on the second shield trio, the one with Piggy in it, had already been reduced to five, and the other two groups were intact. No one was maneuvering against the pipefighter, which was still pouring laser energy in three directions—no, one direction, as the two greater pipes shut down, leaving just the smaller pipe to fire energy at the center of the pipefighters' long-distance formation.

A stream of plasma cannon projectiles poured past her X-wing, at a distance of fifty meters or so, close by starfighter battle standards but not close enough to worry her. These coralskipper pilots weren't the best the Yuuzhan Vong had to offer; she could tell by the difficulty they had in maintaining pursuit of her squadron's starfighters, by the fact that incoming fire was not drifting close enough to be terrifying. Even the comm chatter suggested the comparative lack of danger the squadrons were facing; the voices of Rogue Squadron and Blackmoon Squadron conveyed tension, but not as much as in more challenging exchanges.

Jaina led her shield trio around in a wide loop that kept them ahead of their pursuers but brought them to within firing range of the skips assaulting Twin Suns Seven through Nine. She gave Kyp a little confirming flicker through the Force; he chose another target and fired. This skip pilot managed to veer away and get his void up behind his narrower profile, intercepting the lasers of both Jaina and Kyp, but Jag's, at a slightly different angle and fired at a slight delay, sprayed around the void and tore out the skip's underbelly. The coralskipper veered away, barely under control, and began a long loop away from the combat zone.

"This is a trap." It was Piggy's voice, and Jaina saw that the message was being routed directly to her through her astromech; none of the other pilots would be hearing it. "I recommend we return to base."

Jaina frowned. The five skips pursuing her shield trio were now in a wedge formation, the boldest of them well out ahead of the others. "Explain that, Piggy."

She reached out to Kyp, feeling for a moment his hand on his X-wing's yoke. She handled both her controls and his, simultaneously, identically, and both X-wings decelerated and gained altitude relative to their pursuers. Jag, left out of their Force link, leapt ahead.

Jaina gave Kyp the cue. He targeted the lead skip and fired just as she did. Jag, in his more maneuverable clawcraft, inverted in a maneuver tight enough to send an X-wing out of control and fired at the lead skip's bow. The skip's dovin basal brought its void up to capture Jag's lasers, but Jaina's and Kyp's fire shredded it, sending glowing yorik coral chunks in all directions.

Jaina and Kyp kept up their fire, concentrating on the port side of the coralskipper formation. Jag drifted to his starboard, flashing by those same two targets as he fired, his shots intercepted by voids but keeping those spots of darkness from swallowing the X-wings' fire. In moments, those two skips, though not destroyed, were charred by laserfire and venting atmosphere. Jag looped around and came up behind Jaina and Kyp as they dropped into position behind the coralskipper formation.

Meanwhile, Piggy was talking. Talking and talking. "Listen to the comm chatter. We've been attacked by forces sophisticated enough to time simultaneous assaults on the other three squads, but they didn't jump us until the other three were fully engaged. This is a ploy designed to make sure we're pinned in place and happily hunting easy kills, while they set something up."

"Copy." Jaina trained bursts of laserfire on the skip ahead. Her Force connection with Kyp slipped as she focused on Piggy's words.

He was right. All evidence pointed to the new Yuuzhan Vong commander being canny and experienced. He'd never set up a sophisticated assault with second-rate pilots except as a distraction, a bluff, or a trap.

But they couldn't just flee whenever they faced a trap. The Yuuzhan Vong would come to recognize their skittishness, and then begin to exploit it.

"Piggy, we're going to weather this one out," she said. "I want you to broadcast that warning, the short form, in the clear on fleet frequencies. Try to sound panicked, would you?"

"Copy." A moment later, his voice sounded across the fleet frequency, at a higher volume and pitch: "Great One, this is Twin Suns Five. I feel a trap closing around us. We have to flee."

Jaina snorted to herself at his melodramatic words,

then responded appropriately. "Be calm, Piggy. Have faith. You feel their trap. They're about to feel mine."

Now, she told herself, *all we have to do is figure out what they're trying to do, keep them from doing it, and do something worse to them. Easy.*

Sure.

The beam from the lesser end of the pipefighter ceased. Its part in the operation was over for now. She switched to squad frequency. "Starlancer One, get out of there. Head back to base."

"Copy. Starlancer One on our way."

THIRTEEN

Borleias Occupation, Day 39

The streams of laser energy from Starlancers One, Two, and Three converged on Starlancer Prime, the pipefighter with the three extrusions arrayed in equal angles. Each stream entered one of the pipe openings.

Starlancer Prime's last extrusion, the one aimed at the Coruscant system, fired, channeling its constant, meter-thick beam of laser light toward the former home of the New Republic government several light-years away.

Jag had made a clean solo kill against one of the starboard skips. That left two damaged, one unhurt, of the six that had come against them. Jaina's sensor board showed that one of her pilots, Twin Suns Ten, was drifting powerless, but Eleven had reported that Ten was still alive.

Then there was something else on her long-range sensors, two large red blips arriving from the opposite directions at high speed, just now slowing as they reached the vicinity of the target zone. They were the right size for Yuuzhan Vong corvette analogs, and as Jaina watched, the blips fired off many more, smaller blips—signs of a coralskipper launch. "The second wave is here," she told her squad. "Rogues, Blackmoons, Wild Knights, watch out for reinforcements at your end."

She received three sets of acknowledgments but barely registered them as her wing trio scored quick kills on the undamaged coralskipper and one of the damaged ones. The last Yuuzhan Vong pilot from the original six turned away, toward one of the oncoming flood of coralskipper reinforcements.

Jaina let him go. Other survivors of the two first Yuuzhan Vong squadrons were also scattering back toward their reinforcements. None of them appeared to be pursuing the rapidly retreating Starlancer vehicle or the drifting Twin Suns Ten. Jaina called for her squad to muster in the few seconds available to them. "Rogues, have they sprung the same trap at your end?"

"Negative, Twins Leader."

"Wild Knights just have the original squads, though resistance is stiffening."

"Same with Blackmoon, Twins."

"These are interdictors, Leader." That was Piggy's voice. "They're not here for the Starlancers. They're here for *you*."

"Plot us a course out of here, Piggy. Away from the Starlancers' escape vector."

A bare second later, a projected course sprang up on Jaina's nav computer. It didn't lead through the area showing the most open space. Jaina wondered why Piggy had deliberately ignored that most logical option—and then realized that he'd probably done so because it *was* the most logical option, and one the Yuuzhan Vong had doubtless planned on her choosing. He had to have seen other things she'd missed for him to decide on this course.

Whatever his reasoning, she oriented along his escape vector and fired her thrusters at full acceleration. The rest of Twin Suns came up smoothly behind her. Ahead, Yuuzhan Vong coralskippers began to congregate on her escape route; behind, more skips turned in her wake, accelerating to catch up. Her sensor board suggested that the eleven Twin Suns pilots now faced five times as many skips.

A microjump away, a fraction of a light-year outside the Pyria system, Han and Leia listened to the holocomm traffic from their daughter's battle zone. "I'm going back," Han said.

Leia looked as ashen as Han felt. Slowly, she shook her head. "We can't help her."

"The hell we can't. I can get her escape vector, and we can drill a hole in from the other side before the Vong know we're coming—"

"Fine. What do you want me to tell our passengers, the children?"

Han gave an inarticulate growl. He sat with muscles locked, listening to find out what would become of his daughter.

"We screwed up," Wedge said. As usual during missions of any importance, he stood in the control chamber beside the hologram displaying the mission zone.

Tycho nodded, looking glum. He didn't elaborate on Wedge's words.

He didn't need to. The two of them had had the mission and the Yuuzhan Vong response plotted out in great detail. The Yuuzhan Vong would, at some point, make an attempt to grab the Starlancer vehicles. The pilots of the pipefighters would be theoretically able to detach their cockpits, which had their own rudimentary thrusters, and escape, destroying the pipe assemblies with primitive mechanical self-destruct systems that were unlikely to be affected by enemy countermeasures, leaving behind just enough clues to give the Yuuzhan Vong a hint of what was going on.

But that whole approach assumed that the Starlancers would be the Yuuzhan Vong target. Instead, it appeared that Jaina Solo was the target.

And since only Jaina's squadron had been attacked in this fashion, it meant that Yuuzhan Vong spotters on the ground or in Borleias orbit had identified her and correctly determined her course, suggesting that they were even more on the ball than Wedge and Tycho had guessed.

"How long before we can get anyone to her?" Wedge asked.

Tycho shrugged. "Two minutes to get the frigate *Lunar Tide* to the site. And that'll just get *Lunar Tide* destroyed. Five minutes for the task force now leaving Borleias's mass shadow."

Wedge weighed the numbers, not forgetting that among them were numbers of the living crew of the vessels involved. How many lives was Jaina Solo worth? More important, how much harm would it do to them, to their plans, to demonstrate the New Republic habit, considered a weakness by the Yuuzhan Vong, to risk and probably doom a greater number of people to save a smaller number?

"Tell *Lunar Tide* to get into position to jump . . . but not jump until we give the order. They'll wait for the task force unless we say otherwise."

Tycho nodded and turned to his comm board.

With the discipline of decades, Wedge was able to conceal the way his decision tied his insides up in knots, and he prayed that he wouldn't have to tell Han and Leia that he'd doomed their daughter.

* * *

"I can get the squad out of here," Jag said.

"Care to share the information?" Jaina asked.

"It'll take too long, Goddess. Care to trust me?"

Jaina weighed the question for part of a second and found that she did—if he said he knew how to get them out alive, then he did. "We're your wing," she said.

"You and Kyp, launch shadow bombs. Have them follow me at a distance of a few meters—as close as you can manage. You'll know when to drop them. Hang back, let me lead you by a few kilometers." Without waiting for further authorization or acknowledgment, Jag hit his thrusters and pulled out ahead of the Twin Suns formation.

Jaina felt slight confusion from Kyp, a sort of question mark. She offered up a mental shrug. She armed and launched one shadow bomb, then reached out to grab it with the Force and hurtle it along in Jag's wake. She dimly detected Kyp's similar efforts; his shadow bomb was well ahead of hers.

The foremost oncoming coralskippers were almost on Jag now, but he executed a starboard turn, as close to a right-angle turn as a TIE pilot could manage, and headed directly toward one of the Yuuzhan Vong interdictors, the one between their position and the safety of Borleias.

The oncoming coralskippers vectored to follow Jag. Jaina opened fire, spraying them with stuttering red laser bolts, and heeled over in Jag's wake; she saw laserfire from her fellow pilots flashing into the cloud of skips, saw one of the Yuuzhan Vong craft detonate.

This was hard going. She had to fly, fire, and keep track of her shadow bomb in the Force—and the latter task was one of the more difficult, because Jag was jinking and juking as only a TIE or A-wing fighter pilot could, dodging incoming plasma cannon fire from the interdictor so nimbly and acrobatically that the chief danger to him was that he'd twitch into the path of a plasma projectile rather than having one seek and find him. Keeping the shadow bomb tucked in right behind him was proving an almost impossible task. Her bomb strayed to either side of Jag's clawcraft with every sideslip he performed.

Then she felt Kyp reach to her through the Force. She could suddenly see his technique; she saw Jag's living presence in the Force, and there were the two unliving things that were his shadow bombs, and Kyp had connected them as if encasing all three in a bubble so that whenever Jag moved, he himself drew the bomb along with him. Kyp was supplying the energy, but Jag, unknowing, was directing it. Jaina tried to do the same, tried to draw a connection between her bomb and Jag . . . and though, in that instant, she knew she hadn't developed the degree of control Kyp had, she could tell that her shadow bomb was now shadowing Jag more effectively.

The coralskippers they'd been heading toward mere moments ago had now turned in their wake. Jaina put most of her discretionary X-wing energy into her rear shields and concentrated on flitting like a piranha-beetle, keeping the pursuing Yuuzhan Vong pilots from getting a good shot in at her. Her other pilots were doing the same.

Jag had increased his lead to several kilometers, and up ahead loomed the bulk of the Yuuzhan Vong interdictor. Its squadrons of coralskippers, which had dispersed to head off the Twin Suns' escape were congregating again, but they'd been caught off guard by the run against the interdictor. Of course they had. From a logical point of view, it was the dumbest thing the New Republic pilots could have done.

Jag aimed straight in at the capital ship's bow, the node

where its dovin basals were concentrated—the dovin basals that dragged the ship through space, that projected the voids that drank incoming damage, that projected gravitic fluctuations into hyperspace to drag ships in transit back into realspace—and to keep nearby craft from making the jump into hyperspace. And finally Jaina knew and understood Jag's plan.

His evasive maneuvers became tighter, faster, more random as he neared the interdictor and its full array of plasma cannons opened up on him. Jaina, through her tentative Force connection with Jag, could feel little spikes of alarm and adrenaline go through him, something she would never have guessed, given his calm demeanor in every situation.

"Coming up on drop point," Jag said, his tone as indifferent as if he'd just ordered a meal he didn't look forward to eating. "Three, two . . ." His clawcraft began spraying laserfire in a spiral pattern, the interdictor's voids greedily sucking it all in. Jaina could see the voids concentrating there before Jag's clawcraft, anticipating the spread of his attack.

Anticipating. He was so good at anticipating, predicting, that he could use the anticipation of his enemies as a weapon against them. Jaina shook her head.

". . . one, drop."

Jag's clawcraft vectored again, another angle only a TIE craft could manage, but he continued to direct his laserfire against the flank of the interdictor. Its voids tracked, staying ahead of his lasers.

Jaina yanked her shadow bomb away from Jag, kept it almost on his original course, pulling it to port. Kyp maneuvered his up and to starboard. A void sprang up before Kyp's.

But Jaina's hit, detonating in a brilliant flash mere meters from the dovin basal node. She felt another jolt of alarm from Jag, but he did not disappear from her perceptions.

She looped around the dying interdictor, spraying fire at a pair of coralskippers approaching from ahead to port, and her laser attacks were joined by those of her squadmates. The two skips were reduced to superheated yorik coral rubble in a matter of moments . . . and suddenly there was nothing between her squad and Borleias but open space. Coralskippers were angling in from the sides, but none could manage an intercept course capable of catching her X-wings. She breathed a sigh of relief.

Then her breath left her. Her unit consisted of only ten blips. Twin Suns Three wasn't back with them. She found Jag on the sensor board, back in the vicinity of the dying interdictor, at an angle that was carrying him back into the midst of the coralskippers.

"Twins Three, this is Leader. *What* are you doing?"

"Sorry, Leader." Jag's voice sounded pained. "I was grazed by a singularity effect. My shields are stripped and the yank put me off course. I'll have to catch up to you later."

That was just pilot bravado. Jag had nearly two squadrons of coralskippers converging on him from all directions. No available exit vector would let him use the clawfighter's superior speed to just speed past opposition; he'd have to fight his way out, and without shields, he didn't have a chance. His skills might let him last a few seconds, perhaps a minute. Then he would be dead.

Jaina wavered. Jag was one of her pilots. She couldn't leave him behind. Couldn't.

But Kyp was still in contact with her, still connected through the Force. She heard him across the comm unit: "No, Jaina. If you go back, you've just thrown away what he did for you. *You can't be captured.*"

"I know," she said. Her voice sounded weak to her. She watched as the closest of the coralskippers came within firing range of Jag. He resumed his evasive flying; the little blip representing him on the sensor board blurred as the sensors tried to keep up with his movements.

"Let's go," Kyp said. His voice was solemn, and she could feel that his regret was genuine.

"Yes," she said. "Twin Suns, set course for Borleias, jump when ready. Let the planet's mass drag you out of hyperspace." She saw Twin Suns Eleven jump almost immediately; Tilath must have had the course already plotted.

Over the next few moments, the others jumped, all but her and Kyp, while on the sensor screen Jag's blip became surrounded by an increasingly thick screen of red dots.

"I'm waiting for you," Jaina said. She could barely hear her own voice. There seemed to be a haze over her eyes, a cloud of white noise in her ears.

"I'm waiting for you," Kyp said.

"Together, then." Jaina took a deep breath, watching the ever-tightening web of coralskippers around Jag. They were channeling him, leaving the screen lighter in one direction, and he was inexorably moving toward the other interdictor. "On three. One, two, three, *jump*."

Neither X-wing jumped.

"Blast it, Kyp, go home." Jaina yanked on her yoke, sending her X-wing in the tightest turn she could manage back toward the combat. Back toward the stream of coralskippers pursuing her. And she found, in that moment, that the haze over her eyes and white noise in her ears disappeared.

"Jaina, *no*." Kyp stayed with her. "You can't do this. You can't save him. You can only kill yourself."

"Shut up." He wasn't dead. Jag was still flying, he still

had a trigger under his finger, he wouldn't die. She would get there. She would save him.

The first of her pursuers began firing. They weren't firing plasma cannons. Space around her was suddenly riddled with grutchins, the burrowing insects that could disable a craft. She twitched her yoke, allowing the Force to guide her evasive maneuvers, and switched discretionary power to her forward shields. So far, there were none of the distinctive *ping* noises of a grutchin hit.

"Jaina, this is Colonel Celchu. This transmission is scrambled and coming through your astromech. General Antilles is issuing a direct order. Do not reenter the combat zone. Return to base. Do you understand?"

Part of her did. Part of her knew that Wedge Antilles had concluded that Jag Fel was lost, and was not willing to exploit even the faint chance Jaina Solo offered to save his own nephew. That's how bad it looked.

"Don't tell me the odds," she said, her voice nearly a whisper. She flashed past the first squadron of pursuers. They looped wide to turn in her wake without getting in the way of the second squadron. Now grutchins were coming at her from two directions.

"I didn't *tell* you the odds." For once, Tycho sounded confused.

"Good."

Kyp hung doggedly at Jaina's side, firing as constantly as his lasers would recycle. Jaina wasn't firing. Her mind was somewhere else, not even acknowledging the coralskippers as threats, only her reflexes keeping the grutchins off her. Kyp nailed one oncoming coralskipper, his lasers hitting the dovin basal and then shearing through into the skip's main body. He checked his sensor board. Only forty-nine skips and one interdictor to go.

Then it was forty-eight. The number on the board

dropped and one little light near Jag's blip winked out. But Jag was now awfully close to that interdictor.

Then the answer came to Kyp. "Jaina, I can save him, but I need your help."

He felt a flicker from her. "How?" she asked.

"Aim straight in for the other interdictor's bow. Go ahead and punch through the cloud around Jag to give him some relief. And protect me. I'm going to be too busy to shoot."

"Kyp, the shadow bomb thing can't work again. They'll be looking for it."

"That's not what I'm going to do. Do you trust me?"

"Do it."

They traded places then, Jaina suddenly opening up with her weapons, Kyp handing the task of flying evasively over to his reflexes while his mind went elsewhere.

Luke Skywalker had done this once, a couple of years ago. He'd mentioned it to the other Jedi. No one else had tried it because it had exhausted Luke to the point of collapse, and Jedi were seldom in a position to survive a technique that tired them so completely.

They were past the second wave of coralskippers now and heading toward the cloud surrounding Jag. Beyond it, not far now, was the second interdictor. Kyp knew that other skips had to be converging on him and Jaina. He didn't bother to look at his sensor board. They weren't relevant now.

And he didn't think he'd be as terribly drained as Luke by the technique. He was stronger in the Force than Luke Skywalker.

He'd known that almost since they'd met—that he had more pure power than the legendary Jedi Master. But this was, perhaps, the first time he'd been able to say it to himself without a little thrill of pride. He was just stronger, and that was all. It usually didn't matter. Now it did.

They reached the edge of the coralskipper cloud around Jag. Jaina and Kyp flashed by the skips that had turned against them, dodging their incoming fire, Jaina spraying return fire. Suddenly they were in the middle, with Jag's clawcraft turning in their wake, and the interdictor was before them.

Absently, barely aiming, Kyp squeezed the trigger of his lasers. His red beams flashed out against the interdictor, and a void moved in position to intercept the beams.

Within the Force, within the broader range of senses it gave him, he tried to feel the presence of that void. He couldn't feel the Yuuzhan Vong or their creatures, but he could feel distortions in space, hard little nuggets of wrongness where there should be nothing.

He felt many of them, but didn't know which belonged to the interdictor, which to the coralskippers, and this rarefied sensory data didn't precisely translate to exact directions and distances. A void that felt far away could be from a coralskipper close at hand.

He armed a proton torpedo and fired it. He felt its physical presence as, in a matter of seconds, it closed the distance between him and the interdictor . . . and was swallowed by another void.

He felt it enter the void, felt which of the many singularities it was.

And he seized upon that void, directing all his Force abilities and discipline against it.

It was like using a thin metal rod to push a grounded landspeeder. Too much pressure and it would bend, becoming useless. Too little and nothing would happen. He had to find the right pressure to budge it, to set it into motion and keep it going that way . . .

For a moment, the only things in the universe were him, Jaina, and the void. He moved the void, turned it around, moved it back the other direction.

Then he was himself again, in the cockpit, watching the flank of the interdictor distort. The void had moved back and touched the interdictor, and now the interdictor elongated into it, extending what looked like a pliant extrusion of what he knew to be hardened yorik coral into the singularity.

The portions of the interdictor in closest proximity to the void accelerated faster into its maw so that portions farther back tore, venting gases into space. But the incredible gravity of the singularity didn't allow the remainder of the ship to tear away and be free. It dragged greater and greater portions of the interdictor into it, compressing them, rending them, and in a moment the interdictor was gone.

Kyp felt obliterated, bone-tired, as though he'd run for days, drawing on the Force to sustain him, and had finally settled down for rest. His diagnostics board was beeping at him and he spared it a glance. "I've taken damage," he said. "A grutchin, I think."

In fact, a portion of his cockpit, to starboard, was starting to blacken, with acrid smoke pouring off it. Idly, he pulled his lightsaber from his belt and oriented its head toward the blackened area.

A moment later, the metal parted and insectile eyes shoved their way into the cockpit. Kyp thumbed his lightsaber on and the energy blade plunged through the creature. Kyp turned it off again. Its noise was muted by the fact that almost all the atmosphere in the cockpit had disappeared through the hole in those few moments; Kyp's flight suit activated, its energy shield technology holding atmosphere in around him, keeping pressure on his skin. "Grutchin problem solved," he said.

"Sorry about that," Jaina said. Her voice was muted.

Kyp glanced at his sensor board. He, Jaina, and Jag were outbound from the engagement zone. Maybe twenty coralskippers were in pursuit.

But there were now other friendlies on the board, a cloud tagged Rogue Squadron, a capital-ship-sized blip tagged *Lunar Tide*, approaching from the approximate direction of galactic spin. "Let's go that direction," Kyp suggested.

"We'll do that, Kyp," Jaina said. "Thank you."

"Think nothing of it."

Han sat, limp and gray, in his seat and forced himself to take deeper breaths.

Leia didn't look any better than he felt. "We raised her that way, Han, whether we intended to or not."

"I know."

"So we can't exactly criticize her."

"Since when does logic interfere with my right to complain to her? Especially when she does something that stupid?"

"Han."

"I'm twenty years older than I was this morning. Twenty years, Leia."

"You're starting to sound like Threepio."

He scowled at her. "Am I really?"

"Just fly. The faster we get to the Maw, the faster we can return."

FOURTEEN

Yuuzhan Vong Worldship, Coruscant Orbit

The laser beam, a meter thick, flashed from the depths of space to strike Tsavong Lah's worldship.

It hit with the force of a turbolaser battery, pouring damage onto the worldship surface, superheating the yorik coral there, scarring deeply into it.

Less than a second later, a void materialized beneath it, intercepting it, swallowing all the damage. The void remained there as the damage continued to rain down. Then, a minute later, the laser attack ceased, and the void disappeared.

In the worldship control chamber, Tsavong Lah took the news of the attack with puzzlement in his manner. "Extent of damage?" he asked.

"Minimal," Maal Lah said. "The damage is already regenerating. Within a day, there will be nothing but a battle scar."

"And you have not found the vehicle or emplacement that fired it."

"No, Warmaster. Though it appears that it was fired from beyond the orbit of this system's outermost planet, and took considerable time to reach our worldship."

"Demonstrating merely that they have enough spotters on the planet below, and that those spotters have enough communications gear, that they can keep track of this worldship's position while it remains in orbit."

Tsavong Lah shrugged. "Why would they demonstrate this knowledge in a way that gains them no advantage?"

"I do not know, Warmaster."

Tsavong Lah considered, barely distracted by the twinging sensations brought on by the parasites burrowing their way through the flesh of his arm.

A thought occurred to him, a discouraging one. "Trace the course of that laser attack."

"We have already done so, Warmaster."

"Trace it beyond the Coruscant system. What other planetary systems are directly along that line?"

Maal Lah gestured to one of his analysts, and within moments the analyst brought them the answer. "Pyria," Maal Lah said.

"Open the villip to my father. And bring Viqi Shesh to me."

Borleias Occupation, Day 39

Though the doors to the special ops docking bay were open, and the X-wings of Rogue Squadron were maneuvering through them to land, Jaina, Kyp, and Jag were directed to land in the kill zone, only a few dozen meters from the front entranceway, in an area where no other vehicles were situated. One officer stood there alone, and as they came in for a landing, Jaina recognized him: Colonel Celchu.

Her heart couldn't sink much. It was already somewhere around her ankles. But she felt it descend the final few centimeters to her toes.

As the pilots emerged from their starfighters, Tycho looked between them. "Anyone hurt?" he asked.

They all shook their heads. Kyp, though undamaged, leaned heavily against the wing of his snubfighter, and Tycho gave him a second look. "You, go lie down," he said.

"Happy to." Kyp glanced at Jaina. "By your leave, Great One."

"Get some rest, Kyp."

Tycho turned to Jaina. "General Antilles wants to see you, now."

"I expect so."

"And me?" Jag asked.

"Later," Tycho said. "Though he did want me to extend his congratulations on that shadow bomb tactic. Since kills can't be awarded to more than two people, he thinks that first interdictor should be awarded to you."

"I agree," Jaina said. "I'll sign off on that."

"Me, too," Kyp said.

They walked into the biotics building. Kyp managed not to stagger as he left them for his quarters.

At Wedge's office, Tycho left Jaina and Jag to enter the inner office, then stuck his head out a moment later to say, "It'll be about five minutes."

"Understood," Jaina said.

When Tycho had withdrawn again into the inner office, leaving them with Wedge's protocol droid, Jag said, "I need to talk to you. Privately."

Jaina couldn't tell, from his quiet, controlled manner, what he intended to convey to her, but she had a good idea. "There's a little conference room down the corridor."

"That'll do."

She knew what he was going to say. His face would turn pale with his anger, highlighting the scar on his forehead, and he would cut her with his words. *You abandoned your mission objectives for one pilot,* he'd say. *You almost wiped out the rest of your squadron. You al-*

most wrecked the plan. No one's life is worth that. Not mine. Not yours. You're a complete failure as a leader, as an officer.

He'd say that, and she wouldn't have any words with which to defend herself, because he'd be right.

He'd stare at her with an expression made up of analytical calculation and hard experience. He'd tell her what he thought of her. Then he'd turn and walk away. He'd find himself a unit to command, a unit that could be counted on to perform up to his professional standards.

A sharp pain sprang up in her gut, as though she'd inadvertently swallowed a vibroblade and her movements had finally switched it on. But she held herself straight. She had to be able to look him in the eye when he started in on the verbal beating she knew she deserved.

They reached the conference room, its door open, its interior cool and dark; Jag turned on the overhead lights, closed the door behind Jaina.

She faced him, hoping that what she was feeling wasn't reflected in her expression. "I know what you're going to say," she told him.

"I don't think you do." Oddly, his face was not the stern mask she'd expected. If anything, he looked uncertain, unlike the Jag Fel she was used to.

"You're going to tell me that I screwed up. You're going to elaborate until you're certain I can't take it anymore. Then you're going to leave." Her throat, constricting, caused her to lose control of the last few words; they sounded high and hoarse to her.

"No. We both know that your command decisions were far afield of common sense and effective strategy. We don't even have to discuss that. What I have to know . . ." He hesitated, and if anything looked even less sure of himself than before, "What I *have* to know is this: Why did you do it?"

"I don't know."

"You do know. You have to know. Nobody else but you *could* know." He leaned in closer. It wasn't a posture of intimidation; he stared into her eyes as if he hoped to find an answer, any answer, written in tiny letters on her pupils. "Answer me."

"I . . . I . . ." Her voice hoarsened until she was sure she could no longer use it, but finally words emerged, words that seemed to be coming from a child. "Everyone is going away." Tears blurred her vision. "They keep going away and I can't stop it. I didn't want you to go away."

Then the tears did come, and Jag was transformed into a wavery block of black uniform with a wavery block of pale skin atop it. She could no longer read his expression but knew it had to be one of puzzlement or distaste or outright contempt—

Then he took her by the shoulders and pulled her to him, drawing her head against his chest, resting his own head atop hers, an embrace that startled her so much that she should have jumped away. But she didn't. She leaned against him, a half collapse, her legs no longer willing or able to bear all her weight, and though she did not sob, her tears ran down her face and soaked into his uniform.

"I won't go anywhere," he said.

"Why?"

"Why what?"

"Why won't you go anywhere?"

"Because I don't want to." He tilted his head down and hers up, and suddenly she was kissing him, holding him tight enough to cause a vacuum weld.

Her confusion didn't disappear, but it was joined by a

soaring sensation, as though she'd just taken off and left her X-wing behind. There was also an abrupt relief of pressure, unbearable pressure that she had never felt descending upon her, had never noticed until it was gone.

Gavin Darklighter departed Wedge's office. Wedge and Tycho looked up as Jag entered and saluted.

"I've known Jaina Solo since she was tiny," Wedge said. "You're not her."

Jag kept his attention fixed on the wall over Wedge's head. "I came in her place, sir."

"She asked you to do that?"

"No, sir. I told her to go get some rest. That I'd speak to you and get things sorted out."

"Sorted out." Wedge exchanged a glance with Tycho, but his second-in-command had retreated behind the safety of his sabacc face. "Do I need sorting out, Fel?"

"I believe so, sir, through no fault of your own. If I may answer a question with a question, how old were you before you first disagreed with a commanding officer—and later found out you were right?"

"Twenty. Which is when I first had a commanding officer."

"I'm about the same age, sir, and I have something to recommend before you talk to Jaina Solo."

"Very well. At ease. Sit down. Let's hear what you have to say."

Jag did as he was told and finally met his uncle's eyes. "Sir, I think that disciplining her now would be like hitting a bar of metal when it's superheated."

"Meaning that you'll change its shape."

"Yes, sir. And not for the better."

"What about her reliability in combat? I need to take her off the line. She's not rational."

"That would be disciplining her, sir, probably with the results I predict. I recommend against it."

"Despite the fact that she deliberately disobeyed orders and risked a high-priority mission to pursue a personal agenda."

"Yes, sir." Jag cleared his throat. "Sir, I'd fly again with her tomorrow, and not out of gratitude. I think that what happened today was an anomaly. I don't think it will happen again."

"Care to tell me why?"

"No, sir."

Wedge let a silence fall between them, let it stretch into long seconds. "You know, I would not, from a command point of view, be able to accommodate you on this, despite the fact that I do have appreciation for your views and experience. It's the sort of thing that undermines discipline. But we already have orders in place that demonstrate that Jaina receives special treatment. This is a more extreme variety of special treatment than I'd prefer to accord her, but there you are."

"Yes, sir."

"All right, then. I'll do as you recommend. And get my answers later." Wedge leaned forward, his posture becoming more casual. "Let me take my rank insignia off for a second, Jag, and say how glad I am that you made it today."

Jag managed a smile. "Thank you, sir—uh, Wedge."

"Still difficult to address me informally, isn't it?"

"Yes. Yes, it is."

"Good. That gives me one more way to make a know-it-all nephew uncomfortable." Wedge heaved a sigh. "Back to work for me, so I'll let you get back to your duties, as well."

"Sir." All business again, Jag stood, saluted, and left.

When the door closed behind him, Tycho said, "That was interesting."

"He deliberately countermanded one of my orders," Wedge said.

"He was furtive."

Wedge nodded. "Sneaky, even."

"We'll make a Rebellion-style pilot of him yet."

The Maw

Han navigated through the danger zone of the Maw with the grace, intuition, and delicate skill he could demonstrate whenever the need arose—but which he preferred to demonstrate only when no one was watching, as careful, meticulous flying of this sort ran counter to his image as a cocky and careless flyboy. Behind the *Millennium Falcon*, in single file, followed two X-wings and a freighter, each meticulously duplicating his course changes.

The Maw, from far away, was visible only as a big splotch of color with dark singularities sucking in colorful gasses. It was a convergence of black holes, their random placement almost completely enclosing within it an area of space. The extreme gravitational and light distortion caused by the overlapping fields of effect made it impossible for light within that space to escape and made it fatal for any ship to try to enter or depart along a straight path. The routes to the interior space were complicated and devious, skirting areas made impossibly dangerous by the black holes' gravitational exertion. Only a very good pilot could navigate one of the known approaches. Only an extraordinary pilot could find a new one.

Today Han was playing it safe, traveling along one of the known approaches. Knowledge of those routes was confined to a very few people. Leia knew Han could probably feel his way through a new approach, but now, with a ship full of children and teens aboard, with Yuuzhan Vong conducting activity at the nearby Kessel system, was not the time to explore.

Eventually Han made the final course correction and vectored toward Shelter, the space station growing at the center of the sheltered space of the Maw. He breathed out several minutes' worth of tension and said, "There it is. Uglier than ever."

Shelter was an ad-hoc collection of parts assembled by Lando Calrissian and a collection of advisers and patrons he trusted. Cobbled together into its structure were remains of the original Maw Installation, a collection of hollow planetoids that had housed the workers and technicians who had fabricated Imperial superweapons, plus components of old space stations, modules stripped from cargo vessels, and extrusions whose origins Leia couldn't identify.

In minutes, they were docked at their designated berthing area, a domelike attachment—whose base was about four times the diameter of the *Millennium Falcon*, and whose surfaces, a matte silver decorated with patches of rust, hinted at similar antiquity—which had not been in place the last time they'd visited, several weeks before. Waiting for them as they descended the ramp was a tall woman whose elegance and expensive dark clothes spoke of aristocracy . . . and distant times and places where aristocrats might enjoy the benefits of their station.

Leia hurried ahead of the descending line of Jedi kids and embraced her. "Tendra! I didn't know you were here."

Lando's wife gave her a return smile. "You almost missed me. I brought some matériel and I've spent the last few days making sure it was up and running."

"What matériel?" Han asked.

Tendra waved her hand, her gesture taking in the entire docking bay and, by extension, the rest of the dome. "This. It's a deep-space habitat module used by worldshapers. It has its own gravity generator, even a crude old hyperdrive. It's been in storage on a Corporate Sector scrap heap for generations. I was able to pick it up for, well, less than it's worth."

"And now it's the core of the Jedi portion of Shelter?" Leia asked.

"Yes. I've made sure some of the areas originally intended for worldshaping materials have been restructured for training halls. It's pretty short on supplies—"

"We brought supplies," Han said. "In the other freighter, as well as the *Falcon*. Food, fabrication machinery, energy cells and fuel, recordings . . ." His gaze fell on the Jedi children spreading out through the docking bay, looking at the cargo loaders and Tendra's ship, the *Gentleman Caller*. "And brats."

"Hey." Valin Horn, Corran's son, stopped a couple of meters away and gave him a scowl. "I'm not a brat."

"No, your dad's the brat in the Horn family."

Valin smirked. "I'm going to tell him you said that."

"You do that. Scoot, kid. Go beat up a rancor or something." Han returned his attention to Tendra. "If you're about to leave, you can wait just long enough for us to give the *Falcon* a check-over and then we'll escort you out."

"You're not staying?"

"Too much to do at Borleias. Keeping your husband out of trouble, watching our daughter get *in* trouble . . ." He exchanged a long-suffering look with Leia. "So we're going right back."

"I'll be ready in half an hour." Tendra gave him another smile and headed back to her ship, her heels ringing on the metal floor of the docking bay.

Leia sighed after her. "What I would have given to be that tall."

"I've got a thousand credits that say she's always wished she was petite. And another thousand that if you two got together to talk about how much you envied each other's height, the conversation would devolve into what pains your husbands are."

"No bet. Our husbands *are* pains."

"Well, they were Imperial credits anyway. Ready to help me go over the *Falcon*?"

"No, first I need to say good-bye to . . ." Leia looked around the docking bay, identifying each of the people moving about. "Where *is* Tarc, anyway?"

"I've got a thousand credits that say he's hiding on board the *Falcon*."

"*Stop* that."

Han gave her a smile he knew to be insufferable and thumbed his comlink. "Goldenrod, where is Tarc now?"

C-3PO's voice, sounding distinctly aggrieved, came back a moment later: "He's in the upper quadlaser cupola, huddling in the seat so he can't be seen. And sir, I do have a name."

Moments later, they stood at the bottom of the access into the turbolaser shaft. "Tarc?" Leia said. "You want to come down?"

"No," the boy said. He didn't even lean over so his face could be seen.

"It's time, Tarc." Leia made her voice gentle. "If you get in line early you may get better quarters."

"And then I'll be stuck with *them*. The Jedi."

"There's nothing wrong with Jedi. I'm a Jedi."

"Yeah, but you're different. You're not creepy. I want to go back to Borleias with you."

Han said, "It's safer here, Tarc."

The boy finally did look over the arm of his chair. He

stared down at Han with an expression that combined pity with condescension, a forceful *you have no idea what you're talking about* look. "No, it's not," he said. "The scarheads are looking for Jedi. If they come here and find the Jedi, they'll get me, too."

"Don't say 'scarheads,' " Leia said. "It's not nice."

"Besides," Tarc added, pulling back out of sight, "if they don't come, and people come for these Jedi kids, no one will come for me."

"Of course we will," Han said.

"No, you won't. The only reason I'm still alive is 'cause I look like Anakin Solo. And it hurts your feelings every time you see me. I can tell."

Han looked at Leia. She paled and started to fold over. Han moved to put his arms around her, and slowly she straightened.

Han whispered, "Did you teach him to argue?"

"Nobody had to teach him to argue," she whispered back. "All kids argue like senior politicians. Except that not all senior politicians can cry on cue."

"So what do we do?"

She shrugged. "Maybe we *shouldn't* leave him here. In a place where all the other children have powers he can't compete with. Except for Wedge's kids, who'll probably just subvert the administrators here to get whatever they want."

"What do we do instead? Take him back to Borleias, put him in front of the Vong? Ship him off to a refugee camp run by strangers? At least we *know* Kam and Tionne."

"I just don't know, Han."

"But you know *everything*."

"Only by comparison with my husband."

"Ouch." Han stopped whispering. "Hey, kid."

"What?" Tarc looked back over the arm at him.

"Never get married."

"What does that mean?"

"It means strap yourself in. You're going back to Borleias for now."

The boy's eyes widened. "Really?"

"Just for the time being, kid." Han let real anger creep into his tone. "And don't pull that *because I look like Anakin* skifter. Not ever again. Do you understand?"

Tarc's expression froze. "Yes, sir."

"Remember this face, kid. It's telling you that I mean what I say." Han drew Leia along with him toward the cockpit. "I'll figure out how to convince him next time."

"I've got a thousand credits that say you don't."

FIFTEEN

Borleais Occupation, Day 47

It was the dead of night, but the former biotics facility was never truly asleep. Tam could hear movement down side corridors, distant conversations, a rumble in the walls that signified the takeoff of a patrol of starfighters outside.

But this corridor was comparatively still. Guarded day and night against entry by unauthorized personnel, it was empty of traffic at this hour.

Tam paused outside the door to Danni Quee's laboratories and felt himself rocking in place, moved by the racing of his heart.

But pausing was failure to comply, and the faintest throbs of a new headache joined the rhythm of his heart.

He cursed and moved to the wall opposite the doorway. Reaching up, he brushed his fingers along the wall's surface, near the ceiling, until he found it—a slick patch as though someone had sprayed oil there.

It wasn't oil. It was a thing of the Yuuzhan Vong, another living apparatus that they had given him. It had a texture much like the villip—smooth, slick. He rubbed it until he found the crease that was its activation point, and he stroked that more deliberately. Then he wiped his hand on his shirt.

That spot on the wall changed color. Though he knew it remained flat as a sheet of fine flimsiplast, it seemed to him as though it gained depth, transforming into a duplicate of the security keypad and blue readout beside Danni's door.

As though it were a holorecording, a hand came into view and punched numbers into the keypad. It was a woman's hand, young, unlined, probably Danni's. Tam watched the keys as they were depressed, memorizing the sequence, and glanced at the readout that showed the values of the keys.

They weren't the same. He repeated the letters and numbers he'd seen pressed, and they differed from the ones on the readout in two places.

That meant—what? Either he'd misread the keys as they were being punched, or the readout played back an incorrect sequence.

He nodded, satisfied. It was a security measure. A recording of the readout would yield a password that either wouldn't work or would alert a security office of an intrusion in progress. Only Tam's visual memory, very strong and accurate, one of the reasons he'd become a holocam operator in the first place, had saved him from being trapped by this subterfuge.

He wished he'd been trapped. He wished he'd failed.

The headache began to increase in intensity.

He touched the Yuuzhan Vong recording apparatus and watched it fade away to transparency. Then he keyed the password—the correct password—into the keypad. The door slid aside.

Tam froze. Inside the room, two meters from him, Danni Quee sat at her usual desk. But she was motionless, her head down, colors from the monitor before her playing across her hair.

Danni didn't move, other than from the rhythm of her breathing, and Tam forced himself to enter the office.

It was dim, lit only by monitors and desk lights, and no one other than Danni was present. Tam moved around her station to stand beside her, taking great care not to brush against anything; if he moved slowly enough, he could compensate for his awkwardness. Awkwardness that had caused him to trip when he was being pursued on Coruscant. Awkwardness that had led to his capture. His enslavement.

Danni's monitor showed something, an object with facets like a gem. There was a lot of writing on the screen, technical terminology he couldn't grasp, phrases like *reflectivity index* and *refraction* and *power augmentation*.

He squinted at it. His eyes were fine, but he had to squint to alert the little creature now sharing his ocular orbit with his eye that now was the time for it to wake up and begin recording. He felt the thing twitch; then his stomach twitched as nausea rose within him.

Tam moved through the laboratory, looking at each of the other screens in turn, looking at handwritten notes and datapad screens. At the station beside Danni's lay a couple of data cards; slowly, silently, he brought out his own datapad, inserted the cards in it, copied off their contents, and returned them to their original positions.

There was nothing more to do here.

He felt his headache rise in strength. No, there *was* something more he could do here. His orders were to acquire information . . . and to aid the Yuuzhan Vong in general in any way he could that did not lead to his capture and exposure.

Danni Quee was here. Tam could overpower her while she slept. She was an enemy of the Yuuzhan Vong, and eliminating her as a New Republic resource would definitely help his masters.

There was no way he could smuggle her out of the biotics building, no way he could even smuggle her out of this hallway. No, to eliminate her as a threat, he'd have to kill her.

He could do it, too, in such a way that there would be no likelihood of blame falling on him. In one of his pockets was a gob of material restraining a razor bug. He could pull it out, free the creature, fling it at Danni. It would chew her to pieces.

And he'd go back to the shuttle and receive praise.

He stood in place and his headache mounted. He cursed himself. Just by thinking of a way to help the Yuuzhan Vong, he'd obligated himself to do it, or suffer the consequences. Danni Quee had to die now.

He stood behind her. He didn't bother wondering what might have been, had they met in different circumstances. He was a big, clumsy, inarticulate thing and she was an intelligent, beautiful woman with the stamp of destiny on her. Had they been stranded together on an otherwise deserted planet, nothing would have happened between them. They would have ended up friends. Just good friends.

Tam reached out a hand to brush it, ever so carefully, against one of her blond curls, now colored scarlet by light from the screen before her. Then he reached into his pocket and found the razor bug.

He stood and did nothing. The pain increased until it affected his breathing, making it short and halting.

The problem was, no matter how much he wanted the pain to end, he knew it would keep coming. He knew that Danni Quee deserved to live. He knew that he deserved to die.

He turned away. Pain shot through him as though a metal spike had been hammered through both his temples with a single blow. He staggered and had to put a hand on the floor to keep from falling over.

But the pain didn't kill him. He strained against it, rose, made it as far as the door. He had to lean for long moments against the doorjamb to give himself strength enough to continue. Then he could open the door and leave.

As he walked, his steps made unrhythmic by the hammering within his skull, he reminded himself that he was taking data to his controller. He was succeeding in his primary mission. And the pain diminished.

But only a little.

As soon as the door slid shut behind Tam, Danni raised her head to stare after him.

She typed a command into her keyboard. The screen before her changed views to follow Tam as he staggered away down the corridor.

When he was well out of earshot, she keyed her comlink. "He's gone," she whispered. "He was either memorizing or recording everything on our screens."

Iella's voice came back, not a whisper, but the comlink's volume was dialed down low. "Did he leave anything?"

"I don't know. I'll begin analyzing the recordings now. Out."

"Good work. Out."

Danni brought up the first of the recordings made by the holocams positioned at hidden points around the room. She felt her shoulders twitch. She wasn't sure what Tam had been up to in the long minutes he stood directly behind her, and was desperate to be sure that he hadn't spread Yuuzhan Vong creatures throughout this office.

Yuuzhan Vong Worldship, Coruscant Orbit

In the operations chamber, surrounded by analysts and advisers, blaze bug displays and recording creatures, banks of villips and standing rows of guards, Tsavong Lah sat at the center of things and listened to reports.

Most of them came from Maal Lah and Viqi Shesh. As they spoke, Tsavong Lah reflected that some things never changed. Normally, it would be Nom Anor and Vergere standing before him, interpreting, offering advice, sniping at one another, one of them a Yuuzhan Vong warrior and the other a clever female of a lesser species. Now, with Nom Anor and Vergere performing other tasks, their roles were still being acted out by others.

"It is a *superweapon*," Maal Lah said, using the Basic word rather than the Yuuzhan Vong equivalent. "They have a history of creating devices that can travel faster than light and smash entire worlds, and this is a new one."

"It's Danni Quee's doing," Viqi said. "It has to be. She's the only one who could integrate Yuuzhan Vong and New Republic technology this way. I'm going to make that idiot Tam suffer for not killing her when he had the chance."

Tsavong Lah raised a finger. Viqi bit back on further ranting words. "I just heard heresy," Tsavong Lah said. "First, the works of the Yuuzhan Vong are not technology. They must never be referred to as such."

Apparently stricken, though Tsavong Lah suspected it was merely acting, Viqi bowed her head. "I am sorry, Warmaster. I don't know a word to encompass both disciplines."

"Perhaps, during your punishment, you will find one. Second, our works could not be melded with infidel technology. The gods would never allow it."

Viqi and Maal Lah exchanged glances, and it was Maal Lah who dared to correct the warmaster. "This turns out not to be correct. It has already been done. We know that, some time ago, Anakin Solo reconstructed his lightsaber with a lambent crystal . . . and it appears that he passed knowledge of this technique to others before he was killed. It is also with a lambent crystal that this new device is concerned."

"Go on."

Maal Lah gestured to Viqi. She turned to activate the recording creatures on the table behind her. Each, in turn, began to shine, the light above it showing one of the images Tam Elgrin had recorded.

Maal Lah pointed to the image that had been on Danni's screen. "That is a lambent crystal. Rather, it is a diagram of one. According to the information Viqi's agent seized, it is being artificially grown in a laboratory in the depths of their garrison building. According to other information we read in these images, they tried to grow the crystals on their ships, but they grow only in true gravity, or dovin basal gravity—their infidel technology gravity ruins them."

Tsavong Lah offered Maal Lah an expression of revulsion. "So their *Jeedai* will have more lightsabers? We will not allow it."

"It is worse than that, Warmaster. The diagram you see represents a lambent crystal as tall as one of our warriors."

"As tall as . . . what sort of obscenity could they produce with such a . . ." And then Tsavong Lah knew what they were producing. He found himself standing, shaking in anger, and did not remember rising. "Bring me my father's villip," he said.

In moments, he stared into the villip's blurry but recognizable simulation of his father's features. With impatience, Tsavong Lah rushed through the customary greetings. Then he got to the subject of his communication: "I now know what their Starlancer project is. It is another accursed superweapon. The coherent light these vehicles project to one another will at some point be focused through a giant lambent crystal being fabricated in the depths of their building. When this happens, the beam will be of sufficient power to destroy a worldship. The attack we suffered not long ago was a test-firing, perhaps to attune the weapon's beam to the target."

"Interesting," his father said.

"We cannot allow them to perfect this device," the warmaster continued. "So I now direct you to commit yourself to an all-out assault on that facility and destroy it. Immediately."

Czulkang Lah was silent for long moments. The villip representing his face froze into such immobility that Tsavong Lah wondered if it had suffered some sort of failure. Then his father spoke again. "To do so would be a strategic mistake," Czulkang Lah said. "We have not yet gauged our enemy's tactics or resources. His repertoire of surprises is not fully known. At best, our losses will probably be inappropriately high. At worst, with such a premature attack, we could sacrifice large numbers of warriors needlessly . . . and still lose. It is too early, my son."

"My orders stand," Tsavong Lah said.

His father's features assumed an expression that all but said, *I expected better of you.* It was an expression Czulkang Lah wore whenever a student had failed him for the last time. It had never before been directed at Tsavong Lah, and the warmaster took an involuntary step back.

But Czulkang Lah said nothing aloud, no words that would shame his son. Instead, he said, "It will be done."

"May the gods smile upon your actions," Tsavong Lah said. He gestured at one of his officers, who stroked the villip. It inverted.

The warmaster stood, his breathing heavy. His father's final disapproval, so implacable, was like a physical blow to him.

When he was under control again, he turned to Maal Lah. "Issue this directive. When Borleias falls to us, it will no longer be the home of the Kraal. Instead, it will be given to the priests of Yun-Yammka, a haven for their order, in thanks to the god for the gains he has brought us."

Maal Lah nodded. He, too, said, "It will be done."

That, the warmaster thought, *should send the priests of Yun-Yuuzhan into a fit, and if there truly are conspirators within their orders and the shapers are against me, I will soon know it.* He glanced down at his left arm. *I will soon feel it.*

Borleias Occupation, Day 48

"It has all the characteristics of a major push," Tycho said.

He, Wedge, and Iella stood before the control chamber's hologram display. It showed the compiled readouts from all the garrison's ground-based sensors, including the gravitic sensors Luke's Jedi had planted in the jungle beyond the kill zone, and incorporated live feeds from starfighters out on patrol.

At the center of the display was the large friendly signal marked "Base." Out at a distance of a few hundred kilometers, in every direction of the compass, were masses of red blips; Iella counted sixteen separate groups. "What are they doing?" she asked.

"One or two groups are landing personnel, vehicles, everything an invasion force needs," Wedge said. "The others are distractions. We're supposed to divide up our attention among them in a desperate attempt to figure out where their landing zone is, and we're supposed to become nervous because we're not succeeding."

" 'Supposed to,' " Iella said. "Meaning that you're not? Not doing either one?"

Wedge shook his head. "Oh, we're sending out scouts to all these sites, but they're under orders to show up, stay alert, and then make a run for it if anything comes after them. We don't want to lose pilots acquiring information we essentially don't need."

"So you don't care where their landing zone is?"

"It doesn't matter."

"Why?"

"Because, sometime in the next day or two, they're going to attack us *here*—and that's exactly what we want them to do."

"And when they do," Iella said, "who are you going to face them with? The New Republic or the Rebel Alliance?"

Wedge and Tycho exchanged a look, and both grinned.

"Neither," Wedge said. "We're going to face them with an enemy they've never had the displeasure of fighting. We're going to hit them with the Empire."

"They're not going to like the Empire," Tycho said.

And they told her about Operation Emperor's Hammer.

Borleias Occupation, Day 48

This time, when the *Millennium Falcon* arrived on Borleias, it did so in the middle of the night, to no fanfare, no welcoming committee other than a handful of refuelers. Leia saw Han breathe a sigh of thanks, celebrating the absence of ceremony.

Han took Tarc to find him some quarters—the rooms that had been assigned to the underaged Jedi students, where Tarc had previously been staying, would have been reassigned by now, and Han, though he liked the boy, didn't want him in their own quarters. Leia went in search of her daughter.

Jaina's X-wing was in the special operations docking bay, a mechanics crew working on it, but Leia could not find her daughter in her quarters or in the former incubation chamber that now served the special operations squadrons—Rogue, Wild Knights, Twin Suns, and Blackmoon—as an informal lounge.

Leia couldn't call Jaina on her comlink, couldn't give her the impression that she was keeping tabs, even though that's what she desperately wanted to do. Eventually, having had no luck in her search, she returned to her own quarters.

And it was there she found Jaina—stretched out on the bed, lying on her side, in her pilot's jumpsuit, her boots and other accoutrements kicked off to the foot of the bed. Jaina was asleep, and Leia took a moment just to look at her.

Though in engagement after engagement Jaina had been at the controls of one of the New Republic's deadliest fighter craft, racking up kill after kill against savage enemies, her features were now relaxed in sleep, and she looked as innocent as a child. But she was no child now. She was a young woman, her childhood suddenly, irretrievably gone, and an ache constricted Leia's heart. *We should be away from all this now,* she thought. *Han and Jaina and Jacen and Anakin and I. And Luke and Mara and little Ben. In a field of flowers. On Alderaan.*

Moving slowly and quietly so as not to awaken Jaina, Leia lay down on the bed and put an arm around her. It was a closeness, a protracted closeness that Jaina no longer permitted her in times of wakefulness. Too soon, she heard Jaina's breathing change as her daughter awakened.

Jaina looked up into Leia's face and offered a slight, sleepy smile.

"I'm sorry. I didn't mean to wake you."

"It's all right." Jaina reached up to pull Leia's arm more tightly around her. "Since you left, I've come here sometimes because I knew I could smell you and Dad here. You'd be all around me even when you weren't here."

Leia managed to keep an expression of incredulity off her face. Those words seemed so unlike Jaina—so unlike the person she'd become across the last couple of years. "Are you all right?"

Jaina shook her head. "I don't think so." She lay her head down on the pillow again. "I don't think I know who I am anymore."

"Is it this goddess thing—?"

"No. That doesn't confuse me in the least. It's just a confidence game. No, the problem is all being a Jedi, which seems so crystal clear in what you should do and what you should say at any given time . . . and then being the rest of me, where nothing is clear." Her expression, what Leia could see of it at this angle, seemed bleak.

Leia chuckled. "Jaina, I've been wrestling with the same question since I was only a little older than you are now, and I *still* don't have a good answer. Sometimes I'm Jedi and sometimes I'm not. Jedi teaching says that you must turn away from fear. But as a politician, I have to experience fear. Not just my own. The fear of my allies. The fear of my opponents. If I can't feel it—if I can't *be-*

come it, in a sense—I can't predict which way they're going to jump when trouble hits. Sometimes being a Jedi just runs completely counter to your other goals. The methodology is just too different." Softly, she stroked her daughter's hair, silently willing her daughter's torments away.

"That's part of it, too," Jaina said. "It took me a while to figure it out. I'm afraid."

"It's all right to be afraid. You're surrounded by fearsome things. Being afraid will keep you alive."

Jaina shook her head. "That's not it. I'm not afraid of dying. I'm afraid of *surviving* . . . and getting to the end of the war and discovering that I'm all alone. That everyone I knew and cared for is gone."

"Jaina, that won't happen."

"It's already been happening. I mean, it was like having part of me cut off when Anakin died, but with Jacen it's even worse. As far back as I can recall, no matter what was going on, no matter what was wrong, I could turn around and Jacen would be there. We could be on some distant hideout world or lost in the underbelly of Coruscant or wandering around on parts of Yavin Four no thinking creature has ever seen, and there Jacen was. I never had to be bored, I never had to be afraid, I never had to be alone. When we lost him, I was cut in half. Half of me is gone." Now the tears came. Jaina wiped them away.

Leia shook her head. "Jacen's not dead. I know he's in trouble, but he's alive. I would have felt him go. I felt it with Anakin."

The tension in Jaina's shoulders didn't ease, but she chose not to argue that point. Instead, she said, "I keep having these thoughts. That I should be planning for the future. Just recently, they've gotten, well, even more frequent. But I can't bear to do that. I can't plan to have a home on a world when it might not be there tomorrow, or for a career in a service that might be gone, or to spend time with people who keep throwing themselves against the Vong until they stop coming back."

"I know. That's what it was like all those years ago, when Palpatine seemed to be an unstoppable force and we were always on the run, and your father was just this ridiculously attractive man who always seemed to be on the verge of leaving us. And do you know what I learned?"

"What?"

"At times like that, you plan for your future by bringing people into your life. You know that they can't all survive what you're facing. But those who do, they're part of your life forever. No matter what, when you fall, they'll catch you; when you're hungry, they'll feed you; when you're hurting, they'll heal you. And you'll do the same for them. And that's your future. I've had whole *worlds* taken away from me . . . but not my future."

Jaina was silent, seemingly thinking about Leia's words, for long moments. Finally she rolled over onto her back to look into Leia's eyes. "Actually, I'm glad you got back tonight. Part of why I kept coming here was because I wanted to tell you something. I wanted to let you know that I finally get it."

"You get—get what?"

"I had a talk with Mara a few days ago and it really bothered me. It took me until after that really bad furball in space, the one where we almost lost Jag, to figure it out. I finally understood about you sending us, Jacen and Anakin and me, away when we were little. Having to be away all the time even when we were on Coruscant. I'm not stupid, I always knew why. Responsibilities." Jaina looked off into the distance of time for a moment. "But I never really understood how badly it had to have hurt you."

"Oh, baby. Of course it hurt. I tried to tell you, time after time. But there aren't even words for that kind of pain."

"I know." Jaina sat up and Leia let her. "I've got to go. Reports to write. Goddess stuff to do." But first she embraced Leia, squeezing her with fierce strength. "I love you, Mom."

"I love you, Jaina."

Borleias Occupation, Day 49

Wedge, in Luke's X-wing, transcribed a lazy arc through vacuum in low planetary orbit. Far below was the near-continuous Borleias jungle. He gave the yoke a hard pull and his course suddenly became a tight circle. He went through 360 degrees of arc, starry sky giving way to jungle outside his canopy, then becoming starfield again, as centrifugal force in excess of the X-wing's inertial compensator tugged him deeper into the pilot's couch.

He smiled as he leveled off. "Good to get out once in a while, even when you're not flying missions, isn't it?"

R2-D2's beeps of response came across his comm board. They sounded like an agreement, but not an enthusiastic one.

"Don't worry, Artoo. Luke will come back. There's no one in the galaxy who knows how to survive bad places better than Luke Skywalker."

R2-D2 beeped again, his tones sounding somewhat more encouraged.

Then a voice broke over his comm system, Tycho's. "General, this is a heads-up."

"I read you."

"For the last half hour or so, we've had some odd

traffic on the sensor board. Anomalous readings out beyond the kill zone. Becoming more frequent."

"Your guess?"

"I'd say the push is on. They're coming in from all directions."

"About time. Alert Luke's team to prepare for departure; they'll leave during the confusion of the attack. I'm coming in." Wedge put the X-wing back on a course for the biotics building.

"You're sure about this." Luke gave Lando a skeptical look.

Lando nodded, his manner easy. "I'm sure. Every so often I need to remind the universe that I'm a damned good pilot. With people like you and Han and his daughter around, everyone tends to forget."

They stood in the killing field before the *Record Time*, the troop transport that had been part of the first invasion wave to reach the planet's surface.

Seven weeks before, *Record Time* had been an antiquated cargo vessel working reliably through late middle age. Then it had seen one combat mission, the Borleias landing, and had been shot nearly to pieces. Now, after weeks of as-time-allows repairs by the garrison's mechanics, the skin of its two main sections was so irregularly patched as to look scabrous, and reinforcing bars welded to the narrow section connecting the two ends merely accentuated the fact that the whole thing looked ready to break in half at any moment.

"Who are you trying to kid?" Luke gave him a skeptical look. "You're one of two men who blew up the second Death Star. You don't have anything to prove."

Lando shrugged. He ran a hand down his tunic to smooth it. It was a rust-red, long-sleeved garment, delightful to the touch, and had cost more than he'd made in lean years. It perfectly complemented the cream-colored hip cloak he wore. He wanted to look good for his funeral or his triumphant return to Borleias, whatever would come. "All right, you've got me. It's about the scam, Luke.

"People hear about me, they see what I do, and they think I'm all about the profit motive. And, sure, I like wealth. I like it enough that sometimes I'll even do honest work to get it." He offered Luke a mock shudder. "But that's secondary. The *trick* is what makes everything sweet. Take someone who thinks he's got you, put him through the machinery of your mind and your skills, and bring him out the other end stripped of all his goods, but absolutely convinced that he's had the better of you—so convinced that he's even willing to be nice to you, to be generous to you—and you've accomplished something great." He gestured at the ship. As if on cue, a hatch cover near the top of the bridge, beside one of the sensor arrays, popped free; it rolled down the bow's sloping hull and then dropped to the duracrete with a tired clang. "This is a scam. We're going to take this heap of junk in and the Yuuzhan Vong are going to think our hopes are pinned on it. They're going to blow it up and think they've wrecked our hopes. They'll be doing exactly what we want them to—they'll be our personal servants for those few moments, which would kill them if they knew—and they'll never realize just how much they've helped us. Until we choose to tell them. That's sweeter than any wine, Luke."

"If you say so." Luke took a hard look at the bow, doubtless cataloging where the hatch came from so a repair crew could fix it in the little time they had left. "Who's your copilot on this?"

"No copilot. Just a weapons officer. YVH One-One-A."

Luke frowned. "Isn't that one of your combat droids?"

"It is."

"You're going to use this mission to field-test a droid."

"That's right."

"Not a good idea."

Lando shrugged again. "I'm captaining that flying landfill. My choice. Wedge has authorized it."

"Sometimes I think you're as crazy as Han." Luke checked his chrono. "I'd better get with my team. Some last-minute packing to do."

"I'll be here." Lando watched Luke leave.

He had no interest in field-testing his droids on a mission like this. No, he just had no faith in his ability to get out of this operation alive and didn't want to lead another living thing into death with him.

That was bad, dark thinking. But he'd scammed Luke about his motives in having a droid weapons officer. He smiled to himself. Luke wasn't the naive young man he'd been when Lando had met him. Scamming him was tougher these days. And always a pleasure to pull off.

He walked over to stand near the ramp into the bay he and his droids had occupied so many days ago. He stood well to the side of the sparks drifting out from the bay; he didn't want anything charring his tunic.

The bay had now been partitioned off by a temporary bulkhead into two parts. In the front third, suspended in a metal brace hung from the bay ceiling, was a two-seat B-wing fighter, old but—he'd been guaranteed—reliable.

The rear portion of the bay was filled with boulders. Well, they were not boulders exactly. Hanging from cables were pieces of debris, many of them chunks of downed coralskippers. *Dead* coralskippers, he reminded himself. They'd been hollowed out by volunteer crews who'd later decided they never wanted to field-dress one of the organic spacecraft again. Now they were shells, each one capable of holding one or two members of Luke's team. There was other wreckage in the bay, as well—pieces of Yuuzhan Vong and New Republic ships, chunks of permacrete. The press of a button from Lando's bridge or a comlink carried by Luke would sever all those cables and activate an inertial compensator mounted on the bulkhead opposite the ramp door, shoving the debris and the insertion team out through the door.

The work crew's final welding of the bulkhead between the forward and rear portions of the bay was what was generating the sparks. Lando approved. He wanted that bulkhead to be strong. He didn't need debris to come crashing through to wreck his B-wing.

He wasn't as familiar with B-wings as he'd like to be, but the vehicle should be able to get him and his droid back home—if he could reach the docking bay from the bridge. If he had time. If not, he'd be launching in an escape pod. He'd be captured by the Yuuzhan Vong. He'd be enslaved and tortured.

No, he decided, if he couldn't reach the B-wing, there would be no escape pod for him. He'd ride the wreckage of the corvette all the way down to Coruscant's surface. And he'd look good while doing it.

Lando was on the bridge when Luke's team came up the temporary ramp into the landing bay. It was Luke and Mara, Tahiri, several of the Wraiths, whom he'd barely met—the bald one, the tall one, the Devaronian, the skinny bearded man, and the severe-looking woman—and a final surprise, Danni Quee.

He shouldn't have been startled. He should have known that the persistent scientist would have insisted on being a part of the mission to find out what was going wrong with Coruscant's planet shaping to learn whatever she could of the Yuuzhan Vong.

R2-D2 waited at the bottom of the ramp. Lando knew

that Luke wasn't taking him along, and why; the astromech droid wasn't mobile enough to navigate the difficult terrain the insertion team expected to face, and would certainly be an instant victim of Yuuzhan Vong wrath if captured.

R2-D2 tilted backward, as if leaning back to stare up at Luke, and Lando could imagine the plaintive noises and musical tones he'd be making. Luke stopped at the top of the ramp, still within range of R2's holocam view, and turned back to his droid companion. His gesture was conciliatory, reassuring.

"Pretty sad, huh?" Lando asked.

His own droid companion, YVH 1-1A, looked up from its sensors. "Sad," it confirmed, but without inflection.

"Ready to face the danger?"

"I am ready," YVH 1-1A said. "Of course I am ready. I am programmed to be ready. Always ready. Never uncertain about facing danger."

Lando gave the droid a little frown. It sounded as though the combat droid had picked up some conversational mannerisms from a protocol droid like C-3PO. But YVH 1-1A still didn't have the linguistic modules to help him develop idiosyncrasies like that. Oh, well. Something to worry about when they got back. He hit the switch on his comm unit. "Borleias Control, this is *Record Time*. Ready for takeoff."

"We'll give you the word. The assault is anticipated within the half hour."

"Hey, what odds am I getting that I'll blow up before getting out of the atmosphere?"

"Um, about one in a hundred, sir."

"I'll put a thousand credits on surviving at least to orbit."

"I'll take that, sir. I could use ten credits."

"How do you collect if you win?"

Silence answered him. Lando grinned at YVH 1-1A, but the droid merely stared back at him, humorless.

The alarm cut through the biotics building, the temporary docking bays built outside it, the kill zone surrounding it. Pilots scrambled for their starfighters. Mission controllers reached their stations and began coordinating the units they managed.

Jaina, racing for the special operations docking bay, skidded to a halt as a large man staggered into her path and turned pleading eyes on her. He was young, not unpleasant looking, but awkward of posture, with mussed hair and eyes more bloodshot than she'd ever seen in a human, worse than her father or Lando after the most extravagant night of drinking. "Do you need help?" she asked.

The big man shook his head. "I'm going to die." His words were slow, pained.

"Then you definitely do need help." She brought out her comlink. All around her, pilots and crew ran into the docking bay and toward vehicles parked in the kill zone.

"I'm a Yuuzhan Vong spy, and I'm going to die. I'm supposed to capture you now, with the bugs in my pocket, and carry you to the edge of the kill zone. But I'm not going to."

"Thank you." Jaina switched on the comlink. "Twin Suns Leader to Control. I'm in front of the special ops docking bay. I have a civilian male here. He's, uh, experiencing distress and needs medical help right away."

"Acknowledged, Twin Suns."

"I've won." The big man offered her a broad, idiotic smile. Blood suddenly began pouring down from his nose, running over his lips, spilling to the ground. "I don't have to do what they say. All they can do is kill me."

"Of course." She edged around him. Whatever his situation, she had to get to her X-wing.

"I took the bug off your X-wing," he called after her. "So don't worry."

"I won't," she promised, then turned to race after her pilots.

Tam watched her go.

He knew she hadn't believed him. Everyone had seen shell-shocked refugees here after Coruscant's fall. He must look just like one of them.

It took him a long time to work his way through that thought. With every beat of his heart, another spike of agony was pounded through his skull and into the deep portions of his brain. There wasn't room for brain matter anymore. That had to be why it was so hard to think.

But it was important that some people believe him, so they could finish undoing what he had done since arriving on Borleias.

He could see medical personnel running toward him now. He'd never be able to make a full confession to them, not before the pain ate completely through him and he died. But he didn't need to. He reached into his pockets. His right hand drew out the jellylike container still half full of Yuuzhan Vong bugs. His left drew out the data card, the one on which he'd written "In The Event Of My Death."

Suddenly he was looking at the sky. He hadn't felt the impact of falling. He put the bag and data card on his chest, where they were sure to be found.

Then the sky was full of faces, men and women saying things he couldn't understand. He smiled at them, to reassure them. Maybe they *could* save him. But if they couldn't, it was important they understand that he didn't blame them, that he wasn't mad.

He was still trying to form the words to tell them this when unconsciousness claimed him.

Jaina dropped into her X-wing's cockpit. Still somewhat rattled by the encounter with the madman, she began her power-up checklist. Her astromech, a gray-white R2 unit with burgundy lines and decorations, was already in place. "Hey, you," Jaina said, "I never asked. What's your name?"

Her comm board trilled and she looked to find a line of text appearing on it. *I DON'T HAVE A NAME. MY DESIGNATION IS R2-B3.*

"No name? That's terrible. You can't become famous without a name. Do you want one?"

THAT WOULD BE GOOD.

"How about Cappie? For a friend of mine, a pilot named Capstan."

I AM CAPPIE.

"All right, Cappie, give me the engine readouts . . ."

Jaina went through her checklist with her customary speed. This time, though, she didn't push herself to finish. She *knew* that Jag would be done before she was; she no longer had to look through his viewport for confirmation. On the other hand, when she was done, she did look. She saw him leaning back in his pilot's seat, relaxed. She gave him a smile and a thumbs-up.

He pulled his helmet off and gave her a return smile. It was a half smile, the left side of his mouth, brief but encouraging, for her alone. Then he pulled his helmet on again and was the anonymous pilot once more.

The expression caused something to flutter in her stomach. *Have to remember,* she told herself, *he may have been raised among the Chiss, but he's still full-blooded Corellian.*

* * *

A few meters away, Kyp Durron also saw the exchange of looks. He pulled his gaze away and concentrated on his diagnostics readout instead.

Since Hapes, Jaina had kept Kyp at arm's length. She'd kept everybody at arm's length. Now it was obvious that Jag Fel had gotten past her guard.

So what's it going to be? he asked himself. *Show him up? Let her interest in him run its course, then be on hand when she needs a friend to console her?* He wished he disliked Jag. That would make things easier.

Another voice, another thought, intruded. *Maybe you ought to figure out what she is to you before you make any decisions.*

He grimaced. That required more honesty than he wanted to experience.

Because he knew he wasn't in love with Jaina Solo. He just liked being around her.

She was intelligent, talented, brave, beautiful. Strong in the Force. Important to the New Republic. He could make her happy.

Why did he want to? He suspected it was because she *hadn't* been happy, and her pain, which he'd felt through the Force every time they'd connected, called to him, even when she'd fooled herself into thinking she could make it go away by keeping the whole universe at bay.

But he'd been interested in her before the loss of Anakin and Jacen. So why?

Maybe it was because of Han. He owed Han so much, from the time years ago when they'd met, from the help Han had offered in bringing Kyp back from the dark place he'd been in when he'd destroyed whole worlds. He might not be alive if not for Han. Make Jaina happy, make Han happy. It was a simple formula.

Besides, he had repaid that debt, or some of it. He'd helped Jaina come back from the steps she'd recently taken toward the dark side, and would continue to help as long as she needed him.

"Twin Suns Two . . ." That was Jaina's voice, artificially sweet, and it jolted Kyp out of his reverie.

"Yes?"

"Status, please? All the other little Twin Suns are ready to go."

"Oh. Uh, I'm—" He did a quick scan of his readouts. He'd finished his checklist automatically, as if on autopilot, and hadn't even registered the fact. "Ready to go. Sorry, Great One."

"Liftoff in ten, nine, eight . . ."

Kyp smiled ruefully to himself. So much for acting like a Jedi Master.

SIXTEEN

Borleias Occupation, Day 49

"All special ops squadrons have launched," Iella called out above the clamor of the command chamber.

"We have contact," Tycho said. "Yuuzhan Vong capital ships nearing Borleias, far side of the planet."

Iella said, "Commander Davip is requesting permission to pull *Lusankya* out of geosync to engage the enemy before they reach our location."

Wedge smiled at her. "Of course he is. Tell him no. Transmit to him the details of Operation Emperor's Hammer."

"Done."

Yuuzhan Vong Worldship, Pyria Orbit

"They are not sending forces into orbit," Czulkang Lah told the villip. "Instead, their orbital capital ships are sending some squadrons of small fighters down into the atmosphere."

The villip with his son's face said, "Meaning that they are aware of the approach of your ground forces."

"Correct. We somehow failed to disable all their

sensor devices on the ground and they have not been fooled."

"I will not offer advice. You are Czulkang Lah. You will crush them despite their state of readiness."

Czulkang Lah remained silent. An honest reply, his estimate that the infidels had surprises in store for the Yuuzhan Vong forces, that they might not win today, would only cause embarrassment for the warmaster.

After moments of awkward silence, Tsavong Lah added, "Good fighting." His villip inverted.

Twin Suns Squadron took up position a few kilometers north of the biotics building, high enough that Yuuzhan Vong attacks fired from the ground would have to travel for several obvious seconds before reaching them. Her pilots—twelve again, ever since Pastav Rone had been released from the bacta tanks—waited.

The Wild Knights were arrayed to the east, Blackmoon Squadron to the west, and the Rogues to the south; other squadrons from the Star Destroyers overhead were arriving to fill in the broad gaps in that defensive circle.

Jaina the pilot didn't like waiting. She shook her head and became Jaina the Jedi, to whom patience was a way of life.

But even as a Jedi she couldn't quite shake some thought eating at her.

The fear she'd discussed with Leia was back. It was under control, but always present. With it was worry—for Jag, for Kyp, for her other pilots, for friends, even for Cappie.

She felt it cleanly now. It had, she supposed, been with her since her return from Hapes, but she'd built up an insulating layer around her and kept it distant, muted. Now the insulation was gone.

And, oddly, she didn't mind the fear. Where she'd been

for the last few weeks, she hadn't been quite alive, completely present. Now she was. The worry, the fear, the pain they brought her, told her she was among the living, among her kind, part of everything she cared about. They might be counted as negative emotions, but now she found them welcome reminders of who she was and of the importance of what she had to do.

That thought stopped her. In a way, it was so like what she'd heard from and about the Yuuzhan Vong, whose desire for physical pain seemed so alien. All of a sudden, she almost understood it. Their pain was evidence of their life.

"All right," she told herself. "I'm going to give you some more evidence."

Her comm board clicked with the voice of the chief controller. "Coralskippers now reaching geosync point. Squadrons from *Lusankya* and *Rebel Dream* engaging."

Jaina's fingers twitched. She needed to be where the fighting was. She was Jaina the Pilot again.

She forced herself to wait. She knew it wouldn't be long.

"Intrusion detected in west quadrant."

Captain Reth didn't have to be told. Two kilometers ahead of his E-wing unit, the broad, swaying backs of two *rakamats*, the giant reptiles the Yuuzhan Vong used as ground-based battle vehicles and troop carriers, crested the top of the jungle canopy as they approached.

Reth keyed his comlink. "This is Blackmoon Leader. We're on it." He switched to squadron frequency. "Blackmoon Two to Eight, come with me; we're going to do a couple of strafing runs and see what pops up. Nine and Ten, lay down a firebreak in their path and then spread it around to encircle them."

His pilots clicked acknowledgments. No unnecessary

talk. He liked it that way. He kicked his thrusters and began laying triple-linked laserfire down on the enemy forces.

Jaina sprayed laserfire across the foremost of the *raka-mats* approaching her position. There were three of them, just their spiny backs visible at a distance of two and a half klicks.

Kyp's and Jag's laserfire joined hers. All of it was swallowed by voids on the target ahead. The same was happening with the laserfire being laid down by the other shield trios of Twin Suns Squadron against the other two *rakamats*. Jaina accelerated toward the enemy force, her pilots keeping pace.

"More voids than usual," Jag said. "These *rakamats* are reinforced."

They flashed over the *rakamat* formation; all twelve Twin Suns pilots looped around for another firing run. As they began their turn, plasma cannonfire erupted from the ground, from the *rakamats* and all around them. The streams were wide at first, shots meant to gauge distance, but rapidly closed on their targets.

"They have coralskippers at ground level," Piggy said, unnecessarily. "Using the jungle canopy to soak up our damage and make their precise locations uncertain."

Jaina stood her X-wing on its starboard S-foils and veered from her course just in time to elude a stream of plasma gobs. "What do you recommend?"

"Keep doing what we're doing . . . or do what they're doing."

"Huh. Interesting. Piggy, take command of the squad. Continue aerial assaults. Jag and Kyp, you two come with me."

She veered away from the engagement area and fled back toward the biotics facility.

* * *

"Make it fast, Commander." Wedge's face filled the hologram area of Commander Davip's private communications chamber. "We're sort of busy here."

"Sir, this Operation Emperor's Hammer . . ."

"You've got a problem with it?"

"Not with the plan itself, sir. It's . . . interesting. Potentially very effective. But . . ." Davip steeled himself against what he had to say. "Sir, I don't have confidence in my crew to carry it off with the precision you need. It's something that hasn't been done in twenty years! Sir, I'm commanding mostly misfits, and those misfits could cost you your life."

Wedge nodded, sympathy evident in his expression. "Misfits. I understand. I've been there."

"I don't know why Command assembled this incredible collection of screw-ups . . ."

"I do. It was so they'd all die here and deprive the New Republic Navy of the officers and crew who have offered it the most trouble. Including you. Including me." Wedge shrugged. "The orders stand, Commander. You can either figure out how to convince your crew to perform, in which case we survive down here, or you can't, in which we die. Now, listen. Command of the *Lusankya* isn't a ticket to promotion anymore. It's a ticket to obscurity and early retirement, and you'll deserve them if you don't learn how to think outside your training. *Lusankya* is your last command, Davip, unless you get the job done today. Any more questions?"

Davip shook his head, not bothering to conceal his pained expression. "No, sir."

"Antilles out." The general's hologram faded to nothingness.

Davip exited the chamber and returned to *Lusankya*'s

bridge, to the walkway above and between the tremendous banks of officers and technicians at their stations.

The walkway afforded an incredible view through the forward viewports of the coralskipper-on-starfighter duels taking place just outside the range of the Star Destroyer's weapons. The surface of the walkway itself was so clean, so white, so spare.

Just like Davip's mind at the moment. He always wanted things clean and spare.

Maybe that was it. Maybe he needed dirty and cluttered. Dirty and bloody and confused and unclear . . .

He called down to his chief weapons officer, "Transfer command of one of the turbolaser emplacements designated for Emperor's Hammer to my station. Make it the one belonging to the weapons officer with the worst composite score from simulations."

"Yes, sir."

Several of the officers below, those whose current tasks didn't demand their full attention, looked up at him, confusion evident on their faces. He supposed he'd done something he'd never done before. He'd issued a command that didn't make immediate and obvious sense.

He turned his attention to his communications officer. "Open a line to all the weapons stations designated for Emperor's Hammer. I need to address them now." He pulled out his comlink.

"Yes, sir." The officer typed in a quick command and nodded at him.

"This is Commander Davip. I'm assuming personal command of one of the laser stations for Emperor's Hammer. During the operation, any gunner whose accuracy rates worse than mine is in for it. He or she gets transferred down to the planet's surface immediately after the battle is done and will be put on the crews handling the bodies of our dead. That'll be your position through the duration of our stay insystem, and no transfers will be accepted. That is all." He gave the comm officer a nod to indicate he was through.

That officer, and the others who had been looking at him before, stared blankly, as though they'd just realized they'd been taking orders from a talking bantha in an officer's uniform.

He grinned at them. Why, if he'd known how much entertainment he'd derive from baffling his subordinates, he might have tried it years ago.

Jaina's and Kyp's X-wings crept along just above the jungle floor. They were perpendicular to the ground, their repulsorlifts whining with the unaccustomed demands of having to fly sideways just above a planetary surface. The snubfighters' bows crashed through branches and fern-like vegetation as they moved—not exactly stealthy, Jaina decided, but still invisible from the air.

Jag's clawcraft was not in sight; sensors said that he was about two hundred meters ahead and slowly increasing his lead. The clawcraft's more compact shape was better suited to travel through these surroundings without becoming snared on heavy foliage.

And with Jag's fighter, hovering behind it at a distance of no more than four meters, were two shadow bombs, armed, drifting along in the grip of the Force. Jaina sweated as she divided her concentration between flying this way and controlling her shadow bomb, and once again she envied Kyp's effortless control over all matters of the Force.

All matters not involving his own motivations and actions, that is.

Jag said, "I've managed to set down in some heavy growth just beside a riverbank. A sort of hunter's blind. I have pretty good visibility. If you want, you can set the bombs down behind me. Gently."

Jaina did so, grateful for the relief. "How close do you think you are?"

"Pretty close. I'm looking right at them. About twenty meters off, ahead to starboard. There are two masses of reptoid slaves escorting coralskippers. The skips are moving about a meter off the ground. Their voids aren't visible . . . I suspect they're directing their voids to reinforce the *rakamats*. I see only five skips, but their formation suggests a broad line of them. Hold on." He was silent for a few moments. "Vibrations in the hull suggest that one or more *rakamats* are headed this way. I think we placed it pretty accurately." Then there was a loud bang and a curt laugh from Jag. "A tree just took some laserfire from one of us."

"Try not to get hit with your shields down, dummy."

"Good advice, that. I'd never considered it before. Wait a second."

"What is it?"

"I see a *rakamat* . . . I think it's a range. Something big, shoving down whole trees in front of it. Who wants to try this one?"

"I do," Kyp said.

"All right, lift the shadow bomb up, traverse it ten meters forward, and lower it slowly . . . I see the bomb. Very good. All right, take it ahead dead slow . . . a little to the right . . . no, not that much to the right—Stop! Can you back it up a meter and sideslip a little to the right?"

"This will never work," Kyp said. "I can't sense all the vegetation with the accuracy of seeing it. I can't just steer around things."

"Yes, you can," Jaina said. "Can you direct its movements through hand motions?"

"Well, yes, but it's no better if I still can't see it."

Jaina grinned. "Kyp, set down here and slave your controls to Jag's."

"All right . . . done. Now what?"

"Jag, you use your control yoke like it was a joystick in a game. Direct the shadow bomb's movement. Kyp, keep your hand on your yoke, let its feedback direct where your hand goes . . . and control the shadow bomb through your hand motions."

"Whoa." Kyp sounded impressed. "All right, I'm game."

"Nice of you to be so willing," Jag said. "You're not the one sitting meters away from an armed proton torpedo being directed by a blind man in a two-way hookup. Well, here goes."

Jaina set down her X-wing, lowering it onto its landing gear, and crossed her fingers.

"Hey, it's working," Jag said. "My control is sloppy, but much better than verbal. I've got it past the trees . . . lowering it to a few centimeters off the ground. Good, Kyp, we're getting better. Cruising it forward, dead slow . . . Stop it here, set it down. Good. It's right in the path of the *rakamat*. I can see the *rakamat* clearly now, and there's another one behind it, a little to port. The near one is about thirty meters, the second one, I'd estimate, twenty meters behind it."

"Go ahead and take the second bomb," Jaina told Kyp.

Reth brought his squad around for another pass and cursed. He'd lost two E-wings on the last pass, one in a clean kill, one with comprehensive thruster damage that sent it limping back to base. That left him eight. The Yuuzhan Vong ground force was moving into his firebreak zone, its reptoid troops, coralskippers, and *rakamats* exposed to view from above, but they were soaking up his squad's damage with impunity. And now the coralskippers were coming up off the ground to engage them.

There were a lot of them. Dozens of skips. Hundreds or thousands of reptoids. And the *rakamat*. One squad of E-wings wasn't going to be enough to put a dent in them.

He switched over to command frequency. "Control, this is Blackmoon Leader. We're facing a superior force and could use some reinforcements."

The voice that responded was Iella Wessiri's. "Blackmoon Leader, Control. All our ground forces are engaged. Fight defensively and make a fighting retreat back our way."

"Control, copy." Reth gritted his teeth. This wasn't going to end well. It would be another Hoth, another Dantooine, with not even an opportunity to count up their dead.

Jag looked dispassionately at the reptoid who'd just walked into his viewport. The reptoid stared at him, mouth open to suggest anger or surprise, and looked around to gauge the size of Jag's clawcraft. "I estimate about ten seconds before the Yuuzhan Vong figure out I'm here."

"Get out of there, then. Come back to us."

"No, it's more than ten seconds before the *rakamat* are in position. We need to time this exactly."

"No, come on back now. Do you trust me?"

"No fair using my own arguments against me."

The reptoid was in a frenzy, shouting something back toward the advancing line of coralskippers. Jag activated his shields, heard and felt the increased engine demand thrum through his clawcraft. He rolled his craft over backward like a ball, rotating it along its directional axis so he ended up facing the other way but right-side up, and goosed his thrusters.

Behind him, his hiding place exploded as plasma cannon ejecta rained down on it. Then the trees surrounding it shattered, splintering, as coralskippers gave chase.

Jaina let herself drift, staying in tentative contact with the distant life-forms.

She could feel them, the collective them, and every few moments a new group of them, a few meters away from the last, offered up a second or two of fear as their world shook around them.

They were insects, lizards, other life-forms native to Borleias, and she was sure she was feeling their fear as the impact tremor of the *rakamat's* giant feet shook the ground around them.

She could also feel, with a different set of Force-sensibilities, the shadow bomb she controlled.

The two sets of feeling were coming closer together.

She felt a twitch from Kyp. His range was right over his shadow bomb. *Wait,* she told him.

Closer, closer, and then they were almost together. *Now,* she told him, and triggered her shadow bomb. She opened her eyes.

In the distance, fire erupted into the sky—fire, propelling into the sky tons of charred flesh that had been *rakamats*. A shock wave rippled out from the site of the explosions, shredding trees near it, shaking them farther away, causing nothing more than a ground tremor where Jaina and Kyp sat.

"All right, Twins," she said. "Let's go back in and deal with that last range, and Jag's pursuit."

"Twin Suns, this is Control." In fact, it was Wedge's voice. "Negative on that. Fall back. Fall back."

"Fall back, understood." Jaina struggled with herself,

then assumed her most regal tone. "We want to know why we're being summoned back when we're winning."

"Because you're holding up the Yuuzhan Vong advance."

She lost her godly demeanor. "*What?* I thought that's what we were supposed to do!"

Wedge laughed at her. "Goddess, as usual, you're doing your job too well."

SEVENTEEN

Coruscant System

The *Record Time* dropped out of hyperspace close to Coruscant, close enough for the planet to fill most of her forward viewports.

Lando immediately began broadcasting. "Survivor Cell Thirty-Eight, this is Rescue Two. We're inbound and ready for pickup. Make yourselves ready at Target Zone A-Nineteen. Over."

There was no reply. Of course there wasn't. There was no Survivor Cell Thirty-Eight. There was no Target Zone A-Nineteen. No one was monitoring this comm frequency.

"Sensors show frigate analog incoming," YVH 1-1A said.

"Shields up. Commence firing." Lando plotted a course revision that would carry them away from the other Yuuzhan Vong command ships in the area, a course that would, in theory, get them to the vicinity of the edge of Coruscant's atmosphere. He ran the numbers and winced. The incoming frigate would be on them before they could get into position. *Record Time* was going to soak up some damage.

He keyed the comm unit again. "Survivor Cell Thirty-Eight, this is Rescue Two. Why don't you answer? Why don't you answer?" He clicked it off and grinned at 1-1A. "What did you think of that?"

One-One-A began firing, meticulous shots with the ship's turbolasers at too great a distance to be effective. "Stress analysis of your transmitted words suggests high emotional content. From a search-and-rescue perspective, you sound like an emotional civilian."

"Good. How about the repetition? Too clichéd, or did it work for you?"

"That is outside the scope of my programming." One-One-A continued firing. "The frigate is launching coralskippers. I have destroyed one."

"I suggest you destroy a second one."

"I have destroyed a second one."

"I suggest you destroy a third one."

"If I may ask, are you managing a subordinate, or taunting me?"

"I'm taunting you, One-One-A. All in the spirit of fun."

"I have destroyed a third one."

"I suggest—"

"I have destroyed a fourth one."

Luke waited in the darkness of the cargo hold.

Strapped to his feet was the descent unit the Wraiths had given him. Its bottom was attached with adhesive to his descent pod, a portion of a coralskipper reshaped into an oblong spheroid by creative application of duracrete and paint. Its hatch was dogged shut.

He wore a set of Yuuzhan Vong–styled armor—not one of the true vonduun crab sets, one of the artful simulations. He'd suspected that it might not be appropriate for a man with a mechanical hand and an all-too-useful lightsaber to make use of one of the authentic sets; he suspected he'd have to shed any Yuuzhan Vong disguise too often and too quickly.

Over the Yuuzhan Vong armor, he wore an environment suit, a big, bulky, ancient one no one would miss when he had to shred it upon landing.

He reached out to Mara, felt her in the Force, felt her living presence. She reached back, an absent gesture; he knew her mind had to be elsewhere, on their mission, on their child.

Lando's voice came over his helmet speakers. "We're getting into range." The ship, and everything in the cargo area, shuddered. "Sorry about that. Little bit of plasma goo." His voice was replaced by 1-1A's for a moment: "I have destroyed a sixth one." Then Lando was back: "Knock off the running tally, would you? Um, we'll go into a lateral maneuver in just a minute and punch you out. If you find yourselves in vacuum before then, just go on without me."

"I have destroyed a seventh one."

"I told you—"

"I am teaching myself to taunt you."

Lando pulled a pilot's helmet on. His fancy tunic and cloak concealed a far more ordinary pilot's jumpsuit, and he checked its connections to make sure it was ready to seal him off in case of pressure loss. A piece of plasma had already burned its way through the transparisteel of the forward viewport, and air was hissing out through it.

The *Record Time* shook every few seconds now. Its tail section was taking the brunt of the damage—plasma cannon fire, barely reduced by the failing shields, from both pursuing coralskippers and the trailing frigate analog—while the forward section was suffering from hit after hit launched by a single coralskipper.

But they were almost in position. Lando keyed his helmet microphone. "Coming up on launch zone in fifteen seconds. There's not going to be a countdown. When we're there, I'm going to punch you out."

"Force be with you, Lando."

"Luck be with *you*, Luke." Lando switched off the comlink and returned his attention to the controls.

This was tricky. He put the ungainly, disintegrating freighter into a slow port turn, bringing its starboard side around to face the sunny side of the planet below. "Ready yourself, One-One-A." Then he tripped the newly installed switch labeled GO.

The ship's inertial compensator kicked off. Though he tightly gripped the arms of his chair and was strapped into place, Lando felt himself yanked to the right, heard the post his seat was bolted to creak from the sudden pressure.

All around the forward section of the ship, explosives attached to the outer hull would be going off. They weren't high explosives; they had just enough detonating power to fire chaff and thick smoky residue out in all directions. From outside, it would look as though *Record Time* were experiencing a series of internal explosions.

The smoke and chaff concealed the starboard cargo bay door, which should have been slung open by the maneuver and loss of artificial gravity. Lando saw that its gauge registered that it was open, that its atmospheric pressure was approaching zero, that its own temporary inertial compensator had activated.

He looked out the starboard viewport. There, a cloud of debris was tumbling away from the freighter, directly toward Coruscant's surface far below.

He keyed his helmet microphone again. "Survivor Cell Thirty-Eight, this is the final transmission of Rescue Two. Sorry we couldn't get to you. Hope you have better luck next time." That message, he knew, would be picked up by a New Republic scout ship at the edge of the Coruscant system and relayed to Wedge Antilles; it meant that Luke and his party were safely away.

He turned to 1-1A. "All right, let's get—"

A blast of plasma from the frigate analog hit the center of the span joining the two sections of *Record Time*. The span parted, and the ripple from the impact shook the length of the ship. This time, Lando's chair post did break, bouncing him, still strapped into his chair, into the air. With the ship's artificial gravity dead, he rose until he banged into the bridge ceiling, bounced off, and began drifting toward the fist-sized hole in the forward viewport.

"Oh, I have a really good feeling about this," he said.

Luke felt abrupt weightlessness, then sudden acceleration as he was punched out of the cargo bay and, he hoped, toward the planet.

He checked the sensor readouts glued to the pod surface before him. They showed course—correct. Number—correct; all of his comrades were with him still. As he watched, the inertial compensator in the unit at his feet activated, rotating him so that he approached Coruscant feet-first. Minor repulsor bursts would be keeping him in close proximity to the others.

He shook his head, dissatisfied. He didn't like to be in any small vehicle when he wasn't at the controls. And this was a vehicle only by a very generous broadening of the definition of that word.

Lando got himself unstrapped from his chair and kicked against the viewport. The move carried him away from it, but also caused cracks to appear where his heel had struck, cracks that reached the plasma hole and radiated in other directions as well.

One-One-A pushed himself free from his seat, a trajectory that carried him past Lando and toward the door out. He caught Lando around the waist as he traveled, Lando's mass barely causing a change in his direction, and reached the door recess. He clamped his feet down at the bottom of the recess and, with his free hand, sheared through the metal door.

Atmosphere behind it poured through, tugging Lando, but 1-1A merely shoved his way through the ruins of the door and into the passageway beyond.

"Good work," Lando said.

"Is that more taunting, or a compliment?"

"Neither, really. In this case, it stands in for a 'thank-you,' which is what it really means. Now can you get us into the bay? Because that last blast seems to have pushed us toward the atmosphere, and we're going to be carbon dust in a few seconds to a minute."

"You're welcome." One-One-A kicked again, and they were floating weightless down the passageway.

Luke could feel the heat now; for all the Wraiths' claims, heat soaked into the descent unit and was transmitted into the pod, cutting through his environment suit, through his armor, causing him to burst into sweat from scalp to toes.

The sensor board before him winked out. Then, beyond it, he saw the pod interior surface go from black to red, to yellow—and then flame was licking at it there, flame that grew and spread.

The pod rocked. Luke knew that friction had to have caused a pit in the bottom of his pod; atmosphere was getting a foothold in the pit, causing greater friction, causing the whole unit to sway. He felt a rumble in his feet as the repulsorlift there increased power output to keep the unit upright.

Abruptly there was a bright flash and the top of the

pod was gone. Luke found himself in a column of fire, streaming yellow flames that reached from the edges of the descent unit at his feet straight up into the air; he could see nothing beyond it. For a moment, a memory over twenty-five years old rose before him, the vision of the smoking remains of his Uncle Owen and Aunt Beru, as they lay on the sands in front of his home on Tatooine.

He forced the memory away and tried to gain a little perspective. *If this is bad for me,* he thought, *what is it going to be like for Tahiri? A teenager?*

Luke felt a jolt under his feet, sudden deceleration; his knees flexed as he absorbed the shock. The deceleration remained constant and the flames began to diminish, to waver.

In moments he could see his surroundings through them. Mara was no more than ten meters away, her face not visible through her environment suit and Yuuzhan Vong armor. The others were all nearby.

They were less than two kilometers above the world's surface, still falling, but not at terminal velocity. And though he'd lived on Coruscant for many years, this wasn't the surface he remembered. Great buildings lay toppled, their angles no longer conforming to those of the structures around them. Everything was coated with green, a poisonous shade of the color. At least the orange-and-brown clouds in the distance, full of rain and lightning, were the same, one reassuring piece of familiarity.

"Interesting ride, farmboy." Mara's voice was clear over the comlink; any interference brought on by the atmospheric friction of their decent was now ended.

Luke repressed a snicker. "Not too bad."

"Face?" That was Tahiri's voice, faint, full of emotion. Luke winced. He and Mara would need to offer her some reassurance.

"Yes?"

"*I want one!* I've got to have one of these when we get back. Oh, what a ride! Can we do it again?"

Luke shook his head and felt Mara laughing at him.

One-One-A had to use his blaster on the main door into the cargo bay. Once it was shredded and gone, the atmosphere from the passageway nearly blew the two of them into the bay itself, but the combat droid held fast.

Lando poked his head in. The B-wing seemed to be secure. The cargo ramp door was still down, maybe gone, and he could see starry space beyond—space, and, as the remains of the ship rotated, a coralskipper still pouring fire into its side as the ruins descended toward the atmosphere.

Cold began seeping into Lando's bones. "Let's go."

A minute later, just as the outer edges of the *Record Time* began glowing from friction, Lando's B-wing erupted from the cargo bay, turning away from the pursuing coral-skipper, away from the frigate and other skips that had chosen to hang back once their task was done. With 1-1A silent in the passenger seat, Lando plotted a course that would carry them out of Coruscant's mass shadow, to a point where he could make a jump, any jump, to hyper-space and get clear.

He turned to look at the combat droid. "And I did it looking good," he said.

"Is this taunting, too?"

Borleias

The biotics facility was in clear sight now. Jaina could see it, her squadmates, the surviving starfighters and blast-boats of the other eleven squadrons defending the site, and fires—dozens of fires raging in the jungle outside the kill zone. She poured her lasers into distant targets: ranges, coralskippers. She saw a Yuuzhan Vong frigate analog a dozen kilometers away, in the zone defended by Rogue Squadron. The frigate blossomed in fire and blood as a proton torpedo found its mark. But there were more frigate analogs, other capital ships, all converging on the biotics facility.

She shook her head. The Yuuzhan Vong force marching toward the facility was too great; the defenders could not hold the site.

Until now, she'd been silently raging at Wedge Antilles. Whenever she'd manage to make inroads against the enemy assault, he or one of his controllers would order her to withdraw a half kilometer, a hundred meters. It was as if they didn't want her to win. But now she could see that too much success on her part would serve only to cut Twin Suns off from the other units, to doom her and her pilots. It was probably best that she'd been ordered to fall back at the same rate as the other squadrons.

The mind of Jaina the Goddess woke up. Jaina frowned. *Fall back at the same rate.* She consulted her sensor board. That was exactly what was happening. The New Republic Forces had withdrawn where they were too strong, and been reinforced where they were too weak, and now every live unit of those forces was within a kilometer of the kill zone.

"Jag, I need to apologize to your uncle," she said.

"Why?"

"I'll tell you why later."

"All units, fall back to kill zone," Iella said. "All units, fall back to kill zone. You have fifteen seconds. Fourteen. Thirteen."

Jaina led her squad back, taking up position directly over the landing zone in front of the biotics building, directing their lasers back the way they'd come. "Twin Suns Squadron, on-station." Using her repulsorlifts, she drifted to port and a stream of plasma whipped past her, splashing onto the blue transparisteel panels on the face of the building; she directed laserfire back at her attacker.

Other unit commanders called in readiness as the countdown neared its end. Not all did. Jaina winced. She couldn't hope that no friendlies were out there; she knew some were, pilots who'd been shot down but might still be alive.

"Zero," Iella said. "Hold positions."

And it began to rain.

It didn't rain water. It rained columns of destructive energy, massed fire from turbolaser batteries far overhead, brilliant needles of light that poured into the jungle all around the kill zone.

The turbolaser blasts tore through vegetation, through everything beneath it. Blasts hitting trees detonated them in clouds of smoke. Beams hitting ponds and creeks and stagnant water sent up clouds of superheated steam. Beams flashed down through those clouds, but the manipulators of voids couldn't see them coming, couldn't maneuver the voids into place in time.

Jaina sat transfixed. This was orbital bombardment, what the Empire's Star Destroyers had been built to do, what no Star Destroyer under the command of the New Republic had *ever* done. Jaina had heard about it, but it was just history, just some old-timey thing that no one ever had to worry about.

And now she was seeing it. *Lusankya* was finally fulfilling the purpose for which she had been built, before Jaina had even been born.

For four minutes, death rained down from overhead, in a circle neatly surrounding the kill zone. Then it stopped, and the rumbles, the screams uttered by bodies of water suddenly superheated, the bellows of distant *rakamats* meeting their doom, all died away.

Jaina jumped as her comlink crackled back into life. "Ground forces," Wedge said, "commence mop-up."

Coruscant

The repulsors on the descent units activated for the final portion of the descent. All the members of Luke's group set down on the same roof—except for Kell Tainer, who hit the roof correctly, punched clean through its disintegrating duracrete surface, and ended up three stories down. "Not hurt," he shouted up. "Hey, they've left behind some holodramas I haven't seen."

Luke pulled off his scorched environment suit as the others did the same. He took a look around. In the distance, he could see a flight of four coralskippers; they were not aimed this way, but if he could see them, their pilots might be able to see him. "Let's get under cover," he said. "Shove all the trash into the hole Kell made. Look out below."

Mara, somehow stylishly savage in her vonduun crab armor with its helmet off, surveyed the landscape. Her lips twitched in a momentary grimace. "Welcome home," she said.

Luke shook his head. "This isn't home. I wonder if it will ever be home again."

Yuuzhan Vong Worldship, Pyria Orbit

Czulkang Lah blinked. How had that particular use of the infidels' triangle ships eluded him?

Nom Anor, he decided. Nom Anor had been the Yuuzhan Vong spy in this galaxy for decades. Like an idiot, during all those years, he had failed to discover that humans gave birth to twins so often that it was a matter of little interest to them, and this failure had cost them dearly—it had allowed the notion of Jacen and Jaina Solo as sacred twins to become a weapon in the hands of the infidels.

Now, it seemed obvious that Nom Anor had failed to inform the Yuuzhan Vong military command of a little-used but critical tactic employed by the enemy's senior capital ships. Unforgivable. Unforgivable.

"Recall the ships and coralskippers harassing their orbital forces," he told his aide. "This engagement is done."

"It cannot be done," the officer whispered. "We have been embarrassed. We have *failed*."

"If you can't live with it, find a way to kill yourself," Czulkang Lah answered. "And I will find an aide who has intelligence as well as courage." He turned away. He would have to give his son unpleasant news.

Borleias

As night fell, Jaina finished her power-down checklist. She exited her X-wing, gave it an affectionate pat, waved at Cappie, and turned toward the docking bay exit.

But waiting for her, as he usually did now, was Jag. He wore the slight smile Jaina suspected that only she could see. "What's up?" she said.

"Calrissian got back from Coruscant alive. So, being Calrissian, he's throwing a party for family and friends. And friends of friends, and anyone who looks interesting. He says he has pre-invasion brandy. Care to go?"

Jaina felt herself start to shake her head, the refusal

that had become second nature to her since she'd come to Borleias, but she caught herself in time. She linked her arm through his and smiled up at him. "Love to."

Twenty-one years after the death of Darth Vader and the fall of the Empire...

Luke Skywalker, Han Solo, and Leia Organa Solo, the original Rebel heroes—along with the next generation of freedom fighters—wage an even greater battle against a ruthless new enemy.

THE NEW JEDI ORDER

The epic, all-new *STAR WARS* series featuring five original hardcover and fourteen original paperback novels—by authors including R. A. Salvatore, Troy Denning, James Luceno, Aaron Allston, Matthew Stover, and others.

Catch up on what you've missed...and prepare for what's coming—as *STAR WARS* enters a new era, where anything can happen!

Find out more at www.starwars.com

Del Rey/LucasBooks
www.delreybooks.com